THE
LAURENTINE
SPY

THE
LAURENTINE
SPY

Emily Gee

SOLARIS

First published 2009 by Solaris
an imprint of BL Publishing
Games Workshop Ltd
Willow Road
Nottingham
NG7 2WS
UK

www.solarisbooks.com

ISBN-13: 978 1 84416 603 9
ISBN-10: 1 84416 603 1

10 9 8 7 6 5 4 3 2 1

A CIP catalogue record for this book is available from the
British Library.

Designed & typeset by BL Publishing

Printed and bound in the US.

*I would like to thank the following writers –
Lisa Chaplin, Alison Leake, and Maurice Gee
– for giving feedback that helped me shape
this novel into what it is now. And thanks to
my agent Richard Curtis for the title!*

PROLOGUE

THEY SMELLED THE *Dacha Gorge* before they reached it: carrion. "Stay back from the edge," his uncle said as they dismounted.

The stench of death filled his mouth and nose, choking. He saw mountains, dark fir trees, sheer walls of rock.

"This is what history looks like, boy."

Soldiers' bodies. Hundreds. Thousands. Too many to count. Corhonase, Marillaqan, lying like broken dolls at the bottom of the gorge.

Bile rose in his throat. He turned away.

"Don't throw up on me, boy." His uncle's hand was on his shoulder, gripping strongly.

He clenched his eyes shut. He could still see the bodies, still smell them. "Why?"

"Corhona seeks to expand. They always do." His uncle released his grip. "This time we won."

He opened his eyes. "But those aren't our soldiers, sir."

"It doesn't matter whether the battle was ours or not. Whenever Corhona loses, Laurent wins. Remember that, boy."

"Yes, sir."

His uncle turned and looked back into the gorge. "It doesn't always have to be like this, boy. Sometimes it's possible to win before it comes to fighting."

7

CHAPTER ONE

SOMETHING MOVED AHEAD of her in the catacombs. Pebbles shifted against stone. The sound echoed through the dark galleries.

Saliel halted and reached for her knife.

Silence stretched for long seconds—black, cold, empty—while her heart thudded hard and fast beneath her breastbone and her ears strained to hear.

More pebbles rolled across the sandstone floor, a thin rattle of sound. There was a sudden scuffle of movement in the darkness. A rodent squealed.

Saliel inhaled a shallow breath. *It's only rats.*

But she didn't relax her tight grip on the knife. She waited, counting a hundred breaths, two hundred, three, until she was certain no one moved in the darkness. No soldiers. No thieves. No living person except herself.

The knife slid noiselessly back into its sheath. Saliel stepped forward. The brush of her gloved fingertips over the cold stone made a faint whisper of sound. Her eyes were useless; the dark was too dense, too absolute.

She descended another level, deeper into blackness and silence. The route through the labyrinth of passages and galleries was as familiar as her own face in the mirror. No candle was necessary; she knew every crook and turn, every fall of rock, every shrouded and disintegrating skeleton.

Here.

The alcove was shallow, an arch, a single step, nothing more.

Saliel paused to listen. Nothing moved in the darkness. She squeezed her eyes briefly shut—*please, let the guardian set me no task tonight*—and leaned her weight against the sandstone.

The wall pivoted with grudging slowness.

Her shoulders brushed rock on either side as she slipped through the narrow opening. The block of stone swung quietly back into place, shutting her in stale darkness.

She was no longer alone. She saw nothing, heard nothing—but she knew.

Saliel drew her knife. She gripped it tightly. "I saw three rings around the moon tonight."

"I saw none."

Saliel relaxed at the familiar voice. She sheathed her knife.

"You're late."

"Yes." She'd left the ball as early as she dared, but it had taken the maid long minutes to unlace the gown, to unpin her hair and replait it in a single long braid, to bring hot water to wash her face and warm honeyed milk to drink. "I apologize."

The guardian grunted. Saliel heard the rustle of cloth as he moved. Stone grated against stone and faint light leaked into the ancient storage room. For a moment the man was silhouetted in the doorway—bulky, hooded like an executioner—and then he stepped back to let her pass.

The chamber beyond was vast. Centuries ago it had been used to prepare the dead. Stone tables stood in the centre of the room, grooved and stained, and dark-lipped gutters dissected the floor. A single candle burned. Shadows towered in the corners and swallowed the ceiling.

One and Two were already seated. Their heads turned as she entered. Her eyes knew which was which. In daylight in the court she'd never recognize them; here, cloaked and hooded, she knew them.

The men rose, One tall and solid, Two slighter, narrow-shouldered.

"You had difficulty?" Two's voice was faintly anxious.

"I had difficulty leaving the ball. Nothing more." Saliel sat down on an upturned urn.

"It was a crush, wasn't it?" One sat beside her. His posture was relaxed, his voice calm.

"Yes." Saliel glanced at him. *Did I dance with you?* "There were many naval officers."

"And there are many warships in port," the guardian said, sitting. "Too many. I fear they're up to something."

"Admiral Veller was in unusually high spirits this evening," One said.

She nodded. The Admiral had been flushed with alcohol—and something more than that. There'd been an undercurrent in the vast ballroom, a soundless whisper that had prickled over her skin. She'd seen a gleam in men's eyes—the Admiral and his aides, the clusters of naval officers—and been unable to find a word to describe it. The word came to her now. *Anticipation.* She shivered and drew her cloak more closely to her. "He's excited about something."

One nodded. "Yes."

The guardian grunted. He pushed to his feet and began to pace. His footsteps echoed flatly.

Saliel looked down at her hands. She clenched her fingers together. *Please don't ask me to—*

The guardian halted in front of her. "The Admiral's wife may know something. Three, speak with her and see what you can find out."

Saliel swallowed. She raised her head and looked up at him. "I shall."

The guardian turned from her. "Two—"

"I'll have a word with his valet."

"Good." The guardian shifted his attention to One. "The Admiral should be in the courtesans' salon tonight."

"I hadn't planned on attending," One said. His voice was neutral, without inflection.

"I suggest that you do."

One shrugged his shoulders. "Very well."

Saliel looked down at her hands. She unclenched her fingers. *A simple task,* she told herself. *It will be all right.*

"Is there anything else?" the guardian asked.

"No," said Two, and she looked up to see One shake his head.

"Three?"

"No." She shook her head too. "Except... the Consort still speaks of an investigation. She's certain there are Laurentine spies in the citadel."

"Still? Curse the woman."

Across from her, Two shifted slightly. His tension was tight-shouldered and silent. The folds of his black cloak fell to the floor in sharp lines.

One spoke quietly: "Fortunately the Prince doesn't share her conviction."

Saliel watched as Two's shoulders relaxed.

"We must hope he never does," the guardian said. "Is that all?"

Saliel nodded. "Yes."

"Then we meet in two nights. Be very careful. All of you."

Saliel unclasped her hands and stood.

One rose to his feet. He bowed to her, hooded, faceless. "Goodnight."

"Goodnight." She watched as he and Two crossed the chamber. They didn't use the catacombs; their route lay through the ancient sewer system. Shadows swallowed their cloaked figures. She looked away and walked to where the guardian held the heavy stone door open for her.

"You'll speak with the Admiral's wife?"

I would give anything not to. "Yes."

"Be careful."

"Yes." *Always*.

Saliel stepped into the darkness of the storage room. The door closed behind her. There was a moment when her eyes strained to see and her lungs told her there wasn't enough air, but then it passed, as it always did.

"ENJOY THE SALON," Two said, as they parted in the disused sewers. His voice held a note of envy.

"I shall," Athan said. It was a lie; he didn't think Two would believe the truth.

The ancient sewer tunnels were broad and low and as black as pitch. Athan ducked his head and walked with noiseless care, his gloved fingers barely touching the damp stone walls.

As a youth he'd fantasized about Corhona and its courtesans' salons: salons filled with beautiful, eager women. Women schooled in the provision of physical pleasure and eager to perform any sexual act a man could desire. Women whose ardor was as legendary as their skill.

He grunted silently. *Idiot*.

He'd been a fool to fantasize about whores, just as he'd been a fool to agree to spy in the citadel. This was no adventure. It was a dangerous game, where one slip could mean death for himself and his fellow spies, for Three.

She hadn't spoken much during the meeting. Athan went over her words in his mind, remembering what she'd said, trying to reconcile her voice with those of the ladies of the court. It was impossible. Corhonase was a guttural language, as different from his native Laurentine as a battle chant from a lullaby. *Who are you, my lady?*

His hood brushed the ceiling. Black wool snagged on the rough stone, and he ducked his head lower. *I wish—*

He'd asked the guardian once, casually, who she was, and been told such knowledge was dangerous. The man was correct: to know there were other spies was one thing, to know their identities was something else entirely. *Still, I wish—*

There was no change in the darkness, but Athan's ears told him the sewer tunnel was widening. He stayed close to the wall, feeling with his hands. He pulled himself up on the stone ledge and then stooped to enter the service tunnel. The passage forked almost immediately. To the left a stone staircase led upward.

Athan hunched lower and began to climb the ancient stairs. The walls and the ceiling, the stale air, the darkness, crowded him. He counted the steps off in his head, concentrating on the numbers, disliking the cramped space, the tightness and the narrowness. The weight of the citadel pressed down on him. Fifty steps, and then a hundred. One hundred and fifty. Two hundred. Each step took him closer to the courtesans, to candlelight and wine and sex.

His pace slowed—part weariness, part reluctance. Athan stifled a laugh in his throat. *I used to enjoy it, and now...*

It wasn't that the whores were unwilling. On the contrary, there was keen competition for positions in the salon; the lifestyle was luxurious, decadent even.

But the legend was a lie. The courtesans weren't wanton; they were businesslike, bored.

The gaudy courtesans' salon no longer featured in his fantasies. Instead, his dreams were of private intimacy, and his fantasies were about one woman: Three. He didn't know who she was or what she looked like. It didn't matter. What mattered was that she didn't share her body with anyone but him and that no one else was present when they made love. Most often he imagined that they met in darkness and he never saw her face. He would undress her slowly and her body would be slim and soft and clean, and not smell of other men. And when he kissed her, her mouth was sweet and innocent, and when they made love, she was never bored.

Space opened out ahead of him. The ceiling lifted and the walls pulled back. It was dark still, but he could stand to his full height, could stretch out his arms if he wanted to.

Athan stifled a grunt of relief. The cellars on these lower levels were disused, but caution was an ingrained habit. His life depended on the care he took to avoid detection. And not only his life. Three's too, and the others. He stretched his spine and wished he could forgo the salon tonight.

SALIEL INHALED THE cold air of the catacombs. There was no scent of death or decay. The people who lay interred here were centuries dead, their bones dry and brittle.

Her path took her along twisting passageways and through wide galleries. Here lay the priests and priestesses of a long-dead empire, the warriors and the poets, the nobles and the courtiers. She couldn't see them, but she knew they were there, resting in their niches of cold stone. Hair rose at the nape of her neck at the thought of bony fingers reaching out to pluck her cloak. She fought the urge to hurry, to get out of the darkness and silence as quickly as possible. It was always worse—the return journey—when her skin crawled with unease and it took a conscious effort to keep her pace slow.

It was foolish to be afraid of crumbling skeletons when there were more important things to fear: discovery and torture and death. Yet she had nightmares about this place. The dead woke in her dreams, angry that she disturbed their rest. They hunted her in the darkness and she'd stand still and hold her breath and hope they wouldn't find her. But they always did.

Saliel shivered and shook herself mentally. *It's the living I need to fear. Not the dead.*

Her path took her steadily upward, to the wall that sealed the catacombs from the citadel. Stones had been extracted from the crumbling mortar. She ducked her head and stepped through the low opening.

The beating of her heart slowed now that the dead no longer surrounded her. *I'm a fool to let my imagination frighten me so.* There was nothing to fear in the catacombs. It was here—within the walls of the citadel—that the greatest dangers lay. Saliel moved a short distance up the passageway and stopped and listened, her hand on the hilt of her knife. These passages had already been rediscovered once, by a Laurentine scholar. The details were there for those who knew where to look.

But tonight she had the secret pathways to herself. No candlelight flickered in the darkness, no cloth whispered against stone, no soldiers' boots trod cautiously. Saliel removed her hand from the knife and placed it on the wall to guide her. The stone was smoother than in the catacombs, the passage narrower and steeper. Stairs led upward and she grew warm as she climbed.

She was in the women's wing now. Drafts stirred the air and peepholes let in murmurs of sound and gave glimpses of candlelit rooms.

The secret passages didn't extend to the newer portions of the citadel—the men's wing and the royal chambers, the rooms where matters of military intelligence were discussed. If they did, there'd be no need to ask questions and draw attention to herself, no need to guide conversations to risky subjects. *The Admiral's wife, tomorrow.*

Dread sat beneath her breastbone, tight and familiar. Saliel ignored it. She placed one foot in front of the other, climbing higher and higher within the walls of the citadel, growing warmer. The passage became narrower, the stairs steeper.

Saliel stopped. Here was her bed chamber, high in the tower that housed the unmarried ladies of the court. She leaned close to the peephole and examined the scene. The candle had burned low and the fire was almost out. In the dim light she saw that her door was still bolted from the inside.

A few steps further up the passage was a niche, above her head. It had held candles once; now her nightgown lay folded there. Saliel pulled off the black hood and stripped off her gloves, then crouched to unfasten her soft leather boots. The stone floor was cold beneath her bare feet. Swiftly she removed the sheathed knife and her remaining clothes—cloak and breeches and shirt— and laid the items in the niche. Her nightgown was as cold as the stone it had lain on. She shook out the folds and pulled it over her head. Her skin shivered in protest.

Saliel closed her eyes and concentrated on fastening the long row of pearl buttons by touch. They were cool and smooth beneath her fingers and by the time she'd fastened the last one, high at her throat, the warmth she'd acquired while climbing was gone.

* * *

ATHAN PAUSED AS he entered the main salon. His nostrils flared at the mingled scents of alcohol and perfume, sweat and sex. The air was warm and heavy. It settled on his skin, faintly oily, and he tasted it on his tongue, overripe. Musicians played on the dais, but the music was almost lost beneath the clamor of drunken voices, male and female. A servant bearing wine glasses on a tray approached him.

"Lord Ivo," the man said, bowing low. The crystal glasses and gilded tray gleamed in the light of the chandeliers.

Athan took a glass and motioned the servant away.

The salons opened out from one another, full of noise and heat. He moved slowly through the rooms, sipping the wine, his gaze sliding from one face to the next. The Prince and his cronies were in one of the smaller salons. Athan turned away, searching for easier prey.

Admiral Veller was in a far alcove with two courtesans. Athan watched for a moment and then shifted his attention to Lord Seldo. The man was on the military council—and a self-important rambler when drunk. "Seldo," he said. "Mind if I join you?"

Lord Seldo looked up from where he reclined on a couch. He focused his eyes with obvious effort. "Donkey? Of course, of course."

Athan sat, arranging his limbs in a careless sprawl. "Admiral Veller is in high spirits tonight."

Seldo followed the direction of his gaze. He sniggered.

"I wonder why?" Athan said idly.

Seldo sniggered again. "Thought of action excites the Admiral."

"Action?" Athan raised his glass and drank. The wine was smooth on his tongue. It tasted of dark plums and spice.

Seldo hiccupped. "More wine," he said loudly.

Athan waited until a servant had refilled Seldo's glass. "A campaign?"

"More of an acquisition." Seldo reached out to grab the skirts of a passing courtesan. Wine slopped from his glass. "Here." He thrust the woman at Athan. "This one's for you, Donkey. I don't like redheads."

I don't want her. "My thanks," he said, while the whore settled beside him.

Seldo had hold of another woman, who leaned obligingly into his embrace. She bit his earlobe lightly, then licked where she'd bitten. Seldo hiccupped again.

Fingers stroked up Athan's thigh. He ignored them. "An acquisition?" He raised his glass again and swallowed. Dark plums. Spice. "You're too cryptic for me, Seldo."

Seldo turned a flushed face to him, drunk, eager to display his knowledge. "They shall give us what we want." The words slurred together as he spoke.

"Oh?" Athan took care to make his tone desultory, almost bored. He yawned. "Why?"

Seldo leaned close. "A little trickery," he whispered. He raised his glass to Athan and drank greedily.

A little trickery? What did that mean? Athan looked at the redheaded whore. Plump white flesh spilled out of her scanty costume, but he had no desire to touch her. He smelled alcohol and sweat on her, and the scent of other men's pleasures. Her fingers were busy unfastening his breeches and her pretty, painted face wore a look of false excitement.

We're both bored by this, you and I.

Athan leaned his head back against one of the brocade cushions. He closed his eyes and groped for a fantasy, something that would arouse him and enable him to perform as expected.

His imagination came to his rescue. It was no bored courtesan who touched him. It was the prim and noble Petra, her red hair coiled neatly on top of her head. Never mind that Lady Petra didn't like him, the fingers that stroked him were hers, as were the skilled mouth and tongue.

Thoughts of Lady Petra pleasuring him aroused him very nicely.

THE BLOCK OF stone swung aside. Saliel ducked her head and stepped down into her bed chamber. The secret door pivoted shut with a touch of her hand. She leaned against it. *Safe.*

No. The light and warmth gave an illusion of safety, but she was no safer here than she'd been in the passageways. Less, perhaps.

She sighed and straightened and looked around the bed chamber, reassuring herself that everything was as she'd left it. Black stone walls, dark tapestries. The furnishings were sumptuous and the bed narrow, as befitted a virgin of noble birth.

Saliel shivered, less from cold than from the bleakness of the room, and went to sit beside the fire. She caught a glimpse of herself in the mirror and halted. It was an unnerving sight. She looked ghostly, her face pale above the stark white of her high-necked nightgown. The only color was the long plait of red hair that hung over her shoulder. Her image looked trapped inside the ornate and heavy frame of the mirror, caught in some terrible place. *Which, in truth, I am.*

Saliel turned away from her reflection and sat on the rug before the fire. She drew her knees up and hugged them, shivering. Sometimes it was hard to remember why she'd chosen this life. There were moments when the fear and the loneliness seemed beyond all proportion to the prize at the end. But the prize was worth it. It *was*.

"A cottage," she whispered. There was no one to hear her, but she spoke in Corhonase because in this room she was Lady Petra. The guttural words roughened her voice. "By the sea."

She stared at the glowing embers, imagining it. *A home of my own.*

CHAPTER TWO

SALIEL SAT ON the stool, her hands folded in her lap, while the maid pinned up the heavy braids of hair. The woman's busy fingers tugged and pulled and twisted.

If she slid her eyes sideways she could see the window. The distant summer fields were distorted by the tiny panes of glass. The window was open, and if she shifted on the stool—a movement that made the maid huff slightly through her nose—she could see through the narrow opening. The patchwork of green-gold fields was unblurred. Wind rippled the wheat in a sinuous movement, as if muscles flexed beneath the pelt of a giant beast.

Above the fields, faint in a pale morning sky, hung the moon. Its rings were visible, thin and glinting. *A witch day*, the old women in the Ninth Ward would say, and make gestures to protect themselves from the Eye. But those slums, those women, were half a world away, and the Corhonase had no name for mornings like today.

Saliel bowed her head and looked down at her clasped hands, and the maid huffed faintly through her nose again. A witch day. A day when witchcraft was strong, even such tiny magic as she possessed, little more than sleight of hand and fierce concentration.

She unclasped her fingers and opened her hands, turning them out to see the palms. A lady's hands, soft.

A pickpocket's hands. It was a long time since she'd used that skill. She had left thieving behind when she'd left the Ninth Ward—and left behind fear of being caught and punished: a finger thief's punishment, or worse, a witch's punishment.

Saliel closed her hands, remembering the undercurrent of excitement in the ballroom last night and the almost feverish flush on the Admiral's face as he danced. Things were happening in the citadel, things she didn't understand. *I'd be a fool to ignore the only advantage I have.*

Her fingers clenched around each other. She couldn't bend people to her will, but she'd still be called a witch and punished as witches were: with burning, with a high pyre and hungry flames.

But the punishment would be even worse if she was found to be a spy, not swift, but slow and drawn-out, unendurable. She'd be broken long before they allowed her to die. Unless the slight magic she possessed saved her life or sped her dying: a key filched from a jailer's belt, a knife stolen.

Saliel raised her eyes. The moon's rings gleamed faintly. A witch day. The safest day to practice her skill.

She waited, sitting on the stool, encased in her day gown—stiff petticoats and tight bodice and starched lace ruff—while the maid finished pinning the braids around her head. *Be calm. It's merely a matter of holding her eyes. You've done it before; you can do it again.* But fear was tight in her chest as she stood and turned to face the woman.

She caught the maid's eyes easily. Brown eyes, as dark as leaf mould on a forest floor, slightly protuberant.

Calm, Saliel told herself, staring into the woman's eyes. *Be fast.*

The maid stood motionless, caught and unaware, unblinking, as Saliel reached out and touched her. She saw her hands move, dimly, at the edge of her vision. Slow. Clumsy. She straightened the woman's white collar with fumbling fingers, undid one of the buttons on her apron and did it up again, pulled the cuffs further down the plump wrists, holding the woman's gaze while a sharp ache grew behind her eyes.

When she'd used this tiny magic as a child—picking pockets and taking coins from well-filled purses—she'd barely needed to think what her hands were doing. Now she strained to concentrate. The pain in her head intensified. It took effort not to glance down and watch her fingers pluck the woman's handkerchief from the pocket at her waist and drop it on the floor.

Saliel let her eyelids close in a long blink. When she opened them the maid had come out of her trance.

"You have dropped your kerchief," she told the woman.

"Oh." The maid bent, flustered, to pick it up. "I beg your pardon, noble lady." There was no hint of suspicion in her face or voice, no awareness that for half a minute she'd been caught by her mistress's eyes.

Saliel inhaled a slow, shaky breath and turned to look out the window again. The hard knot of fear in her chest began to ease, but the ache behind her eyes was sharp. She pressed fingertips to her forehead.

SALIEL CURTSEYED. "NOBLE Gerda, may I join you?"

"Of course, my dear," the Admiral's wife answered.

The Royal Consort favored spending her days in the formal gardens atop the citadel, her ladies gathered around her, gossiping and embroidering. On fine mornings the servants erected a canopy and spread thick rugs on the grass and piled them with silk cushions. Saliel settled alongside Lady Gerda and arranged the full skirt of her gown modestly around her. There was tension in her shoulders. *Relax. Do it as you planned.*

She opened her embroidery basket and began to thread a needle. "Excuse me," she said, feigning a yawn and hiding it behind her hand.

"Tired?" Gerda looked up from her embroidery silks. Her figure was full-bosomed and motherly, her face plump-cheeked, but her posture was unyielding and her mouth tightly held.

"A little," Saliel confessed, keeping her voice shy and deferential. "I did so enjoy the ball last night."

"I found it somewhat tedious," her companion said dampeningly. "But young people like these entertainments."

"Surely not only young people... The Admiral was..." Saliel lowered her eyes. "Forgive me, most noble Gerda. I did not mean to..."

"You are quite correct, my dear," Lady Gerda said, faint contempt in her tone. Her mouth, when Saliel glanced up, was thin with disapproval. "My husband did enjoy the ball."

"He seemed in very high spirits," Saliel ventured.

"Yes. It grows wearying. Fortunately one does not have to endure it much longer."

"Ma'am?" Saliel allowed herself to sound bewildered.

"Men are a tiresome subject of conversation." The Admiral's wife held up two strands of silk. "Which shade of green do you prefer?"

THE SKY WAS blue and the sunlight bright and warm, but beneath the canopy there was cool shade and the gentle murmur of voices. Servants circulated, bearing trays of sweetmeats and juice in crystal glasses. Saliel glanced around. A Laurentine poet would liken the

ladies of the court to exquisite flowers, clustered sweetly about the Royal Consort, their voices as soft on the
ear as running water. A Corhonase scholar—for there
were few poets—would snort at such hyperbole and
note that the ladies were attired in a manner befitting
their station and that they spoke in well-bred tones.

The scholar would have been the more accurate of
the two, but Saliel missed the poetry in life. She stifled
a sigh and bent her head over her embroidery.

"Petra."

Saliel looked up. The Consort stood before her, a
round, sleek woman with cold eyes and a small smile.
Her stature was short, but the force of her personality
made her appear tall. She wore no crown, not even a
circlet of gold in her dark hair. Her status was pro-
claimed by the keys hanging at her waist.

"Walk with me. There's a subject I wish to discuss."

Saliel obediently put down the embroidery and rose
to her feet. A servant handed her a parasol trimmed
with dainty tassels of colored silk. She opened it as she
stepped from beneath the canopy. *Relax. You're Lady
Petra. There's nothing to fear.*

The paths were fashioned of crushed white marble
that crunched delicately beneath their feet. Saliel
walked a respectful half-pace behind the Consort, her
eyes meekly lowered. The Consort's keys clinked
together faintly with each step, silver against silver,
musical.

"I've been giving thought to your betrothal," the
Consort said.

Saliel's head jerked up. "But your Eminence, the
mourning period!"

"You've been with us for nearly two years." The
Consort paused by a fountain in the shape of rearing
horse. Its stone nostrils flared wide. "You'll soon put
off your mourning clothes."

A faint breeze lifted the parasol, tugging it slightly in her hand and stirring the fringe of tasseled silk. "I... I hadn't thought to marry so soon."

"Marriage is a necessary evil, my dear Petra." The Consort touched the gleaming keys at her waist. "Without a husband, a woman is nothing. And you are one-and-twenty. It's imperative that you marry as soon as possible."

"Yes, your Eminence."

"Many would consider you past the age of marriage."

Saliel bit her lip. One-and-twenty and unwed? No, she was *three*-and-twenty and unwed. The woman's voice would rise an octave in horror if she knew.

The Consort patted her arm. "My dear Petra, I'm not chastising you. I'm merely pointing out the truth. It was a great shame your parents died before you were married. The timing was most unfortunate." She shook her head. "A double mourning period. *Two* years. And at your age! Very inconvenient."

Saliel swallowed her amusement, and her dislike of the woman.

"But don't worry, my dear Petra. I'll find a husband for you."

Gratitude, she told herself. *Reverence.* "Thank you, your Eminence."

"In fact, I have given considerable thought to the matter," the Consort said. "And I believe that Lord Ivo will make you a suitable spouse."

"Lord Ivo?" Saliel's grip tightened on the parasol. With effort she relaxed her fingers and made her tone timid and hesitant: "Your Eminence, I have conceived something of a... a dislike for Lord Ivo. I would prefer another man as husband, if it pleases you."

"Dislike?" The Consort's thin eyebrows arched in astonishment. "Nonsense. Lord Ivo will do very well for you. Why should you dislike him?"

Why should I like him? The man hadn't had an original thought in his life. "Is there no other nobleman—"

"My dear Petra." The Consort's voice was edged with impatience. "You cannot afford to be fastidious. Not only are you of an advanced age, but you have no fortune and you are—somewhat plain."

Saliel blinked as if to hold back tears. "Forgive me, your Eminence."

The Consort tutted. "Don't cry, my dear Petra. I'm certain Lord Ivo will be content to have you, despite your hair and those unfortunate freckles." Her eyebrows pinched together in a frown. "What *was* your poor mother thinking, to allow you in the sun?"

Saliel bowed her head and looked down at the path. The chips of marble shone whitely in the sunlight. *My mother? I never knew her.*

"So it's settled," the Consort said briskly. "I'll inform Lord Ivo. The betrothal will remain secret, of course, until the end of your mourning period."

Saliel raised her eyes and smiled at the woman. She tried to look overwhelmed with gratitude. "Thank you, your Eminence. You are most kind."

SALIEL ATTACKED HER embroidery. Lord Ivo! How could the Consort have chosen him? Of the men in court, he was one of those she disliked the most. His mouth was wide and slack and foolish, and he was always on the verge of sleep. *I doubt he's even aware of my existence.*

Her stitches became less fierce. In a sense, it was rather amusing. *Lord Ivo will be extremely disappointed when he discovers who his bride is.* The

Corhonase liked their women plump and dark-haired, and she was neither.

Saliel swallowed a laugh. How fortunate that the marriage would never take place. The end of her mourning period was the end of her time at the citadel. She'd leave all this behind her: the tedium of court life, the constant fear.

She tied a knot in the silk thread, snipped off the excess, and looked at her embroidery with a critical eye. *Passable.*

Saliel reached for a new skein of thread and paused. Raising her head, she looked across at Lady Marta. Marta was newly arrived in court, young and modest and sweet-natured—and more importantly, married to one of the captains of the Fleet.

"MAY I WALK with you?" she asked Marta that afternoon, as the ladies prepared to stroll through the gardens.

"By all means." The young woman's expression was one of shy pleasure.

Saliel raised her parasol and fell into step beside Marta. "Shall we take this path? It's quieter." *And safer for asking questions.* She inhaled past the tightness in her chest and smiled at her companion. "I wished to ask you something."

"Me?"

Saliel nodded. "My betrothal will be announced at the end of my mourning period."

"Oh," said Marta. Conflicting emotions crossed her face. She looked as if she didn't know whether to offer congratulations or commiseration.

"What is it like to be married?"

Marta's cheeks flushed with color. "Oh," she said again, faintly.

They strolled in silence for a moment. A breeze rustled the well-clipped hedges. Marble chips crunched softly beneath their slippers. "You are recently married yourself," prompted Saliel.

"Yes."

"Lord Soder looks to be a fine man."

Marta's blush deepened. "Yes."

"You must be very happy."

"Yes," said Marta, but her voice was little more than a whisper, neutral.

Saliel looked sideways at her in frustration. *Talk to me.* "Forgive me for asking, but..." She hesitated and bit her lip.

Marta glanced at her.

"Is it... is it as *disagreeable* as they say?"

"It?"

Another monosyllable. Saliel fluttered her hands as if searching for a euphemism. "A wife's duty," she said in a whisper.

Marta's mouth pursed in distaste. "Yes," she said. "It is extremely disagreeable."

"Oh," Saliel said. She walked a few steps in silence. "But it doesn't happen often, does it?"

Marta was silent. They reached the wall that bordered the formal gardens and halted. From this vantage point the citadel was a disorganized jumble of terraces and ramparts and towers. Its history was easy to trace in the black stone the original builders had used and the gray marble the Corhonase favored. There was as much gray as black. Within a mere two generations the Corhonase had doubled the citadel's size. *You would have done well to explore more thoroughly before you settled in. The black walls hide secrets.*

The ancient scrolls spoke of plots and intrigues, of secret passageways, but the Corhonase hadn't cared to read them. They weren't interested in an empire that had been dead for centuries.

Beneath the muddle of buildings—black and gray—the sandstone cliffs fell like spreading skirts, with the dirty sprawl of the town clutching at their hem. A causeway wound its way down the rust-colored escarpment. Pedestrians and carts labored upward.

Beyond the town lay the harbor. Saliel counted seventeen naval vessels.

She turned away from the view and sat on a marble bench, smoothing her gown. Her mourning clothes were the color of ashes. "I have distressed you. Forgive me."

"No." Marta shook her head. "Don't apologize. You're asking questions I didn't have the courage to ask myself." She sat alongside Saliel and clasped her hands in her lap. "What occurs in the marriage bed is unpleasant," she said, not looking at Saliel. "But the act itself is quickly over. And... and a husband should not visit his wife's bed above once or twice a week."

"Should not?" Saliel asked softly. Something in Marta's tone prompted the question.

Marta grimaced. "My husband wishes me to be with child before he leaves. So he visits my bed every night."

"Leaves?" Saliel took care that interest didn't sharpen her voice.

Marta nodded.

"When?"

"Soon. At the end of the month."

"A campaign?"

"He doesn't talk to me about such matters." Marta plucked at her skirt. "I wish he wasn't going, for then he wouldn't visit me so often, and..." Her fingers tightened on a fold of cloth. She finished in a rushed whisper: "And I wish he wouldn't grow a beard."

"A beard?"

"It makes it seem even more... *primitive*."

"Perhaps if you ask him to remove it?" Saliel suggested tentatively.

Marta shook her head. "He says it's necessary."

"Necessary?"

Marta nodded.

"Why?" Saliel allowed herself to sound perplexed. Beards weren't common among the noblemen of the court. They wore their hair long and their faces clean-shaven.

"He wouldn't say."

"He'll soon be gone," Saliel said soothingly. "Perhaps, if you close your eyes?"

"I do." Marta shuddered delicately. "I dislike seeing him... that is to say, I don't like to see him when he is..."

"Unclothed."

Marta shuddered again. "Yes."

Saliel knew that the male body differed from the female. She'd seen boy-infants in the poorhouse; there was an appendage, small and odd-looking. She was unclear about its appearance on an adult male. The graffiti in the slums had been rough and imprecise and clearly exaggerated.

"Do you know who your husband is to be?" Marta asked.

"Nothing has been decided yet." It wasn't wholly a lie. *Lord Ivo may refuse me.* "The Consort is arranging my betrothal."

"I'm sure she'll choose well."

"I have little to commend me," Saliel said. "I don't expect so fine a husband as yours."

Marta blushed prettily. She was a beauty by Corhonase standards, with a sweet, heart-shaped face and dark eyes and a plump figure. "Your hair is a... a nice color," she said shyly.

"Thank you," Saliel said. "But there are few who share your opinion."

Marta shook her head, with its chaste coil of dark braids, but didn't deny this truth. She smoothed her gown, which was crumpled where she'd clutched it. The marriage keys pinned to her bodice shifted against each other, clinking slightly.

Saliel looked at the keys glittering in the sunlight. The moon was no longer visible in the sky, but she could remember how its rings had looked that morning, pale and delicate. A witch day.

She glanced around. Tall hedges shielded them. She heard no footsteps, no voices. They were quite alone. *Dare I?* Her heartbeat was suddenly loud in her ears. "Marta?"

Marta lifted her head. "Yes?"

Saliel swallowed her fear. She smiled at her companion and caught her gaze.

Marta's eyes were a warm brown, flecked with gold, unblinking and glazed. Holding them required no effort, but when Saliel reached for the keys it became more difficult. Her own eyes wanted to watch the movement of her hand.

An ache began to build in her head. *Concentrate.* But her fingers were clumsy and slow as she struggled to undo the pin.

Marta's eyelids flickered.

Saliel froze, with her hand outstretched and the keys cool against her palm. She stared into Marta's eyes, while her heart pounded in her chest. *You can do this.* Her concentration steadied. Brown eyes, flecked with gold. Unblinking eyes.

Saliel forced herself to breathe. She undid the pin. The marriage keys were smooth in her hand. They clinked slightly against one another.

For a moment she sat, holding the keys, holding Marta's eyes, taking slow, deep breaths and gathering her concentration. Then she tried to pin the keys back on Marta's bodice.

The silk was heavy and stiff with embroidery. Her fingers fumbled, slow. *Calm*, Saliel told herself, while the ache increased inside her skull. *Concentrate*. But she knew she couldn't hold Marta's eyes long enough to fasten the keys.

Panic squeezed her throat, making it impossible to breathe. There was sudden perspiration on her skin. She couldn't inhale, couldn't exhale, couldn't think what to do—

The pin slid into the fabric.

Saliel sat back, trembling, her palms slick with sweat. The pain behind her eyes was intense. It felt as if her head would split open.

Marta blinked. Her eyes were wide and guileless and without suspicion. "Yes?"

Saliel's mouth was dry, her voice slightly hoarse, "Your pin has come undone."

"Oh." Marta looked down. "Thank you." She refastened the catch. Her fingers hesitated, touching the keys.

Saliel's heart stopped beating for an instant. Fear froze her to the marble seat.

"It is unpleasant," Marta said, glancing up. "And somewhat painful. But it's over swiftly, and… it is our duty."

Saliel managed a weak smile and a nod.

Marta released the keys. Wife's keys. Smooth and cool and silver. She rose to her feet. Her smile was shy. "I hope I've answered your question sufficiently?"

"Yes." Saliel had to clear her throat to speak. "Thank you."

'Don't be afraid, Petra.'

Saliel watched her leave. Her hands trembled as she wiped perspiration from beneath her lower lip. *I was a fool to try that.* The skill she'd had as a child—the easy concentration, the quickness of finger—was gone.

No more. Never again.

CHAPTER THREE

ATHAN DIDN'T USUALLY visit the courtesans' salon two nights running, but the citadel was bursting at the seams with newly-arrived naval officers. Whatever Corhona planned involved a lot of ships.

He strolled through the rooms, wine glass in hand. Sounds and scents swirled around him. He saw mouths stretched wide in drunken laughter, bare flesh and groping hands.

The gulf between the behavior expected of noble men and ladies was vast. *Do they not see how odd it is?* But the gulf between honor and trickery was no less vast. Death before dishonor was the code the Corhonase lived by—and yet they planned trickery.

Athan tasted his wine. It was rich and smoky, full of dark fruit—brambles and blackcurrants. He strolled further. Ah... there was Admiral Veller, taking his pleasure in one of the alcoves.

Athan drank idly. Brambles and smoke. A wine that smelled and tasted of autumn. When he judged the Admiral had caught his breath he sauntered slowly over. "Admiral," he said, by way of greeting.

Admiral Veller opened his eyes. "Donkey. Do join us." His wave was expansive.

"Thank you." Athan sprawled on the cushions. The whore shifted to rub herself against him.

"You're overdressed," she said, coy, businesslike. Her fingers trailed up his arm, over lace and plum-colored satin. She began to unbutton his doublet.

Athan ignored her. "I hear you'll soon be acquiring new property for the Empire." He raised his glass. "I toast your success."

Admiral Veller grunted. Sweat glistened on his face. "Thank you." He drained his glass and belched. "More wine," he said, and the courtesan rose obediently to her feet.

"I trust it won't cost the Empire many sons," Athan said. He swallowed another mouthful of wine, savoring it.

The Admiral laughed. "There's little chance of that."

'No?' Athan said, yawning.

The courtesan returned and the Admiral took the glass she offered. "No," he said, leaning back against the cushions and scratching his belly. "We'll be acquiring by invitation, Donkey.' He belched again and drank deeply.

"Invitation?"

The Admiral grunted. He closed his eyes.

The courtesan lay down beside Athan and began to stroke his thigh. He looked at her. He wanted to push her hand away. Instead he lay back and forced himself to relax. Invitation?

"A WIFE?"

"YES," said the Consort.

"Who?" Athan asked, struggling to stay seated in the same slouched pose. His hands wanted to clench. He kept them loose and relaxed.

"Lady Petra. She'll make you a good wife."

It took effort not to say *no*, a short, sharp, forceful monosyllable, not to push to his feet and stride from

the atrium, to not be Athan, horrified, instead Lord
Ivo, languidly surprised. "Oh?" he managed.

"Yes," the Consort said. "She is very biddable and
docile."

Athan looked at the woman from beneath half-
closed eyelids. Docility was not an attribute he sought
in a wife. He wanted spirit and intelligence.

"And she is modest."

Athan acknowledged this with a grunt. Lady Petra
could be nothing other than modest; by Corhonase
standards she was exceedingly plain.

"And she is chaste and virtuous."

Athan nodded, and searched for words of refusal
that wouldn't cause insult. He glanced around. The
atrium was empty except for the Consort's attendants,
standing at a discreet distance. The smooth gray marble, the stern busts set in niches, offered no
inspiration.

"As you are aware, her parents died in tragic circumstances."

Athan nodded again. The events of Lady Petra's
orphaning were well known: in the space of one night
the earth had opened and the sea had risen, and the
island colony of Gryff had been swallowed. The
Corhonase Empire had lost its farthest outpost and
Lady Petra had lost her family.

And her fortune.

Athan sat up straighter on the bench. "I understand
she is penniless," he said. "As my affairs stand—"

"A respectable dowry will be settled on her." The
Consort's voice coolly overrode his. "Her parents died
in the service of the Empire, and I am fond of her."

An image flashed into Athan's mind: himself drown-
ing and grasping desperately at sticks to stay afloat.
His hands flexed as he struggled not to clench them.
"But—"

"The Prince agrees this is a suitable match."

"He does?" Athan said, as the water closed over his head. A royal suggestion was tantamount to a command. He was trapped.

The woman's sharp black eyes assessed him. "Yes."

Athan swallowed his protest. He forced himself to relax. "Very well, I agree."

"Good." The Consort stood. "The betrothal will be announced as soon as Lady Petra's mourning period is over."

Athan rose to his feet. It was difficult to keep the movement lethargic.

"You won't regret your decision."

He bowed.

The Consort inclined her sleekly-coiffed head in response. Her attendants came forward. Something in the way she accepted the fawning attention reminded him of his mother.

Athan watched as the party walked down the colonnade. When they'd passed from view he sat again and stared down at the marble flagstones. They were smooth and cold, gray streaked with white.

A Corhonase wife.

He swore under his breath and squeezed his eyes tightly shut. *This can't be happening.*

CHAPTER FOUR

SALIEL GLANCED AROUND. The ballroom was crowded to its farthest extent. Many of the throng were naval officers in their black and maroon uniforms. The murmur of voices rose to fill the heavy, vaulted ceiling and the musicians labored to be heard. To her Laurentine ear the melody was unexciting. But then, it always was.

She'd never attended a ball in Laurent, but she had stood in darkened hallways with other servants, listening to the music. Sometimes she'd even danced quietly, in stockinged feet, when no one could see her. In Laurent the music made a person *want* to dance—it was gayer, giddier, more infectious, quite unlike the stately and martial melodies of Corhona.

She'd peeked through partially opened doors at the dancers too, envying their gaiety. Compared to those scenes, Corhonase balls were dreary affairs. In Laurent the colors were bright, the laughter frequent, the fashions flamboyant. She'd seen dancers smile and flirt with one another. Here there was no such interaction. It was all humorless and respectful formality.

Her eyes passed over Lord Ivo—tall, black-haired—where he stood with several of his cronies. Irritation stirred in her breast. Didn't the man know how to close his mouth? It gave him the look of an imbecile.

Saliel looked away, to where the Prince and his Consort sat upon the dais. The Prince looked bored. It was said that he found the nightly balls tedious, that he preferred the dancing of the courtesans to that of his court. The Consort sat to his side, at a lower elevation. Her round face was composed into an expression of docility and her hands were clasped demurely in her lap, but her eyes were alert as she watched the noble men and women of the court mingle. Ornate silver keys gleamed at her waist: the key to her husband's strongbox, the keys to the properties he'd inherited, to the citadel. There was no real power in those keys, and it was well for Laurent that her authority was limited to arranging marriages; her mind was razor-sharp.

Saliel turned her head slightly and focused on a bearded face. She studied the man. *Why are you growing a beard? And why is the officer alongside you not?*

She turned to Marta. "The officers look so handsome in their uniforms. Don't you agree?"

Marta nodded.

"There are so many of them and they all look alike. I swear, I can't tell them apart! I can't even make out your husband."

Marta obligingly pointed. "There he is, standing with the Admiral."

"Of course," Saliel said. "How clever of you. Can you tell all the officers apart?"

Marta shook her head. "No. Only those on my husband's ship."

"And which ones are they?"

Saliel observed carefully as Marta indicated the men in question. Every one of them had facial hair. *Finally, it begins to make sense.*

SALIEL SMILED POLITELY at her dance partner. "I notice that beards are becoming quite fashionable."

The man touched his chin in a self-conscious gesture. "Yes." The straggling whiskers on his chin were a different shade of brown to his hair.

"You shall all look like pirates soon," Saliel said, wide-eyed. *I sound like a fool.*

The officer laughed uncomfortably. "Yes."

"Are you a captain?" she asked, noting from his epaulettes that he was a junior officer. "Which is your ship?"

"The *Glorious Conquest*," the man said. He didn't correct her assumption of his rank.

She and the officer were parted by the dance. Saliel traced her way sedately through the intricate steps and halted opposite her newest partner. She looked at him with distaste.

"Noble Petra."

She sank into a curtsey. "Lord Ivo."

Lord Ivo bowed leisurely and held out his arm. Saliel placed her fingertips on his sleeve. The puce-colored satin was warm from his body.

"I spoke with the Consort this afternoon," Lord Ivo said as he sauntered beside her, keeping lethargic time with the music.

"Oh."

"I understand that you're desirous of entering the married state."

Saliel stiffened. "I beg your pardon?"

"Perhaps I was mistaken. I confess I wasn't paying strict attention to her words." Lord Ivo glanced at her from beneath half-closed eyelids. "But my understanding was that we were discussing a marriage. Yours and mine."

The dance parted them briefly. When Lord Ivo claimed her hand again she kept her eyes downcast.

"The Consort speaks highly of you," he said.

"The Consort is most gracious."

Lord Ivo yawned. His attention seemed to wander. "I've recently purchased a piglet."

"I beg your pardon?"

"For racing."

"Oh." Saliel stared at the floor. It was paved in squares of dull red and black stone.

"Her coloring is similar to yours. I believe I shall name her Petra, in your honor."

She glanced at him sharply. "There's no need to do so, my lord."

"But she reminds me of you." Lord Ivo's smile was amiable, foolish.

ATHAN WATCHED LADY Petra out of the corner of his eye. She danced with one of the officers of the Fleet, moving sedately through the sequence of steps. Her hair was bright above the gray of her gown.

He'd almost decided that it wouldn't be terrible to marry her. Certainly, she was docile and biddable—which were synonyms for boring—but she had the wit to dislike him. Perhaps it was perverse, but he enjoyed the spark of irritation in her eyes when she looked at him and the careful, disdainful politeness in her voice. True, her figure and coloring were unfashionable, but her slimness gave her an undeniable grace and the red-gold hair coiled so neatly on top of her head was quite striking.

Athan allowed himself to imagine for a moment that Lady Petra was his wife. He imagined unbinding that fascinating hair and watching it tumble down her back, rich against her pale skin. And then he imagined her lying in the marriage bed, shrinking from his touch and wishing the act over with.

No, he didn't want a Corhonase wife. A woman should enjoy sex with her husband, not endure it.

But if I teach her—

No, that way lay disaster. Lady Petra would be shocked if he suggested sex could be agreeable. And she'd be suspicious. A lady's value lay in her virtue. No nobleman would encourage his wife to enjoy the physical pleasures of the marriage bed. To do so would be insulting in the extreme. Lust, passion, desire, sexual gratification... such things were the realm of courtesans.

And courtesans didn't become pregnant. They ate herbs that rendered them barren. If he visited Lady Petra's bed—as he must do if they married—then he would likely sire a child with her.

A Corhonase child.

Athan's throat became dry at the thought, and he reached out and plucked a wine glass from a tray. How to avoid this marriage?

SALIEL WAS PLEASED that she was the first to arrive. The chamber was empty save for the guardian and herself. Shadows sidled across the floor and the far walls were lost in darkness.

"I'm to be wed."

"What?"

"The betrothal will be announced when my mourning period is over." She sat on one of the stone urns and folded her hands in her lap. "But I'll be gone by then, won't I?" *I sound like Two: anxious.*

"I've already begun preparations for your departure."

Saliel's tension eased. "Will I be replaced?"

"I hope so. It's been useful having a spy in the ladies' court."

Saliel nodded. There were always two spies in the citadel: One, a nobleman, and Two, a servant. She was the first Three.

"Who's your betrothed?"

She said the name with distaste: "Lord Ivo."

"Who?"

"Lord Ivo."

"You don't like him?"

"The man's an ass."

The guardian coughed and cleared his throat. He began to pace. "Lord Ivo... This could be useful."

"Useful? How?"

"A reason for your departure." The guardian leaned against one of the stone tables. He stood at the edge of the dim circle of candlelight. The hem of his black cloak melted into the darkness. "They'll be less likely to investigate if they think you're fleeing an unwelcome marriage."

Saliel chewed thoughtfully on her lower lip. "It will be unusual."

"But not unprecedented."

Saliel nodded. He was correct. "The Consort is aware of my disinclination to marry Lord Ivo."

"Good. I'd like you to make your feelings evident to others in the court. Subtly, of course."

Saliel nodded again.

"Excellent," the guardian said. He straightened and rubbed his hands together. "Your disappearance will be unexpected, but not without reason. Excellent."

"I SAW ONE ring around the moon tonight," Athan said.

"I saw none." The black figure stood aside for him to pass.

"Guardian, I must speak with you privately."

"Very well," the man said. "Afterward."

Tonight Athan was the last to arrive; the others were already seated. He looked at Three as he crossed the floor. The bulky cloak disguised her very effectively. She could be any one of a number of young noblewomen. *I wish the Consort had chosen you to be my bride.*

There was no chance of that. Whoever Three was in court, she was unmarriageable. Laurent would never ask that of her: to share her bed with a Corhonase nobleman, to bear Corhonase children.

Athan looked at her with renewed interest. Did she play a widow? A wife whose husband was stationed half a world away?

"Good evening," he said, as he sat on an urn beside her.

"Good evening."

"There's a lot of activity at the docks." The guardian's voice was terse. "Our sources suggest a squadron will sail shortly." He sat. "What have you learned, Three?"

"The squadron leaves at the end of the month."

"Where?"

She shook her head. "I don't know."

"One? Two?"

Athan shook his head as well, but Two spoke, "The Oceanides."

"The Oceanides?" The guardian's head jerked around. "Are you certain?"

Two lifted his shoulders diffidently. "The Admiral's valet is looking forward to the voyage. He says they're going someplace where the women..." He cast a quick glance at Three.

Athan grunted. He knew what the women of the Oceanides were famed for. Three clearly didn't. He saw curiosity in the angle of her head.

"The Oceanides. It makes sense," the guardian said. "We're the closest naval port, but..."

But it *didn't* make sense. The island chain was crucial to trade routes—and as such had negotiated treaties of independence with both Laurent and

Corhona. To take the Oceanides by force would be an act of warfare that Laurent couldn't ignore. *And ours is the superior fleet.*

"It won't be a campaign," Athan said.

"What then?"

"I don't know," he said, frustrated that he'd managed to glean so little information. "An acquisition. Through trickery, according to Lord Seldo."

"Trickery?" The guardian sounded baffled. "But the Corhonase value their honor so highly."

"If the prize is great enough." Athan shrugged. "They've tried subterfuge before. The invasion of Marillaq—"

"And look at the result," the guardian said. "I doubt they'd try such a thing again."

"Perhaps the Prince is planning an unauthorized operation?" Two suggested.

Athan hesitated—*he is certainly fool enough*—and shook his head. "He wouldn't dare. The Emperor has other nephews who can take his place."

"But if he thought to gain favor?"

"With so many ships, it must be on the Emperor's command," the guardian said. "One, what did the Admiral say?"

Athan shrugged again. "That they'd be acquiring by invitation."

"By invitation?"

"Yes. With little loss of men."

"The Oceanides would never *invite* Corhona…" The guardian fell silent.

"What form of trickery?" Two asked.

Athan shook his head, wishing the scraps of information made sense.

"The officers on eight of the ships are growing beards," Three said tentatively. "Perhaps there's a connection?"

"Beards?" The guardian rose abruptly to his feet. "What could beards possibly have to do with acquiring the Oceanides?"

Three shook her head.

The guardian began to pace. His steps were sharp with frustration.

Athan frowned at the floor. He'd assumed the beards were a new fashion among the naval officers. *But if it's only the men on eight ships...*

There had to be a reason for the beards.

"Pirates," Three said suddenly.

Athan raised his head and stared at her.

"There are no pirates in the Northern Ocean. Laurent destroyed their bases." The guardian stopped pacing. His voice became thoughtful, "I wonder..."

Athan didn't wonder. "The Corhonase will masquerade as pirates." The statement hung in the air for a moment—absurd, utterly preposterous, and yet he knew it was correct.

"Pirates," the guardian said. He sat down again. "Eight ships. With a hundred men aboard each—"

"The Oceanides can't defend themselves against so many," Athan said.

"No. It will be a slaughter."

A slaughter.

Memory came. Bodies lying like broken dolls. Too many to count. Hundreds upon hundreds. The smell—

"Eight ships plunder the islands," he heard the guardian say. "Disguised as pirates. What then?" And beneath that was his uncle's voice in his ear. *Don't throw up on me, boy.*

Athan swallowed. He pushed the memory aside.

"The rest of the squadron sail in, offering protection?" suggested Three.

"Perhaps," the guardian said. "Although—"

"She's right." The plan fell into shape behind his eyes. He saw it clearly. "The pirates plunder—and Corhona offers protection. On the condition that the Oceanides become their territory." *Simple*.

"The Oceanides needn't accept," Two said.

"They will." His voice was flat. *Bodies lying like broken dolls*. "If the slaughter is great enough, they will."

"But Laurent—?" Two sounded confused.

"Laurent can protest, but the Oceanides are free to join the Corhonase Empire if they choose."

"We can fight," Two insisted. "We have the larger fleet. We can take the Oceanides for ourselves."

The guardian shook his head. "That would be unwise."

"But Corhona will take them—"

"Through an act of benevolence. For Laurent to then take them through force wouldn't reflect well on us."

"Corhona would occupy a position of high moral ground," Athan said. "And we'd lose allies." Anger built inside him.

"But—"

"Don't worry," the guardian said. "Corhona won't acquire the Oceanides."

"There's time to warn Laurent?"

"Yes."

Athan's tension eased. "A welcoming committee for the pirates?"

"Undoubtedly."

He was aware of satisfaction—solid in his chest—and a strange sense of rightness. *Sometimes it's possible to win before it comes to fighting*. The decision he'd made nearly two years ago hadn't been a mistake. This moment made it all worthwhile—the lies, the danger. *I did the right thing becoming a spy*.

The guardian laughed. "I foresee loss of Corhonase face."

"Not just loss of face." Three's voice was quiet, thoughtful. "The Emperor's judgment will be questioned, his honor brought into doubt—for the second time in his reign. It may threaten his position."

Athan looked at her. "A power struggle within the imperial family?"

She shrugged.

"Let us hope that's the case." The guardian rose to his feet. He rubbed his gloved hands together. "This is a great day for Laurent. You've all done exceedingly well."

Three stood, anonymous in the black cloak and executioner's hood.

"We'll meet in two nights' time," the guardian said. "Be careful."

Athan nodded. He stood and bowed to Three. Did she feel it too? The satisfaction, the rightness?

Two started in the direction of the sewer tunnels, and halted after a few steps. "Do you come?"

"I must speak privately with the guardian.'

"Very well." Two hurried into the shadows.

Athan turned his head. He watched as the guardian opened the door to the storage room.

"Be careful," he heard the man say. And he heard Three's low response: "Yes."

She stepped through without a backward glance. The guardian closed the heavy stone door. Athan shivered. It was a journey many men would shrink from: the catacombs, alone and in the darkness. *She has courage.*

"What is it?" the guardian asked as he came back to the candlelight.

Athan shook his head to clear it. "The Consort has arranged a marriage for me."

"Marriage? With whom?"

"Lady Petra."

The guardian nodded.

"I can't do it," Athan said. The words were short and tight. "I can't take a Corhonase wife."

"Would it be such a bad thing?" The guardian's voice was amused.

"What if she becomes pregnant? What then? What if I sire a child with her?"

"Relax," the guardian said.

"Relax?" said Athan. "I do not want a Corhonase wife!"

"You won't have one."

"No?" His hands clenched. "Perhaps you didn't hear me correctly. The *Royal Consort* has arranged the betrothal."

"The marriage won't take place," the guardian said calmly. "You have my word."

"But how can you possibly—"

"Don't let the matter concern you. There'll be no marriage."

"But the Consort herself—"

"Trust me," the guardian said.

Athan looked at him. "You won't harm Lady Petra?"

"No harm will come to her," the guardian said. "And no suspicion will fall on you."

"Very well." He accepted this with a nod. His hands unclenched. "Will you tell me how?"

"No," the guardian said. "But it would help matters if you made yourself disagreeable to her."

"I beg your pardon?"

"It would help matters if Lady Petra disliked you."

"She already does," Athan said, his voice dry. *Which is why I like her.*

The guardian shrugged. "Well, then. Take care that her dislike persists."

"I shall."

CHAPTER FIVE

THE FIRST FULL moon of autumn was the anniversary of the Great Burning. The morning passed as it always did—with embroidery and sweetmeats—and in the afternoon Saliel went out into the great courtyard with the lords and ladies of the citadel. Wind gusted around them and clouds scudded across the sky.

Marta stood beside her, wide-eyed and with glowing cheeks. "I love bonfires."

Saliel huddled into her cloak. "So do I." She pretended to listen, hearing only snatches of the Prince's words as he spoke.

"On this day, nearly three hundred years ago, the Great Burning began. Nations united in one cause and fires burned around the world."

She raised her head and looked up at the sky. "Witches died in their thousands," she heard the Prince say from his dais. "And the sky was black for months."

The sky wasn't black today. It was pale, with swift gray clouds. *No screaming crowd. No stench of burning witch.* She smelled only fresh air, heard only the respectful silence of the nobles as the Prince spoke.

"Few witches escaped the Great Burning. We have hunted and burned those that did for nearly three centuries. Each year they grow fewer. Soon the moment will come when the world is purged of evil!"

A roar went up in the courtyard, a swelling, scream-ing sound. Sparrows took flight from the steep-pitched slate roofs.

The roar became a chant as the bonfire was lit. *Burn the witches, burn the witches.* Saliel opened her mouth. "Burn the witches!"

She watched as the fire took hold. Flames roared upward. She felt their heat on her cheeks. Logs snapped and crackled as they burned. Fierce sounds. Sounds that made her feel ill. The wind snatched the smoke, dispersing it.

"Burn the witches!"

When the bonfire had consumed itself, she walked with Marta to the edge of the courtyard. The citadel was a jumble of ramparts and towers and sloping roofs, a muddled patchwork of colors and styles, old and new. As a defensive site, it had no equal. Plague, not warfare, had emptied the citadel of those who built it.

Saliel shivered, hunching into her cloak, and looked out over the town and the harbor. Far beyond the horizon, days and weeks away, lay Laurent. *Freedom.*

"I'm with child," Marta said.

Saliel turned her head. "Are you certain?"

Marta nodded.

"Congratulations."

Marta blushed prettily. "Thank you."

"Your husband will be pleased." Saliel glanced at the horizon again. *Five weeks since the squadron sailed.* "I wonder when he'll return."

"Lady Gerda says that sails have been spotted, out to sea."

"The squadron?"

"Perhaps."

They stood, looking down at the harbor. A pillar of smoke rose from the town.

"Have you ever seen a real burning?" Marta asked.

"Only one." Memory gave her the scent: burning hair, burning flesh.

"I've seen two," Marta said, cheerful. "When I was a child."

"Oh."

"I should like to see another."

"There are few burnings now." Saliel turned away from the view and the column of smoke. "It's cold. Shall we go inside?"

CHAPTER SIX

SALIEL SAT ON a stool by the window. It took effort not to tell her maid to hurry. Through the windowpanes she saw a patchwork of bare fields, white with frost, distorted into skewed shapes by the glass. She couldn't see the harbor, where the maid told her the squadron had arrived during the night, couldn't count how many ships had returned or see what condition they were in.

She winced as the maid began winding the long braids tightly about her head, fixing them there with hairpins. Someone scratched at the door.

"Noble Petra?"

"Enter," said Saliel, holding her head still while the maid anchored the last of the braids in place.

"Noble Petra." The newcomer curtseyed. Saliel recognized her. She was one of the servants who attended the married ladies. "Lady Marta requests your company."

"Now?"

"Yes, noble lady." The woman nodded. "If you please."

"Very well."

Saliel descended the stairs sedately, following the servant, and crossed the wide atrium. The atmosphere was hushed.

They entered the wing where the married ladies resided. Torches burned in the brackets, but the corridors were cold and dark with shadows. The soles of their shoes made quiet, flat sounds that echoed off the black stone. Saliel repressed a shiver as they halted at the door to Marta's suite. *Something's wrong.* The corridors were too silent, too empty.

The servant stepped forward and scratched on the wooden panels.

Saliel laid her hand against the wall while she waited. The stone leached the warmth from her palm.

Marta's maid opened the door. She curtseyed low. "Noble Petra." Relief was clearly audible in her voice.

"Is everything all right?" Saliel entered the parlor. It was a stiff, formal room, with heavy furniture and dark tapestries. Trinkets and tiny ornaments clustered in cabinets of polished, ebony-black wood. The fire was unlit.

"Petra?" Marta's voice was weak and tearful.

The maid hurried across the parlor to the open door of the bed chamber. "Please, noble lady." She beckoned, her face anxious. "Please."

The furnishings in the bed chamber were similarly dark and ornate, but here a fire burned and candles were lit. Marta lay in the bed. Her face was tear-stained. "Petra," she said, holding out her hand.

Saliel hurried over to the bed. "What's wrong?" She took hold of Marta's outstretched fingers. "What has happened?"

"My husband is dead."

Saliel froze, holding Marta's hand. *Is he dead because of me?* She swallowed. Her throat was tight. "How?"

"Laurent," said Marta. Tears welled in her eyes. She began to weep.

I killed him.

Saliel sat on the edge of the bed. Marta clutched her hand. *She trusts me.* She couldn't look at Marta's face. Guilt was bitter on her tongue.

She closed her eyes and listened as Marta's sobbing slowly quieted. Then she raised her head. *Concern, not guilt. I'm Lady Petra, not a Laurentine spy.* But she was a spy—it was all she was in this citadel—and she wiped Marta's cheeks with a lace-edged handkerchief and knew there were questions she must ask. "Do you know what happened? Can you tell me?"

"The Consort told me he died honorably,' Marta said in a choked voice. "She said he took his own life when Laurent demanded surrender. I know nothing more."

Death before dishonor. It was the code the Corhonase lived by.

Saliel looked down at the damp handkerchief in her hand. The entire crew would have followed their captain's example. A hundred men. She closed her fingers around the handkerchief, squeezing tightly, and made herself look up. "A hero." The words stuck in her throat. She had to push them out. "You can be proud of him."

Marta smiled weakly. "Yes. And… I'm grateful to him."

Saliel met her gaze and understood what she was saying. In dying honorably, Lord Soder had given Marta and her unborn child their lives. If he'd surrendered, the dishonor would have been hers, as his wife, and the choice would then have been hers. Death before dishonor. *Truly the Corhonase are fools.*

"Lord Soder was a most honorable man," she said. "A true nobleman."

Marta nodded. Her eyes filled with tears.

Saliel handed her the handkerchief. She turned to the maid. The woman stood at the foot of the bed, quiet and unobtrusive. "Has your mistress eaten breakfast?"

The woman shook her head.

"Bring her something warm to drink, and a little food."

"Yes, noble lady."

Saliel turned back to Marta. Marta hadn't loved Lord Soder, but she had good reason to cry: in Corhonase terms the man had been a very good husband. *I'm sorry.* She shut her eyes for a brief moment and listened to the sobbing. How many other wives had received the same news this morning?

Marta stopped crying when the maid returned. The woman curtseyed with careful balance and placed a tray on the table beside the bed.

"I don't think…" Marta said doubtfully.

Saliel handed her a cup of warm, honeyed milk. "At least have something to drink."

She watched as Marta drank obediently. *Perhaps there's something to be said for docility.* "More?" she asked, when the cup was empty.

"Thank you." Marta glanced at the pastries the maid had brought. "Perhaps I could eat a little…"

Saliel handed her the plate.

Marta chose a pastry filled with fruit and custard. She raised it to her mouth. Her brow creased with new distress. "I shall have to remarry," she whispered. She laid down the pastry.

Saliel reached out and took hold of Marta's hand. "I'm certain the Consort will choose well."

Marta's eyes shone with fresh tears. "But—"

"Don't worry about it," Saliel said softly. "Everything will be fine. I promise."

Marta blinked back the tears. Her smile was small and wavering. "I'm glad you're here."

I'm the reason you're crying. Saliel forced herself to return Marta's smile. "Do eat something."

Marta picked up the pastry again and obediently ate.

* * *

FOR ONCE THERE was no ball; the magnitude of the disaster was too great. Athan had seen the ships for himself from one of the terraces in the formal gardens. There were eight fewer than when the squadron had sailed.

The citadel seethed with rumors. They all had one thing in common: Laurent was cast as villain. That, Athan ignored.

He'd heard that Admiral Veller had given his report to the military council and then taken his own life. The Prince had been in talks with his advisors all day. No statement had yet been released, but the members of the military council had recently exited the debating chamber.

Athan entered the most private of the men's atria and looked around. Braziers illuminated the courtyard, casting shifting shadows over tall columns and elaborate fountains. A figure sat in the semi-darkness.

Athan smiled. *Got you.* He strolled across the courtyard. "Evening, Seldo."

Lord Seldo looked up wearily. "Donkey."

"Care for a drink?" Athan displayed the bottle he carried.

Interest flickered in the man's eyes. He straightened slightly. "Thank you. It's been a trying day."

"So I gather." Athan sat down beside his prey. "I confess I'm confused as to the details." He poured wine for them both. "Here."

Seldo grunted his thanks and drank deeply, gulping the wine. "It's a catastrophe, Donkey."

"Eight ships lost." Athan sipped his own wine. It was savory, pepper and spices. "But I haven't yet heard how."

Seldo drained his glass.

Athan leaned over to refill it. He smiled Lord Ivo's smile—amiable, slightly bewildered. "Tell me, Seldo. How did the squadron lose so many vessels?"

CHAPTER SEVEN

SALIEL'S PACE WAS faster than normal. It was a struggle: haste, caution. She crossed echoing chambers and walked along winding passages. Bones surrounded her—old, crumbling to dust—but she saw only blackness, smelled only stale air.

The guardian wasn't waiting in the storage room. Saliel crossed the small space and felt for the door. Stone grated against stone as she pushed it open.

Three cloaked, hooded men stood in the candlelight. They turned at her entrance. Their voices became silent. One of the figures came toward her, his footsteps echoing flatly.

"I saw three stars fall tonight," she said in a low voice.

"I saw none," the guardian said. "Come. Be seated. We have much to discuss."

Saliel followed him out of the shadows.

"Have you heard the news?" Two asked.

"I've heard very little." She sat on an urn. "What happened at the Oceanides?"

"A disaster for Corhona." Two said, jubilant. "The squadron lost eight ships!"

"And all the men aboard," One said quietly.

Saliel glanced at him. Did he also regret the loss of life? Did he feel some culpability?

"How?" she asked. "What happened?"

The guardian nodded at One.

"Laurent was waiting," One said. "The would-be pirates were heavily outnumbered. Five ships were destroyed in battle. The remaining three were asked to surrender. Their crews refused, preferring to scuttle their ships." He spoke without inflection, stating the facts. "Laurent was able to board at least one before it sank. They found sufficient evidence to implicate the Empire."

"The Oceanidans have decided to join the Protectorate," the guardian said smugly.

Two gave a whoop that echoed in the chamber.

Saliel nodded. Her emotions were mixed: relief Corhona hadn't acquired the Oceanides, regret the islands had lost their independence. She looked down at her hands. *Perhaps I value independence too highly, having none myself.*

"The Admiral is dead."

"What?" She raised her head.

"He accepted responsibility for the disaster and took his life. In the debating chamber. Before the Prince and his military advisors." One's voice was flat.

The guardian shrugged. "Death before dishonor."

Saliel looked down at her hands again. *Another widow.*

"This is a great day for Laurent," the guardian said. "You may feel proud of yourselves."

Proud? There was nothing to be proud of in what they did: lying, pretending. Saliel closed her eyes. *I want to go home.*

"WE'LL MEET IN two nights' time," the guardian said at last, standing. "Take care that your true feelings on this matter aren't apparent to others."

Athan stood. "Guardian, I must speak with you privately."

"Very well."

Three rose to her feet. She didn't stand as Two did, triumphant.

Athan looked at her more closely. "Are you all right?"

"It's been a difficult day." Her voice was low, weary. "There are many new widows in court."

Athan nodded. He could think of nothing to say.

Three turned away. He watched as she and the guardian walked across the chamber.

"Until next time," Two said.

"Yes," Athan said, scarcely noticing as Two left.

The guardian opened the door to the storage room. Athan found that he had to look away. He couldn't watch as Three vanished from sight. *She shouldn't be here. This is no life for a young woman.*

He sat down again and stared at his gloved hands. It seemed to him that he was responsible for the deaths, that he had blood on his hands. The guilt that he felt disturbed him. *Is this how Three feels? Satisfaction and guilt intertwined?*

"Well?" the guardian asked, as he came back across the chamber.

Athan raised his head. "About my betrothal."

The guardian sat. "What about it?"

"I've done as you asked," Athan said. "Lady Petra dislikes me heartily."

"Good."

"And we are still betrothed."

"Don't worry," the guardian said.

"It's been five weeks. Her mourning period will soon be over."

"Don't worry."

Athan exhaled through his nose, a sharp hiss of air. "How can I not worry?"

"You have my word. The wedding won't take place."

Athan stared at the hooded figure.

"Trust me," the guardian said.

"Very well." Athan pushed to his feet. "But know this—" the vehemence in his voice surprised him, "— if you fail to halt the betrothal, I'll leave this citadel. Laurent be damned!"

The threat hung in the chill air of the chamber.

The guardian stood. "There will be no betrothal. You have my word."

Athan gave a sharp nod and turned away. Then he halted. "About Three."

"What about her?"

He turned back to face the guardian. "She shouldn't be here."

"She volunteered," the guardian said mildly.

"She shouldn't be here. This is no place for a woman."

The guardian looked at him for a moment. "Don't concern yourself about her," he said. "She'll be leaving soon."

Athan felt relief, and a deep sense of loss. "Good."

CHAPTER EIGHT

THEY SPENT THEIR days indoors, now that it was autumn. Saliel disliked the Ladies' Hall, with its heavy ceiling and narrow, shuttered windows. Two hundred women sat and sewed, but the Hall seemed to swallow them. They shrank, becoming doll-sized.

She raised her head and looked around, seeing tapestries, sofas with brocade cushions, ornate side tables. The colors she wanted to see—warm reds and yellows, vivid blues and greens—weren't there. The noblewomen wore the colors of virtue: dark colors, pale colors, dull colors.

And gray, the color of mourning. The seamstresses had been busy in the past three weeks; fifty ladies wore gowns of ash-gray silk.

And for each gown, a dead man.

Saliel bent her head over her embroidery.

"Noble Petra."

Saliel looked up. One of the Consort's attendants stood before her, her face round and placid. "Yes?"

"The Royal Consort wishes to speak with you."

Saliel laid down her embroidery frame. She glanced up at the shuttered windows as she stood. *Soon I shall be gone from this place.* It was hard to comprehend such freedom. She inhaled deeply, imagining fresh air in her lungs. *It will be as if I've grown wings and can fly.*

She followed the attendant across the hall, walking slowly, sedately. The Consort sat beside one of the fireplaces.

Saliel curtseyed, low. 'You wish to speak with me, your Eminence?"

"Petra." The Consort's expression was unsmiling, her eyes cold.

She's angry.

Saliel's mouth was suddenly dry. She swallowed, and tried to smile.

The Consort surveyed her for a long moment, and then stood. "Come. There's something I wish to discuss with you."

There was no need to ask what; her mourning period ended in a month. The discussion would concern her betrothal to Lord Ivo. *And my behavior. I am about to be reprimanded.*

Saliel dipped her head and curtseyed again. "Yes, your Eminence."

She stood aside. *A few more weeks and I'm gone,* she told herself. *What she says to me doesn't matter.* But apprehension was tight in her belly as she walked two steps behind the Consort. Only a fool would be unafraid of the woman's anger.

The Consort had a parlor where she spoke privately with her ladies, but today she chose the atrium. Saliel's spirits lifted slightly. No dark tapestries, no shuttered windows. Instead, fresh air.

In the vestibule she took her heavy, fur-lined cape from its peg. Attendants fussed about the Consort, ensuring she was warmly dressed, and then opened the door to the atrium.

Saliel inhaled deeply as she stepped outside, filling her lungs with cold air. The open courtyard was a cheerless place, the marble as gray as the overcast sky. Potted trees, heavy with blossom in spring, were leafless, their branches bare and twisted. *Does she seek to punish me with this?* It was no punishment; she reveled in the iciness of the flagstones through the thin soles of her shoes, in the chill, blustery wind that snatched at her cape.

The Consort began to walk down the colonnade. Saliel fell into step behind her, her eyes narrowed against the wind. "Your Eminence?" she asked, meek and deferential.

The Consort glanced back at her. "You are aware that Marta must remarry?"

Saliel blinked at the unexpected question. "Yes."

"The betrothal will be announced shortly."

Saliel nodded. Corhonase custom required that Marta remarry before the birth of her baby; only a father or stepfather could name a child.

"I have spoken with her on the subject." The Consort's cape swirled in the wind. "And she has indicated a preference in her choice of husband."

Saliel's eyelids flickered with surprise. *Marta was so bold?*

"Given the circumstances I would like to humor her. She is with child, and her husband died honorably. However..." The Consort turned to face her. "It may surprise you that Marta has expressed a desire to marry Lord Ivo."

Saliel stared at her. "Lord Ivo?"

"Yes." The Consort resumed walking. "I was somewhat surprised by her request. I'd thought you would have told her of your betrothal. Your discretion is commendable."

"Thank you, your Eminence." Saliel tried to sound overwhelmed by the faint praise.

"I have no doubt that you would be willing to end your betrothal." The Consort's voice was suddenly as icy as the wind. "You have made your feelings on the matter quite clear."

Saliel bit her lip. She looked down at the flagstones, watching where she placed her feet.

The Consort walked briskly until she came to the end of the colonnade. She halted and turned to face Saliel again. In the thin, gray autumn light her eyes were black. "However, I have another husband for Marta. Your betrothal to Lord Ivo will stand."

Saliel sank into a long curtsey of obeisance. "Yes, your Eminence."

The Consort stared down at her. "The betrothal ceremony will be held next week," she said coldly. "And your marriage one month after."

"So soon?" The timing would be close: her departure, her marriage. "Can't it—"

"No." The word was flat, final.

Saliel bowed her head.

"I trust you have a suitable wardrobe?"

"Yes, your Eminence."

The Consort resumed walking. "Marta has requested that your suite be near hers. There's a vacant one in the same corridor. It is yours."

Saliel rose to her feet. The wind buffeted her as she followed the Consort along the colonnade. "Thank you."

The Consort made no reply. Her shoes made thin slaps of sound on the flagstones.

I am meant to be chastened. "Thank you for discussing this matter with me," Saliel said, her voice humble. "I'm aware there are weightier matters on your mind these days."

The Consort halted. The wind lifted her cape, swelling it around her, as if she had grown wings and could fly.

"It's... it's a difficult time," Saliel ventured hesitantly.

The Consort turned to face her. Her skin was as white as marble. Her eyes glittered blackly. "At least one good thing has come of this disaster."

"I beg your pardon?"

"No one can deny there's a spy in the citadel. How else could Laurent have known?"

Saliel stared at the Consort. Her throat was suddenly too tight for speech. She shook her head.

"Even my husband can't ignore the obvious any longer." The Consort's mouth tightened. "He has sent for a spycatcher."

"Spycatcher?" Saliel stood frozen, while the wind tugged her cape.

"The man who exposed the Laurentine spy in Wrest."

Saliel moistened her lips. "I have heard of him," she said. "His reputation is considerable."

"Yes." The Consort's smile was cruel.

Saliel forced air into her lungs. "When does he come?"

"Very soon."

SALIEL SAT WITH her hands folded in her lap. She surveyed the ballroom. *Calm. Composed.* But terror sat beneath her breastbone, making breathing difficult. "I beg your pardon?"

"The Consort says she will make her decision soon." Marta's voice was low.

Saliel looked at her. "Decision?"

"About whom I shall marry." Marta plucked at her skirt, twisting the stiff gray fabric between her fingers. "I do hope…" Her words trailed off.

Saliel followed Marta's gaze. Lord Ivo was entering the ballroom. His breeches and doublet were a dark purplish-brown, the lace at wrist and throat as white as sea-foam. As always, his expression was vacuous. For a moment disbelief almost smothered her terror. "You like him?"

Marta blushed. "He's a handsome man."

Not handsome. Bovine.

"And his figure is very fine."

Fine? Saliel watched as Lord Ivo gestured for a servant. She saw height and wide shoulders and well-shaped legs. *Odd, I've always thought of him as soft.*

"He's rather lethargic, don't you think?"

Marta's flush deepened. "Lethargy in one's husband is not a bad thing."

So that's why you want to marry him.

A naval officer approached. His face was square-cheeked above the black and maroon uniform. He wore a captain's epaulettes. "Noble Marta, may I have this dance?"

Saliel watched as the pair took their places on the dance floor. Was this the husband the Consort had chosen for Marta?

The musicians began to play. The melody was somehow different tonight. She heard a slow, remorseless beat beneath the dance tune. *Spycatcher*, it said. *Soon.*

How soon—

"Noble Petra."

She looked up.

Lord Ivo stood before her, slack-mouthed. His bow was lethargic. "Do you care to dance?"

"Not tonight, thank you."

There was a moment's silence. Saliel watched the dancers move stiffly across the marble floor.

"Are you quite well, noble Petra?"

She jerked her gaze upward. For a second she almost imagined a sharpness in Lord Ivo's eyes, then he blinked and the illusion was gone.

"I'm perfectly well. Why do you ask?"

His shrug was careless. "You don't seem yourself tonight."

Fool. If Lord Ivo could notice a difference in her manner, then so could others.

"I assure I'm in perfect health." Her voice was Lady Petra's, polite and precise and faintly edged with irritation. "However, if I must dance with you to convince you of that, so be it." She stood.

Lord Ivo blinked again, lazily. "Very well." He held out his arm.

Saliel made sure to thin her lips slightly in annoyance before she placed her hand on his sleeve.

"I spoke to the Consort today," Lord Ivo said as they walked onto the dance floor.

"So did I." Saliel shivered, remembering the icy wind, the blackness of the Consort's eyes, the sudden shock of the woman's words. *Spycatcher.*

Slow-moving couples parted to let them through.

"I look forward to our union."

Here on the dance floor she was prey, trapped. Dancers surrounded them. Panic tightened Saliel's throat. She swallowed, and tried to concentrate on Lord Ivo's words. *I am a Corhonase noblewoman. My name is Lady Petra. I am betrothed to a man I dislike.* "Do you?" she said, her voice cool.

"Yes." Lord Ivo's smile was wide and amiable. "We are well-matched."

Her awareness of the throng of dancers faded slightly. It took effort not to frown at him. "Well-matched?"

"Don't you agree?"

Saliel walked a few paces in silence, and then said, "The Consort is known to choose wisely." To her ears, her voice sounded flat.

"Yes." Lord Ivo's eyes gleamed in the reflected light of the chandeliers.

Is he laughing at me?

Saliel shook the notion off. She smiled stiffly and followed Lord Ivo's lead as he moved through the steps of the dance. He ambled, like a man half-asleep.

"You put off your mourning clothes soon."

"Yes."

The dancers seemed to glance sideways at them as they passed, their eyes sharp and suspicious. Saliel's chest was tight, her throat. It was difficult to breathe fully. *Fool. You imagine it. No one suspects.*

"Our betrothal is to be announced next week."

"Yes." The glittering, watching eyes made her heart beat too fast. Saliel swallowed. She forced herself to look down at the red and black squares of stone she stepped on, to concentrate on the dainty dance slippers and polished boots of her fellow dancers, instead of their eyes.

"Are you quite well, Lady Petra?"

Her gaze jerked up. Lord Ivo was looking at her, an expression of mild inquiry on his slack-jawed face.

"Of course," she said, and realized that she held his arm tightly. She released her grip on his sleeve. "If I appear distracted, it's merely because I'm thinking about... our betrothal ceremony. I'm trying to decide which dress to wear. Lavender or brown. Perhaps you have a preference? The brown is a shade similar to cinnamon and the lavender..."

Lord Ivo's attention wandered. He yawned.

"SPYCATCHER?" TWO'S VOICE was high. Athan clearly heard terror in it.

"Yes," Three said. "The one who caught the spy in Wrest."

Athan looked down at the floor. *A death worthy of nightmares.*

"When?" the guardian asked.

"She didn't say." There was no hint of panic or fear in Three's voice. "Just that it's soon."

"Do we know what he looks like?" Athan asked. He was relieved to find that his voice was as calm as Three's.

The guardian rose and began to pace within the scanty light of the candle. "He's a nobleman. Beyond that, little is known."

"Nothing?" Two's voice held a rising note of panic.

The guardian stopped pacing. His rebuke was short and sternly spoken: "Control yourself."

Two hunched slightly. His black-gloved hands clenched together.

The guardian began to pace again. "A nobleman. Thought to be in his fourth decade. In appearance he's nothing out of the ordinary, although it's said that his eyes are... curious."

There was silence. Athan heard his heart hammering in his chest. *Witch-Eye.* He cleared his throat. "Does he have the Eye?"

"Of course not," the guardian said. "He would have been burned."

Athan discovered that his hands were clenched, like Two's.

"The spycatcher's name?" Three asked quietly.

"His name isn't known."

Two stirred, shifting on the upturned urn. Athan understood his fear. He swallowed and tried to unclench his hands, to relax.

The guardian continued pacing. His footsteps echoed flatly in the chamber. "Three, I've made the arrangements for your departure. You leave in four weeks."

Three nodded.

"If the spycatcher believes you're fleeing him, he may not search the citadel."

Athan frowned. *You cast her as bait.* "Won't that be dangerous for her?"

"Only if she's caught." The guardian spoke mildly. "And there's little chance of that. Trust me."

Athan stared at him. He was no longer sure how much he trusted the guardian. *Your priorities are different to my own.*

"To have no spies in the citadel would be undesirable." The guardian stopped pacing. He sat on an urn. "If the spycatcher believes Three is his prey, then you two may be able to remain here."

"And if he doesn't believe it?" Two's voice was high, anxious.

The guardian shrugged. "Then you'll have to leave."

Athan nodded. Beside him, Two's rigid tension eased slightly.

The guardian sighed, a heavy sound. "I hope it won't be necessary. You're very valuable to Laurent."

They sat in silence, while the candle flickered and thick shadows crowded close. The guardian straightened on his seat. "Thank you, Three. It's well that we are warned." He stood. "We'll meet in two nights' time. Be careful. Do nothing to draw attention to yourselves."

Two nodded jerkily.

"Don't let your fear betray you."

CHAPTER NINE

SALIEL WORE THE lavender gown to her betrothal. It was in the same style as her mourning dresses, with a tight bodice and full skirt and a stiff ruff around her throat, but she almost didn't recognize herself in the mirror. For the first time in two years she wasn't wearing gray.

Embroidered flowers unfurled delicate lavender-blue petals at the cuffs and hemline and across the rigid, boned bodice.

"The color suits you."

Marta was right. The lavender made her eyes look more blue than gray, her hair a richer red. Saliel turned away from the mirror. The lace ruff pricked beneath her chin, tight and uncomfortable. "I'm sorry."

Marta smiled brightly. "For what?"

I would give Lord Ivo to you if I could. Saliel reached out and took her hand. "The Consort will choose wisely for you."

Marta's smile wavered. She nodded and turned away.

THE CEREMONY WAS held in the Great Hall: a huge, vaulted expanse that was part of the original citadel. Cold, gray rain fell outside. It suited Saliel's mood perfectly. Lord Ivo didn't appear to notice the difference in her appearance. His gaze was vague, his smile vacant.

She'd heard the words many times before. This time she wasn't in the audience. *Duty*, she heard the Consort say. *Honor*. And beneath those words: *Spycatcher. Very soon.*

She stood stiffly, aware of hundreds of inhaled and exhaled breaths rustling the air, aware of eyes watching her. Candles burned in the sconces, but the black stone swallowed the light. The faces of those watching were shadowy and half-seen. For a moment they were characters from one of her nightmares, waiting for the candles to snuff out before they hunted her, then she blinked and the fancy was gone.

Dutiful, she reminded herself as the Consort uttered the final phrases of the ceremony. *Obedient. Unafraid.*

The Consort pinned the betrothal keys to her bodice and stepped back. The ceremony was over. In a month her marriage would be celebrated. But she'd be gone before then and the blank, un-notched keys would never be cut.

Would the spycatcher arrive before she left? How soon was soon?

Fear was tight in her chest as she allowed Lord Ivo to take her hand, as she curtseyed deeply to the Consort—*obeisance, gratitude*—as she rose and turned to accept Marta's quiet words of congratulation.

Lord Ivo's hand was warm and limp.

"It was a fine ceremony," Marta said.

"Thank you." Saliel slid her fingers from Lord Ivo's grasp. He appeared not to notice.

"I wish you every happiness."

"Thank you," she said again.

Beside her, Lord Ivo yawned.

CHAPTER TEN

THE SPYCATCHER DID have striking eyes. The irises were
unnervingly pale, almost white within the dark rings
that edged them.

Instinct made the hairs on the back of Athan's neck
prick upright, but common sense told him there was
no magic in that ice-pale gaze; if the man had witch-
ery in his blood he'd be dead.

In appearance the spycatcher was ordinary. His
height and build were medium, his hair brown, his fea-
tures unremarkable. He would have passed unnoticed
if not for the unusual color of his eyes.

His name was Lord Grigor and he had arrived in
court yesterday, three weeks after Three's warning.
His identity as spycatcher hadn't been disclosed and—
so far as Athan had been able to observe—few people
knew who he really was.

The man's manner was amiable. Wherever Athan
went he found him watching and listening and asking
questions. So far the spycatcher had paid him little
attention—a circumstance that made him slightly
nervous. Tonight he was determined to initiate a conversation with the man. *I need to know how
dangerous he is.*

Athan paused as he entered the courtesans' salon.
The smell reminded him of a tropical fruit, over-ripe
and fermenting slightly.

He scanned the room slowly. The mirrored tiles on the ceiling glittered, reflecting candlelight and glimpses of velvet and lace and bare flesh.

A servant approached, offering wine. Athan took a glass, his gaze sliding from face to face, seeking the spycatcher.

There he was. In one of the alcoves with a courtesan.

He slid his eyes away. The man liked it rough. *He enjoys giving pain.*

Athan looked down at his wine and discovered he didn't want to drink it.

Lord Druso jostled his elbow. "Well, Donkey, where to?"

Athan glanced back at the alcove. The spycatcher had finished taking his pleasure; the whore wasn't lingering at his side. He inclined his head in the man's direction. "Shall we make the acquaintance of Lord... uh, Lord Grebber?"

"Grigor," said Druso. He shrugged. "Why not?"

Athan ambled across the salon, the untasted wine in his hand. The spycatcher looked up as they approached. He was struck again by the paleness of the man's eyes. Tiny hairs pricked up on his skin. *Witch-Eye.* Then logic reasserted itself. The spycatcher was dangerous—but not because he was a witch.

Athan yawned, and bowed. "Lord Grebber."

"Grigor," said Druso, laughing. "It's Lord Grigor, Donkey, you idiot." He bowed to the man.

"I beg your pardon." Athan smiled in lazy apology, his eyes half-closed. "Lord Grigor."

The spycatcher inclined his head in greeting. "Lord Druso, I believe. And Lord Ivo. Pray join me."

"Thank you."

Athan sat and leaned back against the cushions.

"I trust you're enjoying the citadel," Druso said courteously.

"I am, thank you." The man smiled. "Very much."

Athan indicated the salon, slopping wine carelessly from his glass. "What's not to enjoy?"

"Nothing." The man's smile widened. "I'm sure I'll find my stay here most pleasurable."

Druso nodded. His eyes passed over the courtesans as he sought one.

"Where are you from?" Athan asked as he sipped from his glass. The wine was spicy on his tongue.

"Wrest," said the spycatcher. The paleness of his gaze almost made Athan shiver. "Do you know it?"

Athan shook his head. "No."

"And you?" The spycatcher's attention shifted. He seemed amused by the length of time Druso was taking to select a whore. "Are you a native of the citadel?"

The urge to shiver faded, now that the man's eyes were on Druso. "No," Athan said. "I'm from Haast."

"Haast?" The spycatcher stopped studying Druso. "I hear it rains a lot there."

The colorless gaze was oddly unsettling. Sweat prickled between Athan's shoulder blades. "More than anywhere else in the Empire," he said, and gulped another mouthful of wine.

The spycatcher smiled. "And do you like rain, Lord Ivo?"

Athan shrugged. "Not particularly."

The spycatcher watched him for a moment, still smiling. "How long have you been here?" he asked. A casual question—except for the intentness of his gaze.

"Bit more than a year," Athan said, sweating. "Same as Druso. We met aboard ship." He smiled at the man and drained his glass.

The spycatcher reached out to halt a passing servant.

"My thanks." Athan leaned forward and exchanged his empty glass for a full one.

"Why come to the citadel?" he heard the spycatcher ask.

Athan settled back on the cushions. "Touring the Empire," he said, raising the glass to his mouth. "As one does." He looked at the spycatcher and found the unnerving eyes intent on his face and almost choked on the wine.

"And you and Lord Druso are still here?" The spycatcher's eyebrows rose slightly in surprise.

Athan shrugged. "A number of us stayed. Druso. Tregar. Irmer."

Druso leaned over and caught the skirts of a courtesan. The woman giggled and slid obligingly onto his lap. The spycatcher's eyes moved to watch as Druso began to unfasten her scanty, lace-trimmed garments.

"The citadel has the best whores outside the Emperor's court, after all," Athan said.

"Yes," the spycatcher said, his gaze still on Druso and the courtesan. "For a principality on the edge of the Empire, it does very well."

Athan sipped his wine. "Do you intend to stay long?"

"No," the man said, his attention on Druso. "My business will soon be concluded."

Athan's chest tightened. "Business?" He infused vague interest into his voice. "What is it? Perhaps I can be of assistance."

The spycatcher glanced back at him. "Thank you, but it's a trifling matter. I require no assistance."

"Oh?" Athan's skin crawled beneath that milk-white gaze. "Well, if you have any difficulty—"

"There'll be no difficulty." The man's tone dismissed him. He turned back to watch Druso.

Athan sipped his wine and forced himself to relax, settling deeply into the soft cushions. Beside him Druso lay sprawled, fondling the whore while she divested him of his breeches.

"I hear that you like redheads." The pale eyes turned his way again.

Not particularly, he'd intended to say, but instead his mouth said, "I'm partial to the color."

The spycatcher turned and beckoned.

Athan frowned at his wine. *What possessed me to tell the truth?* He put the glass down and watched with resignation as the red-haired courtesan crossed the salon.

"She's the one you wanted?" he heard Lord Grigor ask.

Athan closed his eyes. "Yes," he made himself say, as the whore slid onto the cushions alongside him. "My thanks."

He tried to relax his body as the courtesan unbuttoned his breeches and opened his doublet. There was a warm mouth on his skin and deft fingers stroking him, but he felt no stir of arousal. He was too aware of the spycatcher reclining beside him, watching.

"I understand why they call you Donkey."

Actually, they call me Donkey for my lack of wits as much as anything, but I pretend not to realize. Athan opened his eyes. Hair pricked upright on the back of his skull as he met the man's gleaming, colorless gaze. It took all his effort not to tense. He shaped his mouth into a vague smirk.

The spycatcher looked away. "Wine!" he called, snapping his fingers.

Athan closed his eyes again. He was sweating beneath his bunched clothing. *Relax*, he told himself. *Get it over with.*

He built the salon behind his closed eyelids, concentrating on the smells of perfume and wine, on the raucous laughter, on the sound of Druso panting alongside him. It was an evening like any other, familiar and unthreatening. *Relax.*

His body recognized the courtesan's skilled tongue and fingers. It helped, as it always did, to pretend she was Lady Petra. Her voice might be cold when she spoke to him, but her mouth was hot and greedy.

The whore shifted. He felt her warm weight on top of him. His world narrowed to the softness of the thighs that straddled him. *Lady Petra, riding me.*

Athan's skin became tight. He heard himself groan. For a fleeting moment he forgot the spycatcher entirely.

CHAPTER ELEVEN

SALIEL SAT TENSELY, smiling, as the spycatcher bowed over her hand. "May I have this dance, Lady Petra?"

"Certainly." She stood and placed her hand on Lord Grigor's arm. Her heart was beating too fast. *Calm. Breathe. Be Lady Petra.*

They took their places on the dance floor. The musicians began to play.

"Are you a native of the citadel, noble Petra?" the spycatcher asked. He was a good dancer. His movements were neat and precise, light-footed.

Saliel shook her head shyly. "No."

The man smiled at her, courteous and attentive. "Have you been here long?"

"Nearly two years, my lord."

He glanced at the betrothal keys clinking faintly at her waist. "I see you're soon to be married."

"Yes." Saliel nodded and tried to blush. She looked down the floor, as if overcome by modesty.

They paced alongside each other in silence for several seconds, her hand resting lightly on the spycatcher's sleeve, then he asked, "Where are you from, noble Petra?" His tone was polite, conversational.

Saliel stared at the floor. Dull red squares. Black squares. "The colony of Gryff."

Perhaps it was her imagination, but she thought the spycatcher stiffened slightly. "Ah," he said. "A terrible catastrophe."

"Yes, my lord."

"Your parents," he said. "Tell me about them."

Saliel raised her eyes from their scrutiny of the floor. She blinked as if forcing back tears. "It's painful to discuss, my lord."

"Of course," he said smoothly. "I beg your pardon."

Saliel managed a weak smile.

The spycatcher smiled encouragingly back at her. "So you're to be married."

Saliel bit her lip and nodded. "Yes."

"To Lord Ivo."

"Yes," she said again.

"You must be very happy."

"Oh," she said. "Well, I'm…" There was something unsettling about the man's eyes. When he looked at her like that it was difficult to lie.

Suddenly Saliel understood. *He does have the Eye.*

Her heart began to beat more rapidly. *This is a test. Pass it.* She hesitated and then whispered in a rush, "I don't wish to marry him."

The spycatcher smiled, a quick and satisfied movement of his mouth.

Saliel tightened her fingers on his sleeve, clutching at him. "Please don't tell anyone, Lord Grigor! I shouldn't have told you."

"Don't distress yourself, my dear." The spycatcher patted her hand. His fingers were cold. "I shan't tell anyone."

She smiled at him, tremulous, grateful. "Thank you, my lord."

"Not at all," he said smoothly. "It's a great shame your mother isn't here to support you. She would allay your fears." He patted her hand again. "What did you say her name was?"

Saliel was aware of a compulsion to tell him the truth: that she had no idea what her mother's name was. The tiny itch was easily ignored. "Lady Frida," she said, looking into the spycatcher's eyes. "Of Gryff."

The man nodded and smiled his quick, satisfied smile again. His gaze slid away to briefly examine the dancers in their vicinity and then came back to her.

Saliel forced herself not to stiffen and look away.

"When are you to be wed?" the spycatcher asked, his manner polite and attentive.

Never. "In eight days," she said. "Will you still be here?"

She had the impression that the man almost smirked. His eyes gleamed. "I doubt it."

Saliel shivered inside herself. Last night, in the dark hours of the night, she'd dreamt that the spycatcher had stared at her with pale, terrible eyes and said: *I know who you are.* Her panic had been so great that she'd woken, a silent scream in her mouth.

Her throat tightened in memory. For a moment she was unable to breathe. She raised her fingers to her lips and coughed delicately.

"Are you all right?"

Again she felt the compulsion to speak the truth. *No, I'm not all right. I'm terrified.* And again the lie came easily. "Perfectly." She smiled at him.

The dance ended and the musicians laid down their bows. Other sounds were suddenly loud in the absence of music: the rustling of stiff fabrics—silk and lace and satin—and the shuffle of shoes on the polished stone floor.

The spycatcher escorted her back to her seat. He bowed over her hand. The soft touch of his mouth made her want to shiver.

"Thank you, my lord."

"The pleasure was mine."

Saliel watched as Lord Grigor walked away. He paused for a moment, his pale gaze sliding over faces, and then crossed to Lady Serpa and bowed.

I passed the test. But her tension, the fast beating of her heart, didn't ease.

"A pleasant man, is he not?"

Saliel smiled at Marta. "Very pleasant." She rubbed where the spycatcher's mouth had touched her hand, trying to wipe the sensation away.

"I've never seen anyone with eyes quite that color. Have you, Petra?"

She shook her head in response to Marta's half-heard words and stared across the dance floor. One was somewhere in the ballroom. Perhaps one of the noblemen standing talking, perhaps one of the dancers moving slowly across the polished stone floor. *I have no way of warning him.*

Saliel tore her attention away from the dance floor and smiled at Marta. "A very unusual color," she agreed.

She found she was twisting the cinnamon-brown fabric of her gown between her fingers, as Marta was wont to do. She smoothed a hand over the crumpled material and forced herself to relax. She'd see One and Two tomorrow night. Tonight there was nothing she could do except sit and converse quietly with Marta— and hide her anxiety from observers.

She let her hands lie loosely clasped in her lap and smiled at Marta. *It's only one day. Everything will be fine.*

CHAPTER TWELVE

THE DAY PASSED even more slowly than it usually did in the ladies' court. Saliel embroidered, sitting on a sofa with Marta alongside her, she ate lunch, swallowing the food without tasting it, she embroidered again, stitching unfurling leaves in differing shades of green silk. Finally it was time to put away her needles. The evening stretched ahead—a bath, dinner with the unmarried ladies, the nightly ball. It was the rhythm of her days, as regular as the inhalation and exhalation of her breath. *And then the catacombs.*

Saliel stood. Every part of her was tense with anxiety.

The bath did nothing to ease her tension. The water steamed gently, scented with lavender. It was the smell of the ladies' court. No noblewoman would dream of wearing perfume or painting her face—only whores did those things—but lavender in one's bathing water was acceptable.

"Shall I wash your back, noble Petra?" the maid asked.

"Yes."

Saliel sat forward. The bath water swirled around her as she moved. *Yes, please*, she wanted to say. It was difficult to behave as Corhonase nobles did: with careless discourtesy, as if servants were of no worth.

She'd been a servant herself and knew the importance of *please* and *thank you*.

The maid began to sponge her back. Saliel closed her eyes. The scent of lavender was forever on her skin, faint but distinct. The scent of virtue, of modesty and docility. In her mind it was a scent that forbade laughter, a scent that made it impossible to think of picking up one's skirts and running for sheer joy.

When I return to Laurent I shall have no trace of lavender in my home.

"Shall I fetch more hot water?"

"Yes."

Saliel lay back in the bath. She tried to focus on her surroundings—the candles burning in the sconce behind her, the tall screens shielding her from the other women in the bathing suite, the murmur of voices, low and hushed—but the fear was there underneath, tight, squeezing in her stomach.

The maid returned with an urn of hot water, which she poured carefully into the far end of the copper bath.

"Do you require any further assistance?"

"No. You may go." *Thank you.*

The maid curtseyed and left.

Saliel stretched in the water. She leaned her head against the rim of the bathtub. The metalwork screens glinted in the candlelight. Shadows clung to the high ceiling above her. The scent of lavender filled her nostrils—and her mind kept coming back to the spycatcher and his eyes.

She blew out a breath. *Think of something else. Think about how glad I am not to have been born here.* Laurent wasn't perfect; she knew that as well as any foundling from the Ninth Ward, but it was better than Corhona with its—

Saliel became aware of a change in the bathing suite. The sounds were different—shocked murmurs, exclamations. The air rustled, as if an eddy of hushed excitement swept through the chamber.

She reached for the bell to summon the maid. "What is it? What's happened?"

The woman's eyes were wide with excitement. "A spy has been captured, noble lady. Here, in the citadel."

For a moment, everything halted. Saliel sat motionless. She couldn't inhale, couldn't exhale. Her heart seemed not to beat.

She swallowed and tried to speak. Fear was tight in her throat. "Who?"

The maid shook her head. "I don't know, noble lady."

Saliel mimicked the sounds she heard around her—shock, excitement—while terror built inside her. *Get out of here. Run, now.* And beneath the terror was grief, bone-deep. She closed her eyes for a moment—*Please, not One*—and then stood. "I wish to get out."

The maid brought a towel.

Saliel dried herself slowly. *Whatever happens, you must behave as normal*, the guardian had said when they'd last met. *Don't come to the catacombs until night-time.*

Saliel allowed the maid to dress her. She dined with the unmarried ladies of the court. Eating was impossible; the one mouthful she swallowed made her want to vomit. No one noticed. Excited chatter filled the room until the ceiling seemed to resonate with it.

Dressing for the ball was almost as impossible as eating. She stared across her bed chamber at the secret doorway, while the maid tightened the laces of her ball gown. Beyond those blocks of stone was safety.

What if One was telling the spycatcher about the catacombs even now?

But the guardian had been firm. *Not until night-time.* So she sat beside Marta and smiled and nodded and moved her lips to utter polite phrases—and all the while she screamed inside.

The ballroom was a terrible place tonight. The shadows behind the tall pillars were alive. They sidled and crept and gathered darkly at the edge of her vision.

The Prince sat on his dais stroking his chin smugly and the Consort's smile was vicious, triumphant. Wherever Saliel looked she saw faces that were bright with malice. Her ears were full of gleeful whispers.

The spycatcher wasn't present. He was occupied elsewhere—and that thought made the horror reverberate more loudly inside her. She knew nothing other than that the spy was male. No one knew anything else.

It was difficult to breathe. And with each breath that she failed to take, she shrank, became smaller, until the dancers began to tower over her, giant-like, with wide-stretched mouths and huge, gloating eyes. The shadows became bolder. They touched the hem of her dress and hung over her shoulder.

"Are you quite well, Petra?"

The shadows jerked back. The room became brighter and the dancers shrank until they were no larger than herself. Saliel took a quick, shallow breath. "I feel a trifle queasy."

It was hard to look at Marta. Her brown eyes glittered with bright cruelty and her round cheeks were flushed. She had never looked to better advantage.

"Poor Petra," Marta said, her expression sympathetic.

"To think there was a spy in our midst!" Her throat was tight, her voice hoarse. "It's quite terrible. How shall I sleep tonight?"

"But he is caught, dear Petra. There's no danger now."

Saliel managed a weak smile. "I know, but I can't help feeling slightly unwell."

"Your nerves are overset," said Marta soothingly. "You should retire. Come, I'll take you to your chamber." She stood and held out her hand.

"Thank you." Her gratitude was real. She wanted nothing more than to leave the ball.

Marta smiled sweetly.

SALIEL'S STEP WAS cautious, inching, the knife unsheathed and in her hand. She strained to hear above her heartbeat. The catacombs echoed with sounds tonight—the scuff of boots, a hushed whisper. But each time she halted the noises faded and she understood they were in her head.

It took forever to traverse the twisting passageways. She was aware of time passing, of precious minutes ticking away. The first gallery opened out in front of her and she gulped a breath and stared sightlessly across it. Her imagination leapt, telling her the chamber was full of men. Their clothes whispered as they moved, as they drew their blades. The air stirred with a hundred indrawn breaths.

She strained to see, to hear, the knife gripped in her hand, but the blackness was impenetrable and she couldn't hold her breath long enough, couldn't quieten the beating of her heart.

For too long she stood frozen in terror—and then the desperate need to know *who* overrode her fear.

No one touched her as she crossed the gallery, no one plucked her sleeve or grabbed her arm. Nor was there anyone in the passage beyond, or in the next chamber. Saliel's pace became faster. The whispers of sound—imagined or not—were behind her now. They followed, chasing.

She ran the final yards and crammed into the storage room. Her hands shook so violently it seemed she'd never open the door into the chamber beyond.

The door opened with a gritty sound. Faint light leaked into the darkness.

The candlelight showed her two black-garbed men who turned and came swiftly toward her. Saliel stood in the doorway, clutching the knife. She couldn't trust herself to speak for fear of crying.

"Are you all right?" the guardian asked.

Saliel nodded, her eyes on the other man. She swallowed and strove for a semblance of control. "They have Two?"

"We think they're holding him in the old cellars," the guardian said. "It should be possible to locate him."

"We can rescue him?" Hope was painful in her chest.

"Perhaps," said the guardian. "We shall try. You must wait here."

The shadows stirred beyond the candlelight, swelling and shifting. Her heart began to beat louder, faster. "Let me go with you. Please."

"No."

"But what if the spycatcher knows about the catacombs and the sewers? What if he—"

"It's a risk we must take. You will wait here." The guardian turned on his heel and strode away from her.

Saliel looked at One. "Please," she begged. *Don't leave me alone here.*

One reached out and took her by the shoulders. His grip was strong, reassuring. "If it comes to a fight, you'll be safer here than with us."

"I have a knife. I can—"

One shook his head. "I'll fight better if you're here, safe."

"But I can help—"

"I would have to protect you," he said quietly. "It would slow me."

Saliel bowed her head. She squeezed her eyes shut.

"Please stay here."

She nodded. Emotion choked in her throat, making it impossible to speak.

"Thank you." One released her shoulders. "We'll be back. I promise."

Saliel inhaled a slow, trembling breath. She raised her head and looked at him. The black hood hid his identity.

"You'll be safe here."

She believed him. Her fear faded. The shadows in this room were merely shadows, nothing more. "Be careful."

"We shall."

One turned away. She watched the darkness swallow him. The sound of his footsteps, the guardian's footsteps, faded.

CHAPTER THIRTEEN

THEY TRAVERSED THE ancient sewer system cautiously, but once in the service tunnels Athan moved faster. This was his terrain and Two knew nothing of it.

It was his usual practice to leave the tunnels as soon as he could, but tonight stealth was more important than the need to stand upright. Speed was difficult to achieve in the cramped stairwell, but finally the steep, crumbling steps went no higher. They had reached the uppermost level of the ancient cellars.

Athan paused to allow the guardian to recover his breath. The space ahead of them was musty, dank, a tunnel that serviced the cellars on this level.

"Ready?"

"Ready."

Athan moved as fast as he could in the narrow space, crouching, his shoulders brushing rough stone on either side. The air he inhaled smelled of mould. After several dozen paces his gloved fingers encountered a protuberance on the tunnel wall.

"Stop," he whispered.

The guardian grunted and halted. "Access door?"

"Yes."

Athan manipulated the mechanism gently. There was a faint grate of stone on stone and a stirring in the air, a freshness, but no change in the blackness. He slid the door shut. The guardian said nothing.

Dim light leaked in when he opened the fifth door.

After a moment's hesitation, Athan stepped through the opening. He slowly straightened to his full height. The cellars were silent. Ahead, a lamp hung from a bracket, casting a circle of light. He moved aside and heard cloth brush against stone as the guardian followed him.

Athan eased the access door shut. He looked at the guardian and saw his silent nod.

Their soft leather boots made no sound as they walked toward the lamp. It hung at a junction of corridors. Athan knew where he was, although it was an area he normally avoided; his own route through the cellars used more obscure pathways.

They halted. Athan strained to listen. All he heard was his own breathing.

To the left a staircase led up to the newer and inhabited levels of the citadel. Another lamp hung in a bracket on the first landing. To the right were cellars, unused for centuries, their doors lopsided and broken. A third lamp hung outside one door.

In the silence came a sound that made his skin crawl. A whimper, a moan: pain.

Athan bared his teeth in a snarl. He covered the distance to the third lamp with swift, silent steps, the cloak flaring behind him. He unsheathed his knife. The blade gleamed in the dull light.

The guardian's fingers closed about his wrist. "Wait," he breathed.

Athan shook the man's hand off. *Do you take me for a fool?* He leaned his head close to the cellar door and listened.

The door was constructed of timber bound with bands of metal. It had warped with the years and hung crookedly on its hinges. Athan heard movement inside and then the sound of flesh striking flesh.

"Curse it!" It was the spycatcher's voice. "He's fainted again."

"Perhaps cold water, my lord?"

There was the sound of a bucket of water being emptied.

Silence.

"No?" The spycatcher sounded disgusted. "Curse it!"

Someone paced inside the cellar. After a moment the footsteps stopped.

"This is unproductive." The spycatcher appeared to have regained control of himself.

"My lord?"

"I have other prey to hunt, and now is as good a time as any to start. Therlo, come with me. I need to change my clothing. You two, stay here." The spycatcher's voice approached the door.

Athan stepped back. A silent stride took him to the empty doorway of a nearby cellar. He looked around for the guardian. The man was nowhere to be seen.

"Send word when he rouses." The spycatcher's voice became louder as the door opened. "One of you must remain with him at all times. Be on your guard."

"Yes, my lord."

"I'll be in the courtesans' salon."

"Yes, my lord."

The door closed with a dry scrape.

Athan's hand tightened around the knife hilt. *I should kill you now.*

He clenched his teeth together and waited until the flat echo of footsteps had died, then stepped back into the corridor. The guardian joined him. Athan held up two fingers: *Two men.*

The guardian nodded.

With the blade of his knife, Athan gestured to himself and then to the right: *I'll take the one on the right.*

The guardian nodded again and adjusted his hood.

Athan tightened his grip on the knife. Fear flickered in his chest—as quick and bright as the gleam of lamp-light on his knife blade—but he pushed it aside and inhaled deeply, focusing on his rage.

He looked at the guardian: *Ready?*

The guardian nodded.

Athan released his breath in a slow hiss and pushed open the door.

CHAPTER FOURTEEN

SALIEL COUNTED SLOWLY, shaping the words with her lips but not saying them aloud—*one thousand five hundred and ninety-six, one thousand five hundred and ninety-seven*—trying to keep her attention on the numbers and not on what One and the guardian were doing. Had they found Two yet?

Her mind shrank from picturing what would happen when they did. What if they were injured? What if the spycatcher caught them? What if—

Fear was so tight in her chest that it was difficult to breathe. *Don't think about it. They'll come back.*

She hugged her arms and counted—*one thousand five hundred and ninety-eight, one thousand five hundred and ninety-nine.* The chill of the chamber sank through the thick woolen cloak. She began to shiver.

When the shivering became too intense to ignore, Saliel stopped counting and took the candle and explored the chamber. The shadows drew back from the tiny flame. She saw stone sinks along the walls, deep and dark-stained, and drainage gutters, and urns stacked high. The walls were lined with fine-grained black stone. A frieze was chiseled into the tall slabs. The carved images depicted the journey of death as it had been for the ancients who'd built the citadel.

Saliel lifted the candle high and shielded the flame with her hand. Here a corpse lay in state on a bier. A few steps further on, past the main entrance from the citadel—locked and barred—the candlelight revealed a funeral procession, with a bier carried high upon the shoulders of six men. The long train of mourners was particularly detailed. Women wept with their faces raised to the sky, while small children clung to their skirts.

Saliel averted her eyes from the mourners' grief and turned to the next wall. Here were the storage rooms and the secret access to the catacombs. The frieze detailed the preparation of the dead: the process that had taken place in this chamber. A body lay on a table and men with knives stood alongside. It looked as if they removed the corpse's internal organs and stored them in jars. Saliel glanced behind her at the row of stone tables, grooved and stained, and the gutters that criss-crossed the floor. She repressed a shudder.

The third wall was dominated by the official entrance to the catacombs, unopened for centuries. The door towered high, its heavy metal wings corroded with age. On one side, robed priests wrapped the dead man in intricate layers of cloth. On the other side they carried the body into the catacombs and laid it in a niche.

The fourth wall… Here was the low door that led to the disused sewer tunnel. She laid her hand on the rough stone and felt its coldness through her glove.

We'll be back, One had promised.

Saliel turned away. She placed the candle on the nearest table. Its surface was pitted and scored, stained with ancient blood. She sat on an upturned urn and clasped her hands together and waited. She didn't count this time; instead she watched the candle become shorter by tiny increments, watched the flame twist and flicker, watched the wax melt.

It seemed that many hours passed before the door finally swung open. The rush of noise and movement was momentarily frightening, before it resolved itself into two hooded men with black and swirling cloaks carrying the body of a third man between them.

Saliel leapt to her feet and reached for the candle. One and the guardian eased the limp body onto the stone table. She caught her breath at the sight of Two's battered face.

"Is he alive?"

The men were breathing heavily. "Yes," the guardian said in a harsh voice. "He lives. But I don't know for how long." He gestured for the candle. "I think his heart's failing."

One turned away from the table. "I'm going to the courtesans' salon. Perhaps I may learn something from the spycatcher."

"What?" Saliel jerked her head around to look at him.

One didn't glance back, nor did he halt. "I'll be back as soon as—".

She pushed away from the stone table. "No! Wait!" She caught his wrist as he reached for the door. "You must beware of the spycatcher's eyes!"

One turned toward her. His arm was tense beneath her hand. "What do you mean? Witch-Eye?"

She nodded. "His eyes make you want to speak the truth."

"Are you certain?" The guardian left Two's body and came to stand with them.

"Yes. Last night, when I danced with him…" She shuddered, recalling her conversation with the spycatcher. "When he looks at you there's a compulsion to speak the truth."

"And did you?" the guardian asked sharply.

Saliel shook her head.

"I've lied to the spycatcher." One flexed his wrist, freeing it from her grip. "I recall no compulsion to speak the truth."

Saliel's certainty faltered. *Perhaps my eyes make me vulnerable?*

"Were you looking at his eyes when you lied?" she asked.

One was silent for a moment. "I can't recall. Perhaps I wasn't." He rubbed a hand over his hooded face. She thought she heard him sigh. "There is something in what you say, my lady. When I spoke to him I did reveal more than I'd intended."

"Does he suspect you?" the guardian asked tersely.

One shook his head. "No."

Saliel bit her lip. "So... you won't go?"

One glanced at the guardian. "I must."

The guardian nodded.

"But—"

"He's looking for more of us." One's voice was flat. "I must try to learn how many."

Saliel opened her mouth to protest, but closed it without uttering a sound. She shook her head silently.

"Thank you for the warning, my lady." One made a movement of his head that was almost a bow. He opened the door to the disused sewers.

Saliel clasped her hands tightly together. She wanted to grab his arm again and refuse to let him go. *He risks his life doing this.*

"Be careful." The words came out as a whisper.

One nodded, and ducked through the low opening. The door closed.

The guardian turned away. Saliel stayed where she was, her fingers knotted together.

"The wounds are mostly superficial," the guardian said.

She turned to see him bending over the table.

"Stay with him." The guardian straightened. "I'll fetch a stretcher. He can't remain here."

Saliel inhaled a shallow breath and stepped closer to the table. "His heart?" She had no medical knowledge, no notion of how to care for Two.

"It's failing." The guardian handed her the candle. "If he rouses, ask him what you can. We must know what he told the spycatcher."

Saliel nodded, barely hearing his words. Her throat clenched as she looked at Two. Blood. The gleam of bone through cut flesh.

"Thank you," the guardian said. He left.

The spycatcher had used a knife; blood leaked from cuts on Two's brow and cheeks and beneath his chin. His nose was broken and he'd bled heavily. Every finger on his right hand was broken. He struggled to breathe. His lips were blue-tinged and his green doublet dark with water.

Saliel removed her cloak and covered Two. That much—that little—she could do. She pulled off her gloves and touched fingertips lightly to his throat. The skin was cool, clammy, his pulse rapid and very faint.

She brushed wet, brown hair carefully back from Two's brow and took hold of his left hand. Beneath the blood he was young. *Younger than I am.* "Two..." Her voice was hoarse, her throat almost too tight for words. "You're safe now." She squeezed his limp fingers gently and listened to his shallow, gasping breaths. "They can't hurt you any more."

CHAPTER FIFTEEN

THE SPYCATCHER WASN'T present when Athan entered the courtesans' salon. He'd never killed a man before; he trembled inside himself with the shock of it. The scents and sounds swamped him. He took a deep breath, quelling nausea, and signaled for a glass of wine. A servant brought a tray. "Lord Ivo," he said, bowing low.

Athan took a glass. His fingers shook faintly.

The servant turned to go.

"Wait."

Athan recognized the voice. His muscles tensed. He brought the glass to his lips and sipped.

The spycatcher came up alongside him. The servant bowed and offered the tray again.

"Lord Grebber," Athan said in greeting.

Irritation flickered across the spycatcher's face. "Grigor."

"My apologies."

"No matter." He turned away from Athan. His pale eyes scanned the room. There was a sense of barely restrained anticipation about him. *He's like a hunting dog, eager to pursue its prey.*

Athan laid his hand heavily on the man's shoulder. "I see a vacant alcove," he said. "Do join me."

Annoyance tightened the tiny muscles around his mouth. He met Athan's eyes squarely.

The hairs on the back of Athan's neck stood upright. *Walk away*, instinct told him.

"Thank you for the invitation, Lord Ivo, but—"

Athan pushed aside his fear. "Then you'll join me?" He smiled affably and took the spycatcher's arm.

The man hesitated, and then smiled. "Very well. But let us join Lord Tregar. He has a surplus of whores."

Athan looked around the room, allowing his mouth to gape slightly open. He nodded. "By all means." He ambled in the direction of Lord Tregar, his arm still linked with the spycatcher's. The man had bathed. There was no scent of blood on him.

Rage rose in Athan's throat, hot and sharp. *I saw what you did to him.*

He wanted to kill the man; instead he asked, "Are you in good health?" His tone was that of a man making idle conversation. "I don't recall seeing you in court today."

"I'm perfectly well," the man replied politely, glancing at him. "And you?"

Athan suddenly understood what Three had meant: it was impossible to lie with those colorless eyes looking at him. His rage vanished. Terror replaced it. "I feel somewhat nauseous," he was forced to confess, while his heart thudded in his chest. *I should not have doubted you, my lady.*

"How unfortunate," the spycatcher said. He looked away.

An inebriated whore slid off a nobleman's lap and tumbled giggling to the floor. Athan disengaged his arm from the spycatcher and stepped around her. Cold sweat gathered on his skin. "How's your business progressing?" he asked, not looking at the man.

"Extremely well, thank you."

"Oh?" He infused his tone with mild interest. "Then you'll be leaving us?"

"Not just yet." The spycatcher paused to drink deeply from his glass.

Athan watched from beneath half-closed eyelids as the man's gaze slid back to Tregar. He swallowed the fear that clogged his throat. "You have more business here?"

The spycatcher didn't answer immediately. He was intent upon Tregar.

Athan waited. His pulse beat loud and fast in his ears. *Tell me.*

"More?" the spycatcher said absently. He sipped his wine. "Yes."

Athan's fingers tightened around his glass. The sound of his heartbeat became louder. "Much more?" he asked in a disinterested tone. *Is it just me you seek? Or do you search for all of us?*

The spycatcher transferred his gaze to Athan. The pale eyes examined him. He could almost see the question forming on the man's lips: *Why do you want to know?*

Panic clenched in his chest. "Perhaps I can be of assistance," he blurted. He stretched his lips in a smile.

Amusement lit the spycatcher's face. His voice was polite and dismissive: "I require no assistance, thank you." He inclined his head courteously and gestured toward Lord Tregar. "After you."

Athan shrugged and strolled to where Tregar lay with three courtesans. He wiped sweat from his face in a leisurely movement. *I should walk away now.*

He dared not, not after insisting on the man's company.

"Mind if we join you, Tregar?" he asked, forcing his voice into a lazy drawl. He was aware of the spycatcher standing alongside him, taut and almost quivering in his eagerness to hunt. "You appear to have a superfluity of whores."

Tregar's glance was sour. "By all means."

"You know Lord Grebber?" Athan asked, as he reclined on the cushions, trying to relax and not lie stiffly.

"Grigor," the spycatcher said smoothly. "It's a pleasure to meet you, Lord Tregar."

Tregar nodded curtly. "About that pig, Donkey," he said.

Athan waved his glass in negation. Wine slopped on the brocade cushions. "Not for sale, Tregar." One of the courtesans moved to lie beside him. Her hair was as dark and glossy as Lady Marta's, her breasts lush, and her belly softly rounded. She stretched, a sensuous arch of her back, and laid a hand on his leg.

"Pig?" the spycatcher asked.

"Donkey has a russet piglet," Tregar said, his tone resentful. "A very fast creature. And he won't sell her."

Athan shrugged, wanting to push the whore's hand away. Her fingers traced tiny, tickling whorls up his thigh. The nails were gilded. "I'm partial to the color."

Tregar clenched his jaw. He gestured for more wine. A servant approached and knelt, holding out a tray. Tregar snatched a glass and took an angry swallow.

"Tell me, Lord Tregar," the spycatcher said idly. "How long have you been at the citadel?"

"What business is it of yours?" Tregar said. He glanced up and met the spycatcher's eyes.

A shiver crawled over Athan's skin. *Caught.* He scarcely noticed as the courtesan unbuttoned his breeches.

"A year and a bit," Tregar said grudgingly.

The spycatcher smiled. He turned his attention to the woman at his side.

Athan closed his eyes as the dark-haired whore slid her hand inside his breeches. She made a low murmur of appreciation in her throat.

"Tell me, Donkey... may I call you Donkey?"

Athan tensed. He raised his eyelids a fraction. The spycatcher watched as the dark-haired whore bent her head. "You may call me Donkey."

"Thank you," the spycatcher murmured. He glanced up. "Tell me, Donkey..."

Athan experienced a moment of pure terror. He couldn't look away. His eyes were caught.

"Do you like your bride-to-be? Lady Petra."

It was impossible to joke and turn the question aside, to not answer, and even more impossible to lie. With the spycatcher's eyes fixed on him, all Athan could do was speak the truth. "I prefer her to the other ladies in court."

Beside him, Tregar sniggered. The dark-haired whore bent her head lower. He felt soft breath on his skin, a warm tongue.

The spycatcher raised his eyebrows in amusement. He kept his gaze on Athan. "You prefer your betrothed to... let's see... Lady Marta?"

Perspiration trickled down the back of Athan's neck. "Yes."

Lord Tregar snorted his laughter.

"You find Lady Petra attractive?" The spycatcher's voice was light and amused. *This is friendly teasing*, his tone said. His eyes said otherwise. Their gleam— pale and sharp—revealed the man's dislike.

Again Athan was forced to answer with the truth. "I'm greatly attracted to her."

Tregar choked on his wine and began to cough. More sweat slid down the back of Athan's neck. He forced himself to lie relaxed, his half-full wine glass held loosely in his hand, a smile on his mouth as if he didn't know he was being made a fool of.

The spycatcher glanced at Athan's lap and the naked dark-haired courtesan. "And do you think that Lady Petra is pleased to be marrying you?"

Athan shut his eyes. *Of course not. She can't abide me.* "Why wouldn't she be pleased?" he answered, slurring his words slightly.

The spycatcher uttered a soft, laughing sound. "Why not indeed?"

Athan pressed his head back against a cushion, more aware of the spycatcher alongside him than he was of the whore's agile tongue. He dared not open his eyes to see whether the man was watching.

"Tell me, Donkey..." the spycatcher said again.

"Not now." Athan squeezed his eyes more tightly shut, hoping the man would mistake the sweat on his skin for arousal. He groped desperately for a familiar fantasy.

It seemed a violation to use Lady Petra after the evening's ugliness—the blood, the death, the terror. *Forgive me.*

It worked, as it always did. Fear receded as Lady Petra began to pleasure him. Her mouth was soft and warm and her fingers knew just how to touch him. Athan relaxed as slowly, skillfully, she took him out of himself.

CHAPTER SIXTEEN

TWO'S BREATHING STOPPED. The chamber was completely silent. Saliel leaned over him. "Two!"

He inhaled, deeply and convulsively. His eyes opened. Beneath its mask of blood his face contorted into a grimace of pain.

"You're safe," Saliel said hastily. "We're in the catacombs." She squeezed his hand gently.

His fingers flexed in her grasp, clutching weakly back. "Three?" It was more a groan than a word.

She nodded. "Yes."

"Can't breathe," Two said. There was panic in his voice. He struggled to raise his head.

Saliel released his hand and put an arm under his shoulders, helping him to sit. "You're going to be all right," she told him.

Two shook his head. "I told him about you." His breath was shallow, sobbing.

He's crying.

Saliel held him more tightly. "It's all right."

Two shook his head again. "I tried not to tell. But his eyes..." He clutched her arm. "I had to tell him. I couldn't—"

"Hush," she said, stroking his hair.

"I couldn't lie. It was his eyes." His fingers dug weakly into her arm. "You must understand!"

"I do understand," Saliel said. "His eyes compel the truth to be spoken."

"Yes," gasped Two. The grip of his fingers loosened. "Yes."

He sagged against her. His breathing slowly steadied, became less distressed. "How did he find you?" she asked quietly. "Can you tell me?"

Two shivered in her arms. "It was his valet," he whispered. "Therlo. He was asking questions... and I panicked."

Saliel smoothed damp hair back from his brow. "What did you tell the spycatcher?" she asked softly. "How much does he know?"

Two struggled for breath. "At first he just asked... about me. Who I was... Where I came... from. What I was... doing here."

Saliel cradled his head against her shoulder and stroked his hair. "Go on," she whispered.

"Then he began... asking... other questions. He wanted to know... was I alone? I tried not to tell... but his eyes—" Two's voice broke.

She rocked him gently. "You're safe now. He can't find us." *Or can he?* She tensed. "Did you tell him about the catacombs? About this chamber?"

"No," gasped Two. "He asked... at the end... but I couldn't... speak... couldn't... breathe."

Saliel relaxed slightly. She held him while his breathing became calmer. When he was no longer gasping, she asked, "What did you say about us? Can you tell me? Please?"

"Nobles," Two said. "I told him... nobles. You and One... He wanted to know... who... but I didn't know." His voice rose in distress. "He kept asking... *who*."

"Hush," Saliel whispered. "It's all right."

"No." His voice was a faint thread of sound.

Saliel's throat tightened so much that she couldn't speak. She swallowed, hard. "What else did you tell them?"

"I told him... 'bout the... Oceanides... How we found out."

"Anything else?"

Two shook his head, panting.

"The guardian?"

"Yes. Told him... 'bout... guardian."

"But he knows nothing about the catacombs? Or the sewers? You're certain?"

He nodded weakly. "Didn't... tell him. Certain."

The spycatcher hadn't learned everything. They were safe beneath the citadel.

Two sagged more heavily against her. "Told him... 'bout you."

"It doesn't matter," Saliel said.

"Sorry..."

"It doesn't matter," she said again. "We're safe. All of us."

Two groaned. "My chest," he said in a faint, strained voice. "My chest... hurts."

"You're going to be all right," Saliel said, holding him, rocking him gently. "The guardian's gone for a stretcher. We'll take care of you."

Two didn't answer her. The candle flickered and the shadows drew slowly closer. His breathing became more labored. "What's... your... name?"

"Saliel."

"Saliel," he whispered.

She shut her eyes at the sound of her name on his lips. It sounded as if he was saying farewell. "What's yours?"

He gasped for breath. "...Rolen."

"Rolen?"

He nodded.

She smoothed the damp hair back from his brow. "You're going to be all right, Rolen."

His panting became more desperate. "May I... see... your face?"

"Of course." Saliel reached up and pulled off her hood.

Two raised his head slightly. His bloody mouth twisted into a smile. "Red... hair," he said.

Saliel tried to smile back at him. "Yes."

"Nice..."

He slumped back against her. She held him close. His hair smelled strongly of blood. "You're going to be all right, Rolen," she whispered, while tears slid down her cheeks.

Rolen didn't speak again. His breathing grew harsh. And then it stopped.

Saliel drew back. "Rolen," she said, shaking him. His body was heavy and unwieldy. "Rolen!" Her voice rose. "Rolen, *please*."

He didn't inhale and her fingers found no pulse at his throat. Saliel laid him back down on the table and cried, holding him. When she had no tears left she touched his face gently with her fingers. He looked far too young to die. "Goodbye, Rolen."

She put her cloak back on and replaced the hood, but she didn't pull on the gloves. Instead she sat holding Rolen's hand, feeling the warmth drain from him.

The candle was close to burning out when the door from the sewers opened. Saliel turned her head. A large black figure stood in the doorway.

"Two?" It was One. There was hope in his voice.

She shook her head. "Dead."

He closed the door and came to her in four long strides. His cloak swirled, and the flame flickered and nearly died in the draft. He opened her fingers and laid Rolen's cold hand on the table and put his arms around her.

Saliel leaned against him. Hot, silent tears slid down her cheeks.

One didn't say anything. He just held her close. She took comfort from his solid warmth, his strength, his nearness—and most of all from his kindness.

The door from the sewers opened again. One turned his head, but didn't release her. "He's dead," he told the guardian. His voice was low and rough, as if he'd been weeping silently too.

Saliel heard the guardian sigh. She pulled away from One.

"The courtesans' salon?" the guardian asked in a gray, defeated voice.

"I don't know how many of us he's looking for," One said flatly. "Me, we can assume. Other than that—"

"All of us," said Saliel. "He's looking for all of us."

"Two spoke?" The guardian seemed to stand taller. She nodded.

The guardian dropped the bundles he was carrying and came swiftly toward her. "What did he say? Tell me."

Saliel looked at Rolen, lying broken and dead on the stone table. She reached out and took hold of his icy hand. "He said he panicked. He said the spycatcher's valet was asking questions and he panicked."

"The man's valet?" The guardian sounded as if he frowned.

"Thurler, or something like it."

"Therlo," One said. "He was there, in the cellars."

"His valet?" The guardian nodded. "Good, it's well to know these things. Go on."

Saliel gripped Rolen's hand tightly. "He said the spy-catcher's eyes made it impossible for him to lie."

"He spoke the truth," One said grimly. "I learned that tonight."

The guardian's head jerked back. "The Eye?" Fear was sharp in his voice.

"Yes."

For a moment there was silence. The guardian cleared his throat. "What else did Two say?" He turned to Saliel. "Tell me everything."

"The spycatcher knows that One and I are nobles, and that we meet with you. But he doesn't know who we are, or where we meet."

"He doesn't?" The guardian's tension visibly eased. "Excellent. Today isn't a disaster after all."

Beside her, One stirred. "Excellent?" His voice held a dangerous edge. "Two is *dead*."

"It could be much worse," the guardian said. His tone was defensive. "We can save this situation."

"Two is *dead*," One said again.

The guardian lifted his chin. "He knew the risks."

Saliel looked down at Rolen's bloody, disfigured face. He'd known the risks—and been terrified of them. "His name was Rolen." She tightened her grip on his hand. "He said he was sorry."

The guardian said nothing. He shifted his weight slightly. One's hands closed on her shoulders, strong, comforting.

The guardian cleared his throat again. "We must bury him." He bent to the bundles he'd dropped on the floor. "In the catacombs."

One's fingers tightened slightly on her shoulders before he released her. "You have another candle?" His voice was flat, neutral.

The guardian rose and laid a candle on the stone table. "I brought two blankets. One, help me wrap him." It wasn't a request; it was an order.

One hesitated. *He's going to refuse.*

Her shoulders tensed—and then One stepped toward the guardian and picked up a blanket. He said nothing.

Saliel looked away. She lit the new candle and placed it in the holder. Then she drew on her gloves. Rolen's body, wrapped in blankets, was bulky and featureless. *He doesn't look like a person any more.*

The guardian had brought a stretcher. "Three," he said. "Take the candle and lead the way."

Saliel walked across the chamber. She opened the door to the storage room and then the concealed entrance to the catacombs.

The men came behind her, bearing Rolen's body between them. She held the candle so they could see their way through the narrow gap. It was an awkward fit. Their shoulders scraped the stone on either side. A shower of grit and pebbles fell to the floor in their wake.

Once in the catacombs the men stood upright. The gallery they were in was hewn from sandstone. Bands of natural color decorated the walls—pale cream through to rust red. The dead lay in niches carved into the stone. The intricate bindings were gone, for the most part. Bones lay exposed beneath scraps of cloth. Eye sockets gaped and brittle fingers reached out for nothing.

Saliel hadn't seen the catacombs for almost two years; the guardian had ordered her to stop using a candle once she'd memorized the route. She held the candle high and looked around. The sight was both less and more disturbing than she remembered. The dead weren't threatening. It was only in the dark or in her dreams—when her imagination reigned—that they became frightening. They didn't scare her, but somehow the sight of them dragged her spirits down. These had been people once. They had laughed and cried and dreamed, been loved and mourned. *And now they are forgotten.*

Passages opened from the chamber, five in all. "You have somewhere in mind?"

"To the left," the guardian said. "There's a rock fall. We can bury him there."

Saliel nodded and followed his directions. There was a rock fall a dozen paces into the passage. The men lowered the stretcher to the ground. Stones were hastily moved aside to create a shallow grave. Saliel said goodbye to Rolen silently and helped to cover him. They stood, and she found herself weeping again. It was somehow too dreadful for words that Rolen be left hidden beneath the rubble, with no marker to identify him. *He's not alone*, she told herself. *Others share this resting place with him.* But still her silent tears fell.

No one spoke as they retraced their steps. Back in the chamber, Saliel placed the candle on one of the stone tables.

"What now?" One asked.

The guardian leaned against the table. "Does the spycatcher suspect you?"

One shook his head. "No."

"Are you certain?"

"Yes."

The guardian turned to her. "And you?"

"I was able to lie to him. He thinks I'm Corhonase."

The guardian leaned slightly forward, as if examining her. The scrutiny made her uncomfortable. She twisted her fingers together and stood stiffly, grateful for the concealment of the hood. "I wonder why you can lie to him?"

Saliel shook her head. "I don't know."

"Very well." The guardian pushed briskly away from the table. "It's clear what must be done. You must both return to the citadel."

CHAPTER SEVENTEEN

WHAT? HER LIPS parted, but no sound came out. She sat down blindly.

"Why?" One stayed standing. He folded his arms across his chest. "If we go back, we risk losing any advantage we have."

"I'm aware of that," the guardian said, his tone sharp. "But I received orders from Laurent yesterday. We must copy one of the Corhonase code books. The need is urgent."

Saliel shook her head. "The spycatcher is looking for us."

"And doesn't suspect you. Therefore you're in no danger."

"But—"

"You're still scheduled to leave in four nights. That hasn't changed."

"I'm not worried for myself!" The words burst loudly from her. "One dare not return to the citadel! He can't lie to the spycatcher!"

"He must return," the guardian said, curt. "It's imperative the code book is copied."

"But can't you see how dangerous it is for him? If—"

One laid a hand on her shoulder, halting her. "Why is it imperative?" Saliel heard a clear note of warning in his voice. One wouldn't allow the guardian to dismiss his words. "Because Three is correct. If I return to the citadel, I risk betraying us all."

"It's a risk we must take."

"Why?"

"That's not for you to know," the guardian said stiffly.

"I believe it is." One's voice was quiet, and very firm. "If you wish for our cooperation."

The guardian didn't reply. His stillness was brittle. His black-gloved hands clenched.

The silence lengthened. Shadows stopped sidling across the floor. Even the candle seemed to cease its flickering.

"Very well." Saliel shivered at the tight anger in the guardian's voice. "If you insist."

One nodded, and released his grip on her shoulder. "I do."

"Code books were found on one of the ships captured at the Oceanides. We already had one. The other was new." The guardian spoke flatly, his displeasure evident in every word. "It appears that some Corhonase documents have a deeper layer of information than was thought. The second book—the one recovered last month—deciphers that.

"When the new code book was used, it became clear there's a third layer of code." The guardian leaned forward. The black cloak and hood didn't shroud him softly; the fabric fell in precise folds, each crease sharp with tension and anger. "The code book that contains it must be copied!"

One said nothing. His silence made the guardian exhale through his teeth, an angry hiss of sound. "A letter was intercepted several months ago. With the first code book it was propaganda. 'The Protectorate is corrupt. All Laurentine women are whores.' Nonsense like that. When the second code book was used, it became a list of every agent Corhona has in Laurent."

Saliel's breath caught in her throat. *A list of every agent.* For a brief moment—a single beat of her heart—she felt empathy for those unknown spies.

"There are more agents than was thought. Far more. Spies—and citizens who've been bribed or coerced. Naval officers, diplomatic aides, government officials. They've even infiltrated some of the noble houses."

Beside her, One stirred slightly.

"The names are there, but they're unable to be deciphered."

"Hence the third code book," One said. His tone was uninflected.

"Yes." The guardian pushed away from the stone table. Saliel felt the fierceness of his stare. "We must obtain that book. With it we can destroy Corhona's entire network of spies! It will take them years to recover. Decades."

She heard One exhale, a heavy sound. "Why us?"

"The citadel is less heavily guarded than the Emperor's court."

"But there are other minor courts—"

"We're the closest."

"But must it be now?" Saliel asked. "Can't it wait until the spycatcher's gone and we've been replaced?"

"No."

"But if they understood the circumstances," she said. "Surely—"

"We've been ordered to obtain the code book immediately. Regardless of personal risk."

"But the spycatcher's eyes—"

"I will not disobey our orders." The guardian's voice held a cold note of authority. "I advise you not to disobey them either. If you think you can leave

Corhona without my help, you're mistaken. You'd be caught before the day was out."

Saliel looked down at her hands. *He's right.* She squeezed her eyes shut for a moment, and then opened them and raised her head. "How do we obtain the third code book?"

"No," One said flatly. "You're not going back. I'll do it."

Saliel shook her head. "It must be me. I can lie to the spycatcher."

"It has to be One," the guardian said. "The code books are thought to be in the vault behind the debating chamber. No woman may enter that part of the citadel."

There was a short moment of silence. *You don't care that this may kill him, do you? You see us as tools, not people.*

"So the task is mine," One said. His voice was expressionless. "How do I open the vault?"

"With the Key to the Citadel."

One laughed, a harsh sound. "Which is why it's never been done before."

The guardian jabbed the air with a finger. "You must get that key!"

"How?" One asked, an edge of derision in his voice. "Shall I ask the Prince for it? Or shall I overpower his guards and steal it from him?"

The guardian took a step toward One. His hands were clenched.

"The Consort has the Key," Saliel said hastily, standing. "It's one of her marriage keys."

Both men turned their heads to look at her.

"No," said One. The word was a single flat syllable.

"Yes."

The guardian unclenched his fists. "You can steal it?"

Saliel shook her head, seeing the ornate silver key in her mind's eye. "It would be instantly missed. But... I can make an impression. That would take a few seconds at most."

The guardian stepped back and leaned against the table again. "An impression?"

"With soft clay or wax. If you're able to bring me some."

The guardian jerked his head in a short nod. "I can do that."

"No." One rejected the plan with a sharp movement of his hand. "Leave Three out of it. I'll try with the Prince."

"But I can—"

"It's too dangerous," One said, turning to face her. The word *dangerous* hissed on his tongue. "The Consort is no fool."

"And what you propose is even more dangerous! I can get close to the Consort. Closer than you can get to the Prince." *And I can hold her eyes. I hope.*

"But—"

"Are you one of the Prince's cronies?"

One shook his head. "No, but—"

"Then the task is mine," Saliel said firmly. "I'll do it."

"No!"

"Yes. I have the greater chance of success."

One shook his head.

"If I'm caught, I can lie to the spycatcher. You can't." She reached out and touched his arm lightly. "There's less risk for us both this way. Please."

One stared at her in silence. His arm was tense beneath the cloak. He stepped back, breaking the contact, and turned away from her. "If you insist." She heard anger in his voice, flat.

"I do."

"Very well." The guardian straightened. "I'll bring clay tomorrow night. Now hurry. Leave. It's late."

For a moment she thought One would refuse. A draft flickered the candle and lifted the hem of his black cloak, like a hawk flaring its wings. He seemed to tremble with barely suppressed rage. Then he nodded, a short jerk of his head, and turned to face her. "You'll be careful?"

"Yes. But you're in more danger—"

"Don't fear for me. I'll take care to avoid the spycatcher." His hand moved slightly, as if he reached out to touch her. He checked the movement. "Until tomorrow night."

Saliel nodded. She watched as One strode across the chamber. She didn't turn away until the darkness had swallowed him.

"Come," the guardian said brusquely. He already held open the storeroom door. "It's late. You must hurry."

Saliel hesitated at the threshold. She looked back at where One had been. *Be safe. Please.*

The guardian uttered an impatient sound. He pushed past her and opened the concealed exit, grunting as the slab of stone moved aside. "Hurry."

Saliel stepped into the storeroom, trying to ignore the fear that twisted in her stomach. So much could go wrong. "What should I do if One's caught?"

"You must leave instantly. Follow the old sewer down to the town."

"How shall I find you?"

"Wait for me at the bottom. I'll find you."

And so will the spycatcher's men. "But—"

"Hurry," the guardian said again, gesturing at the catacombs. "It's nearly dawn."

Saliel pulled her cloak more tightly around her. Rolen's body lay through that dark opening, buried beneath dirt and rubble. "Can you tell me who One is? In case—"

"No."

Saliel bit her lip. She stepped through into the catacombs. The guardian spoke as the stone slab swung shut: "I'll bring the clay tomorrow."

CHAPTER EIGHTEEN

THERE WAS NO mention in court of Rolen's escape.
Clearly the Prince had decided to suppress the news.
The Consort's gaze was cold and predatory as she sur-
veyed the ladies embroidering in the hall.

She knows one of us is a spy.

Saliel concentrated on her stitches. She found the
Consort almost as frightening as the spycatcher. The
woman was no fool. It wouldn't take her long to com-
pile a shortlist of suspects. And she would be on that
list: Lady Petra, orphan, unknown before her arrival
in court. And the Consort would remember who had
asked what questions and—

The needle jabbed into her fingertip—a sharp prick
of pain. A bead of blood welled up. She'd dreamed of
blood during the short time she'd slept. She'd been in
the catacombs and the spycatcher had found her
because she smelled of Rolen's blood. She'd run with
the light of his lamp at her heels, and the lamplight
and the sound of running feet had disturbed the skeletons. The air had rustled with the movement of brittle
bones as they'd twisted on their stony beds to watch.
And when she could run no more, she'd turned to face
the spycatcher. *Spy*, he'd hissed, his pale eyes bright
with bloodlust, reaching for her.

She'd woken with a scream in her throat. She hadn't
slept again after that.

Saliel sucked her fingertip.

"They say he was Lord Brecher's valet." Marta shivered. "How terrible. To think that one's servant was a spy!"

Rolen had panicked. She would not. Saliel stopped sucking her fingertip. "Yes, terrible." She bent her head over the embroidery again. Three more neat stitches and the flower petal was finished.

"Have you heard what he looked like?" Marta asked.

Saliel closed her eyes briefly—*don't remember*. "No," she said, tying a knot in the thread. She rummaged in her embroidery basket for the scissors.

"They say he was quite young."

Saliel snipped off the excess thread.

"And comely."

There had been nothing comely about Rolen's face last night. *Blood. The gleam of bone beneath cut flesh.* Bile rose in Saliel's throat. She closed her eyes again.

Don't think about it.

She swallowed and opened her eyes and calmly replaced the scissors. She glanced around, at the tapestries showing scenes of patriotism and honor, at the fires burning in the wide hearths, at the noble ladies clustered on the sofas, their fingers stitching busily and their heads bent together as they talked. *Spy*, she heard. *Laurentine*.

She was aware of the Consort seated across the room, her gaze sharp and black. *Relax*, she told herself, and turned back to her embroidery basket. *Choose another color. Gossip. Be like everyone else here.*

"How long had he been in the citadel?" she asked. Her fingers touched silk threads. Red: blood. Brown: the colour of Rolen's hair. Green: his shirt. *Stop it.*

"A year, they say."

"A year!" Saliel made her voice horrified. She looked up. "Think of how much he can have learned!"

Marta's mouth twisted. "Yes."

"Forgive me," she said, contrite. "I didn't mean to remind you of your husband's death."

Marta was silent for a moment, smoothing her finger over an unfurling leaf, tracing the stem of an embroidered flower. She looked up, sweet-faced and pretty. Malice gleamed in her eyes. "I hope the spy's death is terrible."

Saliel had to look away. The scent of blood filled her nose. She heard Rolen's desperate breathing beneath the hushed voices in the hall.

She swallowed against nausea and pretended to search for something in her embroidery basket. Tears burned behind her eyes as she fumbled through the contents. Scissors, skeins of silk thread, a silver thimble. *Rolen didn't die alone. I was there. I held him.*

At the bottom of the basket was the tiny box of inlaid wood that held her needles, and a stylus and tin of wax for drawing embroidery designs. Saliel reached for the tin. It was made of pressed silver, cool beneath her fingers.

Realization came as she held the tin.

Her pulse jerked, and then sped up. She raised her head and looked at the Consort. The woman's gaze was on Lady Serpa. Her expression was coldly thoughtful.

Saliel shivered. *Dare I?*

"It's only five days until your wedding, is it not?"

"Uh..." She blinked and tried to make her brain work. "Yes."

"Are you ready?" The question could have been about her gown or the suite she'd move to in the married ladies' wing, but the expression on Marta's face—anxious—told her it wasn't. *Are you ready for your wedding night?* was the question Marta asked.

Saliel's fingers clenched around the tin of wax. "Yes." Her smile felt stiff. Dread was tight in her chest—but it wasn't Lord Ivo and the marriage bed she feared; it was holding the Consort's eyes.

Marta nodded. The crease between her eyebrows smoothed away. She bent her head over her embroidery frame.

Saliel unclenched her fingers and looked at the tin. It was as wide as the palm of her hand—wide enough for the key to the citadel. She lifted the lid. Wax was molded to a smooth surface inside, smelling of bees and honey and summer. She pressed it with a fingertip. It dented softly.

Saliel exhaled a slow breath and closed the lid.

"YOUR EMINENCE?" SALIEL sank into a low curtsey. Her skin tightened in a shiver as she met the Consort's eyes. "May I speak privately with you?"

The observation lasted several seconds. *Unafraid*, Saliel told herself. *Innocent*. She swallowed and managed a timid smile, while her heart beat loudly in her ears.

The Consort made her decision. "You may." She put aside her embroidery and stood. "Come. We shall walk."

"Thank you, your Eminence." Saliel stepped back and curtseyed again. The tin was a small weight in the pocket of her gown. She cast a quick glance down as she followed the Consort across the Ladies' Hall. The stiff folds of fabric hid the tin. Its outline was invisible.

Her woolen cape hung in the antechamber. Saliel took it from its peg and turned to the mirror, buttoning the cape and adjusting it so that the slate-blue folds fell neatly. She met her own eyes. *I can do this.* Her face was as pale as parchment beneath the tightly-wound braids of red hair.

The reflection showed her the Consort and her attendants. She watched as the women fastened the Consort's cape at her throat and settled it over her shoulders.

The Consort looked up. For a moment their eyes met in the mirror. Saliel managed a smile. She took a deep breath and lifted her chin and turned around. *I can do this*.

An attendant opened the door to the courtyard. Saliel followed the Consort outside.

Cold air gusted at her, stinging in her nostrils and bringing tears to her eyes. Saliel clutched the cape tightly around her.

"Yes?" The Consort began to walk. Her footsteps echoed flatly. The sky was as gray as the marble flagstones.

"I wished to ask you about my marriage."

The Consort halted, swinging around to face her. Anger glittered in her eyes. "I have had quite enough of this, Petra. You dishonor us all with your reluctance to marry Lord Ivo. It is immodest and low-bred and not at all the behavior of a noblewoman!"

Blood rushed to Saliel's cheeks. She lowered her head, submissive. "You mistake me, your Eminence. I am quite reconciled to my marriage. It's my wedding night that I wish to talk with you about."

"What about it?" The Consort's voice was as icy as the wind.

"How do I do my duty as a wife? What is it I must do?"

For several seconds the courtyard was silent except for the gusting wind. Saliel glanced up. The Consort's gaze was dark and cold, assessing. Her eyes seemed as black as the ermine that trimmed her cape.

"Would you mind telling me what I must do?" Saliel asked timidly. "My mother didn't tell me and... and I would ask Marta, but I don't wish to remind her of Lord Soder."

The Consort's expression became less severe. "No. Of course not."

Sweat gathered on Saliel's skin despite the frigid temperature. Her mouth was dry with fear. *Now. Do it now.* But the Consort turned and began to walk again.

Saliel's feet didn't want to follow. She forced herself to take a step, a second step, a third. "Your maid will ensure that you are properly attired. And she'll wait in your parlor until it's over, in case you require anything." The Consort glanced back at Saliel. Her expression was almost compassionate. "You may wish to bathe afterwards."

Saliel bit her lip and nodded.

"As for the rest, your husband will know what to do." The Consort's voice was precise and uninflected. "The whole thing should take only a few minutes. Lie still and remember that union with one's husband is a woman's duty."

Saliel barely heard the words. She slid her hand into her pocket and touched the tin of wax with a fingertip.

"The first time is the worst; the pain will be less after that. Eventually it won't hurt at all." The Consort halted and turned to face her. "Is that what you wished to know?"

Now. Saliel swallowed past the terror in her throat and nodded again. "Yes, your Eminence. Thank you."

"It is something every noblewoman must endure."

Saliel gripped the tin in her hand and caught the Consort's gaze. Sharp eyes. Eyes so dark they were almost black. She concentrated fiercely. *You cannot look away. I have you.*

She did it between one breath and the next: pulling the tin out of her pocket, stepping forward and reaching beneath the Consort's cape. Her fingers found the key effortlessly. It was surprisingly easy, as if terror gave her some of her childhood speed and clarity of concentration. Her focus didn't waver; it was purely on the Consort's eyes. *Dark eyes, clear and sharp*. She didn't have to force herself not to glance down; her fingers knew the difference between the heavy and ornate key to the citadel and the more delicate marriage keys.

Saliel flipped the lid open with her thumb and pressed the key into the wax, aware of the blackness of the Consort's eyes, the touch of the woman's gown beneath her knuckles—the ridges of embroidery and warmth of stiffly-boned velvet.

She released the key. It fell back, hitting the Consort's marriage keys with a faint *clink*. Ermine brushed softly over her skin as she slid her hand from beneath the cape. She closed the tin and placed it into her pocket and stepped back.

Saliel lowered her eyelids briefly.

The Consort blinked. She shook her head as if to clear it. "Accept your duty with obedience and composure. To do anything else is to dishonor yourself as a wife."

"Yes, your Eminence," Saliel said again. "Thank you." She curtseyed deeply and held the position for a long moment. She nearly lost her balance when she rose. She was oddly light-headed. Her legs trembled as if she'd just run a race.

The tin of wax bumped against her thigh as she followed the Consort back to the door. Her heart beat loudly beneath her breastbone, staccato and fast, and she was aware of the prickle of perspiration on her skin. *I did it.*

Pain began to gather behind her eyes. Saliel wiped sweat from her upper lip with fingers that shook and tried to breathe deeply, slowly.

The Consort halted at the door and turned to look at her. "Was that all you wished to speak about?"

Remember who you are, Saliel reminded herself. *You are Lady Petra. Be her.*

She bowed her head humbly. "Your Eminence, I wish to apologise for my earlier foolishness. I am deeply sorry for it."

"I've been most disappointed in you, Petra."

Saliel glanced up. The Consort's expression was icy with disapproval. It was a simple matter to widen her eyes and let the wind sting them, to allow tears to gather and fall down her cheeks. "Forgive me," she whispered.

The Consort's face softened slightly. "Marriage is never an easy thing. And you have not had your mother to guide you."

Saliel nodded and tried to look pitiful, while more tears slid from her eyes and the ache intensified in her head.

The Consort tutted briskly and held out a lace-edged kerchief to her. "There is no need to cry, my dear."

Saliel took the kerchief and wiped her eyes. "Thank you, your Eminence," she said in a choked, tearful voice. "I'm sorry my behavior has been so disappointing. I... I did not mean it to be. I give you my word of honor that it won't happen again."

"Then this matter is forgotten."

Saliel clutched the kerchief in her hands. "Thank you, your Eminence."

The Consort inclined her head graciously and turned to go indoors.

CHAPTER NINETEEN

"I SAW ONE ring around the moon tonight," Athan said.

"I saw none." The guardian stepped aside.

Athan followed the man into the candlelight. A small cloth-wrapped bundle lay on the stone table. Clay, he guessed.

"Let me do it," he said, reaching for the bundle. "It's too dangerous for her to—"

He halted as the storeroom door opened. Three stood in the shadowed doorway, the hem of her black cloak swaying slightly around her ankles.

Athan brought his hand back to his side. He watched as Three waited for the guardian to approach, as she spoke her words of code. He heard the low murmur of her voice and the guardian's reply, but not the words.

He bowed as she came into the candlelight. "Good evening."

"Good evening."

"I have the clay," the guardian said, picking up the bundle and folding back the cloth.

"Wait," said Athan. "Wouldn't it be best if I—"

"I've already made an impression." Three opened her gloved hand, revealing a tiny silver case. She held it out to the guardian. "Will this suffice?"

The guardian snatched it from her hand. He lifted the lid. Athan saw pale wax inside and the impression of a key. "Yes," the guardian said. "This is perfect."

Athan looked at her. "Was it difficult? Does the Consort suspect you?"

"It was surprisingly easy." Three's voice was calm. "And no, she doesn't appear to suspect me."

He nodded.

"And you?" she asked. "How is it with the spy-catcher?"

"Fine," he said. "Don't fear for me."

"But you can't lie—"

"I have ways of avoiding conversation with him."

"If that's all," the guardian said, "we'll meet in two nights' time." He snapped the lid shut. "I'll have a key for you."

"And our departure?" Athan asked.

"Four nights from now."

And my wedding is in five. The tension he'd been holding in his shoulders eased. "Together?"

The guardian nodded. "Yes."

Athan's tension eased still further. He glanced at Three. *Whose face do you have beneath that hood, my lady?*

In four nights he'd know.

CHAPTER TWENTY

THE RACING ANIMALS were housed alongside the stables in a building constructed of brown sandstone. Athan inhaled deeply as he stepped inside. The air was warm and scented with straw and manure. The smell—familiar and earthy—was oddly relaxing. He heard grunts and squeals and the rustle of a servant shifting straw with a pitchfork.

"My lord." A servant hurried forward and bowed. "How may I assist you?"

"I wish to see my pig."

He followed the man at a leisurely pace. The flagstones were damp and freshly-scrubbed. Morning sunlight shone in through the high, barred windows.

His piglet was drinking from the trough in her pen. "An apple," he drawled, and waited until the servant had hurried to do his bidding before whistling softly.

Russet looked up at his whistle. She trotted across the pen toward him. "Hello, girl." Athan bent to rub her head. She pressed against his hand, warm, grunting softly.

The servant returned with a golden-skinned apple. Athan took it and waved him away.

He watched as Russet ate the apple, enjoying her simple pleasure. The piglet's coat was a deep red. As red as Lady Petra's hair. Redder.

What would it be like to marry her?

To be able to lie with her. To feel her smooth skin beneath his hands. To touch her hair...

Athan made a disgusted noise in his throat. There'd be nothing pleasurable about bedding Lady Petra. It would be an act of duty, emotionless and distasteful.

He sighed and leaned against the wooden railing. "I shall miss you," he told the pig in a low voice. He'd bought Russet on a whim; another example of Lord Ivo's foolishness. He'd never expected to become so fond of her.

"Is this your piglet?"

Athan recognized the voice. His skin tightened in fear. "Yes," he said, straightening and turning. He yawned widely.

The spycatcher stepped close to the wooden railing and bent to pat Russet. "What's her name?"

"Russet."

"How old?"

"Six months."

The spycatcher scratched behind Russet's ears. "Fast?"

"Very," Athan said, and yawned again. "Wins all her races."

"I shall have to bet on her. She's a fine pig." The spycatcher turned to face him. His smile seemed genuine.

Athan found that he couldn't look away from the pale eyes. His heart began to beat faster. *Take control. Don't let him ask any questions.* "You like animals?"

"Yes."

"Why?" he asked.

The spycatcher's smile altered, losing its warmth. He shrugged. "Animals don't lie."

"Lie?" Athan repeated foolishly. "Why would they lie? They're animals."

"Which is precisely my point," the spycatcher said, an edge of impatience in his voice. "They don't lie. Unlike people."

Athan wrinkled his brow, as if the concept was too difficult for him to grasp. "Oh," he said.

"People lie all the time. Or didn't you realize that, Lord Ivo?"

The terrifying eyes dragged the truth from him: "Uh, yes." Sweat slid down his throat beneath the stiff ruff of lace. Could the spycatcher smell his fear beneath the scents of straw and manure?

"I'm sure that even you have lied." The spycatcher spoke mildly, but Athan saw malice in the man's eyes. *You wish to make a fool of me.*

"Uh, yes," he was forced to reply. His heart began to beat fiercely. *Think of a question.* But he couldn't. His mind was blank.

The spycatcher's lips parted.

Athan's terror was visceral: a sudden clenching in his chest and in his belly. "Do you prefer animals to people?" he blurted.

The spycatcher hesitated with his mouth partly open, then he laughed. The sound was light and disdainful. "What an absurd question. Why would I do that?"

Sweat was damp on Athan's brow. His throat was almost too tight for speech. "Because animals don't lie."

Slow, terrifying seconds passed while the spycatcher surveyed him, amusement evident on his face. "Tell me, Lord Ivo..." the man's voice was smooth, friendly. "Would you wish to marry your piglet rather than Lady Petra?"

"Uh... What?"

"By your own admission Lady Petra must lie. And your piglet clearly does not. So would you prefer to be married to Russet?"

Athan screwed his face up, trying to look baffled instead of terrified. "No," he said.

The spycatcher laughed again, tilting his head, breaking eye contact for a brief moment.

Athan jerked his gaze away and bent to rub one of Russet's ears. Sweat stuck his shirt to his back beneath the embroidered doublet. His heart beat so loudly that it drowned out all other sounds.

Touching Russet steadied him. The sound of his heartbeat shrank. He could hear other noises—the grunts of feeding pigs, the scrape of a pitchfork on stone, the spycatcher's laughter. "Would you like to feed her an apple, Lord Grebber?"

The spycatcher stopped laughing. "Grigor."

"My apologies." Athan yawned, and then asked the question again: "Would you like to feed her?"

"No, thank you."

"Are you certain?" Athan scratched beneath Russet's chin. His fingers trembled slightly, but his voice was slow and relaxed. "She likes apples."

"No," the spycatcher said again, dismissively. "I'm looking for a piglet to race. I heard there was a litter."

Athan pointed. "Over there." And because he was Lord Ivo, he added, "But they're not red."

The spycatcher exhaled through his nose, a brief sound of disgust. "I'm much obliged to you." His bow was cursory.

Athan raised his head and watched the man walk away.

Russet nudged his hand and he began to scratch her again, his fingers moving automatically. Her coat was warm, rough, clean. He watched until the spycatcher reached the weaning pen, where black and white piglets jostled around a feeding trough. The man leaned his forearms on the wooden railing and studied the animals.

Athan straightened. He turned toward the entrance. It was a struggle to stroll languidly and not take swift steps. He wiped perspiration from his face. *That was too close. I almost gave us all away.*

HE MANAGED TO avoid the man all that day and the next. It meant not visiting Russet again; it was a risk he dared not take.

The spycatcher prowled the ballroom both evenings. Athan knew where he was; he followed Lord Grigor's passage in between yawns and sips of wine. The Consort scanned the dancers from her position on the dais, her gaze lingering on various members of the court. The Prince didn't survey the room. He sat and frowned into his wine glass.

The spycatcher was in the courtesans' salon too. The mirrors made it easier for Athan to watch him asking questions. The man must have spoken to almost every noble man and lady in the citadel. Soon he'd start again, retracing his path, asking new questions. *And then he'll catch me.*

Athan shivered. The whore he lay with mistook it for arousal and made a low murmur of encouragement in her throat. He wanted to push her away; instead he let her straddle him. She was warm and soft, lushly rounded.

He closed his eyes and tried to focus on what she was doing, but his concentration kept slipping. The spycatcher. Questions. *Concentrate.* Release came in the end but there was little pleasure, only relief it was over. He opened his eyes and searched in the mirrors for Lord Grigor. The man was on the far side of the room.

The courtesan made as if to leave. Athan caught her wrist. "Stay." He'd need her if the spycatcher tried to speak with him. *Busy*, he'd mumble and shut his eyes. *Not now. Later.*

CHAPTER TWENTY-ONE

"THE KEY TO the citadel," the guardian said. "Now remember, the first code book is red, the second is green. The third will be another color. We expect it to be thinnest of them."

Athan took the key. The metal was dark and unexpectedly heavy in his hand. "Lead?"

The guardian nodded. "When will you do it?"

"Tonight," Athan said, closing his fingers around the key. "I want this over as quickly as possible."

"I've made the arrangements for your departure." The guardian turned so that he spoke to Three as well.

Three nodded. She sat on the stone urn as calmly as if this was a tea party. Her composure was reassuring; it made some of Athan's tension ease.

"You leave in two nights' time," the guardian said. "I'll have traveling cloaks for you, but dress as warmly as you're able."

"Two nights?" Athan shook his head. "No. Make it tomorrow night."

"That isn't possible."

"But—"

"I've already made the arrangements." The guardian's voice was curt, uncompromising. "It's not possible to alter them."

Athan closed his mouth, clenching the muscles in his jaw.

"This is yours." The guardian handed the silver tin of wax to Three. "All's well?"

"Yes," she said, tucking the tin into the pocket of her cloak.

"The spycatcher doesn't suspect you?"

"No." She shook her head. "He's spoken to me several times, but I've been able to lie. He believes me to be Corhonase."

"And you?" The guardian turned to Athan.

"He doesn't suspect me yet." His fingers tightened around the key. He remembered his conversation with the spycatcher: the scent of straw and manure, sweat on his skin, panic leaping in his chest as the man opened his mouth. "But he's only a question away from unmasking me. He came close yesterday."

"Close?"

His fingers clenched so tightly that the key dug into his palm through his glove. "Very close."

Three turned to the guardian. "Let him stay here. Let me do it."

"No."

"But what if the spycatcher asks the right question? What then?" Her voice was fierce. He heard how afraid she was for him. "He'll do to One what he did to Rolen!"

The guardian stood. "There will be no discussion about this." He spoke flatly, coldly. "The task is One's."

Three rose to her feet. "But—"

Athan stood and took hold of her hand. Her calmness had been feigned. She was as tense as he was, tenser. "It will be fine," he told her.

Her fingers gripped him. "But what if he catches you? He'll *hurt* you—"

"He won't catch me. I promise."

CHAPTER TWENTY-TWO

THE KEY WAS hidden beneath the stiff lace at his cuff. Everything else he carried openly: the tiny bottle of ink with its embossed silver lid was in the pocket of his breeches, the quill and folded sheets of parchment were in the inner pockets of his doublet. The execrable verse he'd scribbled on the first two pages—*The sun was rising in the sky, when Russet op'ed her little eye*—gave reason to carry ink and quill and parchment; it was only the key he needed to hide.

Athan trod lightly. The hour was well past midnight, but candles burned in the wall sconces and guards still walked these corridors. Twice now he'd had to step into an alcove and conceal himself behind a hanging swathe of tapestry.

The guards were ceremonial, their doublets as frilled as his own. They stood at the gates to the citadel and patrolled this innermost sanctum, the ideal of Corhonase manhood: youthful and strong-bodied, with noble brows and resolute chins. Picturesque, but still dangerous. It didn't need a battle-hardened veteran to see him skulking in the shadows; a pretty youth could notice him just as easily.

He'd been this way once before, through the atria and along the corridors, up the flights of marble steps. He'd yawned and displayed languid interest in the items Lord Seldo had pointed out—busts of Emperors and the swords wielded by Corhonase heroes, tapestries depicting ancient battles—and made mental note of the route to the chamber where the Prince and his advisors met. *Left, and up one more staircase, and to the right.*

His memory was correct.

Athan halted. The doorway was impressive: fluted pilasters on either side and the screaming eagle of Corhona spreading its marble wings above. He examined the door. It was solid, tall and double-leaved and inlaid with dark marquetry. Candles burned in sconces on either side, making the silver door knobs gleam.

He glanced around. The shadows cast by the candles were the only things that moved; the corridor stretched on either side, empty. He took note of the nearest hiding places: the alcove fifty paces to the right where a statue of the First Emperor stood, sword in hand, before a tapestry showing the battle that founded the Empire; the alcove to the left, a few paces closer, hung with a tapestry depicting the fall of Sihgil, flames leaping from the rooftops.

Athan slipped two fingers inside his cuff and felt for the key. The metal was warm. He paused for a moment, listening. He heard nothing except his own quiet breathing.

The keyhole was rimmed with silver, tiny in the massive door. Athan inserted the key. There was perspiration on his skin—fear and relief. This was it. *After tonight it will all be over.*

But the key didn't slide easily into the hole. It stuck halfway.

Athan pulled the key out and rubbed his fingers over the shaft and teeth. It felt smooth enough.

This time he inserted the key more slowly. "Work," he whispered. "Curse you, *work*."

As if it heard him, the key slid fully into the keyhole. Athan let out his breath in a hiss. He glanced up the corridor, listening for the guards.

Silence.

But when he tried to turn the key it wouldn't move. "Come on," he whispered to it. "Open."

It took an agonizingly long minute to find a position where the key would turn, angling it up and down, twisting, jiggling, pulling it out a fraction of an inch. Sweat beaded on his upper lip and tension was tight in his chest. His ears strained to hear the sound of booted footsteps.

The key turned a quarter of a revolution—*click*— and then stuck again. Athan turned the key back to vertical and closed his eyes for a moment. *Don't rush this*, he told himself, inhaling a slow breath, exhaling. *Take it slowly. There's no hurry.*

He opened his eyes and gripped key tightly and turned it with slow deliberateness. The shaft snapped.

Athan stood frozen, his mind refusing to accept what had happened—and then horror dried his mouth. *No.* He'd been hot a moment before, sweating; now he was cold.

Half an inch of the key protruded jaggedly from the keyhole.

He shoved the broken shaft in his pocket and tried to pull the key free. His fingers couldn't get a proper grip; it was too short.

Athan was so focused on the key, the keyhole, that it was almost too late when his ears registered the sound of marching feet. His head jerked up.

Panic held him immobile. He couldn't tell whether the guards came from the left or the right—

The right. They came from the right.

He moved with frantic haste. With each stride, he expected to hear the guards' loud shout of discovery.

The corridor was longer than he'd thought, the alcove further away, his court shoes slipped on the marble as he ran—

Athan crammed himself behind the tapestry of Sihgil. The fabric was thick with dust, stiff and heavy. He braced his hands against it—*still*—and tried to slow his panted breaths.

The footsteps became louder as the guards swung around the corner. Louder, closer... and then they halted. Athan squeezed his eyes shut. *Don't see the key.*

The door knobs rattled. "Clear."

The footsteps started again, two pairs of booted feet, out of rhythm. Athan opened his eyes. The tapestry hung a few inches from his nose. It swayed slightly.

He splayed his hands against the fabric and held his breath. The guards came closer, striding in unison now—left, right, loud, louder.

They were level with him. Past him. Gone.

Athan exhaled. The tapestry moved slightly. He closed his eyes and rested his forehead against the stiff fabric. What to do?

Dust choked in his throat. He pushed out from behind the tapestry, struggling not to cough. *Get the key out. And then get out myself.*

But when he tried to pull the key from the lock, it slid more deeply in. There was nothing for him to grasp.

Athan exhaled through his nose, a hiss of air, and squeezed his eyes shut. *Calm,* he told himself. *Think.*

He opened his eyes and crouched. There was a half-inch gap beneath the door.

Athan groped for the sheaf of parchment in his doublet. He unfolded two sheets and smoothed them flat and slid them under the door, pushing until only a sliver of white showed; enough for his fingers to catch hold of, not enough for the guards to notice.

He stood and took the quill from his pocket—a goose feather, shorn clean of vanes. He held his breath as he slid it into the keyhole. *Let this work*. The pointed tip touched the key. He pushed, and felt the key move slightly.

Athan released his breath. He inhaled and pushed again, gently.

It was a slow task. The key moved in grudging increments. Twice he had to pull the quill from the lock and hide behind the tapestry of Sighil. Each time he heard the door knobs rattle and that single, curt word: *Clear*.

His fingers grew slippery with sweat and the linen shirt stuck damply to his back. His hand began to cramp. *Curse you. Just*—push—*come*—push—*out*.

The key fell with a dull thud.

Athan stayed where he was for a long second, bent over the keyhole, and then hastily knelt. He groped for the sheets of the parchment with his fingertips. *Let the key have fallen straight, let it not have bounced, let it—*

The parchment was heavy.

He blew out the breath he was holding and carefully eased the parchment from beneath the door. The key lay squarely on it: notched teeth and a snapped shaft.

Athan snatched it up. He folded the parchment and crammed the sheets into the pocket in his doublet. The quill. Where was the quill?

It lay half under the door, the tip blunted and split. He shoved it into his pocket and stood, his ears alert for the marching feet of the guards.

He heard only silence.

The key was heavy in Athan's hand, the snapped shaft jagged against his palm. He tucked both parts inside his cuff again and wiped the sweat from his face and straightened his clothes.

He walked along the corridor quietly, down the stairs, across an empty atrium. More corridors and stairs and flickering candles in sconces, another atrium with braziers burning to keep back the cold and the darkness.

Athan started across. Shadows loomed behind marble pillars and dark ponds reflected the brazier flames. His footsteps echoed faintly.

"Halt!"

His muscles tensed to run.

Don't be a fool.

Athan swung around, staggering slightly, and squinted into the darkness. "Druso? That you?"

He heard two pairs of footsteps to the right, and two more behind him. He forced himself to relax, to take a lurching step to the nearest brazier. The coals were red hot.

He slipped both parts of the key from his cuff. "That you, Druso?" he said again, turning to face the guards and dropping the key onto the burning coals. He yawned and stepped away from the brazier's heat.

Two guards emerged from the darkness. "Name yourself."

Athan hiccupped and yawned and grinned foolishly at the men. *A nobleman who's drunk too much and lost his way. That's all I am, boys.* "You're not Druso." He slurred the words.

"Name yourself." The command came from behind him this time.

Athan swung around and let himself to overbalance. He clutched at a pillar. "Druso?" He blinked owlishly at the two guardsmen. "Been looking everywhere for you."

"Name yourself." The command was more polite this time. The guards had seen the silver thread embroidering his doublet.

He screwed his face up in a frown. "You're not Druso."

"Your name, my lord."

"Donkey." Athan nodded his head foolishly. "What's yours?"

"Lord Ivo," he heard one of the guards whisper.

"You seen Druso?" he asked, releasing the pillar. "Got a question to ask him." He groped for the sheets of parchment, swaying. "Need a word that rhymes with pig." He pulled the sheets from his pocket, letting go of them with a flick of his wrist. Parchment scattered across the marble floor.

One of the guards swore beneath his breath.

"Oops," Athan said. He lurched to his knees and groped for a sheet. He heard another hissed swearword. One guard began to gather the scattered parchment.

Athan sat on the floor. "I need a word that rhymes with pig," he said with drunken solemnity, looking up.

Three stern-faced guardsmen looked down at him, their uniforms ridiculously frilled and trimmed with lace. The fourth guardsman was chasing sheets of parchment across the atrium. Athan began to giggle.

"Get him to his feet," the senior guardsman, a sergeant, said in a harassed tone.

"I'm writing a verse," Athan said proudly as the men hauled him to his feet. He swayed heavily. "In honor of Russet. She's my pig."

The guardsmen said nothing.

Athan groped in the pocket of his breeches for the ink. "Fastest pig in Corhona," he said, pulling the inkpot free. "She's red."

The fourth guardsman returned, his hands full of crumpled sheets of parchment.

"But I need a word that rhymes with red." Athan said, frowning at the man. "You know one?" He reached for the sheets of parchment, dropping the inkpot as he did so.

The glass shattered. Ink spurted across the marble floor, black.

The sergeant cursed audibly. "A servant," he said, "Quickly!"

One of the guardsmen hastened to obey. Athan watched, his mouth gaping open.

The sergeant bowed stiffly to him. "My lord, these guardsman will escort you to your bed chamber."

"My bed chamber?" Athan frowned at the man and then blinked. "Can't find it. You know where it is?" He turned and surveyed the atrium, lurching so heavily that the guardsmen had to grab his arms to keep him upright. "Is it here?"

"No, my lord," the sergeant said tightly. "Allow my guardsmen to escort you."

Athan beamed at the man. The sergeant didn't return the smile.

He allowed himself to be led from the atrium, swaying as he walked. "You seen Druso?" he asked.

"No, my lord," was the wooden reply.

A flight of steps yawned at his feet. He staggered and almost fell, forcing the guardsmen to clutch him. "You know a word that rhymes with pig?" he asked, once he was safely upright again.

"No, my lord."

"Fig," said Athan, taking a lurching step downward. He hiccupped. "Or... or dig."

CHAPTER TWENTY-THREE

"Is THAT MORE comfortable, noble lady?"

The lace still pricked beneath her chin, but Saliel nodded. Nothing would make the tight ruff comfortable. "Yes."

The seamstress turned her attention to the bodice of the wedding gown. "It's still a little loose, noble lady." Her brow creased in a frown. "I'll just..."

Saliel surveyed herself in the mirror while the seamstress adjusted the bodice. The gown was as white as snow. The color didn't suit her. Her hair seemed startlingly bright, almost garish, and the freckles on her face stood out prominently.

Seed pearls were stitched in intricate patterns across the bodice and skirt. Saliel touched one with a fingertip. *Smooth and cool.* It must have taken someone days to sew each pearl into place. A tedious and painstaking task. A wasted task. She wouldn't wear the gown at her wedding.

Tomorrow. The day she'd marry Lord Ivo and move into a suite of rooms alongside Marta. And tomorrow night, the night Lord Ivo would make his first visit to her bed chamber.

Except that the wedding, the visit from Lord Ivo, wouldn't take place.

Saliel stood still while the seamstress made the final alterations. The calmness was feigned. Excitement hissed inside her. Tonight she'd creep down to the catacombs for the last time. She'd be free of the ladies' court, the citadel, the Consort, the spycatcher and Lord Ivo.

And One will be with me.

Who was he?

Someone tall. Someone who'd come the summer before last. There were a dozen men he could be. Not Lord Kessler, who was too stout, but perhaps Lord Irmer? His manner was calm and he was an amiable man, if a trifle dull. Or perhaps Lord Tregar, with his discontented mouth and disdainful manner. Or Lord Druso, lanky and cheerful. He had the height, and—

"The gown is finished, noble lady." The seamstress stepped back. Her posture was deferential. "Does it meet with your approval?"

Saliel studied her reflection. White satin and lace and seed pearls. Innocence and purity. A virgin bride. "Yes," she said, smoothing her hand over the fabric. *I shall never wear this again.*

CHAPTER TWENTY-FOUR

"THE KEY BROKE in the lock."

"What?" The guardian turned sharply.

"It broke in the lock." Athan walked into the circle of candlelight. He was early; Three hadn't arrived yet.

"The code book?"

He shook his head. "No."

"Give me the key!" The guardian held out a black-gloved hand. "I'll re-forge it."

Athan shook his head again. He sat on an upturned urn and glanced at the storage room. Three would step through the door soon. "I had to dispose of it."

"What?"

He looked at the guardian. "There were guards," he said flatly. "Would you rather I'd let them find it on me?"

"Guards? They saw you?"

"Afterwards, when I was in one of the atria."

"And?"

Athan shrugged again. "They think I was drunk."

The guardian's shoulders relaxed slightly. "Then we try again."

"No," Athan said. "There are other courts, other spies. Let someone else do it."

"This is Laurent's best chance. We try again!"

Athan pushed to his feet. Standing, he was taller than the guardian. "No."

"Don't try to intimidate me," the man said. "Without my aid, you're helpless."

"Helpless?" Athan took a step forward. "You think so?"

The guardian didn't back away from him. He stood in the circle of candlelight, thickset and solid. "You will do as you are ordered!"

"Will I?"

"Yes. You can't leave Corhona without my assistance."

Athan took another step toward the man. "I think you'll find you're mistaken."

The guardian stood his ground. "What about Three?"

"What about her?" His hands wanted to clench into fists. It took conscious effort to keep them at his sides, loose and relaxed.

"You'll have to leave her behind."

"No."

"She's a female, you fool. You think she can travel unnoticed?"

Athan hesitated.

"She won't make it out of Corhona alive. Unless I help."

Athan shook his head. There was a flaw in the man's logic. "If I leave now, you'll have to let her leave too. Three can't copy the code book. You said so yourself."

"I shall copy it."

"You?" He laughed, a humorless sound. "How? You have no right to be in the citadel."

The man lifted his shoulders in a shrug. "I'll pretend to be a servant."

"You'll be caught."

"Probably. And then what will happen to Three?" The man shrugged again. "The choice is yours. Go alone now. Or wait until we have the code book."

Athan's hands clenched. "And Three?"

"She'll leave once the book is copied."

"That will be days!"

"A few, yes."

"But the spycatcher—"

"You've survived thus far."

Only just. His hands clenched more tightly. "And what's to say the key won't snap in the lock again?"

"I'll use iron."

Athan gritted his teeth. "How much longer?"

"A week at the most."

"A week." He turned abruptly away. "I'm getting married tomorrow!"

"So?"

"So!" It was a shout that echoed in the chamber. He swung around. "You said you would stop it!"

"That's no longer possible," the guardian said. "It'll draw too much attention to you."

Breath hissed between Athan's teeth. "And so I must marry?"

"For a few days, yes."

Anger surged inside him. He wanted to grab the man by the throat and shake him until his neck snapped.

"Once the code book's copied, you and Three will leave together. I guarantee safe passage out of Corhona for you both."

If the spycatcher doesn't unmask me. If the guards don't catch me.

Athan cast a glance at the storeroom door. It was shut. "Stop the marriage and I'll stay."

"No. People will talk. What will you say if the spy-catcher asks you about it?"

Words of relief would spill from him. *I want a Laurentine wife. A wife with spirit. Who'll enjoy the marriage bed.* "But if I sire a child—"

"It won't happen. A few days' marriage. A week at the most."

"But—"

"If you want Three to be safe, you will do this."

Athan exhaled through his teeth.

"Do it for her," the guardian said.

Athan turned away before he gave in to the urge to hit the man. "Make another key. And be quick about it!"

"Three must copy it again."

"What?" He swung back to face the guardian. "You don't have the cast?"

"I destroyed it. Like you, I didn't wish to be found with incriminating evidence."

He stared at the man. Dismay held him speechless for a moment. He swallowed. "Three must trick the Consort again."

"She had no difficulty last time."

Athan shook his head.

"She can copy the key tomorrow. You'll have it in three days, four at the most."

If it was just him, he'd turn on his heel and go. *Not without Three. We leave together—or not at all.*

Athan forced his fists to unclench, his hands to relax. "Get me the key and I'll try again." The words tasted bitter on his tongue. "Once."

He glanced at the door to the storeroom. It was still shut. How much longer would she be?

"Don't wait for her," the guardian said. "Go."

"Why?" He jerked his head around to glare at the man. His hands clenched again. "So I can't talk with her?"

"It doesn't matter whether you speak with her or not," the guardian said coldly. "Three's no fool. She won't leave until I allow her. She knows she has no chance without my help."

I am the fool.

Athan exhaled through his teeth. He turned away from the man and sat down on an upturned urn. "I'll wait."

He heard the guardian step toward him. "It's the night before your wedding. Get back upstairs and behave like a man about to be married!"

Druso would be looking for him, and his other acquaintances. They'd want to commiserate, to get drunk, to visit the courtesans' salon.

"You jeopardize your cover. And you jeopardize hers. Get up there now!"

Athan stood abruptly. His hands were clenched, his teeth. *If I didn't need you, I'd kill you.*

He swung away from the guardian and strode across the chamber. The shadows pulled back and flared in his wake. Instinct told him he was making a mistake; reason told him he had to do this. Abandoning Three wasn't an option.

And so I capitulate.

"In two nights," he heard the guardian say.

Two nights. Not one. Because tomorrow night—

Tomorrow night I'll be bedding Lady Petra.

Athan jerked open the door to the sewers and stepped down. The door swung shut behind him. It was utterly black.

He stood for a moment, wrestling with himself. *I don't have to go back.* It would be simple to turn downhill, to walk down to the town, to leave.

Not without Three.

He turned and began to trudge up the sloping tunnel.

CHAPTER TWENTY-FIVE

SALIEL LEANED HER weight against the slab of rock. It pivoted. *The last time*. She walked across the storeroom with her hands outstretched. *The last time*.

The door opened with a gritty sound. She paused on the threshold, relief swelling in her chest, and looked for One.

The guardian stood alone in the candlelight.

Saliel closed the door and walked toward him. "I saw three shooting stars tonight."

"I saw none." The guardian's voice was expressionless.

"Where's One?" She sat on the upturned urn that Ethan had just vacated and clasped her hands together, aware of anticipation, apprehension. Who was he? *Please, not Lord Tregar*.

"He's gone back to the citadel."

Saliel stiffened. "What?"

"He didn't copy the code book," the guardian said, his voice cold and precise. "The key broke in the lock. You must make another impression."

She stared at him.

"You must make another impression," he repeated.

"I can't." She shook her head. "You know I can't!"

"You must."

"But I marry Lord Ivo tomorrow. I have to leave!"

"Not until the code book is copied."

Horror made her mute; her throat was too tight for speech. She shook her head again.

"Yes." The guardian strode to the storeroom. Stone grated against stone as he opened the door. "You must go back."

She couldn't move, couldn't stand, couldn't open her mouth and speak.

The guardian left the door open. He came back, his cloak swirling, and grabbed her arm and hauled her to her feet. "Get back up to the citadel!" His voice was fierce. "Copy the key again!"

Saliel tried to pull away. "No."

"Yes!" The guardian's grip tightened painfully.

Her horror became panic. She tried to wrench her arm free. "I can't marry Lord Ivo. I can't!"

The guardian released her so suddenly that she almost fell. The sound he made was contemptuous. "Don't tell me you haven't spread your legs for a man before."

Saliel's head jerked back. For long seconds she couldn't breathe. "What? What did you say?"

"You're from the Ninth Ward. Don't tell me you haven't whored before."

No. Never. Her lips parted, but no words came out.

"A poorhouse foundling. Wearing velvet and lace and eating sweetmeats for lunch." The guardian made a spitting sound beneath his black hood.

The words, the tone of his voice, made her shiver. "How long have you known?" It was a whisper.

The guardian snorted, derisive. "I've always known." He grabbed her arm again. "Get back up there and spread your legs. Earn the money Laurent is paying you." He yanked her toward the storeroom.

A scream swelled inside her, filling the space in her chest. The chamber was a blur. The floor slid away beneath her feet.

Saliel stumbled and fell to her knees. The guardian didn't release his grip. He jerked her upright. "Which suite are you in?"

No words came out of her mouth. She shook her head.

"Tell me!" The guardian shook her, his fingers digging into her arm. "Which suite in the married quarters will you be in? *Tell me!*"

She tried to twist her arm free, but his fingers tightened. A breath of pain hissed between her teeth. "In the second corridor." Her voice was thin. "Toward the end."

"On the eastern or western side?"

She struggled to think past the pain. His fingers felt as if they dug into the bone. "Eastern."

The guardian's grip on her arm relaxed. "Good." He released her. "There's a passage running inside the eastern wall. All the rooms on that side have access to it."

Saliel rubbed her arm, squeezing her eyes shut against the pain.

"You should have no trouble finding the door. You know what to look for."

She opened her eyes.

"Inside," the guardian said, pushing her toward the storeroom.

Saliel grabbed the doorframe to stop from falling.

"A poorhouse in the Ninth Ward." The guardian made the spitting sound again.

It was familiar: the disgust, the spitting. Saliel straightened, holding on to the doorframe. Tears blurred in her eyes. *I can't go back.*

"Inside!" the man said again.

"You can't make me go back. I can leave. Now." It was shallow bravado; her voice trembled.

The guardian took a step back. He laughed at her. "How far will you get, foundling? With that red hair of yours."

Saliel gripped the doorframe. "What?" The guardian had never seen her unhooded. "How do you know?"

"You think I haven't watched you?"

She grew even colder. *He's seen me through the peephole. In my bed chamber.*

"You won't last half a day," the guardian said. "That hair of yours is too noticeable. You need my help to escape Corhona."

But I can't marry Lord Ivo.

"Copy the key again and you may leave."

She shook her head.

"Yes!" The guardian's voice was a shout. He hit her, striking above her breastbone.

Saliel lost her grip on the doorframe. She stumbled and fell backward.

The guardian stepped into the doorway. "Get back up to the citadel." He no longer shouted. Each word was cold and precise. "You may leave once the code book is copied."

The door swung shut. She heard a grating sound, subdued, and knew the guardian had barred the door. The darkness was absolute. *No*, she tried to say, but her mouth couldn't utter the word.

She lay on the floor while seconds stretched into minutes. Her breath came in choked gasps. Tears leaked from her eyes. *I can't do it. I can't.*

Hours passed. The stone floor was cold beneath her cloak, hard. Saliel began to shiver. *Get up*, she told herself. But she couldn't make herself stand. It would be an admission of defeat. To stand meant that she'd return to her bed, that she'd rise in the morning as Lady Petra and dress in the wedding gown.

That she would marry Lord Ivo.

That he would bed her.

That I will survive Corhona.

Survive?

What price was too great for freedom and independence? For a home?

Women had whored for less; for a mug of porter, for a crust of bread. She'd seen them in the alleys, their skirts raised above their waists. Girls from the poorhouse had done it and laughed afterwards, copper coins clenched in their fists.

If they can do it, I can. I earn more than they did. I earn my life.

After several hours Saliel pushed stiffly to her feet. She took the first step: freedom. A second step: independence. A third: a cottage. Cats sunning themselves on the doorstep. A cow to milk. Hens. A fire in the grate and smoke rising from the chimney.

Her gloved hands met the wall and slid easily into the slight hollows. Saliel closed her eyes. *I can do this. I have to.*

She leaned her weight against the wall. *It's nothing. A few minutes' discomfort and it'll be over. At least he'll be clean. He won't stink of the slums.*

The stone slid aside.

Saliel took a deep breath. Tears shuddered in it, but her eyes were dry. She stepped into the catacombs.

CHAPTER TWENTY-SIX

THE MAID SCRATCHED on the door not long after dawn. Saliel stayed where she was, curled up in the narrow bed. The woman opened the shutters, letting thin gray light into the chamber.

She watched as the maid stirred the embers in the fireplace to life and added fresh coals. The fire didn't warm her. She shivered beneath the bedclothes. Her coldness was inside, where heat and flame couldn't reach.

The maid left and came back with a tray, curtseying before placing it on the little table beside the bed. Saliel didn't bother raising her head to look at it. She knew what it was: a sweet pastry and honeyed milk for her to drink.

She'd been awake all night, but she felt no urge to eat. Dread cramped in her belly, not hunger.

The maid left again and returned with a steaming basin of hot water which she placed beside the fire.

The woman busied herself with laying out the morning's clothes. Stiff petticoats, a corset of linen and bone, a velvet gown. "Noble lady," she said when she was finished, curtseying low. "If you please?"

Saliel's eyes rose to the peephole. A twist of gray fabric blocked it, torn from one of her old dresses. The guardian couldn't watch.

She pushed back the bedclothes and stood. It took effort to walk to the fireplace, to take the cloth the maid held out and dip it in the basin, to wash her face.

She walked through the morning as stiffly as a puppet. *It's what I am: a puppet.* Her strings pulled by the guardian.

It will take a minute or two, she told herself as she sat in the Ladies' Hall and made neat stitches with silk thread. *Five minutes at most.* But she'd had sleepless hours to think about it and the act had grown more unendurable, not less. Lord Ivo would see her, and worse than that, he'd touch her. His hands would be on her skin. And worse than that—far worse—he'd be inside her. His seed would be in her body.

What if he makes me with child?

That was worse than everything else—than being touched and seen and having Lord Ivo in her bed. It made her breath short with panic.

A child. His child.

A child that might have the Eye.

There won't be a child. Not the first time. It won't happen.

But deep inside herself she was afraid.

"Come and have something to eat," Marta said, holding out her hand.

Everything she did was automatic: putting aside the embroidery, standing, taking Marta's hand. She didn't see the sofas and the side tables, the heavy arch of the doorway. *Two or three minutes. Five at the most.*

Marta squeezed her fingers as they passed into the chamber where luncheon was laid out. "Don't worry about it," she whispered.

Saliel's eyes focused. She saw Marta's concern, pinching her mouth and furrowing her brow.

She made herself smile.

Marta's face relaxed.

Saliel forced herself to smile, to eat. Every movement, every word she uttered, was automatic. *A puppet.*

The Consort watched her with something close to approval in her gaze. *I will not cry,* Saliel told the woman silently. *You have no cause to worry.* She was too cold inside for tears, too frozen.

She walked through the afternoon stiffly. Eating, embroidering two leaves and a flower, bathing. Her vision was gray at the edges.

She dressed in the wedding clothes as dusk darkened the sky. The minutes were as long as hours. The maid fussed, plucking at the laces, pulling them tighter, smoothing the seams. Her hair was re-braided, the plaits intricately looped on top of her head.

Marta came. She took hold of Saliel's hand. "Come! See your new suite!"

Saliel walked beside her, her arms and legs as unbending as a doll's.

"What do you think?"

Saliel turned her head, looking but not seeing. Dark walls, dark tapestries, dark furniture.

Other ladies from the court came. They brought gifts: handkerchiefs trimmed with lace, embroidered cushions and delicate vases, a side table inlaid with marquetry. Saliel listened to the words without truly hearing them. She smiled and opened her mouth and said what was expected. They mistook her frozenness for calmness, composure.

Such a lovely gown.

Thank you.

A little gift, a silver candlestick for your bed chamber.

Thank you. It's beautiful. Nodding, smiling. *Thank you. So kind. Thank you.*

It was time. Something rustled through the room. Not excitement; briskness, duty, a sense of bracing, of spines stiffening—and beneath that an undercurrent of compassion. Ladies squeezed her fingers, kissed her cheek.

It's time.

The ceremony was in the Great Hall. The vaulted ceiling towered above her, black. She was as small as a doll, a puppet. The voices of her audience were faint scratchings at the edge of her hearing, the noises of insects. *A dream. This is a dream.*

The hall shrank when the Royal Consort began to speak. Saliel felt herself growing, becoming human not doll. Panic swelled beneath her breastbone.

The Consort's eyes, cold and black, steadied her. *Do this or die*, they told her. The panic shriveled in on itself, becoming a hard knot in her belly.

Lord Ivo stood beside her. She spoke the words that bound her to him. They were sharp-edged in her mouth. In her mind they were as hard as pieces of ice. They fell to the floor and splintered at her feet. *I pledge to be a dutiful wife. I pledge to honour and obey my husband and to bow to his wisdom in all matters.*

A bubble of hysterical laughter rose in her throat. Wisdom?

She felt the urge to open her mouth and scream until the audience covered their ears, to turn and run from the Hall, pushing through the lords and ladies, shoving them aside with hands and elbows until she burst out into sunlight and fresh air.

Beside her Lord Ivo shifted his weight. He seemed to stifle a yawn.

Sunlight? It was dark outside, cold. And there was no escape from this nightmare.

Lord Ivo began to speak, repeating the Consort's words. Saliel didn't listen as his voice droned dully. It was a struggle to inhale, to exhale. *Don't faint. Breathe.*

Lord Ivo turned to her. Silver glinted in his hand: the key to his estate in Haast, the key to the strongboxes that held his wealth. The keys that sealed their marriage.

He touched her. His hands were at her waist, removing the blank betrothal keys and fastening the bridal keys in their place. The urge to jerk away from those fumbling fingers was deep and instinctive, strong.

Saliel squeezed her eyes shut for a moment and then forced them open. *You have to do this*, she told herself. *You have to.*

Lord Ivo stopped touching her. The Consort was speaking again. Saliel watched her mouth open and close, but the words were lost beneath the sound of the scream inside her.

The Consort stopped speaking.

It's done. I'm wed to him.

She curtseyed to the woman, her knees almost too stiff to bend. Lord Ivo bowed and took her hand, helping her to rise.

Sound swelled in the Great Hall: clapping.

It became harder to breathe after that, even though Lord Ivo released her hand. She didn't feel the flagstones beneath her feet as she walked to the banquet hall. It was as if her silk slippers didn't quite touch the floor. Her vision was gray, leached of color.

The evening slid away. She didn't taste the food on her plate. The music in the ballroom was no louder than the hum of insects. She was aware of faces and voices. Words came automatically from her mouth: *thank you, thank you, you're most kind.*

"Lady Petra."

The ballroom snapped into clarity: glittering chandeliers and dark shadows, the sheen of satin and velvet. Moonlight-pale eyes.

Saliel swallowed. "Lord Grigor."

The spycatcher bowed. "May I congratulate you on your marriage?"

"Thank you."

"You must be very happy." His mouth smiled at her; his eyes didn't. "Aren't you?"

No, those eyes urged her to say.

For an instant her mind was blank and she didn't know whether to lie or not. Panic kicked in her chest.

Give him the answer he expects.

She opened her mouth, aware of Lord Ivo standing alongside her and the sharp expectancy in the spycatcher's gaze.

"No, no." The spycatcher laughed lightly. "Don't answer that question, my dear." He patted her hand. "I know the answer."

He plays games. Realization came as the man turned to Lord Ivo. *He knows I can't stand Lord Ivo. My distress amuses him.*

The spycatcher bowed. "May I offer my congratulations, Donkey?"

"Thank you, Grebber."

The spycatcher's mouth tightened. "Grigor."

A look of mild confusion crossed Lord Ivo's face. "Is it? My apologies."

"You're a lucky man." The spycatcher's voice was smooth, his smile wide, but malice gleamed in his eyes. "The Consort chose well for you. Didn't she, Donkey?"

Lord Ivo hesitated for a moment before answering. "Of all the noble ladies in the citadel, I could wish for no other bride." It was the truth; his heavy-lidded eyes were caught by the spycatcher's gaze.

Lord Grigor laughed, a delighted sound. "How charming," he said.

He likes Lord Ivo no more than I do.

Lord Ivo didn't notice the man was mocking him. He nodded and grinned amiably.

"Good evening." The spycatcher bowed. As he straightened, his gaze flicked from her to Lord Ivo and back again. His mouth smirked slightly. *He's thinking of Lord Ivo bedding me.* "And once again, my congratulations on your marriage."

Saliel didn't watch the man walk away. She stared down at the floor, at the red and black squares of stone. *A whore lifting her skirts in an alley. That's what I am.*

She raised her head and looked at Lord Ivo. "If you will excuse me, my lord."

CHAPTER TWENTY-SEVEN

SALIEL WAS NUMB as she opened the door to her new suite, numb as she stood and allowed the maid to undo the laces and buttons that fastened her into the wedding gown, numb as the woman dressed her in a nightgown with a high neck and long sleeves and seed pearls stitched onto the yoke and cuffs.

The maid undid the intricate plaits and rebraided her hair into a single, long plait. She brought hot water and a cloth and a cup of warm, honeyed milk. Saliel washed her face automatically. "No," she said when the maid curtseyed low, offering the milk. Her voice seemed to come from someone else's mouth, distant. "Not tonight."

The maid curtseyed again and left. She was alone in the bed chamber. *A whore lifting her skirts.*

Saliel turned toward the bed, numb.

Spread your legs, the guardian had said, spitting the words at her. *And earn the money Laurent pays you.*

He had watched her in her old bed chamber. Was he watching her in this one?

The numbness vanished. The room came into sharp focus: the wide bed, the dark tapestries on the walls, the armchair beside the fireplace.

There's a peephole somewhere in this room.

Was the guardian already on the other side of the wall, checking to see that she obeyed him? Did he intend to watch while Lord Ivo bedded her?

169

Her horror was so great that everything stood still: the fire in the grate, the candle flames, the shadows in the corners of the room. Her heart didn't beat. She couldn't breathe. *I can't do it if he watches.*

The ability to move returned. Her urgency was almost panic. *Think!* Where was the peephole? *Where?*

The eastern wall, the guardian had said, but the blocks of black stone all looked the same. Which dark mark was a hole and which merely a flaw in the rock?

Saliel hunted frantically, stretching to reach as high as she could, crouching low, feeling cracks and tiny cavities beneath her fingertips. How much time did she have? How long before Lord Ivo came?

Hurry. Hurry.

Was the guardian laughing at her as she searched? Did he find her panic amusing?

There.

Saliel placed her fingertip over the hole. Her body trembled. Each breath was almost a sob. She glanced at the closed door. How long until Lord Ivo came?

Perhaps an hour. Perhaps a minute.

She needed something dark to block the hole—a strip of fabric cut from one of her mourning gowns, one of the black tassels hanging from the tapestry by the door—but she couldn't make herself walk away. *What if Lord Ivo comes now?*

Lace trimmed the cuffs of her nightgown. It tore easily, the threads parting with a sharp, ripping sound.

Saliel rolled the scrap of fabric with shaking fingers. *Calm*, she told herself, but her breath came in gulps. Her ears caught the sound of a door opening and closing, her maid's deferential voice—and a man's baritone answering. Lord Ivo.

Saliel stood frozen.

Spread your legs. She heard the guardian's words as clearly as if he hissed them through the wall. *Earn the money Laurent is paying you.*

Her fingers no longer shook. She bunched the lace and stood on tiptoe and shoved it into the hole. Her chest was tight as she stepped away from the wall.

The maid scratched on the door and opened it. "Noble lady? Your husband is here."

Saliel swallowed. "He may enter."

Lord Ivo stepped into the doorway, so tall his head almost brushed the lintel. His eyes were heavy-lidded, his mouth half-open, slack.

The maid withdrew.

Saliel's throat closed. She couldn't breathe. There was something wrong with her heartbeat: too high beneath her breastbone, too fast, too jerky.

Lord Ivo stepped into the room and closed the door. "Noble wife," he said. "Petra." His hand reached toward her.

Panic rose sharply inside her. She forced herself to inhale a shallow breath, to not flinch from his touch.

A whore lifting her skirts in an alley. That's what I am.

CHAPTER TWENTY-EIGHT

ATHAN HAD DREADED this moment all day. The reality was far worse than he'd imagined: Lady Petra's closed face as she lay on the bed for him, dutiful, her eyes not looking at him as he stripped off his clothes.

With the dread had been fear. *What if I can't do it?* He needn't have been afraid. His body responded to the sight of her, the long plait of bright hair, the curves of waist and breasts beneath the nightgown.

Athan closed his eyes. *I wish—*

He did it quickly—pushing the nightgown up Lady Petra's thighs, feeling her cool, smooth skin shrink from his touch. He couldn't look, just fumbled to push her legs open. She moved stiffly for him, obediently.

There was a moment when he was unable to go any further—and then he clenched his teeth and forced himself to do it.

He felt Lady Petra flinch, heard her catch her breath in pain. She was tight, tighter than any woman he'd ever had. *A virgin.*

She lay beneath him, tense and unbreathing.

Athan squeezed his eyes shut and performed his duty as swiftly as he could, trying not to grunt like an animal. His climax brought no pleasure, only shame. *I'm sorry*, he wanted to say as he rolled off her, as he stood and reached for his clothes.

He turned away from the bed and dressed swiftly, fumbling with buttons and ties. His fingers shook. His breath came in short pants, as if he'd climbed a flight of stairs. As if he tried not to cry.

"Good night, wife," he said, through a tight throat.

He barely heard Lady Petra's reply, barely saw the maid waiting as he pushed through the parlor. He walked back to his bed chamber blindly. "Come back later," he told the valet, shutting the door after the man.

He stood with his forehead pressed to the wall, his eyes tightly closed. Sobs choked in his chest, in his throat. *What have I done?*

CHAPTER TWENTY-NINE

SALIEL CLIMBED OFF the bed. She was cold, numb. Her vision was unblurred by tears. *I did it.*

There should be relief. Instead, there was just numbness. *I did it. I whored.*

The maid brought hot water and cloths for her to wash with. It wasn't enough; a single bowl couldn't clean Lord Ivo from her skin. He'd seen her, touched her. His seed was inside her.

"More water," she said. And when the second steaming bowl came: "More."

The pain had been worse than she'd expected. Blood smeared the cloth she cleaned herself with. Evidence of her virtue, if anyone cared to check.

It's done. Over.

She stripped off the nightgown and scrubbed where Lord Ivo's hands had touched her, where he'd lain on her, where she'd felt his weight and the heat of his body, where his breath had been on her skin and his hair had brushed across her cheek.

She couldn't scrub away the memory, or his seed inside her.

Please don't let me be pregnant.

But even thought of Lord Ivo's child growing in her belly didn't bring tears to her eyes. She was too numb, too cold.

The maid brought a fresh nightgown. She fussed with the bed sheets, smoothing them. She removed the bowls of water, the wet cloths, the damp towel. Then she curtseyed and left.

Saliel stood alone in the bed chamber. She turned slowly and looked at the bed, at the headboard carved of dark wood, the white sheets, the mound of pillows.

He'd bedded her on those white sheets. And she had closed her eyes and let him.

It was impossible to lift her feet and walk to the bed, impossible to climb into it.

Then sleep on the floor. She'd done it often enough.

Saliel took a feather pillow and a blanket and lay down on the rug beside the fire. The pillow was soft beneath her head, the floor hard.

Lord Ivo had bedded her. He'd lain on her, heavy and warm. She'd heard his panted breaths. His seed was inside her.

I did it. It's over. It won't happen again.

The fire's heat didn't warm her. She was too numb. Too cold.

CHAPTER THIRTY

THE MAID RETURNED just after dawn. Saliel heard footsteps in the parlor and the sound of shutters being opened. She pushed herself up from the floor.

She had the pillow and blanket neatly back on the bed before the maid scratched at the door. "Enter."

"Good morning, noble mistress." The woman curtseyed.

Saliel walked to the fireplace. She watched as the maid opened the shutters. Dim light leaked into the bed chamber. The tiny panes of glass were blurred with rain.

Today she had to copy the Consort's key again.

Her head ached with tiredness. Sleep had been impossible; every time she closed her eyes she heard Lord Ivo's breathing. With her eyes open and the candles burning, she heard only the crackle and hiss of the coals in the fire.

Saliel washed her face in warm water and ate the breakfast the maid brought and allowed the woman to dress her. The bruises on her arm were dark, where the guardian's fingers had dug into her flesh. If the maid noticed them, she made no sign.

Today, Saliel told herself while the maid brushed and braided her hair. She looked down at her hands. *The Consort's eyes, today.*

The pain in her head grew worse as the tight braids were pinned up. How could she hold the Consort's gaze when her eyes ached with tiredness? But when she closed them, she heard the noises Lord Ivo had made—soft panting sounds—and felt his hands on her thighs, pushing her legs apart.

Saliel opened her eyes wide. The memory vanished. She heard raindrops hitting the windowpanes. Rivulets of water ran down the glass. *The sky weeps.* She couldn't weep; the tears inside her were frozen, a cold, tight lump in her chest.

The maid stepped back. "I have finished, noble lady."

Saliel stood. "My embroidery basket."

She made a pretence of straightening the items. Her fingers touched silk thread, the smooth wooden box that held her needles, the cool silver lid of the container of wax.

Saliel inhaled a deep breath and lifted her head and stared at herself in the mirror. Her eyes were dark-shadowed and her face pale with exhaustion. "My cape."

Someone scratched on the outer door.

Saliel tensed—*let it not be my husband*—and took the cape from the maid. "Answer it," she said.

But it was Marta, not Lord Ivo, who stepped into the parlor. "Petra," she said, coming to the door of the bed chamber. "How are you?" The question was ordinary, one she asked every morning, but her pretty face was anxious.

Saliel stretched her lips into a smile. "I'm perfectly fine, thank you."

Marta's anxiety vanished. She returned the smile.

The maid fastened the cape at Saliel's throat and opened the outer door again.

Marta took hold of her hand as they stepped into the corridor. "It's bearable," she whispered. "Isn't it?"

Bearable? The sound of Lord Ivo's panted breaths. His seed inside her. If she wasn't numb, she'd vomit. *No, it's not bearable.* "Yes," she said.

Marta gave her a quick smile of solidarity and released her hand. "I shall start a new pattern today. I think... white roses this time."

The long corridors were cold. Saliel pulled her cape tightly around her and stopped listening to Marta. She needed a pretext to speak with the Consort privately. Not her marriage; the Consort's patience on that subject was very thin. *Think.*

But exhaustion and numbness had slowed her wits. She sat alongside Marta in the Ladies' Hall and could think of nothing. She couldn't ask about the identity of Marta's new husband; even Marta dared not ask that question. What then?

Married ladies stopped to speak briefly with her, commenting on the rain, the latest stitch, the choice of color for a new design. Slow-witted as she was, she heard the message beneath their words. *You are one of us,* their voices told her. *You do your duty, as we do. We bear it together.*

The ladies mistook her numbness for composure, for calmness, and smiled approvingly at her.

Servants brought around refreshments. Saliel put down her embroidery frame. *Think,* she told herself.

Sweetmeats nestled on the silver trays: bite-sized lavender and honey cakes, tiny meringues filled with sweetened cream, soft wafers glazed with rosewater syrup. Saliel accepted a plate and napkin and took one of the cakes at random. *Think.*

She watched as Marta hesitated over the selection of sweetmeats and then chose a pastry filled with cream.

"A tisane, noble lady?"

Saliel accepted a porcelain cup that was as delicate as the petals of a flower. What could she speak to the Consort about? *Think.*

The cake she'd chosen was dense and sweet and decorated with tiny pieces of preserved ginger. She chewed slowly.

Marta put her pastry aside with only a small bite taken from it.

"Are you not hungry?"

"The cream tastes too rich," Marta said. "I find I can't eat it."

"Shall I call back the servant? There are sweetmeats without cream."

"No." Marta shook her head. "It was the plainest. The others are too spicy."

Saliel looked down at her plate. Spices showed as dark flecks in the sticky crumbs of cake—cinnamon, cloves, nutmeg. "Too spicy?"

"Yes."

She raised her head. "But you used to like the cakes."

"I find I can't eat them now."

"Cream? And spices?" Relief unfurled in her chest. This was what she could talk to the Consort about. "But what about the soups at lunch? The sauces?"

Marta shook her head. "I can't eat them."

Saliel looked at her more closely. "Have you lost weight, Marta?"

Marta flushed. She glanced down at her lap and smoothed a wrinkle in the fabric. "Perhaps a little."

Saliel felt swift shame. *I should have noticed.* "But you're with child. You need to eat well. It's most important."

Marta looked up. "I'm fine. Please don't worry, Petra."

Saliel put her plate aside and wiped her fingers clean with a napkin. "If you can't eat cream and spices, then you must eat other foods. The cooks can prepare plainer meals for you. I'm sure the Consort will allow it."

Marta shrank back slightly on the sofa. Her face paled. "Oh, I couldn't ask her."

"Then I shall."

Marta flushed again. Her smile was shy and grateful. "You're a good friend."

Saliel looked away. *No, I'm not. I'm using you.* She picked up her cake again and bit into it. She forced herself to chew, to swallow.

CHAPTER THIRTY-ONE

SALIEL APPROACHED THE Consort and curtseyed low. "Your Eminence, I wish to thank you for yesterday." It was the Consort's one power: speaking the words that bound noble men and women together in marriage. "It was a beautiful ceremony. Thank you."

The Consort smiled graciously. "You're welcome, my dear."

Saliel straightened. She took a deep breath. "Your Eminence. May I speak with you privately?"

The Consort took a few seconds to shift slightly on the sofa and rearrange her skirts. The change in her manner was clear. Saliel had seen it many times as a servant: coolness, dismissal.

"It's not a matter concerning me," she said hastily, before the woman could say *no*. "It concerns Marta."

"Marta?"

Saliel nodded. She kept her posture deferential, her voice hesitant: "If... if it pleases you, your Eminence."

She waited with her head bowed for the Consort to reply. Fear was cold on her skin. *Don't refuse*, she begged the woman silently. *Please let me do this today*.

"Very well," the Consort said. "I shall put aside some time for you."

"Thank you, your Eminence." She sank into another low curtsey and held it for a long moment.

Gratitude. Obeisance. The little container of wax bumped against her leg as she rose.

She walked back to where Marta sat with her head bent over her needlework. White roses on dark stems.

Marta glanced up as she sat. Her gaze was full of admiration. "You're so brave," she whispered.

No, not brave. Desperate.

It was difficult to concentrate on the embroidery. Her head ached with tiredness and her stitches were as large and crooked as a child's.

The Consort didn't call for her before lunch. Saliel walked with Marta into the dining chamber and sat beside her at one of the long tables. Silverware gleamed in the candlelight: tureens and ashets and salvers engraved with heavy, curling patterns. The linen napkins were snowy white against the dark, polished wood of the tabletop. She watched as Marta ate buttered rolls and pushed the rest of her food around her plate. All around her, noble ladies dined quietly. They were like cows grazing in a field, placid and well-fed. Nearly two hundred women, but the tapestries swallowed the sound of voices and the scrape of knives on plates.

She'd dined at long tables in the poorhouse—scarred tables, with chipped crockery and tarnished cutlery. There, she'd wolfed down bowls of watery stew and still been hungry. Here, with duck breast and ginger sauce on her plate, she had no appetite.

Saliel laid down her fork. She rinsed her fingers in the bowl of warm, lavender-scented water beside her plate and dried them on a napkin.

The afternoon passed slowly. Her stitches became larger and more crooked. Her eyes were gritty with tiredness. The ache in her head increased.

"Noble Petra."

She looked up.

One of the Consort's attendants stood before her, plump-cheeked and as pretty as a doll. "The Consort wishes to speak with you."

Saliel swallowed. She put aside the embroidery and stood.

The Consort no longer sat beside the fire. Saliel followed the attendant across the hall to the door that led to the Consort's private parlor. Her heart began to beat more swiftly.

The woman scratched on the wooden panels and opened the door.

"Come in, Petra."

Saliel touched the pocket of her gown for reassurance. The tin nestled there, hidden. She took a deep breath and stepped inside.

It was a room she'd never entered before. Like the hall, tapestries hung on the walls and a fire burned in the grate, but the size was much more intimate. Heavy furniture crowded together: sofas upholstered in rich brocades, armchairs with tasseled cushions, small tables inlaid with intricate marquetry.

The Consort wasn't seated. She stood before the fire. Vases and figurines crowded the mantelpiece and a mirror hung above it. The mirror was the most striking item in the room. The wood was honey-gold, a warmer color than she was used to seeing in the citadel. Animals were carved into the frame—birds and dragonflies and lizards with darting tongues— their eyes inlaid with mother-of-pearl. The creatures were astonishingly life-like. They seemed poised on the edge of movement; the birds to shake and preen their feathers, the lizards to blink their gleaming eyes and run down the frame onto the mantelpiece.

The door closed behind her. She was alone with the Consort. "Your Eminence," Saliel said, curtseying.

The Consort gave a slight nod.

Saliel stepped further into the room. "Thank you for agreeing to see me."

The Consort inclined her head again.

"I'm very grateful." She took a second step, a third, a fourth, treading on soft rugs, moving closer to the woman.

"What is it you wish to discuss?"

"It concerns Marta."

"Yes." Impatience edged the Consort's voice. "I'm aware of that. What is it?"

"I am concerned for her health, your Eminence," Saliel said, walking closer.

The Consort's thin eyebrows drew together in a frown. "Is she unwell?"

"She finds it difficult to eat cream, or spicy foods," Saliel said. "She has lost weight."

The Consort's frown deepened. "Lost weight?"

"Yes." Saliel stepped onto the rug before the fireplace. Her chest was tight. She lowered her gaze deferentially and blinked to clear the tiredness from her eyes. "I wondered... is it possible for the cooks to prepare food for Marta that has no cream or spices?" She braced herself for what must come next: raising her head, catching the Consort's eyes.

"Of course it is. I shall arrange for it at once." The Consort turned away from the fire. "Thank you for bringing this matter to my attention, Petra."

Saliel's head jerked up. "I'm worried for her," she said, desperate.

The Consort halted. She turned to face Saliel, a movement that made the keys at her waist clink against one another. Her eyebrows drew together again. "There's more?"

Saliel's mouth was too dry for speech. *Now. Do it now.* She caught the Consort's eyes. Dark eyes. Almost black.

She stepped toward the woman, fumbling to find the container in her pocket, to open it. *Concentrate.* Tiredness slowed her movements. She'd done it swiftly last time; now it took forever. An ache built inside her head as she groped for the keys. Her fingers slid over smooth velvet and stiff seams and ridges of embroidery. *Where are they?*

There. Metal.

Saliel gripped the keys, panting slightly. She stared into the Consort's eyes, straining to hold them. *Do it. Take the impression.* But her fingers couldn't tell the difference between the keys. They were the same, smooth and warm and heavy.

Panic swelled in her chest. It was impossible to breathe. The ache in her head grew larger, pressing against her skull. Her eyesight seemed to blur.

The Consort's eyelids flickered.

Terror held Saliel motionless—and gave her an instant of clarity. The pain in her head was nothing. Her vision was bright and clear. Her fingers knew the key to the citadel.

She pressed the key clumsily into the wax and released it, hearing a faint *clink* as it fell back against the Consort's bodice and hit the marriage keys. She stepped back, almost stumbling, and fumbled to close the container and push it into her pocket.

The Consort's eyelids flickered again and then closed in a blink.

Saliel froze, struggling not to pant, the container of wax gripped in her left hand.

The Consort moved her head slightly, as if to clear it. The frown between her eyebrows deepened. "There's more?"

Saliel shook her head, too afraid to breathe. The stiff folds of the gown hid her hand.

The Consort said nothing. Her frown deepened, as if she struggled to recall something.

Distract her. Hurry.

Saliel swallowed. "I... I like this room very much." She turned toward the fire and took a step away from the Consort on trembling legs, her left arm held close to her side. "Especially the mirror."

She saw the Consort's face reflected in the polished surface. The woman was watching her, narrow-eyed.

"My mother had a mirror that was very similar." Saliel reached up with her right hand, touching one of the gleaming mother-of-pearl eyes with a fingertip. She slid the container of wax into her pocket.

"She did?"

"Yes." Saliel turned back to face the Consort. She forced her mouth into a smile. The container was a small weight in her pocket, hidden. "Very similar."

"Similar?"

"Yes. The creatures with their eyes. I used to love them." She curtseyed, almost stumbling as she rose. "Thank you, your Eminence, you've been most gracious—"

"Your mother had such a mirror?"

Saliel froze. *I've made a mistake.* "It does look similar," she said cautiously.

"I doubt it," the Consort said. "The mirror is from the Illymedes."

Saliel understood her error. Her skin was suddenly damp with sweat. "The Illymedes?" she said, as if she didn't recognize the name.

"Yes." The Consort stepped closer. Her gaze was sharp. "One of the nations in the Laurentine Protectorate."

And only someone within the Imperial household may possess such an item—or be named a traitor.

"Oh." Saliel moistened her lips. She glanced at the mirror. Bright mother-of-pearl eyes stared at her. "How... how do you come to have it?"

"It's from the Emperor's collection."

"Oh," Saliel said again. She tried to smile at the Consort. "I must be mistaken. The mirror only looks similar."

The Consort didn't return the smile. "Creatures with mother-of-pearl eyes?"

Saliel swallowed past the tightness in her throat. She couldn't take back the words she'd uttered. "Yes."

"The mirror could only have been Illymedan work." The Consort's eyes glittered, black. "How did your mother obtain it?"

"I don't know, your Eminence." She creased her brow and twisted her fingers together. *I am Lady Petra, innocent and confused. Whatever your suspicions are, they're false.* "It must have been a copy."

The Consort's brows arched. "A copy? An unusual choice for a diplomat's wife."

"My mother was no traitor," Saliel said, striving to sound tearful and confused.

The Consort smiled suddenly. "Of course she wasn't."

Saliel smiled back, grateful and tremulous. Her eyes were far too dry for tears, but she blinked as if trying not to cry.

The Consort patted her on the arm. "Go back to your embroidery, my dear," she said. "This nonsense about mirrors is of no matter. Don't be upset."

Saliel bowed her head and sank into a curtsey. "Thank you, your Eminence."

She rose. Her heart thudded in her chest as she walked across the room. She glanced back as she opened the door. The Consort stood before the fireplace, studying the mirror.

She knows.

Saliel closed the door and walked across the Ladies' Hall to Marta. *No, she only thinks she knows. She cannot prove it.* The container of wax bumped against her thigh as she sat. She picked up her embroidery frame with trembling fingers. "It went well." She forced her mouth into a smile. "The cooks will prepare plain dishes for you."

CHAPTER THIRTY-TWO

ATHAN SPENT THE day avoiding the spycatcher. He was adept at leaving salons and courtyards when the man entered, at yawning and ambling leisurely in the opposite direction. The rain made it difficult, limiting his choices, but the hours passed without having to speak to the man. He spent much of the afternoon feigning sleep on a sofa in a corner of a drafty salon, with his eyes closed and his mouth open.

He concentrated on memories of home—the estate in the countryside with the tall oak trees and the reed-edged lake, the vineyard on the hill behind, the bunches of grapes ripening and the leaves turning yellow and red, morning mist lying in the dips and hollows in the fields, the scent of honeysuckle in the hedges—but always, beneath the memories, was Lady Petra's face. Her closed expression. Her eyes not looking at him as he undressed.

Shame was tight in his chest. He felt it with every breath he took—shame as he inhaled, shame as he exhaled, shame as he remembered.

When it became too much, Athan went to the stable yard. The rain came down steadily, ice-cold, almost sleet. He splashed through the puddles, hunched into his cape, shivering.

Some of his tension eased as he stepped inside the building where the pigs were housed. The air was warm and smelled of autumn, of hay and apples. He inhaled deeply.

Servants bowed as he walked between the pigsties. He was the only nobleman. No one else braved the heavy rain. "An apple," he drawled, and heard footsteps slap on stone as someone hurried to obey him.

Russet was rolling in the straw. She scrambled to her feet at his soft whistle.

Athan reached down to touch her. "Hello, girl."

Russet grunted. *Hello*, she seemed to be saying back to him.

Athan scratched beneath her chin. The piglet leaned into his hand, her eyes closed with pleasure.

"An apple, noble lord."

He gave Russet the apple and watched as she ate. His tension was less, here, leaning against the wooden railing and watching her. Water dripped from his cape and his feet were wet inside the thin leather shoes, but for the first time today he felt like smiling.

I shall miss you, Russet.

She was a beautiful pig, with her dark snout and hooves, her red coat—

Memory came: Lady Petra in her nightgown, turning away from him, walking to the bed. Her hair hanging down her back in a long plait, bright red against the white linen nightgown.

Athan's throat tightened with shame. "I did a terrible thing."

The piglet flicked an ear and paused in her eating. She raised her head to be petted again.

Athan rubbed her cheek. "There's no way I can make it right," he whispered. *No way to undo it.*

Russet went back to the apple, crunching loudly.

Athan watched her. He was as trapped in the citadel as Russet was in her pen. The piglet did his bidding, running in pointless circles around a courtyard, just as he and Three obeyed the guardian. "Your master is a fool," he said to Russet. "And so is mine."

A fool who holds our lives in his hands.

Athan shivered. His breeches clung to his legs, clammy, and the cape hung heavy and cold from his shoulders. He reached down and patted Russet farewell. "I shall give you to Druso when I leave," he told her in a whisper. "He'll take good care of you."

CHAPTER THIRTY-THREE

ATHAN HAD TO force himself to walk across the red and black slabs of stone to where she sat on the edge of the dance floor, to open his mouth and say her name. "Noble Petra."

His wife raised her head. "Lord Ivo." Her voice was polite and expressionless.

"How are you?" Athan made himself say, looking at her bright hair, not her face. He hadn't the courage to meet her eyes.

"I am very well, my lord," she said in that same polite, expressionless voice. "And you?"

"I'm fine. Thank you."

There was an awkward pause. Shame was tight in his belly. It oozed from his pores as sweat. "Do you care to dance?"

"No. Thank you."

Relief made him sweat even more. "Then I shall bid you good night," he said, bowing.

CHAPTER THIRTY-FOUR

THE SHADOWS WERE the same, the stone tables and the urns, the gutters crossing the floor, the black shapes of Three and the guardian, but the mood in the chamber made Athan's skin prickle with unease.

"You have the impression?" The guardian's voice was cold.

Three reached beneath her cloak. She placed a small container beside the candle. The sound it made—metal on stone—was tiny, and yet it echoed in the silence.

The guardian made no comment. He reached for the container.

"Did you have difficulty?" Athan asked.

Three turned her head to look at him. She moved stiffly tonight, as if exhausted. "The Consort suspects me."

"What?" He tensed. "She thinks you copied the key?"

"No." Three shook her head. "Not at all. She was unaware of that."

"What then?" the guardian asked, brusque.

"I made a... an ill-judged comment. She's suspicious of me."

Athan's mouth was suddenly dry. "And the spy-catcher?"

"She can't have told him yet. He hasn't spoken to me."

"But you can lie to him," the guardian said. It was a statement, flat.

"Yes."

The guardian nodded, a short jerk of his head. "Then we need not worry."

"Not worry!" Athan was on his feet. "She must leave. Now!"

"No," the guardian said.

"The risk is too great—"

"There's no risk. She can lie to the spycatcher."

"What if he uses other methods?" Memory of Rolen was vivid in his mind: the blood, the rope that bound him to the table. Athan swallowed, tasting bile. "What if—"

"Three is pretending to be a noblewoman," the guardian said coldly. "The spycatcher can't lay a finger on her until she's proven to be a spy."

"She should go," Athan said stubbornly. "Tonight."

"Neither of you will leave until the code book has been copied." The guardian's voice had been cold; now it was frigid. "Unless you wish to travel without my assistance. And I can guarantee you'll be caught if you try that."

Athan's lips peeled back from his teeth. His hands clenched.

He felt a touch on the back of his hand. He looked down.

Three's gloved fingertips lay lightly on the ridge of his knuckles. "I'll be fine," she said. "It's for a few days only."

His fists tightened.

"Please," she said. "Sit."

Athan exhaled a hissing breath. He pulled his hand free from her touch—furious with the guardian, furious with himself—and sat again. He glared at the guardian. *I run around in stupid circles for you.*

But it wasn't the guardian he was doing this for. It was Three.

He looked down at his clenched hands.

"I'll use iron this time, not lead. It may take longer."

Athan's head jerked up. "How much longer?"

"A day or two."

His lips tightened. *I'm a pig in a pen. Powerless.* "And if the key breaks again?"

"It won't."

Beside him, Three sat silently. Her posture was stiff, tense.

Realization came suddenly: something had happened between Three and the guardian. The strange mood that he sensed was hostility.

She dislikes him as much as I do. And yet we both depend on him.

"Is there anything else we need to discuss?" the guardian asked.

Athan said nothing. Neither did Three.

The guardian waited a moment and then stood. "I shall see you in two nights' time."

Athan rose. He unclenched his fists and turned to Three. "Be careful," he said, reaching out to take her hand.

Her fingers flexed briefly in his grip before pulling away. "And you."

"I shall."

He watched her walk away. *We leave together, you and I. We will survive this.*

CHAPTER THIRTY-FIVE

SHE DREAMT SHE was burning on a witch's pyre. The court watched. She saw Marta, Lord Ivo, the Consort, the spycatcher. Their mouths stretched wide. She heard shrill cries: *burn witch, burn*. In their eyes she saw dark things—fear, hatred, blood lust—and the shining reflection of flames.

She woke to the roar of a crowd and the smell of her own hair burning. The taste of the bonfire was on her tongue.

Saliel pushed up from the rug beside the fire. *A dream, only a dream*. Her fingers shook as she placed the pillow and blanket back on the bed.

THE CONSORT DIDN'T join the ladies of the court at their needlework that morning. The sofa with its plump brocade cushions was empty.

Saliel bent her head over her embroidery, tense, and placed neat stitches with green thread. Was the woman speaking with the spycatcher?

Servants brought around trays of sweetmeats, and still the Consort didn't come. *Are my rooms being searched?*

Would the maid tell her if they were?

Saliel chose a tiny cake. She bit into it and chewed slowly. There was nothing in her rooms—parlor and bed chamber—to give her away. Her possessions were normal, ordinary. *I'll be fine, as long as they don't find the peephole…*

She put the cake down on her plate. "I wonder where the Consort is this morning."

Marta glanced at the empty sofa. "Tomorrow's the anniversary of the First Battle. Perhaps she's busy with that?"

"Oh." Saliel's tension eased slightly. The Consort was overseeing preparations, not talking to the spy-catcher. "I'd forgotten."

"Another bonfire."

"And privet," Saliel said, striving to match Marta's cheerful tone. She grimaced. "I warn you, I shall sneeze a lot tomorrow."

She spent the day stitching leaves in shades of green and brown—and going over descriptions of people and places in her head. *My mother's name was Frida. She was the fourth child of Lord Kilmer and his wife Lady Hesta. Her brothers—my uncles—were Otto, Viktor, and Elmar. Viktor died in the battle of Sihgil, in the 456th year of the Empire. He was a naval captain. Mother had a likeness of him painted. It hung on the wall in her parlor.*

The details came easily; she'd gone over them often enough in the past two years to be able to remember each name and date and place. It was the things she hadn't been taught that worried her—the things she'd have to make up. *Like what my mother's mirror looked like.*

The Consort ate luncheon with the ladies of her court. Saliel was aware of the woman at the edge of her vision, seated at the head table. She kept her attention on Marta, not lifting her gaze. *Relax*, she told herself. *Converse. Eat.*

The afternoon passed, as all afternoons in the citadel did: she stitched shapes with silk thread, she talked with Marta, she listened to the gossip of other ladies. The Ladies' Hall seemed even colder than it usually was. Shutters covered the windows, fires burned in the hearths, and candles blazed in the sconces and chandeliers, but the dark stone seemed to suck the warmth. She shivered inside herself.

Saliel laid down her needle as dusk fell. The noises in the room changed. Instead of low, polite conversation there was busyness and bustle. Needle boxes snapped shut. Fabrics rustled as ladies rose to their feet.

The next hour was the small freedom of her day, the time she had to herself before dinner. Mothers who hadn't sent their children to country estates used the hour to visit them in the nursery; Saliel used it to bathe. But she couldn't get warm, couldn't relax. The water was too cool tonight.

"More hot water," she said to the maid. *Please.*

The maid obeyed promptly, but it made no difference. Steam curled from the bathwater—and yet Saliel shivered. "A sponge," she said, and when the maid brought one, she dismissed the woman. "I shall wash myself tonight." *And wash off Lord Ivo's touch.* She could feel the imprint of his hands if she allowed herself to think about it.

Saliel scrubbed with the sponge until her skin was red—but she was still cold inside. She rang the bell. "I wish to get out."

She dined with the married ladies of the court. The room was different, the faces, but the words were the same ones she'd heard a hundred times in the unmarried ladies' quarters. She ate pork braised in cream and spices, forcing herself to swallow, while beside her Marta ate plain slices of roast chicken.

It was routine: eating, returning to her bed chamber, dressing for the nightly ball. A glance showed nothing out of place. *Have my rooms been searched?* she wanted to ask the maid. Instead, she bit her lip and stood silently while the woman dressed her.

I am Lady Petra, she told herself as she walked with Marta down the wide staircase that led to the ballroom. The stone balustrade was cold beneath her hand. *I have no reason to be afraid.*

But she was afraid, and her gaze went automatically to the dais where the Prince and the Royal Consort sat.

"The rain has finally stopped," Marta said. "Did you notice?"

Saliel opened her mouth to say *Yes*, but the words dried on her tongue. The Consort was watching her.

Her step didn't falter. *I am Lady Petra. I have no reason to be afraid.* She made herself smile and dip her head in acknowledgement of the woman.

The Consort returned the smile. It was a small movement of her mouth, sharp. Her eyes glittered blackly.

As black as crow's eyes.

Saliel swallowed. "Stopped raining?"

She didn't look in the direction of the dais as she walked around the dance floor with Marta, as she sat and rearranged the stiff folds of her gown, but it was difficult not to snatch a glance. Was the woman still watching her?

Music played, and beneath that was the hum of a hundred conversations and the quiet footsteps of the first couples taking their places on the dance floor. Beside her, Marta sighed. "I shall miss this."

I won't. "When do you think…?"

Marta blushed. Her hand strayed toward her waist. "I think it will soon show."

And Marta would be confined to the women's quarters.

"Noble Petra."

Saliel turned her head. Her skin tightened and the muscles in her stomach clenched. "Lord Grigor." She smiled, shy and welcoming, and gave the spycatcher her hand. "How do you do?"

"Very well thank you, noble Petra." He bowed. His mouth brushed lightly across her knuckles.

Saliel suppressed a shiver.

The spycatcher straightened. "Would you care to dance?"

His pale eyes were on her face. She felt a compulsion to speak the truth: *no.* "That would be most pleasant. Thank you." She stood.

Lord Grigor led her onto the dance floor, finding a space among the other dancers. Saliel took her place alongside him.

The musicians played the opening chords—a sombre upswing of notes—and the dance began. It was slow and elegant, couples circling and passing each other with stately steps. *But this is more than a dance; it's a hunt.*

"You dance well," the spycatcher observed.

"Thank you."

"Did you dance often in Gryff?" It was no idle question. The man's eyes were intent on her face.

"Yes." Saliel met his gaze. The urge to tell the truth was easily ignored. *Be chatty. Lie.* "Balls were held most nights in the Governor's palace."

"The Governor's palace?" The spycatcher's brow creased. His eyes stared into hers, pale. "What was his name? I've forgotten."

Her heart began to beat slightly faster. "Lord Maler," she said, smiling shyly. "His wife was Lady Erma. She was a close friend of my mother's."

"Oh? You knew them well?"

"Yes."

"I believe I met Lord Maler in Jurgenheim. A tall man. Quite thin."

You know this. Relax. Breathe. Saliel shook her head. "He was tall, but his build was heavy."

"Oh? I must be thinking of someone else. His aide perhaps."

She was no longer cold. Perspiration was damp on her skin. "Lord Udo? He was certainly thinner."

The spycatcher held her eyes a moment longer— while her heart beat fast in her chest—and then he nodded. His gaze strayed from her face. He scanned the ballroom.

Saliel concentrated on her steps. It was too soon for relief. She'd convinced the man she was from Gryff; not that she wasn't a spy. She placed her feet with care and searched for words she could use. "Tomorrow's the anniversary of the First Battle."

The man's attention snapped back to her. "So it is."

"It's one of my favorite days of the year."

"Oh?" His eyes were steady on her face.

The pale gaze made her want to shiver. "The ceremony is so stirring! The description of the battle, the names of the heroes. It makes one proud to be Corhonase." *Enthusiastic. Patriotic. Naïve.* "And it's such an honor to wear the privet. Although... it does make me sneeze."

The spycatcher studied her for a moment. "An honor? Yes, I suppose it is."

'But most of all I like the bonfire," Saliel confided.

The spycatcher laughed. His gaze left her face. He scanned the ballroom again.

The music slowed and the dance ended. Saliel curtseyed. "Thank you, Lord Grigor. That was most enjoyable." She met his eyes as she said the words.

"The pleasure was all mine," the spycatcher said, bowing.

Saliel allowed herself to be led from the dance floor. Sweat stuck the linen shift to her skin beneath the tight corset. Her legs trembled with relief. *I did it.*

"I see that your husband has arrived," the spycatcher said smoothly. "He's doubtless looking for you. Shall I escort you to him?"

Her reaction was involuntary, she couldn't help it: she halted.

The spycatcher halted too. His glance was polite and inquiring. "Do you not wish to see him?"

He was playing with her; it was in his voice—the same tone she'd heard him use with Lord Ivo—and it was in the bright, cold eyes. *He plays with people the way a cat plays with a mouse.*

This time Saliel spoke the truth. She had to; it was what the man expected. "I would prefer not to."

The spycatcher's eyebrows rose. She saw amusement gleam in his eyes.

"Forgive me, my lord!" She clutched his arm. "I can't think how I came to say such a thing. I didn't mean to be disrespectful about my husband."

"You're unhappy to be married?" The spycatcher's tone was polite and concerned, smooth.

I am Lady Petra. I am patriotic. "It's my duty to marry," Saliel said. "And I am happy to do my duty."

"Ah, yes," he said. "One's duty."

"Every marriage is for the good of the Empire."

"Indeed." The spycatcher smiled. "Including your own."

"Yes."

The spycatcher's smile widened. "But you would prefer to return to Lady Marta, rather than greet your husband?"

His eyes were on her. She had to say, "Yes."

The spycatcher bowed. "As you wish."

CHAPTER THIRTY-SIX

ATHAN STROLLED WITH Druso into the courtesans' salon, arm in arm. He had to brace himself to enter. The sounds and scents of sex made him feel ill. He turned his eyes away from Seldo, mounting a whore. *That was me, with Lady Petra beneath me.*

He selected an alcove at random and stretched out on the wide sofa, yawning. "More wine."

He chose a glass of wine while Druso chose a courtesan. He didn't watch as Druso divested the woman of her clothes. It was easy to yawn again, easy to let the glass tilt until the wine ran into the cushions, easy to pretend to doze—but it wasn't easy to ignore the sounds, the rhythm. *Did we sound like that?*

No. Lady Petra hadn't giggled, she hadn't whispered as the whore was whispering to Druso, urging him on.

Athan squeezed his eyes shut.

The minutes seemed interminable before Druso was finished.

"Donkey?" He heard his friend ask. "You want her?"

Athan feigned a snore.

He listened as the courtesan dressed. She kissed Druso enthusiastically, and then she was gone. "Wine," Druso called.

He heard the *clink* of crystal, the sound of Druso drinking deeply, silence, and then a familiar voice: "Druso." It was Tregar.

"Do join us," Druso said. "I say, Donkey, wake up!"

Athan uttered another snore. He kept his eyes closed as Tregar called for wine. He tried to concentrate on the tune the musicians played, not the conversation beside him: Tregar's sour, barbed comments, Druso's laughter.

He dozed lightly, the music and the voices blurring together in his ears, and was jerked awake by a sharp elbow in his ribs. "Wake up, Donkey."

Athan grunted and opened his eyes. He yawned. "What?"

"Move over. We have company."

Athan turned his head. Druso was gone. Tregar reclined on the cushions, fondling a whore. Standing watching, his pale eyes gleaming, was the spycatcher.

Fear kicked in Athan's chest.

The spycatcher stopped watching the idle movement of Tregar's hand. "Lord Ivo," he said, bowing.

Athan swallowed. "Lord Grebber."

"Grigor," Tregar said, sharp, sneering. "It's Grigor, Donkey."

Athan yawned again. "My apologies, Lord Grigor." He shifted sideways on the sofa and pushed brocade cushions aside with his hand. "You wish to join us?"

"Thank you."

Athan looked away as the man stretched out alongside him. Sweat gathered on his skin. He gestured for a servant. "More wine."

"How are you finding married life?"

Athan shrugged with a shoulder, not looking at the man. "Fine." He groped for a glass of wine.

"It has its pleasures, hasn't it?"

Athan grunted, a noncommittal noise. He swallowed a large mouthful of wine.

"I'm married," the spycatcher said, his tone idle, conversational. "Did you know?"

Athan gulped another mouthful of wine. *Look at him or he will suspect*. He made himself turn his head. "No," he said, meeting the man's eyes. "I didn't know. Have you been married long?"

"Several years." The spycatcher smiled and leaned close. "Tell me, Donkey. Did you enjoy your wedding night?"

Athan tried to clench his jaw shut, to not open his mouth, not move his tongue, but it was impossible. "No," he was forced to say.

"No?" The spycatcher's eyebrows rose. He uttered a light, delighted laugh. "Why not? You prefer Lady Petra to all the ladies in court."

A bead of sweat slid down Athan's cheek. He wiped it away. "Because she doesn't like me."

The spycatcher's eyebrows rose higher. "She told you that?"

"Of course not," Athan said. "She's a lady."

"Then how do you know?"

His mouth was dry. Fear was a sour taste on his tongue. "I can see it."

The spycatcher leaned back on one elbow, observing him. "How perceptive of you, Donkey. You astonish me."

Athan raised his glass and gulped the wine. He tried to turn his eyes from the man; it was impossible.

"So you didn't enjoy visiting your wife's bed?"

"No."

The spycatcher laughed again, an amused, pitying sound. "Poor Donkey."

Athan managed a weak smile, pinned by the man's gaze, helpless.

The spycatcher leaned close again. "You know, Donkey, there's pleasure to be had in an unwilling bed partner—if you allow yourself to enjoy it."

Athan jerked back. "You mean rape!"

The spycatcher smiled. "How can it be rape? It's your duty as a husband. Something you'll have to do often." His pale eyes gleamed. "I advise you—as a friend—to learn to enjoy it."

Revulsion rose in Athan's throat.

"You want the redhead tonight?" the spycatcher asked.

"No!" It was almost a shout.

The spycatcher smiled pityingly. "Poor Donkey. Your marriage has unmanned you." He turned to survey the courtesans.

Athan squeezed his eyes shut and slid lower on the cushions, sweating, trembling.

"Here," he heard the spycatcher say. "She's not a redhead." The man laughed.

Athan grunted. He didn't look to see which courtesan the man had summoned. He kept his eyes closed as his doublet was unbuttoned, his breeches. But the whore's warm breath, her tongue and clever fingers, failed to arouse him. He saw Lady Petra's face, pale and tense, felt her skin flinch beneath his hands. *I can't do it.*

He let his head loll deeper in the cushions and feigned a snore.

"The fool's asleep."

Tregar sniggered.

"Come here," the spycatcher said, snapping his fingers. The courtesan's warmth left Athan.

He lay with his head turned against the cushions, listening as the spycatcher's breathing changed. *I sounded like that.* The muscles in his throat tightened. *I'm sorry, Petra.*

CHAPTER THIRTY-SEVEN

Saliel woke with a jerk when the maid opened the shutters in the parlor. She scrambled to her feet and had the pillow and blanket back on the bed before the woman opened the door to the bed chamber.

The maid had a sprig of privet pinned to her bodice. The flowers were tiny and white. Saliel's nose itched at the sight of it. She sneezed when her hair was being braided, and again when the maid pinned a sprig of privet to her bodice above the marriage keys.

She wasn't the only person affected by the flowers: ladies sneezed over their embroidery, and the afternoon speeches in the Great Hall were punctuated by the sound of noblemen and women sneezing discreetly into their handkerchiefs. Saliel listened with her lips slightly parted to the description of the First Battle and the founding of the Empire. *Rapt. Patriotic.*

The court dined together, lords and ladies, in the Banquet Hall. Saliel sat beside her husband. Lord Ivo said nothing beyond commonplace courtesies. He yawned several times and seemed on the verge of sleep.

She behaved as the other wives did—making polite conversation, cutting her food into small, neat pieces and lifting them to her mouth. Memory of the wedding night was tightly locked away. *I do not remember.* She chewed and swallowed, chewed and swallowed, but her stomach didn't want the food.

"Delicious," she said, laying down her fork.

They attended the bonfire afterwards. Saliel huddled into her cape and listened as the names of the heroes were read aloud. Flames leapt and roared, devouring the wood, shooting sparks into the air.

Lord Ivo stood alongside her. She didn't look at him, but she sensed his boredom. He shifted his weight and yawned.

Branches snapped and cracked in the bonfire. The sounds made her shiver. *I would burn like that. My skin would shrivel and turn black. My hair would flare alight.* She glanced sideways, searching for the spy-catcher. Did he imagine what it would be like to burn on a witch's pyre?

The throng of nobles was too thick. She couldn't see him.

Saliel looked back at the bonfire. She clasped her hands together and composed her face into an expression of enthralment.

CHAPTER THIRTY-EIGHT

ATHAN ESCORTED LADY Petra inside. The ballroom was warm after the chill night air, but her cheeks remained pale. She looked bloodless.

She sneezed again, six tiny puffs of sounds, *tss tss tss tss tss tss*. He'd never heard anyone sneeze quite like that before, so quietly and quickly.

It was the only time she'd seemed alive this evening; when she sneezed.

"They grow it in an indoor garden," he said, to fill the silence between them.

"I beg your pardon, my lord?"

"The privet. It's grown in an indoor garden." Shrubs forced to flower out of season, just for this one day. *A stupid tradition.*

She made no reply.

"Would you like to see it?" Athan asked. "I hear it's huge."

What words did she think in her mind? *Of course not, you fool. Haven't you noticed how I sneeze?* A week ago, he would have seen a flicker of annoyance cross her face, a miniscule tightening of her lips; now she was perfectly expressionless. "No, thank you, my lord."

Athan stopped looking at her. Shame was tight in his chest. He strolled around the perimeter of the dance floor, aware of her fingers resting lightly on his arm.

She didn't want to touch him, but it was her duty and she did it.

Soon you'll be free of me, my lady. You'll have another husband.

He halted at a row of chairs, stiff-backed and upholstered in dark velvet. Her friend Marta was already seated.

"Do you care to dance?"

"No, thank you, my lord." Lady Petra didn't look at his face when she spoke. Her gaze rested on his shoulder.

"Then I shall bid you good evening."

An emotion almost flickered across her face. He sensed it: relief.

Athan bowed to his wife. *Forgive me for what I have done to you.*

The musicians played the first notes of a new dance. Athan turned from her. As he walked away he heard Lady Petra sneeze quietly again, *tss tss tss tss tss tss.*

"I SAW ONE ring around the moon tonight."

"I saw none," the guardian said.

He had arrived before her; the chamber was empty save for himself and the guardian. Athan crossed the room and sat on an urn and waited, not speaking. It was several minutes before the door to the storeroom opened.

Three stood in the black mouth of the doorway and waited for the guardian to approach. Athan watched, hearing the faint murmur of her voice as she spoke the words of code.

Three didn't walk beside the guardian toward the circle of candlelight; she walked behind him and to one side, distancing herself.

She hates him.

Athan rose and bowed. "You're well?"

"Yes, thank you." The languages were different—one guttural, one lilting—but she sounded almost like Lady Petra. Lifeless.

Athan frowned and watched as she sat. Her movements were stiff. She looked brittle, breakable.

"Is the Consort giving you trouble?"

She looked up at him. Her shoulders rose in a slight shrug. "She suspects me still, but the spycatcher doesn't."

Thought of the man's eyes made Athan's skin tighten. He repressed a shiver.

"He spoke with you?" the guardian asked.

Three turned her head, but didn't look directly at the man. "Yes."

"And you lied?"

"Yes."

"I wish I could lie to him." Athan sat again. He rubbed a hand over his face. The woolen hood was coarse against his skin. "I must answer with the truth." He squeezed his eyes shut, remembering the spycatcher's questions. *Did you enjoy your wedding night?* "How is it that no one notices? The man should have been burned by now."

"They don't notice because they have nothing to hide," Three said quietly.

Athan opened his eyes. She sat with her head bowed, looking down at her hands. *I need to get you out of here.* "The key," he said, turning to the guardian. "Where is it? I'll do it now. We can leave tonight."

The guardian shook his head. "I don't have it yet."

"What?" Athan pushed to his feet. Something bellowed in his chest. He wasn't sure whether it was anger or fear. "What do you mean you don't have it?"

"I had to go elsewhere to have it cast in iron," the guardian said. He didn't stand. "It was difficult."

"Difficult?" Athan spat the word. His hands clenched. "*Difficult* is being up there with the spy-catcher!"

"Do you wish me to bribe a metalsmith who'll run straight to the guards?" The guardian's voice was cold. "The key will be ready in two nights' time."

Two more days. Two more nights. Athan turned away and closed his eyes. Did the man realize what he was asking of them?

Tss tss tss tss tss tss.

Athan's eyelids snapped open. He jerked his head around and stared at Three.

"Excuse me," she said. "It's the privet."

His shock was absolute. It felt as if everything in his body stood still: heart and lungs, blood, breath.

The strength drained from his legs. Athan sat clumsily. *No. It can't be true.*

It was true. He knew it, absolutely and utterly. He *knew*.

Three didn't know. She wouldn't be sitting beside him now if she did.

She wouldn't have let him bed her if she'd known.

His eyes were open, but he didn't see the candlelight and the shadows, the guardian. He saw Lady Petra in her nightgown, her face pale and closed, her eyes not looking at him. He felt her skin shrinking from his touch, the tension in her body as she lay beneath him. He heard her breath catch in pain.

It should not have happened.

Rage surged through him, blurring vision and hearing, burning in his throat. He dimly heard the guardian dismiss them.

Athan rose to his feet. He inclined his head to Three, to Lady Petra, and watched as she walked across the chamber, not waiting for the guardian. *I know why you hate him so much.*

He waited until Three had shut the storeroom door before turning to face the man.

"Well?" the guardian said, brusquely. "What is it? You wish to speak with me?"

Athan tried to breathe, tried to swallow his rage, but it pushed up into his mouth, a silent roar that tasted like blood on his tongue. "She's Lady Petra, isn't she?" His voice didn't sound like his own: it was too loud, too thick. "Three is Lady Petra."

The guardian stood very still. The only things that moved in the chamber were the candle flame and the shadows. Then he turned away. "Nonsense." His tone was dismissive. He picked up the candle.

Athan's lips pulled back from his teeth. He reached out and grabbed the guardian's arm and swung him around. The candle flame almost blew out.

"Let go of me."

"You son of a whore!" Athan's fingers tightened. "How dare you do that to us!"

"I said, *let go of me!*"

Athan ignored the command. He shook the man, making his head snap back on his neck. "How dare you do that to her! *How dare you!*"

The guardian struck his chest. "Release me!"

The blow, the man's imperious tone, pushed Athan past control. He released the guardian with a shove, making him stumble and almost fall, and then hit him with all his weight behind the blow. His fist sank solidly into the man's stomach, making both of them grunt. The guardian doubled over, dropping the candle. Athan swung again. His fist connected with the man's jaw as the candle hit the floor and went out.

The guardian fell, the sound almost lost beneath the clang of the candleholder on the flagstones.

Athan followed the sound, reaching for the man, pinning him as he scrambled to stand. He grabbed at folds of cloak, at arm and shoulder and throat. His rage was too great for words. An animal sound of fury came from his mouth. He gripped the guardian by the neck.

The man bucked beneath him, clawing at his hands.

Athan tightened his grip, throttling the guardian. *How dare you do that to her!*

The man uttered a choked, panicked sound. His fingers became desperate.

A measure of sanity returned. Athan released the guardian and scrambled back. He sat in the darkness with his head bowed, panting, his heart thudding in his chest, and listened to the guardian gulp for air.

He closed his eyes. *I nearly killed him.*

"She mustn't know who you are." The guardian's voice was a croak, wheezing. "It's too dangerous."

Athan opened his eyes. He saw only blackness.

The guardian's fingers plucked weakly at the hem of his cloak. "You mustn't tell her."

Athan pushed the man's hand aside. "Don't tell me what I must do."

His rage at the guardian was no less. The man had made him do something terrible. Something he could never undo.

To Three. *Of all people, not her.*

Athan stood. For a moment he had no idea where north and south were—the blackness swung dizzily around him—and then everything settled into place: urns and tables and storeroom, sewers. He saw them in his mind's eye.

He turned away from the guardian and walked across the chamber, clumsy, blind, feeling with his feet for the gutters. The sound of the guardian's gasped breaths gave him something to walk away from. His cloak brushed a table, a second one, a third, and then his outstretched hands touched the wall. It took a minute of searching before he found the door to the sewers.

He opened it and stepped through into more darkness.

Athan walked fast up the tunnel, stumbling, not caring about the noise he made. His chest and throat were painfully tight. It was difficult to drag in each breath.

The tunnel widened into a chamber he could sense but not see. He felt for the ledge, his gloves snagging on rough sandstone, but didn't pull himself up; instead he bowed his head into his hands and squeezed his eyes shut.

Of all people, not her.

CHAPTER THIRTY-NINE

SALIEL WOKE AT dawn. She blinked her eyes open. The dimness, the hard floor she lay on, the despair, were familiar: she was back in the poorhouse.

Shutters opened in the parlor, the hinges creaking slightly, and reality snapped back into place. Saliel scrambled up from the rug in front of the fireplace. She had the blanket and pillow back on the bed before the maid scratched on the door.

Two nights, the guardian had said. It was a vast length of time. Two seconds, two minutes, were things she could cope with. Two days and nights were too much.

Relax, she told herself as she washed her face. *Concentrate on each moment, not on what may or may not lie ahead.*

She focused on the tight sensation on her scalp as the maid plaited her hair, on placing one foot in front of the other as she walked down the long, cold corridor, on making each stitch as precise and perfect as she could while she sat next to Marta in the Ladies' Hall.

"Noble Marta."

Saliel looked up. One of the Consort's attendants stood before them. She had a doll's face: pink rosebud mouth and plump cheeks, smooth milk-white skin. Her velvet gown was the color of dark plums.

"The Royal Consort wishes to speak with you."

Marta put down her embroidery. "Oh."

Saliel glanced across the room. The hairs on the nape of her neck pricked upright. How long had the woman been watching them?

She smiled shyly and dipped her head. *Respectful, unafraid.*

Marta stood, nervously smoothing her gown. "Why do you think...?" she asked in a whisper.

A husband, most likely.

Neither of them spoke the words aloud.

Saliel watched Marta follow the attendant across the room. *Poor Marta.* Something tightened in her belly, a clenching, a twisting of nausea. *Stop it.* She bent her head over her embroidery. *Don't feel sorry for Marta.*

Every woman in this room would be bedded by a husband, and every woman would find the experience unpleasant—but they would do their duty with pride. Marta would be proud of herself. She'd not feel dirty.

Saliel was stitching the veins of a leaf with pale brown silk when Marta returned. Her face was composed, but delicate color flushed her cheeks. Something in her eyes—shining—and in the way she held herself hinted at excitement.

"I'm to marry."

Saliel laid down her needle. "Who?"

"Lord Renner."

"Lord Renner? I don't believe I know him."

"He arrives today," Marta said, sitting. "He's second in command to the new Admiral."

"Today? Then how is it you're marrying him?"

Marta blushed and looked down at her lap. "He asked for me. Several weeks ago."

"You know him?"

Marta nodded. "He commanded my husband."

"Oh," Saliel said. "What's he like?"

"I only danced with him a few times." Marta glanced up shyly. "I scarcely dared to speak to him. He's a commander."

'What did your husband think of Lord Renner? Did he speak highly of him?"

"My husband didn't discuss such matters with me."

Of course not. Saliel picked up her needle again. "Congratulations. It's a very fine match."

"Isn't it?" Marta's eyes shone.

Saliel looked at her, seeing timidity and pride. *I was a fool to pity you.*

"The Consort wishes to speak with you, Petra," Marta said.

Saliel's chest tightened. "With me? Now?"

Marta nodded. "Yes."

Saliel made herself place the embroidery frame to one side and stand, to speak calmly. "I wonder why?"

She crossed the Ladies' Hall with unhurried steps. *Think before you answer. Make no mistakes this time.*

The attendant stood at the door to the private parlor. It didn't rain or snow outside, and yet the Consort chose to speak to her here. *So I can't run?* Her chest became even tighter.

Saliel stepped into the room. The door closed behind her.

The Consort was alone. There were no guards, no spycatcher.

Saliel relaxed slightly. "Your Eminence," she said, curtseying deeply. "You wish to speak with me?"

The Consort sat on a sofa. Her mouth smiled; her eyes didn't. "Yes, my dear. Come here. Sit." She patted the green and gold brocade.

Saliel made herself smile shyly as she approached the woman. This was an interrogation, not a conversation—the sofa told her that. The Consort walked or paced when she spoke of women's matters, of betrothals and marriages. Today was different; today was dangerous.

"Sit," the Consort repeated, smiling and patting the brocade again.

Saliel sat. *Shy*, she told herself. *Innocent. Eager to please.* "Your Eminence?"

"It occurred to me, my dear Petra, that you must have known a friend of mine. Lady Karla."

"Lady Karla?" She knew the name, but her mind was suddenly blank.

"Yes." The Consort's smile, her eyes, became sharper. "I should like to hear how she was before... before events in Gryff."

"Of course, your Eminence. If it pleases you." *Who was Karla? Think.*

The Consort inclined her head. "It does."

And then it came: *Karla, wife of Lord Ditmer, the military attaché in Gryff.*

Saliel moistened her lips. "Lady Karla was a friend of my mother's. She had a little daughter. A lovely child." She smiled, as if in memory. "Her name was Elsa. She was, let me think... five or six. Lady Karla also had son, a few years older, whom she and Lord Ditmer were most proud of."

The Consort's smile was less wide. She nodded.

Elaborate. Give her details. "Lady Karla had a beautiful garden. Gryff is... was much warmer than this. The flowers were exquisite. Huge blooms—" she opened both hands to show the size, "—and such bright colors. Reds and yellows and pinks."

Saliel paused. She let her hands curl closed. "I do miss Gryff." She blinked as if to hold back tears. "It was very beautiful."

"So I understand," the Consort said. Her voice was sweetly sympathetic. "I should like to hear more about it."

"More?"

"Yes. Tell me about the—"

Fingernails scratched lightly on the door. It opened. "Your Eminence." An attendant curtseyed low. A different woman, with fuller lips and a softer chin. "The Admiral has arrived. Your husband requests your presence."

The Consort's mouth tightened fractionally, then her face smoothed and she smiled. "We must talk more about Gryff, my dear Petra. Tomorrow."

Saliel swallowed. She tried to look flattered, to flush with pleasure. "Yes, your Eminence. If it pleases you."

She spent the rest of the day making neat stitches and remembering every detail she'd been taught about Gryff. *There was a place, not far from the Governor's palace, where a spring came up from the ground. The water was warm and smelled of sulfur. Sometimes it grew so hot that steam rose.* In the evening she sat at the long dining table with the other married ladies. A dozen different conversations twisted together in her ears, a meaningless babble of sound. Candles burned brightly in the chandeliers and the shutters were closed against the darkness. She chewed automatically. Spices and cream were heavy on her tongue.

She went over names and dates and places while the maid dressed her for the ball, while she walked across the ballroom with Marta. She sat alongside her friend and smoothed the gown over her lap, aware of the spycatcher prowling the room, smiling and asking questions, and the Consort watching from the dais. The dance floor was busier than it had been for months: naval officers in their maroon and black uniforms, widows in gray mourning gowns.

"There he is," Marta whispered. "Lord Renner."

"Oh? Where?" She followed the direction of Marta's gaze.

"He looks very distinguished. Doesn't he?"

Saliel nodded. "Extremely. He has an air about him." *And he's old enough to be your father.*

"He's coming over," Marta whispered. She brushed her gown with quick fingers. "How do I look?"

"Lovely," Saliel told her. It was no lie; Marta was one of the prettiest ladies in the ballroom.

Marta became even prettier as Lord Renner bowed low over her hand. The shy blush suited her.

"Noble Marta."

Marta's reply was almost inaudible: "Lord Renner."

Lord Renner had streaks of gray at his temples and an air of command. His mouth was set in firm, inflexible lines. "Who is your friend? I should be pleased to meet her."

"Oh." Marta's shy blush deepened. "May I present Lady Petra?"

Saliel smiled and held out her hand. "Lord Renner."

The man's bow was precise. His lips briefly touched the back of her hand. "It's a pleasure to meet you, noble Petra."

"The pleasure is mine."

Lord Renner turned back to Marta. "Do you care to dance?"

Marta obeyed the unspoken command. "Yes, thank you." She stood.

Saliel watched as they walked on to the dance floor. *Don't pity her. She's pleased to be marrying this man. He'll be an Admiral one day.*

"Noble Petra."

Saliel stiffened. She turned her head. "Lord Ivo."

His bow was as punctilious as Lord Renner's had been; his fingers didn't linger, his lips barely touched her skin. "Would you like to dance?" he asked as he straightened.

There is nothing I'd like less. But Lord Ivo's voice held the same undertone as Lord Renner's. He expected obedience. "Yes. Thank you."

Saliel stood and placed her hand on his sleeve. She could feel where his lips had touched her. It felt as if tiny insects crawled across her skin. Memory stirred. *No. Don't remember.*

"That gown becomes you extremely well," Lord Ivo said.

Saliel looked down at it. Lavender blue. "Thank you."

Lord Ivo made no reply. He yawned.

She concentrated on the sounds around her—the rustle of fabric and murmur of voices, the melody the musicians played—as he led her on to the dance floor.

The dance was slow and formal. She didn't look at Lord Ivo; she looked at his shoulder, clad in beige velvet, at the lords and ladies dancing near them, at the red and black squares of stone beneath their feet. He yawned twice more and didn't speak until the dance was finished.

"I shall visit you tonight," he said, as he escorted her from the dance floor.

Her heart stood still for a moment. The sounds that surrounded her—voices and music—became inaudible. The ballroom was a blur. *No. He didn't just say that.*

He had said it. Her ears had heard it. Tonight.

Lord Ivo led her back to her seat and bowed. "Good evening, my lady."

Saliel looked up at him. "Good evening, my lord." The words were scarcely louder than a whisper.

She watched him walk away.

I can't do it again.

CHAPTER FORTY

ATHAN DIDN'T KNOW what words he was going to use to explain, to apologize. He sweated as he waited for the maid to announce him.

I've come to talk. He'd say that first, so she knew he didn't want to bed her. And then he'd beg her forgiveness. He'd tell her that he'd only discovered her identity yesterday. That if he'd known he would never have bedded her, that he wouldn't have laid so much as one finger on her.

The door to the bed chamber opened. The maid stepped out. She curtseyed. "You may enter."

Athan reached up and tugged at the tight lace ruff. He stepped over the threshold, sweating, dreading. The door closed behind him.

Three sat in an armchair beside the fire, dressed in her nightgown. A shawl lay around her shoulders, wool crocheted so finely that it looked like lace. A candle burned on the small table beside her.

Athan had to swallow to be able to speak. "Good evening." He bowed.

She looked up, not meeting his eyes. Her face was pale and expressionless, her red hair vivid.

I think I love you.

Athan stepped closer. He swallowed again. "Noble Petra."

Three stood, picking up the candleholder, her gaze on the bright flame, not him. "Good evening, my lord."

"I wish to speak with you," Athan said.

She lifted her head, meeting his eyes fully.

The words he wanted to say slid out of reach. For a second his mind was completely blank.

Athan blinked. He shook his head to clear it. "I wish to speak with you," he repeated.

Pain stung the back of his hand—hot, burning. He looked down. The lace cuff was on fire. Flame licked up his sleeve.

Three uttered a cry. She dropped the candle and tried to snuff the flames with her hands.

Shock held him frozen for a moment, as witless as Lord Ivo—and then rational thought returned. "Your shawl!" He snatched it from her shoulders.

She understood. Their hands tangled for a frantic second and then she had the shawl wrapped around his arm. Her fingers gripped him tightly.

Athan stared at her, breathing heavily. His forearm was hot, stinging. The back of his hand felt as if he'd plunged it in boiling water. He smelled burning wool.

She was no longer lifeless. He saw how fast the pulse beat below her jaw. "My lord—" Her voice was appalled.

"It was an accident."

She released him and turned toward the door. He heard it open, heard her calling for the maid.

Athan hugged his arm to his chest. The candle lay where she'd dropped it on the rug. The wick was black and dead.

It had been no accident. He knew it with the same strong certainty that he'd known her identity yesterday. Three had meant to burn him.

He exhaled his breath in a hiss of pain and closed his eyes.

Footsteps crossed the floor. "My lord?"

Athan opened his eyes and turned around. Behind Three was the maid, a bowl of water in her hands.

He held out his arm and let the maid replace the shawl with a wet cloth. The coolness dulled the pain.

Three didn't meet his eyes. "You need to have the burn dressed."

I need to speak with you.

She looked fragile in the white nightgown. Her bare toes were visible beneath the lace-edged hem. He saw her tension, the shallow breaths she took, the stiffness in her shoulders.

The cuffs of her nightgown were singed.

"Your hands. Let me see."

She glanced at him and then obeyed. Her palms were reddened. *You must hate me very much to do this to yourself.*

Athan cleared his throat. "Noble Petra, I... I'm sorry."

"It wasn't your fault." Her voice was low. She didn't meet his eyes.

Yes, it was. I shouldn't have come tonight.

"See to your mistress," he told the maid. He bowed to Three. "Good night."

CHAPTER FORTY-ONE

SALIEL CLOSED HER eyes as the door shut behind Lord Ivo.

"Mistress, are you all right?"

She opened her eyes. Her palms stung—hot—and nausea twisted in her belly. *I burned a man.*

"Mistress, shall I bathe your hands?"

Saliel shivered. She hugged herself. "Bring me a new shawl. I'm cold."

But the coldness had nothing to do with the temperature of the bed chamber; it was inside her.

She sat and let the maid drape a shawl over her shoulders and bathe her hands in water. The shivering didn't stop.

The maid left and came back with a warm drink. "Here, mistress." She curtseyed, presenting the tray.

Nausea rose in Saliel's throat at the scent of honey and milk. "No," she said. "I don't want—"

She stood, pushing past the woman, and made it to the chamber pot before she vomited. The maid fussed over her while she knelt on the floor. The emotions of the day—fear, dread, shame and guilt—were gone.

She rinsed her mouth with water and bathed her face and let the maid dress her in a fresh nightgown, while numbness spread inside her.

"Shall I fetch the physician, noble mistress?" the maid asked timidly.

"No."

"But your hands—"

She no longer felt them; every part of her was numb. Saliel opened her hands and looked at them. The palms were red. "It's nothing."

"Mistress, are you certain? The physician—"

"I want to be alone," she said. "I want to sleep." *And I want to forget what I have done.*

She stood and allowed the maid to help her into the wide bed. "You may go," she told the woman.

Tonight she didn't climb out of the bed and lie down beside the hearth; she was too numb to care where she slept. She turned her face into the pillow. *I burned a man.*

SALIEL COULD FEEL her hands in the morning. The palms were tender, but not sore.

"Good morning, noble mistress." The maid placed the breakfast tray beside the bed and curtseyed.

Saliel sat up slowly. She looked past the woman. Beyond the door was the parlor, and beyond that, the corridors and salons and atria of the citadel—and the Consort and the spycatcher. And Lord Ivo.

I don't want to be Lady Petra today.

She reached for the cup of tisane, making her hand shake as she picked it up. The delicate porcelain cup clinked against the saucer.

"Mistress, are you all right?"

She sipped the tisane, slopping hot liquid on the sheets, and then put it down. "I don't think I can eat this morning." She pressed a hand to her mouth. "I feel... I think I may be ill again."

She lay back and let the maid fuss over her, rearranging the pillows and wiping her face with a cool cloth. "My hands hurt," she said weakly. "Bring me some salve."

The salve soothed the tenderness. Saliel closed her eyes. "Inform Lady Marta I'm unwell. I shall stay in my bed today."

The maid's message brought Marta, full of concern. "Petra? Are you ill?"

Saliel had no tears, they were a frozen lump in her chest, but she told the story in a tearful voice.

"His sleeve was on fire?" Marta's eyes grew wide. She gazed at Saliel in admiration. "I should have fainted. How brave you are!"

No. Today I am a coward. Today I hide in my room.

"I shall stay with you."

Saliel shook her head on the pillow. "Please don't stay, Marta."

"But—"

"My nerves are overwrought, is all." She smiled wanly. "I shall be fine tomorrow."

"Are you certain?"

"Yes." Saliel closed her eyes. "I shall sleep."

The maid escorted Marta from the suite and returned to stand beside the bed. "Do you require anything, noble mistress?"

Saliel raised her eyelids. "No."

"Shall I summon a physician?"

"No. I wish to be left alone. Don't let anyone disturb me."

"Yes, noble mistress." The woman curtseyed. She left the room, shutting the door behind her.

Saliel listened to the silence. She inhaled a deep breath and released it. *Alone. Safe.*

She turned on her side and hugged her arms. She closed her eyes.

CHAPTER FORTY-TWO

ATHAN WENT TO Lady Petra's suite in the middle of the morning, when he thought the maid would be there. She was.

"Noble lord." The woman sank into a low curtsey.

"How's my wife?"

"She's resting, noble lord."

"Resting?" He glanced at the closed door to the bed chamber. "She's here?"

"She was very distressed, noble lord. She's not well enough to be in court today."

Athan almost nodded his approval. *Clever.*

He could have insisted that he see her—a husband's wishes overrode his wife's—instead he said, "You may tell my wife not to be distressed on my part. The burn is minor."

The maid ducked her head in another curtsey. "I shall tell her, noble lord."

Athan yawned. "I have a task for you."

"For me, noble lord?"

"Yes." He dug in his pocket and pulled out a gold coin. "I'm concerned for my wife's health. She's... fragile."

The maid moistened her lips nervously. Her gaze was on the coin. "Noble lord?"

"I wish to know anything that happens to her."

"What sort of thing, noble lord?"

230 The Laurentine Spy

If she's taken for questioning. "Any change in her routine, no matter how small it is. Women's minds are easily disordered."

The maid took the coin and dipped another curtsey. "I shall do as you ask, noble lord."

"See that you do." Athan turned toward the outer door and let the maid hurry past him to open it. He ignored her as he stepped into the corridor. *Thank you,* he said silently as the woman closed the door behind him.

He strolled down the corridor, lighter in his chest now that he had a means of watching Three. *Not that she needs my help.* He touched the bandage on his hand. A resourceful woman.

He wished he could keep to his bed too. The tale had circulated through the court as quickly as the flames had caught hold of his cuff. "I stood too close to a candle," he said a dozen times, two dozen times. "The lace caught fire." And he yawned and let his mouth stay slightly open afterwards, and saw that his words were believed. *That fool, Donkey,* he heard Tregar whisper behind his hand.

The day passed too slowly, full of amused sideways glances. *Hurry up,* he told the clocks as their hands inched toward sunset. *Let this day be done.*

The seconds stretched into long minutes and longer hours. Even the tunes the musicians played in the ballroom seemed drawn-out and slow. The melodies dragged and lumbered.

"Not dancing, Donkey?" Druso asked.

Athan yawned and shook his head. "Not tonight." He beckoned a servant and spent several seconds selecting a glass of wine.

The wine was dark, almost purple, and smelled of earth and dark berries. He tasted blackcurrants and blackberries and something spicy he couldn't put a name to.

He closed his eyes to savor the flavors. Blackcurrants and blackberries and—

"I hear you had an unfortunate accident." Lord Seldo's voice was amused.

Athan opened his eyes. "Yes." He turned to greet the man.

The spycatcher stood alongside Seldo, smiling. "Good evening, Lord Ivo."

Every hair on his scalp felt as if it stood on end. "Good evening." He couldn't look away. He was caught by those sharp, pale eyes.

"A burn, I hear?" the spycatcher said politely. "Not too serious?"

"It's very minor," Athan said, sweating, telling the truth. "A few blisters." He forced his mouth into a smile.

"However did it happen?" the spycatcher asked.

She set my cuff on fire.

His mouth opened to say the words.

Athan dropped the wine glass. The crystal shattered on the red and black flagstones, spraying wine.

The spycatcher cursed. He stepped back.

Athan looked down. "So sorry," he said. "I can't think how…"

The spycatcher cursed beneath his breath again, brushing at the wine on his breeches.

Lord Seldo clapped Athan on the shoulder, laughing. "Perhaps you should take to your bed, as your wife does."

I would, if I could.

Servants gathered the shards of glass and wiped up the wine. In less than a minute the mess he'd made was gone. "I must change my breeches," the spycatcher said. "Excuse me." Irritation edged his voice.

"Please accept my apologies, Lord Grebber."

The spycatcher didn't bother to correct him. He turned on his heel and walked away.

Athan glanced down at his own breeches. "And I must change mine. Excuse me."

THREE ARRIVED MOMENTS after he did. Athan watched her walk into the circle of light.

The guardian watched her too, obliquely. Athan sensed the man's wariness. *You needn't worry*, he told him sourly, in his mind. *She doesn't know. And I won't tell her in front of you.*

"Here's the key," the guardian said. He didn't hand it to Athan; he placed it on the stone table, beside the candle.

You don't dare, do you? You're afraid of me.

Athan reached for the key. It was slightly lighter than the previous one. "I'll do it now," he said. "We can leave tonight."

The guardian shook his head. "That's not possible."

Athan stood. "We leave tonight," he said flatly.

The guardian stood too, moving sideways, putting the table between himself and Athan. "You must leave tomorrow night."

Three glanced from the guardian to him. *Yes, he fears me*, Athan told her silently. He took a step toward the man. "Why?"

"A ship sails from the Bight on the morning tide, the day after tomorrow."

"We're booked on it?"

"No. But the spycatcher will think you are."

"Then why must we wait until—"

"If you leave too soon, pursuit will reach the Bight before the ship sails." The guardian spoke rapidly. His words fell over themselves. "The port will be closed and all ships searched."

Athan exhaled through his nose. "Very well." He clenched the key in his hand. "We travel tomorrow night."

'Be here at nightfall." The guardian stayed where he was, behind the table. His stance was tense, wary. "It will take most of the night to reach the Bight—and you must be there by dawn."

"If we don't sail, what then?"

"You cross the Bazarn Plateau."

"The Bazarn Plateau?" The sharpness of his voice made the guardian flinch. "Are you insane?"

"It is the safest route," the man said hastily. "They'll never think to search there. No one will follow you."

No, we'll just freeze to death in the snow. Athan took another step toward the man. "You risk our lives with this."

"No," the guardian said, moving sideways. "You'll be safe. The code book will be safe."

Athan halted. "We take the code book with us?"

"Yes."

The guardian cared nothing for their lives, but he wouldn't risk the code book. Athan unclenched his fingers and looked at the key. "To Marillaq?"

"No."

He looked up. "But—"

"Our embassy in Marillaq is compromised. The Corhonase have a spy there."

"So where do we take it?"

"The Illymedes is safe," the guardian said. "And Pinsault. Or Laurent itself. You must give the code book to someone ranked General or higher."

"Very well." Athan closed his fingers around the key again. "I'll copy the book tonight."

"Remember, it's neither red nor—"

"I know." He turned to Three. "A final day. Can you do it?"

She nodded.

The journey opened out in his mind: the high snow-covered plateau, the mountains, the gorge. Did she understand what lay ahead of them? "Until tomorrow night," he said, and bowed to her.

She stood. "Be careful." They were the first words she'd spoken tonight. He strained to hear Lady Petra in her voice and failed. The languages were too different: one spoken almost in the throat, the other rising and falling on the tip of the tongue.

He watched her walk away. *By this time tomorrow she'll know who I am.*

Athan turned his head and looked at the guardian. He felt the same rage as two nights ago. Breath hissed between his teeth. The guardian flinched. It brought no satisfaction; the harm had been done. *I can't undo what I did to her.*

He swung away from the candlelight.

Tomorrow Three would learn the truth. He shrank from the thought of it. *How can I tell her? What words will I use?*

Athan pushed open the door to the sewers and stepped into darkness. When would he tell her? Where?

Tomorrow afternoon, he decided as he trudged up the sloping tunnel. Late, when the Consort had released the ladies from their needlework and the sun sank towards dusk. *I'll go to her suite and ask to speak with her. I'll send the maid away. And once we're alone—*

Dread clenched in his belly.

I'll tell her I wish to speak with her.

And he'd say it in Laurentine, so that she knew immediately.

CHAPTER FORTY-THREE

THE IRON KEY slid into the lock. It turned, a stiff movement. The latch lifted on the other side of the door with a soft *click*.

Athan released the breath he'd been holding. He laid his palm against the cool wood and pushed. Two inches of darkness appeared.

He pulled the key from the lock, tucked it into his cuff, and glanced up and down the corridor as he took a candle from his pocket. *Hurry*. He reached up to the wall sconce. The wick took a moment to light, while he strained to hear the tread of booted feet.

Athan pushed the door open, shielding the flame with his hand, and stepped inside the debating chamber. Furniture loomed out of the darkness: high-backed chairs upholstered in brocade, desks made of dark, polished wood.

He closed the door, lowering the latch to lock it again. His footsteps echoed quietly as he walked across the floor. The chamber stretched beyond the light cast by the candle, full of dark shapes.

Shallow marble steps lead up to a dais. The Prince's chair was massive, throne-like. The screaming eagle of Corhona spread its wings across the back. Its feathers were gilded. Athan snorted beneath his breath. *A fine seat for a puppet*. The Prince had no authority; any decisions made in this chamber were approved or rejected by the Emperor.

The wall behind the dais was marble, white, carved with scrolling foliage. Fluted columns stretched high into the darkness.

Athan studied the sculpted designs. Shadows shifted with each flicker of the candle. He held the flame close, squinting to see more clearly. It took long minutes of searching, while hot wax trickled onto his fingers and tension built in his chest, before he found the keyhole.

"Yes." The *s* hissed triumphantly on his tongue.

He took the key from his cuff, inserted it, and turned it cautiously. The lock clicked open. Athan removed the key. The door swung inwards at the touch of his hand, heavy, swinging silently on its hinges.

He stepped into the doorway. The vault was small, cramped. It reminded him of a mausoleum; the low ceiling, the shelves on either side long enough for a man to lie on.

No coffins rested on the marble shelves. Instead there were leather-bound books and rolls of maps.

Athan stepped inside and scanned the shelves, looking for red and green and blue leather. He saw thick volumes and thin ones, gold-embossed and plain—all brown.

Think. Where would they put the code books? Somewhere safe, somewhere secure.

His eyes fell on a small, wooden chest that sat at the end of one shelf. The top was inlaid with Corhona's screaming eagle, pale wood on dark. Gold gleamed around the rim of a keyhole.

Athan stepped closer and bent over the box.

The key to the citadel slid easily into the keyhole. The lock opened with a quiet *snick*.

Athan lifted the lid carefully. He saw red and green, and blue. Relief swelled in his chest.

The third code book was a slim volume. He took it out to one of the desks in the debating chamber. A silver candleholder sat on the desktop. Athan removed the candle, replacing it with the one he held. He sat. The tiny flame lit his movements as he pulled ink and quill and parchment from their hiding places inside his clothes. He opened the book.

Sixteen pages, filled with letters and numbers and symbols.

Athan inhaled a deep breath and dipped the quill in the ink. *Do it carefully*, he told himself. *Make no mistakes.*

After the second page he stopped to rub his eyes. At the end of the third page he laid down the quill and rubbed his face with both hands. He yawned, and heard his jaw creak. On the fifth page he caught himself writing the wrong combination of numbers and letters.

"Stop." He said the word aloud, and then obeyed with his hand, laying down the quill.

Exhaustion was gritty in his eyes. He closed them and sat for a moment, resting his head in his hands. It would be easy to fall asleep here.

Easy. Fatal.

Athan pushed to his feet and walked once around the chamber, treading carefully in the gloom. He sat again and picked up the quill and copied another page with meticulous care, and then walked around the debating chamber again.

The hours passed that way: copying, walking, trying to rub the exhaustion from his eyes and the cramp from his fingers. Four times the door handles rattled as the guards checked them.

Fourteen pages, fifteen.

Sixteen.

It was done.

He did everything more slowly than he wanted to, making sure he made no mistakes—forgetting to lock the box or the vault, leaving the chair he'd sat in pushed out instead of in, not putting the unburned candle back in its silver holder. The copied pages sat beneath doublet and shirt, against his skin—and if he did everything right, no one would ever know that he'd been here.

Athan blew the candle out at the door and waited for the guards to pass. He rested his forehead against the smooth wood. He saw symbols behind his closed eyelids, letters and numbers.

He slept a little, standing, and jerked awake to the sound of booted footsteps.

The guards came closer. Their footsteps stopped. The door handles rattled. "Clear."

Footsteps again, growing fainter—

Athan quietly opened the door.

He stepped out into the corridor and locked the door behind him. His tiredness was gone.

He retraced his route—cautious, alert—walking down staircases and along corridors, crossing silent atria. At the first brazier, he disposed of the bottle of ink; at the second, the quill; at the third, the stub of the candle.

He breathed more easily once the flames had swallowed the candle. Only the pages beneath his shirt could betray him now—and the key hidden inside his cuff.

With each step he came closer to safety—and with each step the skin between his shoulder blades grew tighter. Here was where he'd been found, last time.

Athan stood in the shadows for long minutes, watching, listening. His ears strained to hear footsteps.

Nothing.

He stepped out into the atrium, placing his feet carefully. Sweat stuck his shirt to his skin.

His tension grew greater once he was safely across. *So close now*. His breaths were short and shallow. He had to strain to hear past the beating of his heart.

Two more staircases. Another atrium. A final flight of stairs...

He was no longer the only nobleman in these corridors.

Athan wiped the perspiration from his face. He let his shoulders slouch. *I'm merely another bleary-eyed noble who has drunk too much*. He stumbled slightly as he walked, and yawned widely.

His valet was asleep in a chair beside the hearth. The candles had burned low and the fire was almost out.

The man jerked awake as he entered. "Noble lord," he said, scrambling to his feet.

"Go away," Athan said, an irritable note in his voice. "And don't wake me in the morning." He stretched his jaw in a yawn.

"Yes, noble lord. As you wish."

Athan turned away, not watching as the man bowed. He heard the door open and then shut.

He shrugged out of his doublet, letting it fall to the floor, and unbuttoned his shirt. The copied pages were warm from the heat of his body, limp, damp with sweat. The ink hadn't smeared.

He turned to the bed. The movement caught his eye in the mirror. He saw himself: linen-white parchment, bare chest.

Athan stared at himself. He heard his uncle's voice in his head: *Sometimes it's possible to win before it comes to fighting.*

The pages he held, with their letters and numbers, their strange symbols, would save countless Laurentine lives.

These pages make me a hero.

A few months ago he would have stood triumphantly. He would have cared about what the pages in his hand meant to Laurent, what they meant to his House.

Tonight there was no triumph. His relief had nothing to do with Laurent, or with what his House would think of him. It was more personal; now they could leave.

Athan turned away from the mirror. He slid the copied pages beneath his pillow. *We paid too high a price.*

He stripped, shedding his clothes. It was done.

Only one more day.

CHAPTER FORTY-FOUR

ATHAN FOUND AN empty sofa in the corner of one of the smaller salons. He yawned and wandered over, aware of the parchment hidden beneath shirt and doublet and ruffles of lace. He arranged his limbs in a careless sprawl, stretching one leg along the seat. The puce velvet of his breeches went ill with the dark green brocade.

He pretended to doze, resting his chin on his chest above the pages of code. *What will I say to her?* No apology could be sufficient. Nothing could compensate for what he'd done.

He could give her his name, his House, his wealth. *Marry me. I think I love you.*

Athan tried to imagine her reaction. Would she laugh in his face, or spit in it?

"Wake up, Donkey!" A hand shook his shoulder. "You'll miss the racing."

Athan opened his eyes. "Druso." He yawned.

"Hurry up," Druso said cheerfully. "That pig of yours is running soon."

"Russet? So she is. I'd forgotten." He yawned again and rose leisurely to his feet.

"Forgotten?" Druso grinned and shook his head. "You don't deserve that pig, Donkey."

"You're right." Athan adjusted the lace at his cuffs. The key to the citadel was a hard lump against his wrist, making the band of linen tight. "You may have her."

Druso's grin faltered. "What?"

"You may have Russet."

"I was only jesting, Donkey."

Athan shrugged. "Pigs are too much effort. You may have her."

"But—"

Athan yawned and turned away. "Come, let's watch her race."

CHAPTER FORTY-FIVE

SALIEL JOINED THE noble ladies at their embroidery. A second day in bed would have brought too much attention; she would have had visits from the physician, from Lord Ivo, from the Consort.

Lunch time came and went. She sat alongside Marta, stitching. The last dark-veined leaf. The last unfurling petal. The last—

"Noble Petra."

Saliel looked up. One of the Consort's attendants stood in front of her. Her face was doll-like, familiar.

"The Royal Consort wishes to speak with you."

Saliel swallowed. She put aside the embroidery frame. *Don't panic. She can't do anything to me. There's too little time.*

She rose to her feet and followed the attendant across the Ladies' Hall. The woman scratched on the door to the Consort's private parlor.

Saliel inhaled a slow breath. *Calm.*

The attendant opened the door.

"My dear Petra." The Consort sat beside the fireplace. Her gown was sumptuous, a midnight blue that made her skin seem as pale as milk and her eyes as dark as ebony. "Do come in."

Saliel stepped into the room. "Your Eminence." She curtseyed.

"Have a seat, my dear."

Saliel sat, while the attendant poured tisane into porcelain cups. A silver platter of sweetmeats lay on one of the tables. She folded her hands in her lap. *I am Lady Petra. I'm taking tea and cake with the Consort. I'm excited and nervous.*

The attendant curtseyed and left the parlor.

The Consort opened her hand in a gesture of invitation. "Have something to eat."

"Thank you." She selected a bite-sized cake.

"I hear that your husband had a most unfortunate accident," the Consort said, her hand hovering over the sweetmeats. She plucked one from the tray.

"Yes, your Eminence."

"You put out the flames. With your bare hands."

"Oh, no." Saliel glanced up. "I tried to, but it was Lord Ivo who put them out. He used my shawl." Shame helped her to blush. "I didn't think to do that."

"Your shawl?" The Consort's eyebrows arched slightly. "How quick-thinking of him."

"Yes." Saliel looked down at the cake on her plate. *Surprisingly so.*

"And you didn't faint or have hysterics," the Consort said with cool approval. "I commend you, my dear Petra. Not many noble ladies would have acted as you did."

Was there an edge to those words of praise? Saliel looked up and met the Consort's eyes. "Thank you." She picked up the cake and bit into it, tasting ginger and cloves and honey.

"I wish to speak more about Gryff," the Consort said. "It is comforting to know that Karla lived in so beautiful a place."

Saliel chewed slowly and swallowed. *Calm. You can do this.* "Of course. What would you like to know?"

"Tell me about the Governor's palace. I hear it was quite exquisite."

"It was." Saliel put down the sweetmeat. "I wish you could have seen it, your Eminence. The marble had a... a tinge of pink, as if the stone was blushing. At sunset it was the color of roses."

"Yes," the Consort said. "So I have heard." Her expression was benevolent and smiling, friendly. "Tell me more."

Saliel described the long flights of marble stairs, the colonnades, the gardens with ponds and fountains and peacocks strutting along the paths. The words came automatically—she'd rehearsed them so often.

The Consort watched as she spoke. The dark eyes were fixed on her face. The woman scarcely seemed to blink.

Saliel paused to sip her tea. The liquid was lukewarm. She smelled rosehips. "Is there anything more I can tell you, your Eminence?"

The Consort smiled. "Yes. But do finish your cake, my dear."

Saliel bit obediently into it. Ginger. Cloves. Honey.

A door on the other side of the parlor opened.

"Ah," said the Consort, her smile widening. "Here is my other guest."

Saliel looked around. She saw an attendant curtseying in the doorway, and a corridor beyond, and—

Her throat closed.

"Do come in," the Consort said. "My dear Petra, are you acquainted with Lord Grigor?"

Saliel forced herself to chew, to swallow, to smile at the man. "Yes. How do you do, Lord Grigor?"

The spycatcher bowed. "Very well, thank you." He smiled at her. His gaze was sharp, his tone jovial: "I hear you had a little adventure."

"Petra acted with great presence of mind," the Consort said. "One would have expected a noblewoman to faint in such circumstances, but she didn't. It is most remarkable."

"You are to be commended, noble Petra," the spy-catcher said, and bowed again.

"Oh," Saliel said, putting down the plate. The blush didn't come to her cheeks this time; she was too afraid. "It was nothing."

"Please be seated, Lord Grigor," the Consort said. "Petra was just telling me about Gryff."

"Gryff?" the man said, sitting. "How interesting."

The Consort turned her head and looked at Saliel. Her eyes gleamed, black. "Lord Grigor has an interest in Gryff. I thought he'd like to hear what you have to say."

"Of course." Saliel smiled. *Shy. Innocent. Unafraid.* "What would you like to know?"

CHAPTER FORTY-SIX

THE AFTERNOON WAS gray. A raw, blustery wind blew, tugging at his cape. Athan accepted a tankard of warm mead from a servant, but sipped only a few mouthfuls. He couldn't see the spycatcher in the crush of noblemen.

"Come on, Donkey." Druso tugged at his sleeve.

Athan followed, yawning, holding the tankard ready in case the spycatcher was at the pens. *You'll find that mead is stickier than wine.* But the man wasn't there.

Druso leaned over the wooden railing, scratching beneath Russet's chin.

"She likes an apple after the race," Athan said. "But don't feed her before."

"I've had other pigs," Druso said. His tone was unoffended.

Athan laughed, and leaned his forearms on the railing. "So you have." He inhaled the smell of the sty, of straw and apples and manure, and sipped his mead again.

CHAPTER FORTY-SEVEN

"IN SOME PLACES steam came up from the ground," Saliel said. "It smelled of sulfur." She sipped from her cup; her throat was dry with talking. The tisane was cold and unpalatable. She forced herself to swallow it.

Lord Grigor's expression was courteous, attentive, but he shifted his position slightly on the sofa. It was a restless movement. *He's bored*, she realized. *He thinks this is a waste of time.*

The tension inside her eased. She'd done it. Saliel smiled at the man, shyly, and drank another mouthful of cold tisane.

The spycatcher looked away. It was a relief not to have that gaze on her, pale and intense, urging her to tell the truth.

Saliel glanced at the Consort. The woman sat with a polite smile on her mouth, but anger glittered in her eyes. *She feels a fool.*

"Lady Petra's mother had a mirror similar to the one on my wall," the Consort said to the spycatcher. "Didn't she, my dear?"

"She did?" The man studied the mirror for a moment and then turned to look at her. "It looked like this one? How unusual."

Saliel put down the cup and saucer. She had rehearsed this moment. "The Consort says it's Illy-medan work, but mother wouldn't have allowed such a thing in the house." She shook her head. *Confused. Anxious.* "I don't understand."

The man smiled encouragingly at her. "Are you certain it was similar?" *Tell me the truth*, his eyes urged her.

"Yes," she said, nodding. "The animals were different, but the workmanship is the same."

"Perhaps you could describe it to me?" the spycatcher said, his tone light and friendly, reassuring.

"There were four squirrels," Saliel said. "One in each corner, with mother-of-pearl eyes. And acorns and oak leaves carved into the frame."

The spycatcher studied her for a moment. "Squirrels?"

"Yes." Saliel nodded.

"There are no squirrels in the Illymedes," the spycatcher said. "And no oak trees."

I know. She creased her brow. "There aren't?"

"No."

"Then... it wasn't Illymedan work?"

"It would appear not."

She smiled. "I'm very pleased to know that. Thank you, Lord Grigor."

The spycatcher acknowledged her words with a dip of his head. "My pleasure."

It was a strain to meet those pale eyes. An ache was growing in her temples. Saliel looked away, at the Consort. The woman's lips were pinched together. "Is there anything else you wish to hear about Gryff?"

"No, thank you, Petra." The Consort's voice was cold.

"Excuse me," the spycatcher said. "But I would like to speak more with Lady Petra."

Saliel glanced at him. His gaze had been bored and uninterested; now it was sharp. Her chest tightened. *What did I say?*

She looked back at the Consort. "Your Eminence?"

The woman didn't answer immediately. Her eyes were on the spycatcher.

Saliel turned her head and saw the man give a slight nod. Panic jerked beneath her breastbone. *What did I say?*

The Consort's smile widened. She looked at Saliel. "I would like you to speak further with Lord Grigor."

Saliel moistened her lips. "You would?"

"Yes."

"Now?"

"Yes." The Consort reached for the little silver bell beside the platter of sweetmeats. "I shall have someone escort you to a room where you may speak more about Gryff." She shook the bell. The sound was light and tinkling.

Saliel moistened her lips again. "But... my embroidery."

"I would prefer that you speak with Lord Grigor, my dear Petra."

She swallowed. "If it pleases you, your Eminence."

The door from the Ladies' Hall opened. "Fetch Lady Petra's cape and bring it here," the Consort commanded.

Saliel sat, waiting. *Calm,* she told herself. But panic was tight in her chest. What had happened? She'd said nothing, done nothing—

I looked away from the spycatcher's eyes.

Saliel glanced up at the man. He was watching her. She smiled at him, polite, shy.

The door opened again.

Saliel turned her head. One of the Consort's attendants stepped into the parlor. She held Saliel's cape.

Fool, you looked away again. Saliel rose to her feet. She allowed the woman to settle the cape over her shoulders and fasten it at her throat.

"Show Lady Petra and Lord Grigor to the green parlor," the Consort said.

The attendant curtseyed. "Yes, your Eminence."

"Petra, please answer any questions Lord Grigor may have for you."

"Of course, your Eminence." Saliel sank into a curtsey. "My embroidery basket?" There was a pair of scissors in it, small and silver, sharp.

"I shall have someone take it to your maid." The Consort smiled.

"Thank you. You're most kind."

They were pretending, all of them. Did the attendant sense it? Beneath the smiles and the curtseys, the politeness, a hunt was taking place. *And I am the prey.*

THE PARLOR WAS along cold corridors and up a flight of winding stairs.

"Request my manservant to attend us," the spycatcher said.

"Yes, noble lord." The attendant curtseyed.

The parlor was simply furnished—tapestries showing forest scenes, a sofa and two chairs upholstered in green brocade, a writing desk. A large vase stood on the desk. It was an ugly shade of green. A fire burned in the grate.

There was only one door. A single window was high in the wall, framing a view of an overcast sky.

"What a charming room," Saliel said. She removed her cape and sat, folding her hands in her lap and smiling politely at the spycatcher. *I am as placid as Marta—and as innocent.* "You have more questions, my lord?"

The spycatcher took a seat across from her. He returned her smile. "Yes. I should like to hear of your escape from Gryff. The Royal Consort assures me it's a fascinating tale."

"It wasn't an escape, my lord," Saliel said. "It was merely a journey. I left some days before the disaster."

The spycatcher accepted the correction with an inclination of his head. His gaze was fixed on her face. *Tell me the truth*, his eyes urged.

"I was aboard the *Ocean Pride*, with my mother and aunt, and my cousin Lady Tressa and her husband."

The spycatcher's eyebrows rose slightly. "Did your family suspect a great quake?"

"No." Saliel shook her head and tried to look distressed. "I remember the ground shook a lot that last week, but no one guessed what would come."

"Then why did you leave?"

"My cousin and her husband were moving to Dravek. Tressa was with child." She blinked, as if trying to hold back tears. "She wished for us to be with her when the time came."

"Ah," the spycatcher said. "I see." He steepled his hands. "And were you?"

"No." Saliel squeezed her eyes shut and pressed a hand to her mouth. "Forgive me, my lord." Her voice was choked. "It's... it's painful to speak of."

"There is nothing to forgive," the spycatcher said politely. His voice held an undertone that made her open her eyes.

The man was looking at her intently. She almost felt his gaze, as if a knife blade brushed lightly over her skin.

I did it again. I broke the hold of his eyes.

Saliel swallowed. She lowered her hand. "There was a fire on board," she said. "The ship... it sank. There were only a few survivors. My cousin was not one of them. Nor were her husband or my aunt."

"You have my condolences."

She smiled weakly and felt for the handkerchief in her pocket. "Thank you."

"It must have been a terrifying experience." Lord Grigor's voice was smooth, sympathetic.

"Yes." She made herself shiver.

"But you and your mother survived? You were most fortunate."

"Yes." Saliel dabbed beneath her eyes with the handkerchief. "We made it aboard a life boat. We were... very lucky."

The spycatcher nodded.

"We came ashore at Kressel that night. We thought—" She pressed the handkerchief to her mouth for a moment and then lowered it. "We thought we were safe. We thought everything would be all right."

"It wasn't?" The spycatcher's expression was sympathetic, curious. It was a mask he wore. He must know the tale; the Consort would have told him.

Saliel shook her head. "Kressel had the fever."

"Ah." The man's eyebrows raised. "How unfortunate."

"Yes." She twisted the handkerchief between her fingers, not daring to look away from his eyes.

"Did you fall ill?"

"My mother caught the fever first. And then I did. I... I don't remember what happened after that. I know only what I've been told."

The spycatcher smiled at her, sympathetic and encouraging. "And that is...?"

"My mother died and I... I was very ill. I had the fever for many weeks. I was taken in by a townsman and his wife. They cared for me, but..." She bit her lip and shook her head, touching light fingertips to her temple. "I can't properly remember."

"A townsman? What was his name?"

"Edler." Her head was beginning to ache from the strain of meeting the spycatcher's eyes. She felt a compulsion to tell the truth. *Edler is a Laurentine agent. A clever man, who buried a dead noblewoman in an unmarked grave and requested an agent be found to take her place.*

She made her mouth smile. "Edler and his wife were most kind. They took me to their estate in the country. I stayed there until I was well enough to travel. It took many months."

"And then you came here."

"Yes."

The spycatcher leaned back in his chair. "Why the citadel?"

Because it is a wide ocean away from anyone who knew the real Lady Petra. "My father spent some time here, many years ago. He spoke of it occasionally. The citadel sounded... safe." She tried to look naïve. "I wanted somewhere safe."

The spycatcher's eyes were fixed on her face. "You had no relatives elsewhere?"

Saliel shook her head. "No. They were all on Gryff."

The spycatcher studied her. His finger tapped his mouth. *He doesn't know whether to believe me or not.*

The door opened. Her gaze jerked to the doorway.

A man stood there, dressed in the plain clothes of a servant. He bowed. "Noble lord?"

"Therlo," the spycatcher said. "Wait outside."

The man bowed again. The door closed.

Saliel glanced back at the spycatcher. His eyes were narrow and thoughtful as he studied her face. *I looked away from him again.* Her skin tightened in a shiver.

The spycatcher seemed to come to a decision. He stopped tapping his mouth. "I have an interest in tales of survival such as yours, noble Petra. If you don't mind, I should like to go over it again."

Saliel swallowed, and smiled. "Of course."

The spycatcher leaned forward in his chair. His eyes held hers, moonlight pale. "You left Gryff on the *Ocean Pride*."

"Yes." The intense stare was unsettling. Her tongue wanted to speak the truth.

"With your cousin and your aunt and your mother."

"Yes."

"And there was a fire at sea and the ship sank."

"Yes." Her head was beginning to ache.

"But you and your mother made it aboard a life boat."

"Yes."

"And you came ashore after two nights."

"Yes... I mean, no." Her heart began to beat rapidly. "It was only one night."

The spycatcher sat back in his chair. He steepled his hands again. "And you came ashore after one night."

Saliel swallowed, and nodded. Perspiration beaded on her skin. She understood the reason for the spy-catcher's slow smile, for the gleam in his eyes. *I have just proven that I can lie to him.*

"Excuse me for a moment, noble Petra." The spy-catcher rose to his feet. "I should like to write this down. It's most interesting."

"Of course."

The spycatcher walked to the door and opened it. "I shall only be gone a few minutes," he said, bowing. He stepped outside.

Saliel waited for a moment, listening to the loud beating of her heart, then she stood and crossed the room with quick steps. The door opened smoothly, with no noise. The spycatcher's manservant stood on the other side.

"Noble lady?"

"Fetch me something to drink. I'm thirsty."

The man bowed, an apologetic movement. "My master has commanded me to stay here until he returns."

Saliel swallowed. "Very well." She lifted her chin haughtily and turned back into the room. "Put more coals on the fire. It grows cold."

"At once, noble lady."

She watched as the man knelt before the hearth. *Should I run?*

No. The skirts of her gown were too stiff and wide, the corset too tightly laced. Therlo would catch her in a few strides.

The man's doublet lifted slightly as he reached to place fresh coals on the fire. A knife was sheathed at his hip. The sight riveted her attention. *If I take it—*

She could hide it. And then pretend to feel faint. The spycatcher had no proof she was a spy. He'd have to take her back to her maid, to loosen the corset. *And I can take the knife and—*

She couldn't kill her maid. But she could bind and gag the woman, and open the door into the secret passages and flee.

If she did that, all routes from the citadel and the town would be sealed.

Saliel turned her head and looked out the window. How long until dusk? An hour? Two hours?

The servant stood. "It is done, noble lady."

His bow was respectful, but his eyes—

He believes I'm a spy. It excites him.

"Do you require anything else?" the man asked.

"Fetch me something to drink when Lord Grigor returns."

"Yes, noble lady."

Therlo bowed again—and she caught his gaze as he straightened. Blue eyes, shining with anticipation.

It was like it had been with the Consort the first time: easy. She stepped forward swiftly and slid her hand beneath the man's doublet. She felt the warmth of his body, the movement of his ribs as he breathed, the softness of fabric and the hard ridge of the knife handle.

She drew the knife free of its sheath, staring into the man's eyes.

I could kill him. It would be a simple matter to cut his throat—

I can't.

Saliel stepped back and slid the knife into the pocket of her gown. The hilt protruded slightly. She held her hand to hide it.

She closed her eyes briefly.

Therlo blinked. He shook his head as if to clear it, and turned away from her. Saliel watched as he opened the door and stepped outside.

She walked across to the fire, pressing the knife into her pocket until the blade slit the fabric. The hilt slid deep. It was hidden.

Saliel smoothed her gown. Lavender blue. Her heartbeat was loud in her ears. She inhaled deeply, feeling the tightness of the corset, and glanced out the window again.

Another hour and I can do it.

The door opened. The spycatcher stepped into the room. A manservant followed, carrying parchment and a quill and a flask of ink. "My man tells me you wish for something to drink."

"Yes," Saliel said. She moved to the sofa and sat. "I'm somewhat thirsty." She watched as the servant placed the parchment on the writing desk and laid the quill neatly alongside.

"Fetch a drink for Lady Petra," the spycatcher ordered as the servant put the flask of ink on the desk and opened it. "And a glass of wine."

The man bowed. "At once, noble lord." He hurried from the room, closing the door behind him.

The spycatcher sat. He looked at her, a slight smile on his mouth.

Saliel clasped her hands in her lap and waited, listening to the coals shift in the fireplace. "Lord Grigor?" she asked, when the silence between them had stretched for nearly half a minute.

The spycatcher stroked his chin with a finger. He looked at her for a moment longer without speaking, and then appeared make to a decision. He stood and walked across to the writing desk. He pulled out the chair, but didn't sit. "I should like you to write the tale in your own hand, Lady Petra."

"Me?" It was easy to sound startled.

"Yes." The spycatcher's gaze was intent on her face.

"But... why?"

"Because there's a Laurentine spy in the ladies' court."

Saliel gasped. "A Laurentine spy!" She held her hand to her breast in a gesture of horror. Her heart beat rapidly. *He changes the game.* "How can that be?"

"There is some suspicion that the spy is you," the spycatcher said, smiling politely, watching her face.

"Me?" She pushed to her feet. *Aghast. Horrified. Innocent.* The knife bumped against her thigh.

"Yes."

"But... but I'm not!"

The spycatcher inclined his head in acknowledgement. His expression was sympathetic. "The Consort wishes me to question you more closely."

"The Consort thinks I'm a spy?" She made her face distressed. "I assure you I'm not!" She clutched her hands together. *Agitated. Innocent.* "How can she think such a thing?"

"So you will cooperate with me?"

"Of course!" she cried. "Of course!"

The spycatcher opened his hand in a gesture of invitation. "Then please sit here."

Saliel clutched her hands more tightly together. She tried to look wide-eyed and confused. "Why?"

"So that you may write the tale of how you came to be here."

She creased her brow. "This will help?"

"Yes."

"Then of course I shall do it." She stepped toward the writing desk.

The spycatcher didn't move. He was so close that she could reach out and touch him if she wished. "I think... I have a feeling, noble Petra, that you have been lying to me." His voice was soft, his eyes as sharp and pale as ice.

"I swear to you I haven't!"

The spycatcher stepped back. "Then please sit."

She did, pretending to blink back tears. The knife blade pressed against her leg through the layers of petticoats. Her bodice had grown tighter in the past few minutes. She could do it now, pretend to feel faint, be taken back to her chamber.

Saliel glanced at the window again. *It's too soon.* She would risk their escape; the route to the Bight would be blocked before they reached it.

She picked up the quill and dipped it in ink. She understood this test. *Remember that it's   not ss.*

I left Gryff aboard the Ocean Pride, she wrote. The quill made a light scratching sound on the parchment. The ink was black. *With my mother and my aunt and my cousin Lady Tressa and her husband.* She spelled the name out carefully. *T. r. e.   . a.*

CHAPTER FORTY-EIGHT

"SHE WON!" DRUSO cried, delighted. "Russet won!"

"Did you think she wouldn't?"

"No, but—" Druso grabbed his wrist. "Come! I have to give her an apple."

Athan allowed himself to be dragged in Druso's wake, pushing through the noblemen wrapped in capes against the cold. The courtyard was loud with sound: bets being made, laughter, pigs squealing. Each breath smelled of mead and manure and sawdust from the track the pigs raced on.

He glanced up at the sky. The ladies would be putting aside their needlework soon. It was almost time to speak with Three.

His chest tightened with dread.

Lord Tregar said something behind him. Athan's ears didn't catch the words, but the sour tone was familiar. He didn't bother turning his head and asking the comment to be repeated. *I shall be pleased never to see you again.*

He followed Druso to the winner's pen. Russet grunted at the sound of her name and came trotting over.

Athan smiled, watching as Druso fed her an apple. He'd miss the piglet's enthusiastic greetings and the wholehearted enjoyment with which she ran races, the gleaming curiosity in her brown eyes.

"Promise me you'll never sell her to Tregar."

"Of course not." Druso scratched beneath Russet's chin. "I shall breed from her."

Athan glanced up at the sky again. *Soon.*

"Noble lord?"

He turned.

His manservant stood behind him. The man bowed and held out a folded piece of paper.

Athan took it. "What's this?"

"Lady Petra's maid requested that I give it to you, noble lord."

His mouth was suddenly dry. He unfolded the paper with hasty fingers and scanned the message quickly. The writing was ill-formed, the words misspelled, but the meaning was clear.

Athan cleared his throat. "Druso, you must excuse me." He didn't wait for an answer. He turned away, the note clenched in his fist.

He wanted to run; he made himself stroll.

CHAPTER FORTY-NINE

THE DOOR OPENED. Saliel looked up. It was the second manservant, carrying a tray.

"Tisane, noble lady?"

Saliel laid down the quill. "Yes."

The man poured. He moved like a servant, with neat, unobtrusive movements, but he was the spy-catcher's man. She saw it in his eyes, in the way he glanced at her too boldly. His eyes were almost as dark as the Consort's.

Saliel accepted the cup. The tisane was a clear, pale yellow. Steam rose, lemon-scented.

The servant placed the silver pot on the writing desk, within easy reach, and offered the tray to the spycatcher. A single crystal glass stood on it, filled with wine the color of oxblood.

"You may wait outside," the spycatcher said, taking the glass.

"Yes, noble lord."

The servant glanced at her as he closed the door. Anticipation gleamed in his eyes, as it had in Therlo's.

Saliel sipped her tea. *You wait in vain. I shall not betray myself.* She set the cup down on the writing desk and picked up the quill again.

She'd filled one-and-a-half sheets with writing, curling each *f* with a flourish and dotting each *i* precisely. She reread the last sentence.

We were aboard the life boat for a full day, and came ashore at night on the coast of Kre el. She dipped the quill in ink and glanced up at the window. Not much longer.

She bent her head. *We were four pa engers and three crew*, she wrote. *The pa engers were my mother and myself, and—*

The door opened again. "Noble lord, you have a visitor."

Saliel looked up. The dark-eyed servant stepped into the room and bowed. Behind him was Lord Ivo.

The spycatcher rose to his feet. "Lord Ivo. What a... pleasant surprise."

"Grebber." Lord Ivo acknowledged the spycatcher with a lazy nod of his head. "I must ask, what are you doing with my wife?"

Therlo stood in the doorway, blocking it, but he'd have to step aside if Lord Ivo insisted. Saliel laid down the quill and took a deep breath.

The spycatcher smiled. "Your wife and I are discussing her journey from Gryff. The Royal Consort has given permission."

"Has she?" Lord Ivo shrugged. "But I'm Lady Petra's husband, and I haven't given my permission."

The spycatcher laughed, his manner friendly. "It's merely a discussion—"

Lord Ivo dismissed the man's protest with a yawn. "It grows late. My wife can speak with you again tomorrow."

Saliel rose. She reached for her cape.

"But, Donkey—"

"I must insist," Lord Ivo said mildly.

There was a moment of silence, while Saliel fastened the cape at her throat. She didn't look at the spycatcher or his servants. She kept her movements subdued and obedient.

"Why?"

The spycatcher's tone brought Saliel's head up. The man was staring at Lord Ivo. His eyes were narrow with suspicion.

Lord Ivo's throat worked, as if he tried not to speak. "Because—"

He lunged at the spycatcher. The sharp blade of a knife gleamed in his hand.

Saliel stood frozen, like a fool, as the spycatcher threw himself backward, dark wine spraying from his glass, as the servant leaped forward and Therlo charged from the doorway with a shout.

Lord Ivo slashed at Therlo, forcing him to stumble back, and struck the other servant a blow that made him double over.

The spycatcher hurled his glass aside. He lunged at Saliel, his arm upraised, and struck her across the face, open-handed.

Saliel fell. There was an instant of blankness; she heard nothing, saw nothing. The taste of blood was in her mouth.

Fingers closed around her left wrist, biting in.

She blinked to clear her vision. The spycatcher's face loomed close. His lips peeled back from his teeth. "I have you, bitch." He yanked her wrist, hauling her to her knees.

Saliel scrabbled for the knife. Fabric ripped as she tore it from her pocket. She stabbed with all her strength.

The blade sank deeply into the spycatcher's thigh. He uttered a choked cry and released her wrist.

Saliel pushed upright, reaching for the green vase without thought. Her fingers closed around it. Cool. Heavy. She swung as hard as she could.

The vase struck the spycatcher on the side of the head. He fell without uttering a sound, hitting the writing desk. The porcelain cup tipped over. Tisane spilled over the pages of writing.

Saliel stood looking down at the spycatcher, the vase gripped in her hand. Blood trickled down the man's temple. *Is he dead?* She couldn't inhale, couldn't exhale; her chest was too tight.

A strangled grunt jerked her around. The dark-eyed servant lay motionless, the hilt of a knife jutting from beneath his chin.

Saliel raised the vase again. Lord Ivo and Therlo wrestled in front of the fireplace. Lord Ivo gripped the manservant's throat, his fingers digging in. Therlo's face was suffused with blood, savage. He clawed at Lord Ivo's eyes.

The men broke apart. Lord Ivo scrambled to his feet. Therlo bellowed and pushed up from the floor.

Lord Ivo punched him. The blow was solid. Therlo fell as the spycatcher had fallen, heavily and without sound.

Saliel lowered the vase.

Lord Ivo swung around. He stared at her, panting. Strands of black hair had come loose from the band at the nape of his neck. There was nothing sleepy about his face. His eyes were wide open, clear and fierce. "Are you all right?"

It was One's voice, Laurentine, coming from Lord Ivo's mouth.

The world shifted dizzyingly beneath her feet. Saliel turned away. The vase dropped from her hand. It cracked as it hit the floor, splitting into three pieces. It was the same ugly shade of green inside as it was out.

I think I'm going to be ill.

CHAPTER FIFTY

"I DIDN'T KNOW it was you," Athan said. He gulped for breath. His heart hammered in his chest.

She stood with her face averted.

"Three…" He stepped over the servant's body. "If I'd known you were Lady Petra I would *never*—"

She jerked away from his outstretched hand. "Don't touch me."

"Three," he said desperately. "Please—"

"We must go. It's nearly night." She spoke with Lady Petra's voice, cold and clipped, distant.

He glanced up at the window. The sky was darkening toward dusk. "But—"

"Not now!" Three didn't look at him. She almost ran from the room, the full skirt of her gown making a *whisk* of sound.

Athan followed, shutting the door firmly. He hurried down the stairs after her. Apologies crowded on his tongue.

Three halted at the foot of the stairs and waited for him. He didn't have to tell her to take his arm; she laid her fingers lightly on his sleeve, barely touching him. She didn't look at him.

They walked along the corridor silently, calmly. *A man and his wife, strolling together.* Athan tried to steady his breathing. His heart still raced in his chest.

Each step brought them closer to freedom. They crossed one atrium, and another, while the sky grew darker. Fresh candles burned in the corridors. Athan dipped his head to nobles and ignored their servants. *Closer. Closer.*

Three released his arm. Athan opened the door to her suite and bowed. Her skirts rustled stiffly as she walked past him.

"Leave us," Athan told the maid as he stepped inside. "I wish to speak privately with my wife. Come back in an hour."

The woman curtseyed. "Yes, noble lord."

Athan closed the door behind her. He stood with his back to it, gripping the handle. "Three—"

"Not now!"

He pushed away from the door, following her into the bed chamber. "I didn't know," he said, his voice edged with desperation. *Listen to me.* "I only found out three days ago. If I'd known—" He swallowed. "I wouldn't have done it."

Three didn't look at him. She reached for a candle-holder.

"You're the one person in this citadel I would never harm. You must believe me!"

She lit the candle and held it out to him. "Take it," she said, not meeting his eyes.

"Three..." He swallowed. "Let me make it right. Please. Marry me."

Her eyes jerked to his. They were gray and wide, shocked.

"You'll have my name and my House and every-thing else I can give you."

She shook her head, not uttering a word.

"I won't touch you. I promise." He swallowed again. "Please."

Three turned away and put the candleholder down. She walked to the wall and crouched and pressed her fingers to a block of stone. It turned inwards. Athan watched as she reached inside and seemed to grasp for something.

A doorway opened in the wall.

Three stood. "You'll need the candle." She stepped through the doorway without looking back at him.

Athan grabbed the candleholder and followed hastily, ducking his head. Two shallow steps led up into a narrow corridor. Black shadows lunged back from the candlelight.

The door slid shut. *We're safe.*

"Three." Her hair gleamed in the candlelight, beautiful. "Please, listen to me—"

"I said, not now!" Her voice was low and fierce.

Athan stepped back. "My apologies."

He followed her along the passage, not crowding at her heels. *Fool. Triple times a fool. Now isn't the time.*

Anger grew in his chest—at the guardian, at the spy-catcher, at himself. He went blindly down hundreds of stairs while his cape brushed stone on either side.

Awareness of where he was came snapping back as they entered the catacombs. He saw the candle flame. He saw Three's shining hair. He saw crumbling skulls and broken-fingered hands and shreds of cloth.

Athan stepped closer to Three. His breath came more quickly. He began to sweat.

He tried not to look at the skeletons, but with each chamber that opened out, there were more. Dozens, hundreds, thousands. Toothless skulls grinned, watching as he walked past. Bones rustled behind him, stirring.

Athan squeezed his eyes shut. "Wait." His voice choked in his throat.

Three's footsteps stopped. "Are you all right?"

He gripped the candleholder and tried to steady his breathing. *I can't look at them*.

Her voice came closer. "They're dead."

Athan opened his eyes. He fixed his gaze on her face, trying not to see the skeletons. They beckoned for his attention, pale and brittle.

"They're dead," Three said again, meeting his eyes. "Many years ago they were people, as you and I are, but now they're dead. They can't harm you."

He gulped for air. Shame was hot in his cheeks. "It feels as if they're watching."

She didn't laugh at him. Her gaze was serious. "No," she said. "They're not. They can't."

Her calmness, her matter-of-factness, steadied him. He followed as she began to walk again, gripping the candle tightly, focusing on the red-gold hair. Their path took them downward, deeper. The citadel sat heavily above him. The air was cold and stale. Skeletons lay in their niches, staring at him from empty eye sockets. *Don't panic*, he told himself with each step. *Don't panic. Don't panic.*

At last Three halted. Relief came as sweat, dripping off his skin. He recognized this chamber, this shallow alcove. He'd been here before.

He watched as Three pressed her hands against the wall. Stone grated against stone as the slab swung aside.

Athan ducked his head and followed Three into the ancient storeroom. He crossed the room while she sealed the entrance to the catacombs. He opened the door. Faint light shone in. "After you, my lady."

She hesitated, and then stepped past him.

Athan had seen her emerge from the storeroom a hundred times; now it was he who walked out into the shadowy chamber. He saw the stone tables and the urns, the dark gutters, with relief. His chest became less tight. It was easier to breathe.

"What happened?" the guardian asked sharply, striding swiftly across the floor.

Athan closed the door. "The spycatcher took Three for questioning."

"What? Tell me!"

Beside him, Three said nothing. Athan glanced at her. She stood with her head slightly averted. Her expression was tight, closed.

She hates him.

"Later," Athan said. "It won't be long before we're missed. We must hurry." He held out a hand to Three.

She didn't take his hand, but she did walk past the guardian, not looking at him.

The man followed at their heels as they crossed the chamber. "Tell me," he insisted.

"When we're free of this place."

"But you have the code book?"

"Yes." Athan jerked open the door to the sewer. "After you."

The guardian hesitated. "But I want to hear—"

"Later," Athan told him flatly.

The guardian stood his ground for a mere second, then ducked his head and stepped through the doorway. *You're right to be afraid of me. I despise you more than you can ever know.* Athan's mouth tightened. He turned to Three. "My lady?"

He didn't offer her the support of his hand; he let her step down into the sewers unassisted. Then he followed, still holding the candle.

CHAPTER FIFTY-ONE

ATHAN HAD NEVER been this way, down to the township. The tunnel was wide and low, the gradient awkwardly steep. He walked with one hand braced against the wall. Each step took him closer to freedom. *First the Bight, and then the Bazarn Plateau.*

He shook his head. Crossing the plateau in winter was madness. It was no journey for a young woman from the nobles' court.

But she's no ordinary woman.

The guardian halted. Ahead, the sewer tunnel widened. There was a ledge on the left, and a steep and crumbling staircase. Athan craned his neck and looked up. Darkness.

The guardian hoisted himself up on the ledge. He reached down and caught hold of Three's wrist. "Hurry!"

She jerked back, breaking the man's grip. "Don't touch me."

The guardian uttered a hissing curse. He leaned down and grabbed Three's arm.

Athan's fury erupted. He had no recollection of pushing up onto the ledge; he was simply there. His hand was at the guardian's throat, forcing the man's head back.

The guardian uttered a choked sound. He released Three's arm.

Athan shook the man, his fingers digging deep. "Don't you dare touch her!" Fury roared in his head, hot, blood-red—and beneath that was sanity, cool. He released the man, pushing him away.

The guardian sprawled on the ledge, sobbing for breath.

Athan stood over the man. "You've done her too much harm already."

"But she's only a—"

Athan hissed, a sharp exhalation of air. He bared his teeth.

The guardian cringed back on the rough stone.

Athan crouched and ripped the hood from the man's head. He didn't see the guardian's face; he saw only his eyes, wide and frightened. "If you lay one finger on her again, I swear on my House I'll kill you."

The man believed him; Athan saw it in his eyes.

He stood abruptly. His breath came in pants, like the guardian's. He turned and stared down at Three.

She stood with her face averted. He saw only her profile. Her head was bowed, her eyes shut. She hugged her arms beneath the cape.

"Three," he said softly.

Her eyes squeezed more tightly shut, and then she turned her head and looked up at him. Her face was paler than it had been before, more closed.

Athan swallowed. He stepped back. "Come." It wasn't an order; it was an invitation, quiet. He didn't offer his hand; she wanted his touch as little as she wanted the guardian's.

He turned his head away.

He heard Three pull herself up on the ledge, heard the guardian stand, still gasping. *I shouldn't have let her see me do that.* He inhaled a slow, calm breath—

but he wasn't calm inside. Rage still vibrated in his chest. His fingers curled into his palms, clenching. "Let's go," he said, not looking at either of them. "We have to be at the Bight by daybreak."

CHAPTER FIFTY-TWO

IT WAS STILL night when they reached the Bight, but the sky was lightening and dawn not far off. The moon hung heavily over a black sea. Its rings were razor-sharp.

Athan reined his horse on the brow of the last hill. The ground was hard and white with frost. The animal's breath plumed in the frigid air.

Three halted beside him.

"You all right?" he asked. His voice was hoarse with fatigue.

She nodded. He couldn't see her face; the hood of her cloak was pulled forward.

Athan followed her gaze and looked down at the town. A haze of wood smoke hung over it. Within the crooked streets a few glimmers of light were visible. Beyond the buildings was the harbor.

Athan glanced behind him, half expecting to hear the sound of hooves galloping. He gathered the reins. "Ready?"

Three nodded again.

He urged his mount into a slow walk. They entered the Bight quietly.

The *Seafarer Inn* was still shuttered, but faint light seeped through the cracks. Athan slid stiffly from his horse. He ached, muscle and bone.

He turned to assist Three, but she'd already dismounted. She leaned against her horse for a moment.

Athan reached out a hand to her, and then checked the motion. "Are you all right?"

She straightened and nodded.

Athan rang the stable bell and went to stand at her side. He held his arm out to her, silently. *We must still pretend.*

Three laid her gloved hand on his arm. Her fingers shook faintly.

They stood silently, shivering, their breath gathering like white fog before their faces. After a long minute the stable door creaked open. An ostler appeared. He squinted at them and bowed. "Noble lord? Noble lady?"

"Take our post horses." Athan held out a coin. He was Lord Ivo still, and he let his mouth gape open. The air was painfully cold against his teeth. "See that they're well cared for." *They've been ridden hard, poor beasts.*

The ostler ducked his head again and took the coin. "Yes, noble lord." He gathered the reins. The horses moved slowly, as exhausted as their riders.

"Wait."

The ostler looked back. "Noble lord?"

"Which way to the harbor? Our ship sails this morning."

The man pointed. "That way, noble lord."

Three took her hand from his arm as soon as the ostler disappeared from view. She glanced up at the lightening sky.

"We must hurry," Athan said.

They headed for the docks, walking fast on rough cobblestones. The sky grayed. The sun was yet to rise, but he could see more clearly where to place his feet. Three kept the hood of her cloak well forward, hiding her hair. It would stand out, even in this half-light.

Athan held out his hand to halt her before they reached the waterfront.

They stood silently for a moment, listening. He scanned the empty street, the shuttered windows, and then nodded. "This way."

The lane they turned into was narrow and deep with shadows. It stank of sewage. Athan held the furred collar of his cloak to his nose, trying to breathe shallowly as he counted the buildings. They weren't houses; they were shacks, leaning into one another, with broken shutters and holes gaping in the roofs.

Their destination was little more than a hovel. Refuse piled in the gutter and rats scurried at their approach.

The door was warped and unpainted. Athan released the collar of his cloak and felt for his knife. He inhaled, smelling rotting garbage and raw sewage. "Ready?"

"Yes." Her whisper was as low as his, barely audible.

Athan gripped the knife. He tapped lightly on the door.

He counted the seconds in his head, *one, two, three*—

The door swung open.

His grip tightened on the knife hilt. He saw nothing but shadows inside. "The spider sends his greetings."

"Friends of the spider are always welcome here." The voice was low and gruff. "Come inside. Quickly."

They stepped inside. Athan closed the door and blinked in the darkness. His nose wrinkled at the smell. *Unclean.*

Their host was a dim shape. He vaguely saw a hand beckon. Together they followed the man down the hallway. Bare floorboards creaked beneath their feet. A door opened—and finally there was light.

The room was squalid. Candlelight revealed a scarred floor and walls streaked with filth. The furniture was ramshackle, battered and grubby. A fire burned in a broken grate, casting warmth.

"You must change. Quickly. There's little time."

The man spoke in Laurentine this time and his voice, although gruff, was well-educated. Athan turned to look at him. He was as unprepossessing as the room, with stringy dark hair and a grimy, furrowed face, but his eyes were bright and fiercely intelligent.

"Here." The man handed Three a bundle of clothing tied with coarse string. His fingers were blackened with dirt, the nails ragged and filthy. "You may use this room. You." He jerked his head at Athan. "Follow me."

Three pushed back the hood of her cloak. Her face was shockingly pale. The shadows beneath her eyes looked like bruises.

Athan sheathed his knife. He clenched his hands to stop from reaching for her. "My lady, are you all right?"

She glanced at him, a brief flicker of her eyes. "Perfectly."

Athan swallowed. He turned to the man. "She'll be safe here?"

"Of course. Now hurry."

Athan glanced at Three as he followed the man from the room. She didn't watch him leave. She stood with her back turned to them both.

CHAPTER FIFTY-THREE

SALIEL UNTIED THE string and opened the bundle of clothing on the table. It appeared that everything, including her undergarments and footwear, was to be replaced. Hesitantly she lifted an item to her nose. It smelled clean.

She stripped as quickly as she could. The long row of buttons down her back proved almost impossible to unfasten. Her fingers fumbled with fatigue and haste and she was nearly in tears by the time she removed the gown. She pressed her hands to her face and took a deep, slow breath—*don't cry*—and unlaced the tight corset and peeled off the last of her clothing: petticoats and linen shift, stockings.

The new garments were looser and less restricting than any she'd worn in the past two years, the fabric coarser. She pulled on leggings, long and warm, and then a full skirt, a blouse, a thick sleeveless vest of felt, and woolen stockings and boots. The only items left on the table were a heavy cloak and a scarf for her throat.

Saliel looked down at herself. Everything—cotton and wool and felt—was a drab grayish brown. Peasant clothes.

But her hair was still dressed in a noblewoman's intricate coronet of braids.

She pulled out the pins that anchored the braids in place and sat on a stool beside the fire and unplaited her hair as swiftly as she could. Her fingers and arms ached long before she was finished.

Her hair fell past her waist when it was done. Saliel hugged her arms. She closed her eyes for a moment. *I want this day to be over*. But a chilly dawn was breaking beyond the shutters and long hours stretched until nightfall.

She was plaiting her hair into a single braid when someone tapped on the door.

Saliel tensed and looked up from her task. "Yes?"

The agent stepped into the room. He held a pair of shears in his hand, and a headscarf. "Leave it," he said, when he saw what she was doing. "I'm sorry. I must cut your hair."

She was too tired to protest. Too tired to even care. She took the headscarf and held it in her lap as the man stepped behind her. She felt his hand at the nape of her neck. Cold metal touched her skin. The blades came together with a *snick*.

The agent stepped back. Her hair hung in his hand, part-braided, almost touching the floor.

Saliel watched as he laid the shears on the table and roughly coiled her hair. She raised a hand to her neck. One twist of braid remained, unraveling as she touched it. Her head felt wonderfully light. *Lady Petra is gone*.

"You must keep your hair covered until you reach Marillaq," the agent said. "No one must see it. Do you understand?"

Saliel lowered her hand. The Bazarn Plateau was under Corhonase administration. It was as dangerous as the Bight, as the citadel. "Yes."

Someone knocked on the door. "Enter," the agent said.

Saliel looked away. She picked up the headscarf and turned it over in her fingers.

Floorboards creaked as someone entered the room. The person halted. "Your hair."

Saliel looked up. Peasant's clothing, coarse and bulky, a face dark with stubble. He was Lord Ivo—familiar—but he was also a stranger.

"It was necessary," the agent said. He laid the coil of hair on top of her discarded lavender-blue gown.

"She'll still need to keep it hidden," One protested. "Did it have to be cut?"

"Others will take your places on the *Silver Fern*." The agent gestured at the items on the table. His meaning was obvious: someone else would wear her clothes and hair.

One looked at her a moment longer, then turned to the man. "Do you need mine?"

"No. Black hair was easy to find." The agent gathered her clothing together and took the bundle One held. "Wait here. I'll only be a moment." He left the room with hurried steps.

Saliel turned her head away. She tucked the chin-length strands of hair behind her ears and began to put on the headscarf.

For a moment there was silence. She heard the coals burning in the fire. Then One spoke. "I meant what I said." His voice was low and intense. "I offer you my name and my House and—"

"No."

"Let me make it right." She heard him take step toward her. "Please."

Saliel turned her head to look at him.

One stood tensely. She saw emotion shining in his eyes: shame, remorse. "If I'd known it was you I would *never*—" He swallowed. "Please, let me make it right."

She should feel sympathy for him; he was One. But all she saw when she looked at him was Lord Ivo. *I look at you, and I want to be ill.* "No."

His brow twisted. "But I owe you—"

"You owe me nothing."

"I do! I—"

"I'm a poorhouse foundling," Saliel said flatly. "From the Ninth Ward. You owe me nothing."

His nostrils flared, as if he smelled the stink of the slums. The muscles in his face tightened. He swallowed again. "No," he said. "You're lying."

"I'm from the Ninth Ward." She said it in the dialect of the slums this time, coarse. "Laurent's Cesspit."

His nostrils flared again. He took a step backward.

Saliel looked away. Her fingers trembled as she tied the headscarf in place. One would keep his distance. *At least I've gained that. My presence now disgusts him.* A laugh choked in her throat, bitter and unuttered. He'd offered her his House, but the servants would never let her through the door. They'd cast her into the street and spit on her.

The agent came back into the room. He no longer carried the bundles of clothing. "Are you ready?"

One's face smoothed free of expression, becoming blank. "Where do we go?"

"Across the marshes."

"How?"

"I'm taking a coal barge across," the agent said, and the grime etched into his skin suddenly made sense.

"We need to eat," said One. "And sleep."

"You can do both on board."

One nodded.

"You're peasants. Your names are Petter and Franta." The agent paused to let them absorb the information.

Franta. Another name. Another role to play.

"You're signed up on a migrant caravan across the Bazarn Plateau. It leaves tomorrow morning. You're on your own until you reach home."

Home. The distance was vast. How many months would it take? *With him.* Saliel looked down at the filthy floor. *I don't think I can—*

"I've arranged supplies and donkeys for you." She looked up to see the agent hand a pouch to One. "Corhonase money. Not much. You're very poor, seeking a better life."

One took the pouch.

"The border with Marillaq is closed," the agent said. "But there are smugglers who'll take people across—for a high price." He held out a second pouch, much larger than the first. "Marillaqan money. I suggest you pose as someone more prosperous once across the border. A merchant perhaps. There must be no connection with the migrant caravan. I understand you both speak Marillaqan?"

Saliel nodded. One nodded too, and hefted the second pouch in his hand. "Our passage home?" he asked.

"From that. And payment for the smugglers. It's mostly gold. There should be enough."

One stowed the pouches beneath his vest.

"Are you ready?"

No. She reached for the scarf and cloak. Franta's scarf and cloak. *I am Franta now.*

CHAPTER FIFTY-FOUR

ONE DIDN'T SHUN her. Nor did he ask her to marry him again. She caught him watching her, a baffled expression on his face, as they disembarked from the coal barge, and again as they parted with the agent in the bare dirt paddock of the caravansary. Noise swamped them: shouts, children's wails, the sound of dogs barking and mules braying, the clatter of ironware being hefted onto wagons.

One said nothing. He just looked at her, a tiny crease between his eyebrows.

Saliel turned away, hugging the cloak more tightly to her. *Don't look at me. Don't speak to me.*

But there were no opportunities for private speech in the frantic bustle of the departing caravan, and no time to think about what lay ahead. The afternoon was a confused blur of cooking pots and food and blankets, of tents and donkeys. Her ears strained to understand the words being spoken around her. The Corhonase was rough, almost unintelligible. She spoke in careful monosyllables, afraid her tongue would betray her. *I'm Franta. I'm a peasant.* The precise vowels of the court, the clipped consonants, sat in the back of her throat, wanting to be uttered.

On the first evening One offered to share his food, silently, as they sat around a fire with other peasants.

He held his bowl out to her. His portion was twice the size of hers.

She looked at the stew, the thick slices of bread, but all she saw was his hand. He had touched her with those fingers. He'd pushed her legs open—

I'm going to be ill.

She stood abruptly.

The nausea subsided as she hurried between the groups of peasants eating. She halted by the line of mules and donkeys and looked back across the caravansary. The paddock was alight with campfires. Sparks swirled upward. Tents and wagons were dark shapes.

The moon rose slowly in the sky. The air was fragrant with wood smoke and stew. *I should go back to our fire.* But she couldn't make her feet move. She stood, listening to the murmur of voices and the *nicker* of mules.

Rely on no one but yourself. She'd learned that in the slums. But the slums had taught her other lessons too: *do what you must to survive.* She had to do this— be with him—to survive, to get home.

The mule beside her shifted its weight. It touched its nose to her shoulder.

Saliel laid her hand on the animal's neck. She felt its warmth, the roughness of its coat, its aliveness.

The moon rose higher. To the east lay the Bazarn Plateau, high and cold. It would take two months to cross that stretch of land.

In spring I'll be home.

She closed her eyes. A home of her own, with cats sunning themselves on the step. A garden with vegetables. A cow to milk. She saw it behind her eyelids: the cottage and the cats, the smoke rising from the chimney, tall hollyhocks and beans climbing a stone wall, a cow grazing.

Saliel opened her eyes. She lowered her hand and pulled her cloak more tightly around her and walked back through the campfires. She didn't look at One as she sat down beside him.

IT BECAME EASIER to understand the conversations around her as the caravan climbed toward the plateau. Two days became three and then four, and the vowels that came to her tongue were broad, the consonants deeply guttural. She no longer needed to think about each word before she spoke.

The stubble on One's cheeks and chin, his throat, grew into a beard. He was unrecognizable as Lord Ivo. It was more than the clothes and the beard, the peasant's voice; it was his manner. There was nothing vague or lethargic about him.

He still tried to share his food with her. She saw his guilt, his shame, each time he held the bowl out to her. "Don't," she said shortly, on the fourth evening. *Your shame makes me remember.* "I don't want your food."

One's face tightened. His gaze fell. He pulled back the bowl.

And now it's I who feel shame.

She stared down at her own bowl. The sounds of the caravan surrounded her. Male voices rose in a shout of laughter, logs shifted on the fire, a goat bleated. She pushed the stew around with her spoon, remembering One's words. *I didn't know it was you. Let me make it right. Please.*

He'd been the guardian's pawn. They'd both been.

One hadn't come to bed her, that second time. He'd come to tell her who he was. *Please sit*, he'd said. *I must speak with you.* And she'd caught his gaze and set his clothes on fire.

Saliel laid down the spoon. She closed her eyes. *I owe him an apology.*

It was an impossible apology to make.

She opened her eyes. She saw firelight and a dark, night sky. Flames hissed as they devoured branches of wood. Embers glowed red-hot.

Saliel shivered. She picked up the spoon. *Forget what happened in the citadel.* She scooped up a spoonful of stringy meat. *He's not Lord Ivo. Think of him as Petter.*

CHAPTER FIFTY-FIVE

THE PLATEAU STRETCHED—wide, white—to a range of mountains. The snow didn't soften them; they stood strong and sharp. He could see their bones: thrusting ridges, deeply scoured gullies.

His donkey stumbled. Athan steadied the animal. He looked behind him. The caravan straggled—slow, lurching wagons and weary pack-animals. The track they left was wide and dirty, snow churned with mud.

Athan clicked his tongue, urging the donkey forward. He'd expected the snow and ice, the cold, knifing wind that came off the mountains; he hadn't expected the mud. *Cursed stuff.* It bogged down the wagons and exhausted everyone—donkeys and mules, peasants.

On overcast days the mud stayed frozen and the plateau was bleak and traveling swifter. On days like today—

Athan raised his head. Sunshine. Snow. Mud.

The plateau, the mountains, were beautiful in their own way. It was an austere beauty: strong, stark.

He cast a quick, sideways glance at Franta. She walked alongside him, leading her donkey. She'd pushed back the hood of her cloak. Not one strand of red-gold hair escaped from beneath her headscarf. Her face was thinner than it had been a month ago, when they'd started this journey.

He looked away before she could catch him watching her.

A BLIZZARD BLEW up in the evening. Pitching the goat-hair tent was difficult; anchoring it before the wind tore it from the ground was a battle. They shared the tent with another couple, peasants as poor as themselves. Tonight they'd share it with the donkeys too—or find them dead in the morning.

Athan laid a boulder on an edge of flapping fabric. Beside him Franta leaned into the gusting wind. She was wrapped tightly against the cold. All he could see were her eyes.

"Another?" The wind tore the words from his lips.

She shivered, hugging her arms, and nodded.

Athan's eyes watered as he turned into the wind. The moisture trickled down his cheeks and froze. He lowered his head and bulled his way forward. Hard pellets of snow whipped past him.

His bones ached with cold. Hunger cramped in his belly. *I wish I was back at the citadel.*

The words sat in his mind as he bent to pick up a large boulder, as Franta crouched to help him.

Back at the citadel for a night. All the food he could eat. A hot bath. A warm, soft bed. An evening in an overheated salon, surrounded by drunken noblemen and whores—

No. I wouldn't go.

The answer surprised him into stillness. *Wouldn't I swap this for that? For one night?* Warmth and alcohol, sex.

The answer was still *no.*

Franta levered her fingers under the boulder, grasping it. Athan grunted as they stood. The sound was part-laugh. *I'm insane. The cold has driven me insane.*

He tried to take as much of the boulder's weight as he could, but their progress was slow and staggering. The wind howled, snapping his cloak around his legs. Snow came more heavily, thick and horizontal.

They placed the boulder on the last flapping edge of frayed fabric. "That should do it," he shouted. The roar of the wind swallowed his words.

The tents and wagons were huddled together tonight, as if warmth could be gained from proximity. A single campfire burned. The flames were thin and wind-whipped, struggling to survive. Inside their tent, order reigned. Osker had tended to the donkeys; the animals lay across the opening, fed and watered. His wife Lenka was spreading out bedrolls and blankets.

Athan ducked his head and stepped over the donkeys. Osker, a morose man, looked up and grunted. Lenka spread the last blanket. She reached for the stew pot.

Athan shrugged off his cloak. It was crusted with snow. His fingers moved stiffly as he pulled off gloves and scarf and boots. The scent of food made his mouth water. Hunger growled in his stomach.

The stew was lukewarm—lumps of meat, floury root vegetables. They dined in silence. Athan ate slowly, trying to make the meal last. He wiped his bowl with the last of yesterday's bread, dry and stale, and chewed stolidly. He was still hungry when he'd finished.

Lenka took the rough wooden bowls and placed them in the pot to be washed. Darkness fell rapidly. Osker lit the lantern. It illuminated the tent and made it almost cozy. A fine trick; they and their belongings were worn and drab-colored. The only brightness in this place was hidden.

Athan glanced at Franta. The headscarf covered her hair.

He looked away and rubbed his face. The beard rasped beneath his hand. He squeezed his eyes shut for a moment, remembering how her hair looked. Rich and warm, gleaming, as bright as copper.

Osker rummaged in a saddlebag. He was a thin man who expected defeat at every turn. Lenka had once been more cheerful; there were laughter lines about her eyes. Now she was as haggard and careworn as her husband. Their children had died, that much Athan knew. This journey was an escape—from memories, from poverty.

Osker turned back to the light, a flask in his hand. This was the routine they'd established during the past month: dinner, followed by a mouthful of raw, fiery liquor. And then bed. Sleep was always quick to come after the exhaustions of the day.

Athan watched as Franta raised the flask to her lips. She swallowed and grimaced and wiped her mouth with the back of her hand. *A foundling from the Ninth Ward*, she'd said. At this moment he could believe it. She looked like a peasant, sitting cross-legged on her bedroll.

But so do I. He hadn't shaved in a month, or bathed or changed his clothes.

Franta held the flask out to him.

Athan took it. He shuddered as he swallowed. The liquor burned its way down his throat. *Vile*.

He handed the flask to Osker and glanced around the tent. Everything was worn, dirty: the taut goat hair fabric thrumming in the wind, the thin bedrolls and darned woolen blankets, the stained clothes he wore. His fingernails were ragged and filthy. He knew he stank of old sweat.

It was better to be in this tent—full of shadows and lantern light, surrounded by darkness and wind and snow—than the citadel. Better to fall asleep on a lumpy bedroll with hunger in his belly and the taste of liquor burning on his tongue, listening to the wind roar overhead.

Better. Safer.

Each night in this tent brought them closer to home.

THE BLIZZARD HAD died by dawn and so had two of the migrants. Stones were piled high to cover their bodies; the ground was too hard to bury them.

Snow stretched as far as the eye could see—white plateau, white mountains—and the sky was intensely blue. Athan felt as if he'd climbed to the top of the world, a place so far from the citadel that the court and its inhabitants ceased to exist. Lord Ivo was gone. Lady Petra, gone.

He hefted the heavy, unwieldy bundle of the tent on his shoulder and walked to where Osker was loading the donkeys. The animals stood patiently, their eyes half-closed.

The donkey that carried their food had a light load. There was meat enough for one more pot of stew, flour for three more loaves of bread. After that, they'd go hungry.

Neycha and the shelter of the caravansary, the market where they could buy supplies, was two days' journey away. Athan turned and looked east. He saw nothing but white, stretching to the distance.

He glanced back at the pile of stones, the graves. The plateau—for all its startling beauty—was a dangerous place. *We could all die here.*

CHAPTER FIFTY-SIX

NEYCHA, WHEN THEY arrived in the raw wind of dusk, was an unappealing and dismal settlement. The town fought a losing battle with mud. Buildings wallowed in muck, seemingly resigned to a slow and choking death. Athan could almost taste the town's defeat in the cold air.

He inhaled, smelling wood smoke and something acrid, something unpleasant. He glanced at Franta. "Is that—?"

Her face told him she'd recognized the smell too. She stopped walking. The donkey she led halted.

"Are you all right?"

He saw her swallow. She groped for her scarf and pulled it up over her nose. Her eyes squeezed shut.

Athan reached for her. "Are you all right?" he asked again.

Franta didn't flinch from him; she didn't even seem to notice his hand on her arm.

"Franta…" He tightened his grip.

Her eyes opened. She looked at him above the twist of scarf. "That smell. It's—" She swallowed. "I hate it."

Others had smelled it too: wood smoke, the scent of burned hair and flesh. There was a stir in the caravan. *Witch-burning.*

Athan kept his hand on Franta's arm as the caravan skirted the town. The smell became stronger. "Don't look," he said as a bare field came into sight, a fire still smoldering at its centre. The snow was churned with footprints. Sluggish black smoke rose into the sky. The stink of burned meat almost made him gag.

The caravan straggled as it passed the field. Some migrants hurried past, others slowed. Athan heard hushed whispers of fear, of disappointment that a spectacle had been missed. Franta said nothing. She didn't turn her head to see the skeleton of the bonfire: charred logs, charred bones. She walked with her gaze lowered and the scarf held to her nose.

The caravansary lay on the far side of Neycha. The fenced yard was a quagmire, thick with the churned-up filth of previous caravans.

"Where shall we pitch the tent?"

Franta didn't answer. She seemed not to have heard the question. The bustle of the caravan surrounded them—donkeys and mules, wagons, men and women and children, a bleating goat.

"Franta," he said more loudly. "Where would you like to pitch the tent?"

Her head lifted. He watched as her eyes focused. She glanced around.

"Are you all right?" he asked beneath the noise of the caravan.

Franta looked at him. "I don't like this town."

"Neither do I."

Falling darkness hid the squalor, but in the morning the ice-encrusted grime and piles of refuse offended Athan's eyes again. It was the slovenly, careless filth of people who no longer cared. The sense of despair was almost tangible. The buildings of the caravansary— inn and stable—sagged, defeated by their surroundings.

His mood was sour as he counted out copper coins. *I pay to sleep in a dungheap.* He trudged across the yard and pushed open the door to the inn.

The taproom was dark after the sunlight. Athan paused, blinking as his eyes adjusted to the dimness. He saw a smoke-stained ceiling and walls, a fire in a grimy hearth, scarred benches and tables.

Straw was strewn on the floor. An unpleasant smell rose from it as he crossed the room. The tables hadn't been wiped in a long time. They were littered with crumbs. Food lay where it had been spilled.

The innkeeper was as repugnant as the taproom, as the yard outside. He didn't appear to have washed in months. He smelled of liquor and stale sweat.

"For the two nights," Athan said. The coins clinked thinly as he laid them on the grubby counter.

The man took the coins without bothering to speak. His fingernails were black with dirt.

Athan turned away.

"You want food? Liquor?"

Athan looked back at the innkeeper. *I want nothing your hands have touched.* "No."

The man shrugged. "A bath?"

Athan turned around fully. "You have baths?"

The innkeeper nodded, and spat on the floor.

"Hot water? Soap?"

The man nodded again.

Then why don't you bathe? Why don't you wash the filth off yourself? "How much?" he asked.

ATHAN HUNKERED DOWN by the tent and opened the pouch of money. He tipped the coins into his hand. They barely filled his palm.

"They sell baths here." He touched a coin with one finger and looked up at Franta. "Would you like one?"

She shook her head.

"Are you certain?" He held the coin out to her.

Franta put her hands behind her back. "Spend it on food."

"One coin won't make much difference."

She shook her head again. "You're too thin."

He looked up at her. "So are you."

She shrugged.

Athan returned the coins to the pouch. "As you wish."

CHAPTER FIFTY-SEVEN

THE MARKETPLACE WAS as dirty as the caravansary. Mud and refuse squelched beneath his boots.

The stalls were ramshackle, their goods sparse. Athan glanced around. There was no bustle, no cheerfulness. Men lounged, sour-faced, talking and spitting. *A mean little town.*

He tied up his donkey beside the drinking trough. A scum of ice lay on the water. Osker fastened his donkey alongside. His expression was dour.

Athan scanned the marketplace. He saw meat, vegetables, leather, bread—

And Corhonase soldiers, two of them.

They looked nothing like the guards in the citadel—clean, alert. Their faces were stubbled, their metal buckles and leather boots unpolished.

Athan turned away from them.

Haunches of meat and strings of onions hung from the nearest stall. The meat was gray, the onions withered. He slouched as the soldiers strolled past. *Just another starving peasant, boys. Nothing of interest.*

"How much?"

The price the stallholder asked was absurd. When Athan told him so, the man sneered and spat on the ground.

There was nothing good-natured about the bartering, not at that stall or the next. Osker became more dour. They strapped a sack of potatoes on a donkey's back, onions and meat on the other. Athan turned and surveyed the market, aware of the soldiers. What else did they need to buy?

Flour.

The sky was gray. Snowflakes began to drift down.

They found a stall selling flour. It was coarse, gritty. "How much for a sack?"

Athan haggled, while the soldiers strolled around the marketplace. He held onto his temper as he handed over coins—too many coins. Osker hefted the sack on his shoulder. His expression was as sour as the stallholder's.

Jeers rose to Athan's left, a shout.

He turned his head. What he saw—the handful of men, the stones—made him push away from the stall.

Let it go. Beware of the soldiers. But his feet were already striding. He pushed through the group of men. "Stop."

One of the men shoved him aside. "Out of the way, peasant."

Athan turned to him. He bared his teeth in a smile.

"Didn't you hear me, peasant? Get out of my—"

He hit with his full weight behind him. All the frustrations of the past few hours were in the blow.

The man went down like a felled tree.

Athan swung round to face the other men. *Three against one. Not good odds.* "Who's next?"

The second man took two blows to the head before he fell. Athan shook his fist out. *Two to one.* But it was more than that—four, five, six men, attracted by the prospect of a brawl.

Walk away from this. Now.

It was too late. Men ringed him.

Athan blew out a breath. He flexed his hands and clenched them again. *Go for the biggest man. Bring him down first—*

"What's happening?" The two soldiers pushed through the cluster of men.

Athan unclenched his fists. "Nothing."

The townsfolk who surrounded him stepped back and turned away. The first man he'd hit scrambled unsteadily to his feet and followed them, lurching.

"Explain yourself," one of the soldiers demanded. His hand rested on the hilt of his sword.

Athan opened his hands in a shrug. He tried to look mild and unthreatening, confused. "I was just buying flour."

The guardsman surveyed him. His face was unshaven, his uniform wrinkled, his gaze narrow and suspicious.

"That's right." It was Osker, the sack on his shoulder. "Flour."

The soldier glanced at Osker and at the fallen man, before looking back at Athan. He didn't release his grip on the sword.

Athan stood with his hands open and relaxed. Snowflakes floated down.

The soldier cleared his throat and spat. "Make any more trouble in this marketplace, peasant, and you'll spend the night in gaol."

"No more trouble," Athan said. He dipped his head humbly.

The soldier grunted. He turned away. The second guardsman eyed Athan a moment longer, then followed his companion.

Athan watched them walk away. The man at his feet groaned and pushed up onto an elbow. Blood streamed from his nose.

"What was that about?" Osker asked.

"This." Athan turned and crouched.

The kitten had hidden itself behind a broken plank of wood. It cowered away from Athan's hand. He grasped it by the nape of the neck and stood.

* * *

FRANTA AND LENKA were mending rips in the tent. They talked as they sewed. Athan couldn't tell their voices apart; their accents were identical. *How does she do it?*

He carried the kitten gently. It was thin and wet, shivering.

The women looked up. They stopped talking.

"Do you like kittens?" Athan held the tiny creature out to Franta. Its coat was gray striped with black.

She put down her needle. "Where did you find it?"

"At the market."

"You bought it?" She reached for the kitten.

"Ah... no."

Franta wrapped the kitten in a fold of her cloak. "What then?"

"They were stoning it."

Her face tightened. Her hand cupped protectively around the kitten. "Who? Children?"

"Some of the stallholders. Men." The cruelty fitted with the town; the squalor, the ugliness. *A miserable place, this.*

"You rescued it?" It was the first time she'd smiled at him.

"Knocked down two men." Osker's voice held grudging admiration. "He's a good fighter, your husband."

Franta's smile faded. "I know."

CHAPTER FIFTY-EIGHT

THEY CALLED THE kitten Solo. It seemed an appropriate name. The little creature cleaned up well and seemed quite content to spend his days curled up on top of a donkey's load. Whenever they paused to rest or eat lunch, Solo played among the tussocks and the boulders. In the evenings he chased shadows inside the tent, provoking even Osker to laughter.

Athan narrowed his eyes against the midday sun and chewed his bread slowly. Franta sat beside him on a boulder. He watched as she plaited strands of tussock together and trailed them before the kitten.

Solo crouched low and pounced. He captured the tussock and began to do battle with it, rolling and springing upright and then falling over backward on his prey.

Franta laughed. "Solo, you have no dignity." She picked up the kitten and hugged him. Her face, when she turned to Athan, was alight with laughter.

Athan smiled back at her. There was an odd tightness in his chest: relief. *She's forgiven me for being Lord Ivo.*

Franta let Solo down again. He scampered off to pounce on the hem of Lenka's cloak.

Franta leaned close. "I think we should give them Solo," she said in a low voice. "We can't take him with us."

"No." He'd realized that. There could be no connection between the peasants on the plateau and the well-to-do citizens in Marillaq, not even a small striped kitten.

"They like Solo. Osker especially. They'll treat him well."

"Yes." Athan turned the piece of bread over in his fingers. "I'll get you another one when we're home."

Franta drew slightly back. She shook her head. "I'll get myself one."

She still sat beside him on the boulder, but there was a distance between them that hadn't been there a minute ago. *I shouldn't have mentioned home.*

Athan took another bite of bread. The contentment he'd felt sitting in the sun, watching her laugh, was gone.

Franta stood. She brushed breadcrumbs off her cloak and walked over to the donkeys. Athan watched as she unfastened her pattens and bent to strap them on over her boots.

He finished the piece of bread. He was still hungry, but hunger was a constancy; like the air he breathed, it was always there. He'd learned to ignore the dull, gnawing ache—or at least to pretend to himself that he ignored it. He stood and stretched and walked to where Lenka and Osker sat. "May I have that?" He gestured to the heel of the loaf, which lay amid crumbs on a ragged cloth.

Lenka handed it to him.

"Thanks."

The bread was heavy and dry, baked that morning in the ashes of the communal fire. Athan chewed, standing, and looked around. A few more weeks and they'd reach the end of this journey, where the mountains crowded close and the Dacha Gorge marked the border with Marillaq. On the flanks of the mountains were the lumber towns—and work. Labor in the forests for the men, or the sawmills and charcoal pits; for the women, cleaning and cooking in the taverns. Or for the unfortunate, whoring.

Athan swallowed the last of the bread. He rubbed a hand over his face, disliking the feel of his beard, and cast a final glance at the mountains. He walked to where his donkey stood. Thick mud squelched beneath his boots.

He donned his pattens and rechecked the loads. Osker joined him, running his hands over the donkeys' legs and examining their hooves.

Athan looked around. He saw mules and donkeys and wagons, and figures bundled in drab brown-gray against the cold. Franta was talking with one of the women. Even with her back to him and her hair hidden, he recognized her.

She's not from the Ninth Ward. He saw it in the way she stood, the way she walked. She'd had lessons in deportment, as his sisters had.

Gentry, at the very least.

I can bring her home.

If she would let him.

CHAPTER FIFTY-NINE

LUKIN, THE FIRST of the lumber towns, was a raw, new settlement possessed of a vigorous energy. The migrants felt it. Saliel was aware of an undercurrent of excitement in the camp. Osker walked into the town as soon as the donkeys were unloaded. He came back at a run. "Lenka!"

Lenka looked up from their food stores.

"Work," Osker said, breathless. "In Kazacha. For any man that wants it!" His face was alight with excitement. He put his arms around his wife and hugged her.

Lenka hugged him back. She laughed.

The emotion on their faces brought sudden tears to Saliel's eyes. *They love each other.*

She turned away and walked across the stony paddock, shading her face from the late afternoon sun. Steep slopes rose high, twins to those standing at her back. Marillaq.

She said the word aloud, letting each syllable rest on her tongue: "Marillaq." Another country, another step closer to home.

She couldn't see the gorge. It lay somewhere between these mountains and those. The cliffs were said to be sheer. Thousands of men had fallen to their deaths during Corhona's failed invasion of Marillaq.

Their bones littered the floor of the gorge. It was said the cliff walls still echoed with their screams.

Saliel shivered and hugged her arms. *Campfire tales, to scare women and children.* The soldiers were ten years dead. There were no screams.

A shadow fell across her. She turned her head. Petter stood beside her. He looked at Marillaq for a long moment, and then dropped his gaze to her face.

"Well?" she asked, her voice low.

"The caravan's going to Kazacha."

She nodded. "We stay here?"

"Yes. There'll be smugglers operating from here."

Saliel looked at the mountains. She saw snow and stony scarps, dark trees. In a few days they'd be in Marillaq. She'd miss the camaraderie of the caravan, the doggedness with which hardship had been endured. Life had been uncomplicated during the past two months, simple and pared down to the basics. In Marillaq everything would become complex again. *He won't be Petter any more. And I won't be Franta.*

She hugged her arms more tightly.

"I'll choose a site for the tent."

Saliel nodded. She stayed where she was, staring at the mountains, listening to the crunch of Petter's footsteps as he walked away. The camp behind her, the tents and wagons, Petter—they were safe things, familiar. Marillaq was unfamiliar; and so was the person Petter would be once they were across the gorge.

She turned and looked at the campsite. Solo was curled up asleep on the bundle of their tent. Petter stood looking down at the kitten. His cheeks were hollow beneath the beard, his skin stretched too tightly over the bones. Shadows fell across his face, accentuating his gauntness.

He wasn't Lord Ivo—but nor was he Petter. He was a stranger.

She watched as he picked the kitten up and put him carefully on the ground. Solo shook himself. He yawned—pink tongue, sharp teeth—and stretched.

Saliel inhaled a deep breath. She released her arms and began walking back toward the campsite.

CHAPTER SIXTY

HE HUNG ON the end of a rope in darkness, spinning. The net bound him tightly. Cords dug into his back, his arms. The rope jerked him higher.

They won't drop me they won't drop me they won't drop me—

But he didn't believe it. A scream built in his throat. He couldn't breathe, couldn't drag air into his lungs. The ground was too far beneath him—

He jerked awake.

Darkness. Spinning. A scream filling his mouth—

He wasn't bound in netting. He didn't hang on the end of a rope.

Athan sat up, pushing aside the blanket. He gulped air. Sweat dripped off his skin.

It was dark. The smells of hay and cow and manure filled his nose. He was out of the Dacha Gorge. He was in Marillaq, in a cow byre.

Calmness returned. The bunched tension in his muscles relaxed. He closed his eyes and wiped the sweat from his face.

He heard the cows breathing below him. If he listened carefully he'd hear Franta's breathing—quiet inhalations and exhalations—and the breathing of the other refugees who hid in this barn.

Athan lay down again. It was over: the citadel, the Bazarn Plateau, the Dacha Gorge. He was in Marillaq.

Laurent seemed so much closer—his brothers and sisters, his parents. The estate, with the vineyard growing on the hills.

Soon I'll be home.

He turned on his side and pulled the blanket around him, making the hay rustle. He stared into the darkness. Franta lay there. He couldn't see her.

He wanted to reach out and shake her awake. *Who are you? Please, I need to know.* But they weren't alone, hadn't been alone in the three days and nights they'd been here: three days when they'd talked together in careful Marillaqan and he'd not dared ask the questions that crowded on his tongue; three nights when they'd slept side by side on the straw.

After the second day Franta had spoken like their hosts, with the accent of the mountain people. *How does she do it?* He had to concentrate to speak the right words. The languages blurred together in his mind: Corhonase, Marillaqan, Laurentine.

Athan lay in the dark and stared at where she lay, listening to the cows breathing. *I want—*

The things that he wanted were simple. To go home. To be himself again. To know her name.

THE FARMER BROUGHT breakfast—bread and warm boiled eggs and cheese. "You," he said, pointing at Franta. "And you. Come with me."

Athan paused, reaching for an egg. "We're leaving?"

The man nodded.

Athan climbed down from the hay loft, his cloak bundled beneath his arm and a crude sandwich in his hand. At the bottom he waited for Franta, chewing. "Our clothes have come?" he asked as they stepped outside.

The farmer nodded again.

They followed him across a cobbled yard and into the farmhouse kitchen. The walls were whitewashed, the ceiling low and heavy-beamed. A large pot boiled on the wood stove, hissing.

The farmer walked to the table. It was a solid slab of timber, scrubbed clean. Two bundles lay on it: fur-lined cloaks tied with twine, and inside them—

Soft wool. Finely-woven linen.

"May we bathe?" Franta asked.

"Water's for a bath." The farmer jerked his head at the boiling pot. "One of you will have to wait."

HE SHAVED WHILE Franta bathed. There was a razor and a leather strop in the bundle of clothes, a nightshirt, undergarments, vests and breeches and knitted stockings, riding boots—everything a well-to-do citizen required. The fabric was costly, but the clothes bore no resemblance to those he'd worn in the citadel. The colors were stronger, warmer. There was no satin or lace.

Athan set aside the bowl of shaving water. The farmer's wife kneaded bread at one end of the table with her sleeves rolled up. He eyed her. *People like you are the reason Marillaq nearly fell.*

It had only been ten years. Did she not remember the battle of Dacha Gorge?

He wanted to take her by the arm and shake her. *I could be a Corhonase agent, yet you smuggle me past your border guards. Do you not care? Do you value money more than your country?*

Athan turned away. The door to the yard stood open. He walked across to it. His uncle's voice was in his ear, *don't throw up on me, boy.* He blinked the memory away—bodies lying like broken dolls—and focused on the farmyard.

A hen pecked among the cobblestones. An empty bowl sat to one side of the stone doorstep. A troll bowl.

The bowl brought back even stronger memories of his uncle: his enthusiasm and his endless questions, the scratch of a quill on parchment late into the night—

"You may bathe."

He turned his head. Franta stood in the kitchen, wary, too thin, watching him. Her hair was uncovered. It gleamed, red-gold.

Athan swallowed. "You look…" *Beautiful.* The word dried in his mouth.

The Marillaqan clothes suited her—the forest-green undergown with flecks of brown and gold woven through the wool, the sleeveless overgown embroidered in wine-dark red and saffron yellow.

Athan swallowed again. He stepped away from the doorway and bowed. "You look lovely, my lady."

Faint color rose in Franta's cheeks. She didn't meet his eyes. "Thank you."

He bathed quickly, scrubbing the grime from his skin, washing his hair. He was dressing when he heard hooves on the cobblestones outside.

Athan crossed the bed chamber and ducked his head to look out of the window. He saw three horses and one rider.

It was time to go.

CHAPTER SIXTY-ONE

THEY RODE FOR hours through silent forests, he and Franta and their guide. The snow muffled the sound of the horses' hooves. Fir trees stood tall and dark. Morning became afternoon. They ate while riding and passed a waterskin between them. The guide set a steady pace. He didn't speak.

The shadows lengthened on the ground. It began to snow lightly. Snowflakes drifted down through dark branches.

It was familiar—the fir trees, the snow. He was fifteen years old again. If he turned his head he'd see his uncle. *Trolls don't exist, sir.*

How do you know, boy, until it's been proved?

Dusk was gathering when at last they came to a road. The snow was muddy, churned with hoof prints and the tracks of wagon wheels. "Therac," their guide said, jerking his head downhill. It was the first word he'd spoken all day.

"How far?" Athan asked.

"Half a mile."

Athan nodded.

"Leave the horses at the inn. Someone will collect them."

Athan watched as horse and rider vanished back into the forest. He turned to Franta. "My lady?"

They rode without speaking. Questions gathered on Athan's tongue. He held them back with his teeth. *Don't push her*. The road curved and the forest drew back against the mountainside. He saw snowy fields, smelled wood smoke. Lamplight gleamed ahead.

"What names shall we use?"

Athan looked at her. "Why don't we use our real names?"

"Our real names?"

"Marillaqan names are similar to Laurentine. There should be no danger."

Franta rode in silence for almost a minute. The horses' hooves made soft, wet sounds in the mud and snow. The lights of the town grew nearer, brighter. Finally she said, "Very well."

Athan cleared his throat. *Don't push her*. "What's your name, my lady?"

Franta glanced at him. "Saliel." She didn't name a House. "What's yours?"

"Athan."

Her expression told him not to ask more questions.

HE HUNG ON the end of a rope. *Spinning. Darkness. A scream in his throat—*

Athan jerked awake. He sat up and gasped for breath. His heartbeat hammered in his ears.

He wasn't spinning. It wasn't dark. He didn't lie on straw. Embers glowed in a fireplace. There were sheets and a soft mattress.

Where? Where am I?

He touched his chest, feeling a single layer of linen: a nightshirt. He wasn't wearing his peasant clothes. He wasn't in a cow byre, or a tent—

The inn. I'm in a room at the inn.

Athan released his breath slowly. He lay down. There was a pillow beneath his head.

312 The Laurentine Spy

A pillow.

Laughter choked in his throat, where a moment ago there'd been a scream.

He closed his eyes. The room was silent. No one else breathed but him. For the first time in over two months he slept alone. Franta was in a bed chamber across the hall—

No, not Franta.

He had her name now: Saliel.

ATHAN WOKE AGAIN after dawn. He rang for hot water and busied himself with his morning ablutions—shaving, washing.

It was interesting the difference that so simple and familiar an act as shaving made. It made him feel clean, but more than that, it made him recognize himself. The ritual of it—the movements and the sensation, the sound, the sharpness of the blade, the face he saw in the mirror—all anchored him to Athan. Lord Ivo had been shaved by a valet and Petter had never shaved. But Athan shaved himself; it was part of who he was.

I am myself again.

CHAPTER SIXTY-TWO

"I WOULD PREFER to ride," Saliel said in a low voice, breaking open a roll with her fingers. The bread was still warm from the oven.

"I'm sorry." Athan's regret sounded genuine. "But you're a wealthy man's wife. You must travel in a carriage."

"I rode yesterday."

"And will be remembered because of that." His voice was as quiet as hers. No one would hear it beyond their table. "From now on we draw no attention to ourselves."

"Very well." She spread pale butter on the bread, and then berry-red jam.

"I'm sorry," Athan said again.

Saliel shrugged with one shoulder. "We're in Marillaq; we must do as the Marillaqans do." She bit into the roll. The jam tasted of summer in her mouth, of raspberries and sunshine.

They talked of safer things after that, more loudly, and she climbed into the hired carriage as a prosperous Marillaqan wife would: cheerful, content to be shut in a box instead of riding on horseback with her husband.

Her stomach didn't like the swaying of the coach. *I ate too much at breakfast.* But it was hard not to when food was spread before her: freshly-baked bread and creamy pats of butter, cheeses honeycombed with holes, thick slices of smoke-cured ham, jams that tasted of summer.

The view through the windows—small and jerky—made the discomfort worse. She saw trees, snow, Athan astride a large bay.

Saliel closed her eyes. She concentrated on the coachman's shouts, the crack of the whip, the sound of carriage wheels and hooves on snow, on cobblestones, on snow again. Hours passed. She began to grow cold despite the cloak and gloves she wore. The nausea became harder to ignore.

The sun was high in the sky when at last the carriage halted. Athan opened the door. "We'll stop here for lunch," he said, smiling up at her.

Saliel climbed down from the carriage.

"Shall we eat?" He offered her his arm.

Thoughts of food made her feel even more nauseous. "May we walk a while first?"

The streets were narrow and cobbled, closely crowded with tall stone buildings. Snow lay in the gutters and ice hung from the eaves. Wooden signs swung above shop doorways, carved with images: an apothecary's vials of medicine, a cobbler's shoes. The baker didn't need his sign; the smells of yeast and cinnamon scented the air far beyond his doorway.

They turned back at a smithy on the outskirts of the town. Furnaces flamed red-hot. Men in thick, fire-scored leather aprons beat metal on anvils.

Saliel's nausea slowly faded. Athan strolled beside her, seemingly at ease, but he wasn't relaxed. He was alert, aware of every alley, every doorway, every person on the street.

"What's wrong?"

"Nothing."

She shook her head. "You think we're being watched."

He scanned the street again. "Perhaps."

She glanced around—shops and townsfolk, carriages. "No one's watching us."

Athan halted. He looked at her. His expression was serious. "Corhona's had two months to search for us."

She grew suddenly cold. "You think people could be here, looking for us."

"I think it's possible. I think… we need to be very careful."

She glanced around again. *Marillaq is safe. We're safe.* But they were no longer surrounded by dozens of peasants. They were alone. They stood out.

Saliel shivered. She lifted the hood of her cloak, covering her hair.

They ate lunch at the coaching inn in a cheerful, busy taproom—a pie of chicken with dark-fleshed mushrooms—and traveled on through fir forests and snow, stopping in Herault when night fell. The rooms had whitewashed walls and black-beamed ceilings and bright rugs on the floor. Saliel took her place at the table in the private parlor Athan had hired. She looked at the white walls, the simple furnishings, the rugs. *So much nicer than the citadel.* A serving maid brought soup and curtseyed and withdrew.

Saliel unfolded her napkin, suddenly self-conscious. For the first time in two months she was truly alone with Athan. She picked up her soup spoon.

"Saliel."

She glanced up. "Yes?"

"Forgive me, but I need to ask…" He looked at her intently. "Who are you?"

She sat with her spoon poised over the soup. "I told you at the Bight. I'm a foundling from the Ninth Ward."

Athan shook his head. "No, you're not."

Saliel looked down at the soup. It was creamy, yellow, with leeks floating on the surface. She laid her spoon down on the tablecloth.

CHAPTER SIXTY-THREE

"I'm from the Ninth Ward," she said again.

Athan shook his head.

Saliel folded her napkin and placed it beside her soup bowl. *She's telling the truth.* He saw it in her face and in the way she sat. "But you walk like a lady." It was a protest. "You ride like a lady."

"I'm not one."

He'd never set foot in the Ninth Ward; few people did out of choice. It was a place of squalor and disease and misery, crowded, swarming with vermin. It had many names: the slums, the stews, Laurent's cesspit. Athan inhaled, almost expecting to smell the stench of sewers. *You can tell a Ninth Warder by their stink. It never washes off.*

Everything he'd ever been taught urged him to push to his feet, to stride from the room. He stayed sitting. He inhaled again. No smell of sewers, just leeks, soup.

Athan looked down at his bowl. *I wanted to marry her.* He was aware of regret, deep in his chest.

He pushed aside the bowl. "I don't understand."

Saliel pushed her own soup bowl away. She didn't look at him. "Does it matter?"

"Yes."

For a moment she sat stiffly, looking down at the tablecloth, then she spoke, "When I was seven I was taken to the Aspides. By a diplomat and his wife."

"Seven?" He had an instant's glimpse of the child she'd been, thin and filthy, her hair crawling with lice, gutter language coming from her mouth. "Why?"

"They wanted someone to pass as their child."

A foundling from Laurent's cesspit? *They must have been desperate.* "Why you?"

"She had red hair."

Saliel didn't look up to speak. She sat with her head bowed, looking down at the tablecloth. Athan had a moment of sudden understanding. *She's ashamed of who she is.*

He cleared his throat. "Were they nice to you?"

"They were hospitable."

He frowned. "Is that all they were? Hospitable?"

Saliel glanced briefly at him. She didn't speak.

"Why did they take you then?"

She touched the handle of her soup spoon and moved it slightly, so that it lined up with the rest of her cutlery. "I think they wanted to be the same as everyone else."

Athan rubbed his temples with hard fingers. A dangerous pretence. If anyone had found out—*they'd have been shunned, ruined.* "What was it like living with them?"

Saliel's brow creased slightly as she stared at the tablecloth. "The luxury was... extraordinary. I had a room of my own, a bed I didn't have to share. I had new clothes and toys and shoes. I'd never had shoes before. And there was so much food. As much as I wanted. As much as I could eat."

Athan glanced down at his steaming soup. *I had all that and thought nothing of it.* Shame heated his cheeks. "It must have seemed very strange."

"Yes."

He raised his eyes to her face again. She was still looking at the tablecloth. "Were you happy?"

She shrugged with a shoulder. "I got used to it."

"But were you happy?"

Saliel sat in silence for a moment. The crease between her eyebrows grew deeper. "I was afraid. I was always afraid they'd send me back."

"You think they would have?"

"The nursemaid said they would, if I didn't mind my manners or speak properly." She shrugged again. "It was an effective threat."

"I can see that it would be," Athan said, keeping his voice calm. He imagined her as a child, quiet, watchful, anxious, afraid of making the slightest mistake. "They schooled you. That's why you speak Corhonase and Marillaqan."

"I had the same lessons as the other diplomats' children."

Athan picked up his spoon and stirred the surface of his soup. "How long were you in the Aspides?"

"Six years."

"Then where?"

"They sent me back."

"Back?" His gaze jerked to her face. "To the Ninth Ward?"

"Yes," she said. "When they were recalled to Laurent."

Rage flared inside him. He released his spoon carefully, laying the handle on the side of the bowl. "What filthy people!" But some of his anger, his disgust, was for himself. *I will discard her too, when I return home.*

Saliel seemed surprised. She looked up, meeting his eyes fully. "On the contrary. I owe them a debt I can never repay."

"How so?" he asked, baffled.

"They gave me an education. Without that I'd still be in the Ninth Ward."

"They gave you *half* an education."

Saliel shook her head. "They arranged for my tutoring to continue for a while. I think they felt some responsibility for me."

It wasn't responsibility. It was guilt. "A while?"

"A year. I think... they must have been posted abroad again."

He studied her face. She'd still been a child, thirteen, fourteen years old. "What happened then?"

Her gaze fell. "I paid for the lessons myself." Her lips twisted slightly in a movement he recognized: shame.

Athan grew cold. She'd been a whore. *She wasn't a virgin when I bedded her. She—*

"I was a pickpocket. A finger thief." Saliel opened her right hand and spread her fingers. "I stole to pay for my lessons."

His relief was intense. At its heels was shame, equally intense. *She was a virgin that night.*

"When I was old enough, I found work as a governess."

"A governess? But your birth—"

"My employers were commoners," she said. "Merchants. I never worked for a House."

No noble House would let you through the door. Your birth is too base. Athan looked down at his soup without seeing it. "Did you enjoy it?"

"It was better than the Ninth Ward."

Of course it was. Anything would be.

Without her education she'd still be there, trapped, condemned to a life of grinding poverty. At best she'd be a scullery maid, at worst a tavern wench, a whore, a beggar. Her intelligence would count for nothing, *she'd* be nothing.

Athan rubbed a hand over his face. He raised his head and looked at her. "Why did you become a spy?"

Saliel was silent for a moment, frowning. "Being a governess is all very well. But... I disliked it."

"Why?" he asked, although he could think of a dozen reasons.

Her mouth twisted into a smile that was faintly bitter. "I disliked being a servant—which was foolish. What else can a foundling from the Ninth Ward hope to be?"

He shook his head silently.

"I dreaded my future. Moving from family to family, hoping that each new position would be... not unpleasant. Saving the money I earned so that when I grew too old to work I could rent a room in a boarding house somewhere." She pressed two fingertips to her forehead. "And it was always awkward with the other servants. I was above them in status, but below them in birth. They never knew how to treat me." Athan had an image of her, lonely and excluded. Something in his chest tightened painfully.

"One day an acquaintance of my employer approached me. He'd heard I spoke Corhonase. He asked whether I'd be prepared to spy for money, and I said... yes. I thought I could buy a life for myself, afterwards. Independence. I thought it was worth the risk."

She must prize independence highly, to risk her life for it. Athan looked down at his soup and stirred it with his spoon. "What will you do when you return to Laurent?"

"Buy some land," Saliel said, without hesitation. "By the sea."

It was a good answer. Similar to what his own would be if he had no House. He stirred his soup, round and round. "You like the sea?"

"Yes."

Saliel didn't look at him. Her soup was untouched.
Did she think she shouldn't dine with him?

Athan laid down his spoon again. He looked across
the table at Saliel's bent head. If her birth matched her
voice, if she truly was a diplomat's daughter—

She wasn't. She was a foundling from the Ninth
Ward, and he'd be cast from his House if he married
her.

*Even so, I should make the offer again. I owe it to
her.*

His gaze fell. He stared at the tablecloth. Home.
Family. They were simple words, but what they
meant was huge. The Seresin country estate where
he'd been born, where he'd run wild as a child. The
mausoleum where he expected to lie alongside his
ancestors. The family gallery, where his portrait hung
with his brothers' and sisters'. That portrait would
be removed and burned. He'd be erased from the
family records.

Such a future—to be adrift without Name and blood
ties and birthright—brought cold terror to his skin.
House Seresin anchored him. It was who he was.

*If only her birth matched her voice. If only she was
a diplomat's daughter—*

Athan looked at her. He took a deep breath. "Saliel,
marry me."

Her head jerked up. "What?"

"We'll pretend. We'll say you're from one of the far
colonies."

"No, Athan." She shook her head. "Your House
will check my pedigree. You know they will."

"I'm a fourth son. They won't check that hard—"

"I will not pretend to be noble."

"Gentry, then," he said, leaning forward. "You
don't have to be noble. It's not important I marry
well—"

"No." She met his eyes squarely. "I will not pretend."

He looked back down at the tablecloth, at the bowl of soup. Part of him was relieved. *Too risky a deception. If it was discovered—*

"Eat," he said. "Your soup will be going cold."

She made no move to pick up her spoon. "Which is your House, Athan?"

He closed his eyes. *Not now.*

"Athan, which House?"

He raised his head and looked at her. "Seresin. My father is the Count."

Her mouth opened. She shook her head. He saw how shocked she was, how appalled. She stood abruptly.

He pushed to his feet, almost knocking his chair over. "Don't," he said. "I beg you." *Don't walk away from me.*

Saliel bowed her head. "Your House has royal blood, Athan. I can't be in the same room as you. You know that."

Before Corhona I would have agreed with you. "This isn't Laurent; it's Marillaq. I refuse to shun you."

Her head lifted. She looked at him, her eyes steady. "And once we reach home?"

Athan rubbed his face. "Saliel…"

"You'll have to shun me. You'll dishonor your House if you don't."

He closed his eyes. "I'm sorry."

"Don't be. We both know how it is in Laurent."

He opened his eyes and looked at her. "Saliel, if you truly were a diplomat's daughter—"

"Don't," she said sharply. "Don't say it."

Athan swallowed. It was a struggle to keep his voice steady: "I'm sorry."

She shook her head.

"Sit," he said quietly. "Please."

After a moment's hesitation, she did.

They ate their soup silently. The maid took away the empty bowls. They sat without speaking. Athan could think of nothing to say. *I should have let her leave. It would be more comfortable than this.*

"Athan?"

He looked at her. Bright hair, gray eyes, a pale face. Regret clenched in his chest. *I wish—*

"If you don't mind me asking…" Her voice was diffident, hesitant.

"Anything," he said. "Anything at all. Forget about my House."

"It was your House I wanted to ask about."

"Oh." He looked down at the table. "What?"

"How is it that a Seresin is a spy?"

CHAPTER SIXTY-FOUR

THE SERVING MAID brought the rest of their meal—
roast lamb, vegetables—and a bottle of wine. Athan
carved the meat. He didn't speak. His expression
was inward-looking, frowning. Saliel didn't dare ask
the question again. She put food silently on her
plate.

Athan served himself. He poured two glasses of
wine. He didn't begin eating. He sat looking down at
his plate. "I was in Marillaq when Corhona tried to
invade. I saw the gorge afterward. That's why I
became a spy."

"Oh." She felt herself flush. "Forgive me, I didn't
mean to pry—"

He looked up. "I also became a spy because I was
bored."

"Oh." She picked up her cutlery, aware of Athan
watching her. He wasn't relaxed. *He expects me to
judge him.*

"Why were you in Marillaq?" she asked.

Athan blinked. "Marillaq? I was with my uncle. He
was studying the trolls."

"Trolls?"

"They live in the fir forests," he said. "Little gray
men."

She stared at him. "Really?"

He shook his head. "They're a superstition. But the locals believe they exist. That's why they put out troll bowls."

"Troll bowls?"

"Beside the doorsteps." He gestured at the platter of meat. A portion of lamb lay to one side, cut into tiny pieces.

"That's for trolls?"

He nodded. "To keep them happy."

Saliel began to eat. The potatoes were crisp-skinned and seasoned with rosemary, the lamb tender. "What happens if they're not happy?"

"Milk sours. Calves are stillborn. Hens don't lay." Athan picked up his knife and fork. "Things like that."

Keep talking. It's better than the silence. "Why was your uncle interested in trolls?"

"It's what he did. Studied things."

"And you helped him?"

He nodded. "My parents gave him charge of my education."

"Why?" As a Count's son he'd have had tutors...

Athan frowned. He speared a piece of meat on his fork. "Being in a House is like being in the citadel. It's restrictive and... and *boring*. So I played pranks. One day I went too far. I was sent to my uncle."

"It was a punishment?"

He was silent for a moment, frowning at the meat on his fork. Then he shrugged. "My parents didn't know what else to do with me." He began to eat.

"How old were you?"

"Twelve."

So young to be sent away. "Did you enjoy it?"

Athan's face lightened. "Yes. Very much. I saw the world with him. Marillaq, the colonies, the island nations. We were even in Corhona for a while."

"Corhona? They have trolls?"

"No, but they have a bat that drinks blood. It feeds on cows while they sleep—" He saw the expression on her face. "Forgive me. It's not a topic for the dinner table."

She shook her head. "What else?"

"A snake in the Oceanides that mesmerizes its prey." Athan reached for his wine glass. "It catches their gaze. They're completely helpless."

Saliel looked down at her plate. "Oh."

"It's extremely disturbing to watch," she heard him say. "It's almost as if the snake has the Eye."

"Oh." She pushed her food around on the plate. Vegetables. Meat.

"My uncle studied anything to do with the Eye. It was his particular interest."

Change the subject. "He sounds like an unusual man. How long were you with him?"

"Nearly eleven years."

"Eleven years?" She glanced up. "So long?"

Athan nodded.

"Did you never see your family?"

"We went home every year." He drank a mouthful of wine. "Stayed for a few months. But there was always something new to study."

"And your parents didn't mind?"

"As long as I wasn't making trouble, they were happy."

She looked at him for a long moment. "That must have been some prank."

Athan placed his glass back on the table. "Imagine a herd of goats in a ballroom."

"Oh."

"Ladies shrieking and fainting. Goats running everywhere." He looked down at his dinner. "My father was not amused."

"No. I can imagine not." She busied herself with her food, cutting the meat, the potatoes. "Where is your uncle now?"

"Home. He doesn't travel any more." Athan's voice was flat.

Don't ask. Talk about something else—

"He met someone," Athan said. "A commoner. He asked for permission to marry her."

She glanced up at him.

"He was given the choice to go home or be cast off. He chose to go home."

Saliel laid down her knife and fork. "Your uncle made the right choice, Athan."

"Perhaps." He didn't meet her eyes.

"Family is the most important thing there is."

He sighed and rubbed his face. "I know."

They ate their dinner, while the shutters rattled in the wind and logs shifted in the fire. Athan's expression was frowning, closed. When he'd finished he pushed his plate away.

"You will marry, won't you?" The sound of his voice almost made her jump. "Someone who'll take care of you."

Saliel placed her cutlery carefully on her plate. She looked up, meeting his eyes. "I don't intend to marry, Athan."

He stiffened. "What?"

"I do not wish to marry."

"Why not?"

Because my children will have the Eye. Saliel folded her napkin and placed it neatly beside her plate. "Once I've earned my independence, I don't intend to lose it."

Athan shook his head. "It's because of me, isn't it? It's because of what I did to you."

"No. It's not. I've never wished to marry."

"But... don't you want a family?"

Saliel pushed her plate away. "I don't need one."

"Everyone needs a family."

Not I. She picked up her glass and swallowed the last mouthful of wine. "What will you do when you get home?"

Athan eyed her for a moment. Then he sat back in his chair and folded his arms. "There's a vineyard on one of our estates. I'd like to grow the grapes, make them into wine."

"No travel?"

"I've been away too long. I want to be in one place. I want to be home." Athan uncrossed his arms and leaned forward. "Saliel—"

"No."

"Promise me you'll marry someone."

Saliel stared at the fire. "What does your uncle do now?" she asked, watching the flames. "Does he still study?"

"He drinks. That's what he does now: he drinks."

Saliel looked at him. He was frowning at the table-cloth. "You've been away for nearly two years, Athan. Maybe things have changed."

"Maybe." He raised his head. "Saliel—"

Saliel pushed her chair away from the table. "Good night, Athan."

Athan closed his mouth. He swallowed. After a moment he stood and bowed. "Good night."

ATHAN STRIPPED OFF his day's clothes. He washed his face in the porcelain washstand. Hot water, soap, a soft towel—they were simple things, and yet the difference they made was huge. Memory of the Bazarn Plateau, the peasants, the poverty, was already fading. It seemed years and continents away from this bed chamber—the feather pillows and the clean sheets—not a few days' ride.

There's hardship everywhere. I'm just not used to seeing it.

Athan reached for the towel. He caught sight of himself in the mirror as he dried his face. *I don't look like me.*

It was the thinness, the way his bones jutted from beneath his skin—and it was more than that. It was what was inside him.

Athan stepped closer to the mirror. He studied his face. *I'm my uncle. I'm making the same decisions he did.*

He turned away and hung up the towel. *No, I'm not.* His uncle had never scandalized their House with his pranks, he'd never been a spy—

His fingers slowed, unbuttoning his shirt. *I didn't tell her the truth tonight. It was more than what I saw at the gorge, more than boredom.*

The code book was snug against his chest. The oil-skin wrapping was warm. Athan pulled it out. He turned the package over in his hand—oiled cloth, neat stitching. *I wanted them to notice me.*

They'd notice him now. He was a hero.

Athan hid the code book under his pillow. Sleep was slow to come. He lay awake, staring up at the ceiling. He heard a dance tune in his head. Ladies shrieking. The sound of goat droppings scattering across a marble floor. *I wanted them to notice me.*

Why had he never realized it before?

CHAPTER SIXTY-FIVE

SALIEL ATE LESS for breakfast the next morning, but she felt ill again in the carriage. They stopped for lunch at Selac. Athan walked with her through the busy market square. He didn't appear to see the richly-colored bolts of fabric, the strings of glass beads, the displays of spices and the thick-rinded slabs of cheese. He scanned the square, watchful, alert.

The inn had no private dining parlor; they ate their lunch in the taproom. Sunlight fell across the table in diamond-shaped squares, bright and pale. Athan said little. There was a frown on his brow. He looked inward, not outward.

Saliel chewed her food and swallowed, drank the ale in her mug, but it was tasteless—the bread and cheese and meats, the ale. *His mood is dark because of me.*

It was dusk when they arrived at Epern. The inn had a private parlor. A maid laid the table, curtseyed, and withdrew. Silence built between them as they ate. She heard the logs burning in the fireplace, the clink of cutlery...

"You must promise me you'll marry."

Saliel raised her eyes. "No, Athan."

"It makes you ill, doesn't it?" His mouth was bitter. "Thought of being with a man."

Yes. It does. Saliel put down her knife and fork. "Athan—"

"Let me show you." His voice was quiet, fierce. "Let me show you how it should be."

She flinched slightly, pressing back in the chair. "No."

Athan's face tightened. "It is because of me."

Saliel laid her napkin on the table. "No, it's not."

"Then promise me you'll marry—"

"Athan, please don't discuss this with me again."

He held her eyes for a long moment, and then looked down at his plate. "As you wish."

ATHAN DIDN'T SPEAK with her again about marriage, or about the marriage bed. He was a son of Laurent's greatest House; his manners were impeccable. He was courteous and attentive—and when they were in public, watchful.

They traveled fast, descending from mountains to foothills to snow-covered plains. The winter became gentler. Snow lay less thickly and the ice on the lakes thinned until dark water could be seen.

Saliel was aware of a sense of urgency, a prickling of unease. She looked behind her often. No one watched them, no one followed.

With the urgency and the unease, was nausea. It didn't matter how much she ate at breakfast, how straight or winding the roads were: every morning, nausea.

Her monthly flow hadn't come on the plateau, but it had been like that in the Ninth Ward—too little food, no monthly flow. *It'll come tomorrow. I'm not with child. It's the carriage.*

But her flow didn't come. Each afternoon the illness faded—and her fear grew. *What shall I do?*

It wasn't something she could discuss with Athan. His mood was dark; it would be darker still if he thought she bore his child.

On the tenth day they reached the coast. They halted for the night in Flers. The smell of salt spray and seaweed and fish was strong. There was no private parlor to be had, but the three merchants who dined at the other table ate hurriedly and left, talking in low voices about the price of peppercorns.

A serving man brought pastries filled with crushed almonds and a pot of tea, and busied himself clearing the merchants' table.

Saliel poured two cups and passed one to Athan. "How far to the port?"

"We'll reach it tomorrow," he said. "If the weather is in our favor."

The serving man picked up his tray. Cutlery clinked as he walked across the room. The door swung shut.

Saliel sipped her tea. It tasted as it smelled: of apples and honey. She glanced across the table at Athan.

He was looking down at his plate. His expression was frowning, bitter.

Saliel put down her cup.

Athan didn't notice. *He looks inside himself. And he hates what he sees.*

"Athan?"

His head lifted slightly. His expression became attentive, courteous. "Yes?"

"I'm sorry I burned you. At the citadel."

Athan shook his head. "You have nothing to apologize for."

Yes, I do. She looked down at the pastry on her plate. "When did you discover who I was?"

"First Battle," he said. "When you sneezed in the catacombs."

"Oh." She looked up. "Athan..."

"What?"

She leaned forward. "You have to forgive yourself."

He couldn't. She saw it on his face.

They ate their dessert silently. Saliel chewed slowly, trying to think of a way to erase Athan's guilt, his self-hatred. *What if I accept his offer? What if I let him show me how it should be?*

Dread clenched in her belly.

She drank, not tasting the apple, the honey. Memory of their wedding night was there if she cared to remember: fear, revulsion, pain.

It won't be like that. Everything's different now. I like him.

And Marta had been correct: he was a handsome man.

Even so; dread.

Saliel tried to understand the dread as she drank the apple-scented tea. It wasn't because of who Athan was, or because of his appearance. It was because of his size. He was so much bigger than her, so much stronger. *I won't be able to stop him.*

And yet I'd trust him with my life.

When she had finished she placed the cup in its saucer and looked at Athan. She clasped her hands together and inhaled past the tightness in the chest, in her throat. "Athan."

He lifted his head. "Yes?"

"If you wish, you may show me."

His brow creased. "Show you?"

She saw the instant he understood. He became very still. "I may?"

Saliel nodded.

"Why?"

Because I want you to be happy. What happened wasn't your fault. She looked down at her plate. "You said it should be good between a man and a woman."

"Yes."

She swallowed to clear the contriction in her throat. "I'm not certain of that."

"Then let me show you," he said. "Please."

She raised her eyes. The intensity of his gaze was almost frightening. "Athan..." *I'm scared.*

"I won't hurt you," he said, as if he'd heard her speak the words aloud. "I promise. And I won't make you with child."

You may already have.

"You're certain?"

She looked at him. The self-hatred was gone from his face. Instead of shame and guilt, she saw hope. *I can do this for him.* "Yes," she said.

CHAPTER SIXTY-SIX

ATHAN OPENED THE door and stepped into her bed chamber. Saliel stood beside the fireplace, dressed in her nightgown.

He closed the door.

She was afraid. He saw it in her eyes, in the way she tensed as he walked toward her. *I did that. I'm the reason she's scared.*

"You're certain you want this?"

She nodded.

Athan reached out and touched her hair with his fingertips. Soft. Smooth. Shining. *I should walk away.*

"Just tell me to stop. And I will."

He took it slowly—standing by the fireplace, sitting on the bed—giving her time to draw back, to refuse. He'd never been so nervous with a woman before, so afraid of making a mistake.

She stiffened when he unbuttoned her nightgown, but said nothing.

Athan bent his head. He kissed her throat lightly, tasting her.

The minutes became long and slow, full of warmth and soft, smooth skin. Saliel relaxed gradually. He touched her gently, learning her responses, seeing the pleasure rise in her.

He'd dreamed of this in the citadel, when she'd had no name or face—he'd imagined touching her, had imagined the clean scent of her skin, had imagined her body opening to him. *This is how it should be.*

The candles burned down while he brought her to climax with his fingers, his mouth. "Oh," she said, afterwards. Her eyes were wide and startled.

Athan felt suddenly lighter, as if a heaviness was gone from his chest. He laughed, and laid a hand gently on her midriff. The muscles quivered beneath his fingers. *I did that.*

He didn't dare kiss her properly. Kisses were for lovers. He bent his head and pressed his mouth to her skin—so soft—and closed his eyes for a moment, listening to the shutters rattle in the wind, listening to her heartbeat.

He felt a touch in his hair. Her fingers, stroking lightly.

Athan opened his eyes. *I wish—*

He pushed up from the bed. He cleared his throat and began to strip. He'd taken off his clothes once before, in front of her. Then, she hadn't watched. Now she did.

He felt as shy as her, as self-conscious. He stood awkwardly in front of her, aware of how different their bodies were—size and shape—and how odd he must look to her. How frightening.

He saw Saliel swallow, nervous. She raised her eyes to his face.

"I won't hurt you," he said. "I promise."

Athan lay down beside her. Her body was tense, but she didn't shrink away from him. *Don't rush this.* He touched her gently, drawing pleasure from her. When he judged she was ready, he slid his fingers inside her. He felt her body accommodate him, soft and hot and tight.

Athan withdrew his fingers. He brought himself to lie above her, bracing his weight. "I'll stop if it hurts. You must tell me."

Saliel's cheeks were flushed, her eyes dark. She nodded.

She trusts me.

He entered her slowly. It was harder than he'd thought. His body wanted to—

Saliel tensed slightly.

Athan paused. His head was bowed, his eyes clenched shut. "Does it hurt?"

"I'm... not sure."

He almost laughed, almost lost his control. He gritted his teeth and held himself still, struggling to breathe. *I can do this. I can.* "Do you want me to stop?"

"No."

He held onto his control as he slid deeply into her, as her body moved instinctively to meet him. Time blurred. Seconds. Minutes. This was what he'd dreamed of: the heat, the friction of their bodies, the pleasure spiraling tight, tighter—

Saliel arched beneath him. He felt her climax.

Athan withdrew swiftly. He held her, panting, dragging air into his lungs.

Saliel's fingers gripped his arm. She lifted her face to him. "Athan..."

He bent his head and kissed her. *I love you.*

She didn't draw away. She kissed him back. Her mouth was soft, sweet, shy.

CHAPTER SIXTY-SEVEN

ATHAN PULLED THE quilt over them. He held her as the pleasure slowly dissipated. His warmth and solidity, his arms around her—strong—gave her a feeling of safety. *He won't let anything happen to me.*

She was relaxed in a way she'd never been before, heavy-limbed. The heat of Athan's body and the sound of his breathing lulled her toward sleep.

"Promise me you'll marry."

Saliel opened her eyes. The bed chamber was full of shadows and candlelight. "I can't make that promise."

Athan sighed. "Promise me… promise me that if you meet a man you can love—a good man—and he asks you to marry him, you will."

She watched the shadows dance across the white-washed walls. "I will."

Athan said nothing more after that. She lay quietly, listening to his low breathing, to his heartbeat, storing the memories.

Minutes slowly became hours. At last Athan stirred. His arms tightened fractionally. She felt his mouth on her skin. His kiss was feather-light.

Saliel opened her eyes. The candles had burned out. Only the embers in the fireplace gave light.

"Forgive me," Athan whispered against her skin. "I am too much a coward."

She wanted to place her hand on his arm, to answer him, but the words weren't meant for her to hear; he thought her asleep. *You're not a coward*, she told him silently. *You are wise. You must not leave your House for me.*

"I'm sorry," he whispered.

Athan released her. He dressed quickly, quietly. He bent to kiss her hair, a touch so light she barely felt it. She heard him walk across the room, heard the door open and close.

He was gone.

CHAPTER SIXTY-EIGHT

THEY ARRIVED AT the port of Bressoq at dusk. The coachman took them to a respectable inn near the wharves, where the streets were narrow and the tall stone buildings stood like close-crammed gray teeth. Saliel stepped down onto the cobblestones and drew her cloak more tightly around her. The air was chill and dank, heavy with the smells of coal smoke and sea salt and frying fish.

Athan paid the coachman off and thanked him for his service. The man nodded and took his place on the driver's box, gathering the reins in his hands. She watched as horses and carriage disappeared into the gray dusk, threading their way between pedestrians and dogs, wagons and carts.

Athan turned to her and offered his arm. His face was weary.

The inn was tall and narrow, built of gray stone like its neighbors. Inside, the innkeeper greeted them, smiling in his starched white apron, and welcomed them to Bressoq.

Athan ordered rooms and dinner, and asked the man which ships were due to sail east.

"Well, there's the *Sea Wind*. She sails at midnight for Monserrac, but she's not for the likes of ye." The man bowed.

"Anything else?"

"The *Shining Lily* leaves for Laurent in three days. She's of good quality. Ye'll probably find passage on her."

"Very well," Athan said. "We'll enquire at the shipping office tomorrow."

The innkeeper nodded and smiled and rubbed his hands together. His gaze fell on Saliel and then flicked back to Athan. A curious expression crossed his face. "Ah…"

"Yes?"

"There were two men asking after… They said they were looking for friends. A large, dark-complected man, they said, and a young lady with red hair."

Everything became very still—the flames in the fireplace, her breath. Saliel was aware of a strange sense of inevitability. *We've been waiting for this.*

"Oh?" Athan sounded only mildly curious. "What did they look like?"

"Quite ordinary, sir." The innkeeper shrugged. "But one of them did have unusual eyes. Very pale."

Her throat tightened. The shadows seemed to freeze on the wall. She had the sensation of being unable to get air into her lungs.

"What did they call themselves?" Athan asked.

"Uh…" The innkeeper felt in the pocket of his apron. "They left their direction." He unfolded a piece of paper. "Grigani, it was. From the Aspides."

"Ah, yes," Athan said. "Of course." He held out his hand for the scrap of paper. The innkeeper gave it to him. "Staying at *The Lonely Helmsman*, I see. Where is that exactly?"

"Not far from here. One block closer to the docks." The man gestured vaguely.

"And when was our friend Grigani here?"

"Yesterday."

Athan's arm was rigid beneath her fingers, but his voice was marvelously calm. "Thank you," he said.

"You've been most helpful. It shames me to reward you so poorly, but I believe we'll remove ourselves to *The Lonely Helmsman*, to be with our friends."

The innkeeper's expression of geniality faded.

"Here's something for your trouble, and our thanks." Athan handed the man several coins. "We're more grateful than you can imagine."

The innkeeper thinned his lips, looked at the silver coins in his palm, and managed a smile. "Do ye require a porter?"

"No, thank you," Athan said. "We have little in the way of luggage."

Saliel removed her hand from his arm and bent to take her valise, trying to breathe past the constriction in her throat. She nodded politely to the innkeeper and followed Athan outside, pulling the hood of her cloak forward. She scanned the darkening street. A man walked toward them, his stride brisk and purposeful. A cloaked figure leaned in a doorway, his head turned in their direction. Two men conversed idly across the street. Dogs barked and carriage wheels clattered on the cobblestones, and everywhere there were men.

She crossed the road with Athan, her head held high, her steps calm and unhurried. They walked a few paces into an alley and halted in the shadows. Saliel gripped the handle of her valise with both hands, tightly. "Well?"

"Do you have a knife?"

She shook her head. Athan had a knife—he wore it always at his hip—but she'd not carried one since the catacombs.

Athan crouched and opened his valise. "Here." He handed her a sheathed knife. "You know how to use it?"

Saliel nodded. She'd learned how to defend herself— along with so many other things—during the mad, rushed month before she'd sailed to Corhona.

Athan stood. "You must sail with the *Sea Wind* tonight."

"And you?"

"It will be my pleasure to kill Lord Grigor."

Saliel shook her head. "Forget him. We'll both take the *Sea Wind*."

"And have him reach Monserrac before us?" Athan shook his head. "No."

"Better to take the risk!" she said, her voice low and fierce. "He has a man with him. You can't take them both!"

"We shall see," Athan said, reaching beneath his cloak. "Here, take the code book."

"No. I'm not boarding that ship without you."

"You have to," he said, flat-voiced. "One of us must reach Laurent."

She stared at him. In the gray half-light his expression was uncompromising.

I won't let you die. Saliel tightened her grip on the knife. "If you won't come with me, then I'll go with you." She began walking down the alley in the direction of the *Lonely Helmsman*.

CHAPTER SIXTY-NINE

"CURSE IT, SALIEL!" Athan's fear for her twisted into something close to anger. He took hold of her arm and swung her to a halt. "You are *not* coming—"

"Lord Ivo," came a greeting from the mouth of the alley.

Athan turned, thrusting Saliel behind him. A man stood where the alley opened into the street.

Athan bared his teeth in a smile. "And you are?"

"Therlo. We've met."

"So we have." Athan pushed his valise aside with one foot. He reached for his knife. "The pleasure was all mine—as I recall."

A second cloaked figure stepped into the alley. He was too tall to be the spycatcher. A blade gleamed in his hand.

Athan tightened his grip on the knife. "Saliel," he said quietly. "Run."

"Only if you do."

Athan gritted his teeth. He turned and grabbed Saliel's arm—and ran.

An alley opened to the right, a second and third to the left. He chose their route at random. Saliel pulled her arm free and ran beside him. They met no carriages or wagons; the alleyways were too narrow. It was a place of crooked doors and rancid smells. The few pedestrians shrank aside, offering neither help nor hindrance.

Athan's chest began to burn. He panted as he ran, gulping air. Everything was gray, leached of color. *A few more minutes and we can hide in this maze.*

They reached the end of their luck abruptly, swinging around a corner to confront a dark space hemmed in by the backs of buildings. There were no doors, no windows, just piles of fetid refuse.

Athan swore. He thrust Saliel behind him and spun to face their pursuers.

"Don't move," he said, dragging air into his lungs. "Leave this to me."

The spycatcher's men careered around the corner and halted.

Athan eyed them grimly. He ripped his cloak off and wrapped it roughly around his left forearm.

Therlo laughed, a gasping, exultant sound. He unfastened his cloak, tossing it aside as he stepped forward. The other man flanked him, breathing heavily.

Athan unsheathed his knife and held it lightly between his fingers. "Who's your friend?"

Therlo drew his knife. "Volker."

"And where's your master?"

"You'll see him soon enough." Therlo laughed again, panting. "He looks forward to it. Nothing squeals quite like a Laurentine spy."

Athan crouched low.

"Your… what did he say you called him? Ah, yes. Your guardian. He squealed for us, Ivo. He screamed."

Athan took the knife more firmly in his hand. *Don't listen to him.*

Therlo stepped closer. "I look forward to hearing your lady whore scream too."

Athan shook his head. *Concentrate.* Anger would kill him.

He began to move slowly forward, keeping his body low, shielding the blade with his left arm, making sure he was between Saliel and their attackers. "I had hoped to break your skull, servant," he said softly. "And yet, you live. I'm disappointed."

Therlo lunged at him.

Athan stepped aside and blocked the blow with his forearm. The blade sliced harmlessly into the layers of cloak. He jabbed his knife at Therlo's stomach. The man stumbled back and fell awkwardly.

Volker leapt in, his teeth gleaming in the semi-darkness. Athan spun and blocked the thrust, shredding his cloak still further. His knife opened Volker's cheek. He tried to take the man out fast—while Therlo was still down—but his foot slipped on the cobblestones and his blade slid off Volker's ribs, cutting but not killing.

Volker staggered back, but Therlo was up again. Athan risked a glance behind him. Saliel stood with her back to the wall. His spare knife was in her hand, unsheathed.

Athan flexed his fingers, feeling the balance of the knife in his hand. Months he'd spent in Balzac, fighting with other youths under the tutelage of a grizzled knife fighter. They'd jabbed at each other with charred sticks, feinting and blocking, lunging and slashing. He'd come away from the lessons with red welts raised on his skin, his clothes torn and charcoal-streaked—but he'd learned how to defend himself. How to kill.

A useful skill, his uncle had called it.

"Come on," he said to Therlo. His tone was soft, insulting. "Don't tell me you're afraid."

Therlo snarled and moved closer. Volker circled to the left. The low, crouching movements blurred in the deepening dusk. *Do this fast. Soon you won't be able to see them.*

Athan feinted and then struck—hard—taking Therlo in the shoulder, slicing through muscle and striking
bone, making him stagger and grunt with pain. The
man spat a curse, but retained hold of his blade.

Volker darted in. Athan added another slash to his
cheek. The man stumbled back, but didn't fall. He
remained standing, shaking his head. Hot droplets of
blood struck Athan's face.

He lunged for the kill, while Volker stood dazed, but
Therlo moved too. His knife scored down Athan's
right arm, parting the fabric and leaving a faint, stinging line on his skin.

Athan dropped to the cobblestones and rolled, coming to his feet out of range of Therlo's blade. From the
corner of his eye he saw Saliel step forward. He waved
her back.

For a few seconds no one moved. They were all
breathing heavily. "That's right," Therlo said, panting.
His sleeve was black with blood. "Keep your whore
out of this. We want her unmarked when we bed her."

Athan ignored the words. He wrapped the shredded
cloak more tightly around his forearm and flexed his
knife hand. There was blood on his fingers, warm and
sticky, not his own. He crouched low and beckoned
Therlo forward. "Come on. Why the caution?"

Dimly, he saw Therlo snarl, but it was Volker who
charged. Athan feinted—and saw a chance to take the
man. He thrust hard, with all the weight of his body
behind the blow.

Volker slipped on the cobblestones and fell. Athan's
knife missed flesh, snaring in the man's cloak. He fell
with him. They rolled, struggling with each other, and
then came apart.

Athan scrambled to regain his feet. His knife lay on
the cobblestones, glinting. He reached for it.

Therlo lunged.

Athan saw his own death coming—a gleaming blade—and then Saliel was between them, facing Therlo. He tried to cry out to her, but his voice strangled in his throat.

Therlo slashed at her, a vicious, upward stroke.

Athan's heart seemed to stop beating—and then he saw the blade had missed Saliel. His pulse surged. Something roared inside him. His scrabbling fingers found the knife. He launched himself at Therlo, snarling, knocking him to the ground.

They rolled on the cobblestones, grappling fiercely, and somehow Therlo had a knee in Athan's stomach. "Filthy spy," he hissed.

Athan put his elbow in the man's throat and raised his knife. Therlo screamed as the blade slashed across an eye. He released his grip, keening softly.

Athan came to his knees, looking for Saliel. He lost what little breath he had.

Volker had her. They lay sprawled on the ground, a tangled shadow. Volker was on top—that much Athan could see—and his hands were around her throat.

He's choking her.

Athan scrambled desperately to his feet. Volker screamed, a short, cut-off cry. The figures parted. Saliel rolled away and pushed to her knees. Volker stayed on the ground. He lay curled around himself on the cobblestones, wheezing.

The muscles in Athan's groin tightened in an instinctive wince. "Saliel, are you all right—?"

An arm hooked around his ankles, jerking him off his feet.

Athan managed to twist as he fell, avoiding Therlo's blade. The tussle was short and ugly. He knocked the knife from the man's hand and held him by the throat while he thrust his blade up beneath Therlo's ribs. He must have found the heart. Therlo stopped struggling.

His body spasmed and a strange sound came from his throat. Then he lay still.

Athan pushed unsteadily to his feet and turned to Volker. He lay face down. The cobblestones were black with blood beneath him. Saliel stood silently. Her face was a pale oval in the dimness.

"Are you all right?" Athan stripped the shredded cloak from his arm.

"I cut his throat."

Athan let his knife fall to the ground. He walked over to her, lurching slightly, and took her in his arms. "It's all right."

Saliel pressed her face into his shoulder and shook her head. She was shaking.

Athan held her in silence. He could think of nothing to say. They had both killed. It was—most profoundly—not all right.

CHAPTER SEVENTY

TRUE DARKNESS FELL. "Are you hurt?" he asked.

Saliel shook her head. "Are you?"

"No." Athan closed his eyes. Memory of her standing between him and Therlo was vivid in his mind: the glint of the knife as it slashed up, the heart-stopping moment when he'd thought the blade had caught her. She could have died so easily. It could be her lifeblood on the cobblestones.

He tightened his grip on her.

The things he had feared were nothing, gone. The portrait in the family gallery, the Seresin mausoleum, the country estate—were all unimportant. He could live without his parents, his brothers and sisters, his uncle. He wouldn't be nameless. He had a name: Athan. The Seresin was unimportant. It didn't define who he was.

He didn't need his House to anchor him and make him whole. He needed nothing and no one other than himself. *And you, Saliel. I need you.*

The moon rose, casting light and shadows. Its rings were razor-sharp.

With the moon came a whisper of sound. Athan raised his head. His ears caught the scuff of feet, furtive.

He released Saliel and made a desperate grab for her discarded knife. No attack came. Instead, two dark

352 The Laurentine Spy

figures in the alleyway froze. He caught a glimpse of
eyes wide with alarm and a grime-streaked cheek.
Boys. Adolescents.

He took rough hold of Saliel's wrist and dragged her
from the trap they were in, the knife in his fist.

The watchers made no move to hinder or follow
them, but still Athan ran, pulling Saliel with him. He
turned three corners in quick succession and then
slowed to a walk. He released Saliel's wrist. They were
both gasping for breath.

"What now?"

Athan wiped sweat from his face. "The spycatcher—"

"Do you think you can face him tonight? Truly?"

Athan leaned against a wall. "Truly?" He shook his
head. The adrenalin was gone; he was shaking, sweating. "No."

"Then let us leave." Saliel gripped his arm. "Let's
sail on the *Sea Wind* tonight."

"I should stay—"

"No. We go together, Athan, or not at all."

He reached out to touch her cheek. "Then we go
together."

THEIR VALISES LAY where they'd left them, pushed
against a wall like bundles of rubbish. Athan
crouched and wrenched his open. His spare cloak was
folded at the bottom. He pulled it out and stood, settling it over his shoulders with a jerk. The fabric was
cold at his throat. "Ready?" He held his hand out to
her.

They kept to the main streets, walking briskly.
Torches fixed in brackets burned at each corner. A
light snow began to fall. Athan scanned the shadows,
the dark alleyways. No one appeared to be following
them.

The dockside, when they reached it, was a confusion of noise and movement. Dogs barked and wagon wheels clattered and hawkers advertised their wares loudly. Two bonfires burned. Snow fell with a hiss into the leaping flames. The scent of frying fish stopped Athan in his stride. "Food," he said. "We need to eat."

The fish he'd smelled were small and being fried whole and then laid—crisp—between thick slices of bread. He bought four sandwiches and paid extra for them to be wrapped in sheets of paper. Hot grease leaked through the flimsy wrappings, staining them.

The *Sea Wind* loomed up from the water, a jutting cliff, straining at her ropes. A glance told him she wasn't new—but despite her shabbiness, she was alive, bright with lamps and loud with voices. And beneath the human noises—shouts, laughter, tears—was the soft slap of water against creaking wood.

He stood back to allow Saliel to climb the narrow gangway. A breeze ruffled the black water and swirled snowflakes in his face.

Athan put down his valise. He flexed his fingers and cast a glance behind him. The wharf was a chaos of flame and moonlight, shadow and darkness, noise, movement. Women clutched their children, men shook hands, and the bonfires crackled and hissed. A voice rose drunkenly in song and somewhere a dog yelped.

He picked up his valise and began to climb the gangway. The skin between his shoulder blades, at the nape of his neck, was tight. *We're not safe yet.*

Saliel waited for him at the top. Athan's tension eased slightly as he set foot on the *Sea Wind's* deck. The harassed purser, standing near the head of the gangway, sold them two berths, barely glancing at them as he did so.

The ship was crowded. Everywhere Athan looked he saw crying babies, overexcited children, and weary adults. Torches burned and snow fell and the sea and sky were black.

He drew Saliel to one side. "Let's make sure no one followed us."

CHAPTER SEVENTY-ONE

IT BECAME EASIER to draw breath when the *Sea Wind* was released from her mooring ropes. It felt as if a large weight had lifted from his chest. Athan inhaled deeply and turned to Saliel. "We're safe."

She said nothing, merely nodded.

Their cabins were below deck. He took Saliel to her berth first, down steep stairs and along a narrow corridor lit by smoky lanterns. The door was partially open, revealing an iron kettle sitting on the narrow strip of wooden floor, steam coiling from its spout. Inside, two women talked.

Saliel's face was pale and weary, smudged with dirt. There was a dark mark on the hem of her cloak.

"There's blood on your cloak," he said in a low voice. "Take care they don't see it."

Saliel removed the cloak. She folded it over her arm, hiding the stain.

Athan looked at her carefully. There was a fleck of dried blood on her jaw, a tiny splash. He put down his valise and took hold of her chin. "Blood," he said, and she shivered and stood still while he rubbed it off with his thumb.

Athan released her chin and looked her over a second time. Then he pulled back the hood of his cloak. "Have I blood on me?"

Saliel studied at his face for a long moment, then glanced at the rest of him and shook her head. "No."

He could still feel where Volker's blood had splashed his cheek, but he trusted her. "Thank you." He handed her two of the fish sandwiches. The greasy paper was cold.

A passenger came down the narrow corridor. Athan pressed himself against the wall to let the man past.

"Go," Saliel said quietly. "Have something to eat. I'll see you in the morning."

"Your throat?"

"It's fine, Athan."

He wanted to check for himself, but he saw how tired she was. She looked fragile, as if she'd shatter at the slightest touch. He bent his head and pressed his mouth to her cheek. Her skin was cool, smooth. "Good night, Saliel." He stepped back and picked up his valise.

"Good night."

He nodded and turned away. He heard the door creak as Saliel pushed it open. The conversation inside stopped.

Athan walked slowly back along the corridor. He wanted to be with her tonight. To tell her he loved her. To ask her to be his wife. To hold her in his arms and offer comfort.

His berth was down another flight of steep stairs. The cabin was cramped, with twelve bunks and an empty night bucket in one corner. A small mirror hung beside the door, its surface flecked and spotted. He saw his face in it, saw exhaustion and calmness. *I don't need my House.* There was no panic, just a sense of freedom, a sense of the future opening out before him.

A man occupied one of the bunks, his stubbled face slack in sleep. Athan trod quietly and slung his valise on the last free bed, hard and narrow. He placed his food more carefully beside it. The air was stale. It smelled of sour male sweat and urine.

He rested his forehead against the wooden bunk frame and shut his eyes. He felt years older than he was. *I could sleep here, standing.*

Athan sighed. He opened his eyes and turned away from the bunk and went in search of water to wash his hands and face.

CHAPTER SEVENTY-TWO

IT WAS A raw morning, damp and cold. The sea was a dark, leaden gray and the sky was a paler shade of the same color. He found Saliel on deck, sitting on one of the long benches.

She glanced up. Her eyes seemed to look through him for a moment, and then she blinked and smiled. "Good morning, Athan."

He sat down beside her on the hard bench. "Are you all right?"

"Yes."

No, you're not. You killed a man last night. He studied her face—closed, pale. "Would you like to talk about it?"

She shook her head. "No, thank you, Athan."

He held his hand out to her, wordlessly, palm up.

Saliel hesitated for a moment, and then placed her hand in his.

They sat side by side in silence, looking at the sea, at the slow roll of the gray waves.

"The guardian's dead."

Athan turned his head and looked at her. "Yes."

"I didn't like him."

He released Saliel's hand and put his arm around her, pulling her close. "Neither did I."

"He didn't deserve to die like that." He felt her shiver.

"No. No one does."

The spycatcher was somewhere behind them. *In Bressoq, still. He can't know yet where we've gone.* Even so, Athan looked west, craning his neck. The horizon was empty.

THEY LEFT THE *Sea Wind* at the Red Isle, where it stopped to take on fresh food and water. The ship's destination—the colony of Monserrac—took them too far from where they needed to be.

The hour wasn't long after dawn, but the wharf was bustling. Catches of fish were being unloaded from boats. Everyone was busy—buying, selling, piling fish into baskets and carts.

Saliel scanned the crowd, searching for the spy-catcher. *He can't possibly be here yet.* But she was still tense, still afraid.

They walked together. Athan held her arm. His grip was firm.

The words that filled her ears meant nothing—swift, sibilant, each *s* a hiss. The cobblestones were red, the buildings flanking the wharf were red. Saliel turned her head, looking at the crowd, at the rust-colored stone. *The Red Isle.*

A sleepy-eyed clerk sat behind a desk at the shipping office. "Anywhere in the Protectorate?" His Laurentine had the same hissing sibilance she'd heard on the wharf.

"Yes," Athan said. "As soon as possible."

The clerk seemed unsurprised by the request. He yawned and reached for a sheet of parchment. "There's a ship leaving for the Illymedes this afternoon and one to Hespernay tomorrow morning—"

"The Illymedes," Athan said. "We'll take two berths."

It took the clerk several minutes—yawning—to find the passenger list. It was clear he'd rather be in bed.

He picked up a quill, squinted at the tip, and dipped it in ink. "Cabins below deck?"

Saliel glanced down at herself. Two weeks aboard the *Sea Wind* had not been kind to their clothes.

"No."

The clerk looked up. "I beg your pardon?"

"The finest cabins you have." Athan reached beneath his cloak and pulled out the pouch of Marillaqan money. Coins clinked as he tipped them into his hand.

Saliel almost laughed at the clerk's expression. He glanced at the gold coins and then at their rumpled, travel-stained cloaks. He blinked and cleared his throat. His manner became brisk. "Of course, sir. The finest cabins." He flicked through the pages of the passenger list. "There's... several cabins on the upper deck. And a suite."

"A suite?"

"Yes, sir. It has a bedroom and parlor, and a servant's room and—"

"We'll take it," Athan said. Then he glanced at her. His question was unspoken: *If it's all right with you?*

She nodded.

"Your name, sir?"

The clerk wrote the name Athan gave him—Argante—in neat, concise handwriting. "And your servant, sir?"

"We have none at present."

The clerk didn't show by so much as a flicker of an eyelid that he found this unusual. He counted the coins Athan gave him and locked them in a strongbox, then wrote the ticket and receipt briskly and dusted them with sand. "Here you are, sir."

Athan took the sheets of parchment. "May we leave our luggage here?"

"Of course, sir."

"He thinks us very odd," Saliel said, as they walked down the steps.

"No doubt."

She glanced around. Fishermen unloaded their catch. An errand boy ran with his head down. A man sold hot chestnuts from a handcart. No one watched them.

"Shall we walk?"

Saliel nodded. She placed her hand on his arm.

The wharf became a street, climbing from the harbor to the town. Everything was made of red stone—the cobblestones, the warehouses and inns, the houses. The street became busier. Children ran to school. Housewives hurried past with scarves tied around their heads and baskets over their arms. Everywhere were men— walking briskly, strolling, standing and talking.

The street opened into a square paved in red stone. Market stalls clustered—potatoes and onions, russet-colored apples, strings of sausages and round loaves of dark bread.

At the centre of the square was a burning-pole.

Saliel averted her eyes from it.

"Do you wish to buy anything?" Athan asked.

She shook her head.

The street became steeper. It twisted as it climbed the hillside. They walked slowly. "The Illymedes at spring," Saliel said. "Isn't there a festival?" She vaguely recalled a song: *...bells ring to welcome spring...*

"Yes." His face, when she looked at it, was frowning.

"What, Athan?"

His frown deepened. "There's a circuit of festivities. The route is always the same: the Illymedes for the spring revelries, then the colt races in Qussey, then midsummer in Pinsault."

She remembered tall-masted ships with bright pennants anchored in the harbor at the Aspides. "The noble Houses?"

"Yes."

Saliel walked a few steps in silence. "Your family may be at the Illymedes."

"Some of them, yes."

Her time with him was suddenly much shorter. "That's wonderful, Athan," she said, forcing enthusiasm into her voice. "You'll be able to join—"

Athan halted. "No." He drew her to one side of the street. Steps led down between the houses. She saw the red paving stones of the market square at the bottom. "I won't be going back."

"What? Why not?"

His frown vanished. He laughed suddenly. "This wasn't how I intended it to be."

Saliel shook her head. "What, Athan?"

He looked at her, smiling slightly. "Please marry me, Saliel. Be my wife."

She stared at him. "I beg your pardon?"

"Be my wife," he said again. His eyes smiled at her. *I can't.*

"I know you think you'll lose your independence, Saliel. But believe me, you won't."

She did believe him. *Accept his offer*, said a voice inside her.

Saliel swallowed. "No," she said.

"Why not?" Athan asked, still smiling.

"Because you don't owe me—"

"This isn't because I owe you, Saliel. It's because you're the person I wish to spend my life with."

Her throat was too tight for speech. She shook her head.

"Yes." Athan reached out to touch her face. She felt his fingertips on her cheek. "I love you, Saliel."

She jerked her head back. "But you'll be cast off!"

"I don't care."

He didn't. She saw it clearly on his face: the smile, the calmness.

"Well, I do! Family is the most important thing there is, Athan. You can't—"

"Yes," he said, smiling. "I can."

Saliel stepped back. "I won't let you."

"I'm staying with you, Saliel. Wherever you go. Whether you marry me or not." His voice was quiet, firm. It sounded like a vow.

She felt pain in her chest—sharp—beneath her breastbone. *He truly wants to be with me.*

It would be easy to accept his offer. Easy to open her mouth and say yes. Easy to be selfish. To ruin his life.

Saliel shook her head. "I don't want to be with you."

"Then why did you risk your life to save me?"

She looked down at the red cobblestones.

"Saliel…" Athan stepped close to her. His hand was on her cheek, warm. "We'll make our own family."

She squeezed her eyes shut. She wanted it: him, children.

Children with Witch-Eye.

Saliel lifted her head. She looked at him.

Athan was smiling at her, with his mouth, his eyes. "Nothing you can say will make me change my mind."

She'd been afraid in the citadel. She'd been afraid in the alleys at Bressoq. This fear was worse. She smelled burning flesh as she inhaled.

Saliel swallowed to clear her throat. "Athan, I have the Eye."

Athan took his hand from her cheek. "That's not funny, Saliel."

"I have the Eye," she said again, more loudly.

He pressed his hand across her mouth. "Don't say things like that! If anyone heard—"

I would be burned.

She took hold of his wrist and pulled his hand from her mouth. "I have the Eye. How do you think I copied the Consort's key?"

"You were a finger thief."

"I was. A good one. Because I had the Eye."

Athan shook his head. "Lies won't make me change my mind about you. Saliel—"

"I set your sleeve on fire."

"I know."

"Linen and lace, Athan. How long do you think it took to catch alight?"

"A few seconds."

"Almost a minute."

He shook his head. "No, it was only—"

"I held your eyes for almost a full minute, Athan."

His forehead creased slightly. He pulled his hand free from her grip. "No, you didn't."

"Yes, Athan. I—"

"No." He shook his head again. His expression was stubborn.

He refuses to believe.

"Look at my hands." She held them palm out. "Can you see them?"

"Of course I can." Athan was becoming frustrated. She heard it in his voice. "Saliel—"

She caught his eyes. Beautiful eyes. Brown. Dark. She saw who he was in them: his courage and his integrity, his compassion, his intelligence.

A carriage clattered past. She heard voices speaking in a language she didn't understand, the footsteps of passers-by. She stepped forward and reached beneath Athan's cloak, feeling for the pouch of money hanging from his belt. *There is nothing to see here. We're merely a husband and wife. See, he knows I'm taking the pouch.*

An ache built behind her eyes as she opened the pouch and felt inside with her fingers. One coin. Two.

It took a few seconds to find Athan's hand. The ache expanded inside her head. Pain pressed against her skull. It was a strain to hold his gaze while she opened his fingers—warm skin—and pressed the coins into his palm.

Saliel stepped back. She lowered her eyelids.

Athan blinked. "Saliel, I…" His voice faltered. He looked at the pouch of money in her right hand, and then at the coins on his palm.

"I have the Eye, Athan," she said quietly, handing him back the leather pouch. "You do not want to marry me."

His lips parted slightly. He didn't have to speak; his face told her everything. Shock. Belief. Fear.

He turned away from her abruptly.

"Athan, it's all right. I promise I won't—"

He pushed through the pedestrians, almost running. He didn't pause, didn't look back.

Saliel stayed where she was—on the edge of the street, at the head of the flight of stone stairs. She looked down at the cobblestones.

Square cobblestones. Red.

He has left me.

Minutes became hours. The shadows on the ground shrank. At noon she turned away from the street and walked down the steps toward the market place. Toward the burning-pole.

Hunger cramped in her belly, but she had no money to buy food. Athan had left with the leather pouch clenched in his hand. She hadn't even a single coin.

He has our ticket home.

She should be afraid of being alone and penniless, with only the clothes she wore on her back. She should be afraid of the spycatcher. She was only afraid of the burning-pole. *What if he names me for a witch?*

Saliel halted at the top of the last flight of steps. *I should hide.*

But if she hid, Athan would never find her.

She sat down on the step and hugged her knees. Beyond the bustle of the market, beyond the red buildings and the black slate rooftops, was the sea.

She watched the market. Looking for Athan. Looking for the spycatcher. She saw women with bright scarves covering their hair, sailors with tarred ponytails, children scavenging, a finger thief.

She recognized the way the boy stood unobtrusively and watched, the way he sidled closer to his mark— *yes, I would have chosen her too, stout and prosperous, paying no attention to anything but the bargain she's getting.*

The boy reached swiftly into the woman's basket. She was the only person to see it. The woman didn't notice. The stallholder didn't notice. No one in the market noticed.

The boy walked away, quiet and unhurried, strolling, drawing no attention to himself. The way he moved was familiar, the way he scanned the market for another mark. The hunger she saw in his face was familiar too. *That was me. Hungry. Stealing.*

Saliel looked down at the steps. *It's who I am again.* If she wanted to eat, if she wanted passage home, she'd have to steal.

I earned that ticket home. I earned that money.

What would Athan do if she went down to the wharf?

She sat, hugging her knees, searching for the courage to stand, to walk down the last of the steps, to follow the sloping street down to the docks.

Someone halted behind her on the flight of stairs. A shadow fell across her.

Saliel tensed. She turned her head.

Athan stood there.

If he'd loved her this morning, he no longer did. His eyes were hard, his mouth tight.

"Can you make people do things?"

Saliel swallowed and moistened her lips. "No."

Athan didn't look at her. He stared down at the market place. "What can you do?"

She looked down at her hands. "I can catch a person's gaze and hold it for a few seconds. At most a minute."

Athan didn't speak. She glanced at him. His face was angles and planes, hard, grim.

The silence between them lengthened. A minute passed. And another.

"How long have you known?"

Saliel stared at her hands. "I found out when I was fourteen. I needed money to pay my tutor. I had two choices, stealing or... or whoring. I chose to steal."

Athan said nothing.

"One of the women in the poorhouse tried to teach me. She told me to... to look a person in the eyes so they didn't notice what my hands were doing, and I learned that if I did that... I learned I could hold their gaze."

Saliel closed her eyes. She bowed her head so that her forehead touched her clasped hands. She couldn't look at him; her shame was too great.

"How many times have you done it to me?"

Saliel raised her head. "Once," she said. "When I burned you."

Athan didn't look at her.

He's afraid to meet my eyes. "Athan, I give you my word I'll never do it again. I promise you."

He said nothing. His gaze was on the market.

Saliel turned her head away. It was easier to watch the bustle of people than his face, easier to look for the little finger thief. The boy was still there, thin-faced and dirty. He was younger than she'd been when she'd started stealing. How old was he? Eight? Nine?

Athan stood behind her with a pouch of money beneath his cloak, but she dared not ask for a coin to give the boy. *I'm sorry, child.*

She watched as the boy sidled closer to a well-dressed man. *Not that one. Can't you see? The stallholder is watching you.*

"Get up," Athan said. "We'll be late."

His flat voice, the words, jerked her attention to him. "Athan—"

But he was already walking away, down the steps. He didn't look back to see if she followed.

A clamor rose from the market as she stood. Saliel didn't understand the shouted words—but she knew their meaning: thief.

Run, child. Run.

CHAPTER SEVENTY-THREE

ATHAN PUSHED THROUGH the crowd, too angry to be courteous. Rage trembled in his muscles. He tasted it on his tongue, hot, bitter.

Beneath the anger was something close to regret. *I thought I loved her.* And the regret made him even angrier.

A witch. I thought I loved a witch.

He'd lain with her. Twice. *To have union with a witch is to pay the price.* If the tales were true his genitals would rot and fall off. The burning-pole on the far side of the square caught his eye. *I should—*

He couldn't. However much he hated her, he couldn't watch her burn.

A child darted past him. Athan caught a glimpse of a thin face and panicked eyes before he was shoved roughly aside by a tall, heavyset man.

His rage flared. He swung around with clenched hands.

Saliel stepped aside for the child. She didn't appear to see the man. He barreled into her, knocking her down.

Athan's rage faltered. His hands unclenched. "Saliel!"

He started to run—and then stopped. *What am I doing? She's a witch. What do I care if she's hurt?*

But it seemed he did care.

He strode back and grabbed Saliel's arm, angry at himself, at her, at the man. "Get up."

She lifted her head and looked at him. She seemed to be struggling to breathe.

Athan released her arm. He went down on one knee. "Saliel…"

The man who'd knocked her down was speaking. Athan brushed the words aside with his hand. "Go away."

Saliel tried to stand.

Athan helped her, his hand under her elbow. "Saliel, are you all right?"

She pulled her arm free. "I'm fine."

She wasn't. He heard it in her voice, saw it in her face—pinched and white, in the way she pressed her hand to her stomach.

What do I care?

Athan turned away from her. He wanted to look back; he forced himself not to. But he walked more slowly than he had before. Across the square, down the long street. *Don't look back. Don't wait for her.* At the shipping office he halted and turned around. Saliel was a hundred paces or so behind.

He didn't know he was running. One moment he was standing, watching, the next he was with her. "Saliel—"

Pain was stark on her face. He heard it in her gasped breaths.

And then he saw the blood at the hem of her gown.

CHAPTER SEVENTY-FOUR

ATHAN SAT OUTSIDE the cabin with his head in his hands. *I should have looked back*. He stared down at the deck. He didn't see timber; he saw bloodied cobblestones. *Let her live. Please, let her live*.

The deck of the *Morning Star* moved beneath his feet. Sailors shouted overhead in the rigging. The code book was a solid lump beneath his shirt—

He heard the door open.

Athan pushed to his feet, almost stumbling.

The ship's surgeon stood in the doorway. There was blood on his cuffs. His gray-bearded face was solemn. "Mister Argante, I'm sorry."

She's dead.

Athan turned away. There was pain in his chest, as if something split open inside him. It was impossible to inhale, to exhale, to breathe. *She's dead.*

"Are you all right, Mister Argante?"

Athan couldn't shake his head, couldn't speak. It was all he could do to keep standing upright on the deck.

"I'm sorry," the surgeon said again. "There was nothing I could do to save the baby."

Athan turned his head. "What?"

"It was already too late when your wife came aboard."

"What?" he said again, stupidly.

"The miscarriage," the surgeon said. "It had already happened by the time she came aboard. I'm sorry."

Athan stared at the man. Shock was blank inside him.

"Your wife is sleeping. If you wish, you may see her."

"Sleeping?"

"Yes." The surgeon smiled. "Don't worry, Mister Argante, there's no danger to her life. It was clean miscarriage. I believe there'll be no infection."

Athan could think of nothing to say. He nodded.

"I see no reason why your wife shouldn't become pregnant again. Only... she needs time to heal. At least a month, Mister Argante. Preferably two."

Athan swallowed. "Of course."

The surgeon stepped away from the door. He gestured inside. The bloodstains were dark on his cuff. "You may see her."

Athan swallowed again. He made himself take a step. The deck seemed to lurch beneath his feet.

"I've left Nurse Bruyes with her. Send for me if you need anything."

Athan nodded. He took another lurching step toward the door.

"Good evening, Mister Argante."

"Wait."

The surgeon halted.

"Thank you," Athan said. The words were rough. They seemed to come from deep inside his chest. "Thank you very much."

HE DIDN'T NOTICE the furnishings. He didn't notice the nurse briskly bundling up an armful of bloodied bed linen. He only had eyes for Saliel.

Her face was almost as white as the sheets. Her hair spilled across the pillow, bright.

She's alive.

He reached down to touch her hair. The strands were fine beneath his fingers, soft. He didn't dare touch her face. It was too thin. Exhausted. Fragile. She looked as if her bones would break beneath his fingers.

You were pregnant? Why didn't you tell me?

There was anger in his chest—if he wanted to feel it—and a sense of betrayal. But they faded as he watched the pulse beating beneath her jaw. The pulse, the shallow rise and fall of her chest as she breathed—those were what mattered.

Athan cleared his throat. "I'll... I think I'll go outside again."

The nurse nodded and smiled. His saw sympathy in her eyes.

I'm not going to cry, he wanted to tell her, but he didn't trust his voice.

ATHAN SAT ON the bench outside the cabin until daylight faded. He looked at his hands. He opened them palm-up and stared at them. *She put her life in my hands. I could have had her burned.* He tried to understand why she'd done it.

When it was dark he went inside. One of the ship's servants brought food on a tray. Athan ate in front of the fire and then sat staring at the flames. It was late when he heard the murmur of voices in the bed chamber. He put down his wine glass.

Long minutes passed before the door opened. The nurse stood in the doorway. "Your wife is awake, Mister Argante."

Athan rose to his feet. "How is she?"

"Very tired. She'll sleep again soon." The nurse stepped away from the door. "You may see her, if you wish."

Athan nodded. He walked across the parlor and stepped hesitantly into the bed chamber. A tiny seed of panic sat beneath his breastbone. *What am I going to say to her?*

The room was full of candlelight and soft shadows. Saliel lay with her eyes closed. Her skin was translucently pale.

Athan shut the door. He walked over to the bed. "Saliel…"

Her eyes opened. She looked at him for a moment, then turned her face into the pillow. *Go away.*

Athan stepped closer to the bed. "Saliel… why didn't you tell me?"

Her eyes squeezed tightly closed.

"Saliel." He swallowed, and tried to speak past the shame in his throat. "I'm sorry I left you. I'm sorry I didn't look back. I'm sorry… about the baby." He cleared his throat. "Saliel, why didn't you tell me?"

She didn't answer.

"Please, Saliel, why didn't you tell me?"

She was crying, he realized. Quietly.

He couldn't stand and watch—and he couldn't walk away.

The mattress dipped as he lowered himself onto the bed. He reached for her. "No," he said, as she tried to pull away. "Please, Saliel."

He held her as she cried. "I'm sorry," he said, stroking her hair. "I'm sorry for everything that happened today."

Saliel said nothing. Gradually her body relaxed and he knew that she slept.

Athan didn't let her go, didn't get off the bed to wash his face or take off his clothes. He stayed where he was, holding her. *I'm sorry, Saliel.*

* * *

ATHAN WOKE SOME time after dawn. Saliel still slept. Her breathing was soft and even. He heard the sound of shutters opening. Daylight spilled into the bed chamber.

He turned his head and watched as the nurse drew back the shutters from the second window. "I've rung for hot water and food," she said.

Athan released Saliel carefully. He climbed off the bed. "Thank you." He rubbed a hand over his face and felt stubble, coarse.

The suite had a bathing chamber, with a tiled floor and a washstand and a hip bath. Athan shaved and then stripped off his clothes and bathed.

He rang the bell and gave everything in his and Saliel's luggage to be laundered. "Do you think it's possible to find a new gown for my wife?" he asked the nurse.

"I should think so."

"Perhaps something blue? It suits her."

The nurse smiled. "I'll see what I can do, Mister Argante."

It was nearly noon when Saliel woke. Athan watched from the doorway as the nurse brushed her hair. He'd slept all night holding her, and yet he felt as awkward as a teenaged boy. *I don't know what to say to her.*

Her face was still pale, still shadowed with exhaustion, but an empty breakfast bowl stood on the bedside table.

"You ate something," he said, relieved.

Saliel looked at him—a brief glance—before lowering her gaze. "Yes."

Athan stepped inside the bed chamber. "You feel a little better?"

"Yes," she said politely. "Thank you."

The nurse laid down the hairbrush. "You may speak with your wife for a few minutes," she said. "And then she must rest again."

"Thank you," Athan said. He stood aside for her, and then closed the door. The awkwardness returned. *What do I say to her?*

The silence grew. Saliel didn't look at him. She smoothed a wrinkle in the sheet.

Athan cleared his throat. He made himself walk toward the bed. "Saliel."

"Yes?" Her voice was quiet. She didn't look at him.

He sat on the edge of the bed. "Saliel... why didn't you tell me you were pregnant?"

She stopped smoothing the sheet.

"Why, Saliel?"

"I thought you'd prefer not to know."

"What?" Anger pushed him to his feet. "How could you think that?"

She met his eyes. "A bastard child. A child you would never see. Do you think that would have made you happy, Athan?"

He opened his mouth—and then shut it.

"I thought it would be easier if you didn't know." She looked down at the sheet again. "I thought... you wouldn't feel so guilty."

His anger drained away. In its place was shame. "I apologize," he said. "I didn't realize."

Saliel shook her head.

Athan cleared his throat again. "Yesterday... I'm so sorry, Saliel. It's all my fault—"

"No," she said quietly. "It's better this way."

"What? How is it better?"

She raised her head. "I have the Eye, Athan. The child likely would have too."

Athan swallowed. "Did you... Did you not want the babe?"

"What would I have done if it was a witch, Athan?" Tears shone in her eyes. "What would I have done?"

Athan sat beside her on the bed. He took her hand. "Witchcraft grows less with each generation, Saliel. Not greater. The child probably wouldn't have had the Eye."

"You don't know that."

"I do. My uncle spent several years proving it."

Saliel looked down. Distress creased her brow.

Athan reached out and touched her cheek lightly. "You have the Eye, Saliel, but you're not a true witch. You can't make people act against their will."

"I burnt you," she whispered. The furrows of distress on her brow deepened.

"*You* burnt me. You didn't make *me* do it." He put his arm around her and pulled her close. "Saliel, if you have children, I doubt they'll have the Eye."

"But you don't know," she whispered.

"No," he said. "I don't."

He smoothed back Saliel's hair. It had taken him a day to reach this point. He wished it had taken minutes. *If I'd stayed with you yesterday, none of this would have happened.* "Now you must rest." He bent and kissed her pale cheek. "Sleep, my lady."

ON THE THIRD day, Saliel tried to get out of bed. "No," Athan told her, firmly.

"Women miscarry all the time in the Ninth Ward. And they don't lie abed—"

"This isn't the Ninth Ward."

"But Athan—"

"No."

On the seventh day he gave her a blue gown. "This is for you."

"I can get up?"

He nodded. "The surgeon says it's all right."

He still held her each night while she slept. *I will never leave you again.* It wasn't a decision made from guilt—although guilt was there. It was made from certainty, from knowledge.

He'd watched a painter once, over several days. The man had created his background meticulously, using layer upon layer of pigment. When the painting was completed none of those individual layers had been visible to the eye. With Saliel he'd seen the final result. He'd known who she was as a person—private, relying on no one but herself—without understanding why.

Now I finally understand.

She wasn't unusual; she was remarkable. And he was going to spend his life with her.

He saw the future in his mind's eye. A house built of honey-colored stone beside the sea. A vineyard on the hillside behind. Children laughing. *We'll make our own family, Saliel.*

It was a subject—his not leaving her—that Athan dared not broach. *No arguments*, the surgeon had said when he'd allowed Saliel out of bed. *No excitement. Your wife needs quiet and rest.* And although he was no surgeon, Athan saw what the man meant. She was too thin, too pale, too fatigued.

On the twelfth day, they reached the Illymedes.

CHAPTER SEVENTY-FIVE

THE MORNING STAR docked at noon. Dark clouds massed in the sky. The harbor was crowded. Many of the ships were Laurentine, flying the pennants of noble Houses.

"Do you see the Seresin flag?" she asked as thunder rumbled in the distance.

Athan glanced at her. "Yes."

"Which one?"

He pointed to a pennant with jewel-like colors: sapphire, emerald, ruby.

"Can you tell who it is?"

"Not my father," Athan said. "The background would be gold."

"One of your brothers, then."

"Phelan or Vadel. It doesn't have the heir's border."

"You'll be able to join them."

Athan looked down at his hands, resting on the wooden railing. "Yes."

ATHAN PULLED ON his gloves. "Don't open the door to strangers."

"I won't."

"The port's busy," he said, drawing back the bolt and opening the door. Rain fell outside. The deck was dark with water. "It may take me a while to find a carriage."

"I wish I could come with you."

"In this rain?" Athan shook his head. He pulled his hood up. "I'll be an hour at the most. Bolt the door."

"The spycatcher—"

He turned his head and looked at her. "I think he's close, but I don't think he's here yet." His voice was quiet, serious. "I wouldn't be leaving you if I thought he was."

I know. "Be careful," she said.

Athan laid his gloved hand on her cheek. "Don't worry about me." He closed the door.

The bolt made a quiet *snick* as she drew it across. Saliel walked to the couch and sat and looked down at her hands. *This is it. The Illymedes.*

She closed her eyes and built the image behind her eyelids—the cottage, the garden—but it didn't have the power it once had. The dream she'd held onto for years now seemed empty, lonely.

The rain became heavier. It drummed on the deck. *Don't cry when you say goodbye. You must not cry.*

She filled the cottage, the garden, with details, trying to make them seem less empty: two cats, half a dozen hens, a brown cow. Peas and beans and rows of potatoes. Tall hollyhocks with scarlet flowers—

Someone knocked on the door. "Mistress Argante?" The voice was familiar, female.

She stood. "Nurse Bruyes?"

"I have a packet of herbs from the ship's surgeon, Mistress Argante."

Saliel walked to the door. Thunder rumbled overhead. She hesitated, and then drew back the bolt. "Thank you—"

Nurse Bruyes stood outside. Behind her were three men.

Time seemed to stop. One moment she was pushing against the door, the next she was on the floor with her cheek pressed to the rug.

The room spun dizzily. She saw familiar faces—Nurse Bruyes weeping, the spycatcher.

Everything snapped into focus.

The spycatcher.

"You hit her too hard, fool."

Someone lifted her to her feet.

"Put her on the couch. And you—get rid of the nurse."

She heard the sound of a knife being unsheathed. "No!" She tried to struggle.

The spycatcher laughed. He stepped close. "My apologies, Ottler. Perhaps you didn't hit her hard enough." His lips drew back in a smile. "Lady Petra. How lovely to see you again."

Saliel spat at him.

The spycatcher wiped his cheek. "Your guardian told me you were from the slums. I see we shall have to teach you some manners. Ottler, the couch."

Ottler—large, dark, hard-eyed—forced her to sit, his hand at her throat.

"Search the rooms," the spycatcher said. His voice came from behind her. A knife blade touched beneath her jaw. "She won't move. Will you, my dear?"

Ottler removed his hand.

Hard fingers twisted in her hair. The tip of the knife pressed more firmly against her skin, forcing her chin up. "Will you?" The spycatcher's voice was at her ear. "Answer me."

"No." She choked the word out.

He didn't ease the pressure of the blade. Saliel felt her skin split open.

"Filthy, lying spy." His voice was soft, hissing. "And you... you're filthier than all the others. Lies fill your mouth like maggots."

Saliel closed her eyes. Blood trickled down her throat, warm.

"I've been looking forward to this moment," the spycatcher whispered in her ear. "I'm going to enjoy breaking you. I'm going to enjoy every second of it." He pressed the blade more deeply.

Her breath caught in her throat—a sob, a gasp. She opened her eyes. The parlor was empty. She heard movement in the bed chamber.

"I'll put your eyes out," the spycatcher said. "And then you'll tell me everything. Everything." He released his grip on her hair. His hand slid down her cheek, her throat. "And when I'm finished with you, I shall give you to my men." He caressed her breast with hard, pinching fingers. "You can be their whore. Believe me, by the time they're done you'll be glad to burn on a witch's pyre."

She couldn't drag air into her lungs. *Calm. Think.*

"Nothing." Ottler and the other man came back into the parlor.

The spycatcher removed his hand from her breast. "The luggage. Check it."

Their valises were on the floor beside the couch. Ottler picked one up and tipped it upside down. Athan's belongings spilled from it, across the cushions and floor—nightshirt and shaving kit, Marillaqan clothes, his spare knife. "No." Ottler jerked the other valise open and upended it. Her nightgown tumbled out, her hairbrush, her clothes.

Ottler threw both valises on the floor.

The spycatcher increased the pressure of his knife. More blood trickled down her throat. "Where is it?"

"What?" The word came out as a croak.

His fingers twisted cruelly in her hair. She felt strands come out of her scalp. "The code book."

"I don't know—"

Someone knocked on the door. "Saliel?"

She tried to cry out to Athan, to warn him, but the spycatcher was too fast. His hand clapped over her mouth. "The door. Quickly."

The two men crossed the room swiftly. They stood on either side of the door, one dark, one fair.

Athan knocked again. "Saliel?"

The fair-haired man slid back the bolt.

Athan stepped into the cabin. His cloak was dark with water. "I have a carriage," he said. "It's not the best—"

They took him as he pushed his hood back, hitting hard, bringing him to the floor.

I'm sorry, Athan. Tears fell from her eyes. *I'm sorry.*

CHAPTER SEVENTY-SIX

HE LAY GASPING. Knees dug into his back.

"Search him." The voice was familiar.

Athan raised his head. He saw Saliel and the spy-catcher, he saw the knife, he saw the blood on her throat, on her blue gown.

He snarled and tried to push to his feet.

"Search him," the spycatcher said again.

Someone grabbed his hair and jerked his head up. An arm locked around his throat. He tried to struggle as hands searched him roughly. The arm tightened. His vision grayed, became black.

When he swam back to full consciousness he heard the spycatcher's voice. "Excellent." It was almost a purr. "Excellent."

Athan lifted his head, searching for Saliel again. The weight was gone from his back.

"Hager, take her."

He saw boots, legs walking. He followed them with his eyes. A couch. Saliel.

She looked at him. He saw her distress, the silent tears sliding down her cheeks.

Don't cry for me. But he had no breath to speak.

Hager took hold of Saliel's head, twisting his fingers tightly into her hair. She didn't seem to feel it. Her expression didn't change: grief.

The spycatcher removed his knife. Blood trickled more quickly down her throat.

"Saliel—" Athan tried to push to his feet again.

Someone hauled him upright. The arm was around his neck again.

"Donkey." The spycatcher bowed with a flourish. His teeth glistened as he smiled. "How delightful to see you again."

"Grebber."

The spycatcher's smile tightened. "I have the code book." He raised his hand.

Athan recognized the oiled cloth, the stitching. He looked the man straight in the eyes. "I don't care."

The spycatcher stared at him for a moment. "You don't care," he said, lowering the package.

"No."

The spycatcher leaned close, holding his gaze. "What do you care about then, Donkey?"

"Her." The word was pulled from him. "And I will *kill* you—"

The spycatcher laughed softly. "You love her, do you?"

"Yes—" He doubled over as the man's knee took him in the groin, hard.

The arms that held him let go. Athan fell to the floor.

The spycatcher bent over him. "You love her."

Athan squeezed his eyes shut, trying not to vomit. He couldn't speak, couldn't breathe.

"You love her."

Yes. He opened his eyes and looked for Saliel.

His pain shrank abruptly. His vision cleared.

She had caught Hager's gaze.

He watched as she leaned sideways and groped beside the couch. He saw a hairbrush, his shaving kit—

His spare knife.

Saliel drew it from its sheath. She didn't try to stab Hager. She straightened and slid the knife into the pocket of her gown.

She turned her head and looked at Athan. He saw her shock to find him watching.

"Do you love her?"

"Yes," he said, his eyes on Saliel. "I do." *Wait*, he mouthed.

She nodded, a minuscule movement.

The spycatcher grabbed his hair and hauled his head around. "And tell me, does it hurt to see her like this?"

The pale eyes were impossible to look away from. Athan tried to clench his jaw but the word was forced from his mouth: "Yes."

The spycatcher's smile sharpened. "Do you know she's a poorhouse foundling, Donkey?"

"Yes."

The spycatcher looked startled for a moment—then he laughed. "And yet you still love her. How delicious." He released Athan's hair and stood. "This is going to be more amusing than I'd thought." He turned away. "Bind his hands, Ottler."

Athan was hauled to his feet. For the first time he saw the man who held him. *He's huge.*

"Co-operate," the spycatcher said. "Or I shall have Hager slit her throat too." He gestured at the bed chamber.

Athan turned his head. A woman lay on the bed. He saw brown hair, blood.

"Recognize her?"

Athan closed his eyes for a moment. "Yes." He stood quietly while his hands were tied in front of him. Ottler was thorough. The cord dug painfully into his wrists.

The spycatcher watched, smiling. "And her," he said, turning to Saliel.

Hager tied Saliel's hands together.

"Her cloak."

It lay neatly over the back of the sofa. Hager shook it out and placed it over her shoulders, covering the blue gown. The spycatcher's smile grew wider. He stepped close to Saliel.

She averted her face.

"No." The spycatcher gripped her hair. "Learn to enjoy it." He caressed her cheek, her bloody throat, her breasts. "I shall let every man on the ship have her. Every single one. And I shall make you watch." He looked at Athan. "How does that make you feel, Donkey?"

Athan bared his teeth. "That I want to kill you."

The spycatcher laughed. He released Saliel's hair and pulled the hood forward over her face. "Come," he said. "It's time to go."

Ottler pushed him toward the door. He walked, watching Saliel. One step. Two. Three. Her head lifted. She looked at him from beneath the hood.

The spycatcher opened the door. Rain fell heavily outside.

"Athan—" Saliel's legs seemed to give way. She clutched at him. Their hands touched for a brief moment. The knife pressed into his palm.

He took it while Hager dragged her back.

They walked briskly, the spycatcher holding Saliel's elbow, then Athan with Ottler and Hager flanking him. Hands gripped his arms on either side. No one on deck paid them any attention; they had their heads down against the rain.

The cords were tight. His fingers were numb by the time they reached the gangway. It was wide enough for only one person. Hager walked ahead of him; Ottler behind. Athan slit the cords with rough haste, gripping the knife blade clumsily—*don't drop it*—tearing clothes and skin.

The cords parted. His fingers stung as blood rushed into his hands.

At the bottom of the gangway, Saliel glanced back at him. Her face was pale beneath the wet hood. Athan gave a tiny shake of his head. *Not yet.* There were too many jostling people, too much noise and confusion. It would be easy for the spycatcher to drag her into the crowd. He'd never find her again. *I need space. I need to be able to see you.*

They walked along the wharf, the spycatcher and Saliel, Ottler and Hager and himself. Rain sluiced down, heavy, warm. Athan flexed his fingers. The numbness was gone, replaced by sharp, tingling pain.

Water splashed up with each step they took. The bustle of the *Morning Star* grew less. Rain swallowed the sound of voices, the clatter of wagon wheels.

Steps led down to a lower level of dock. He saw smaller vessels—sloops and ketches, fishing boats— and an empty, drenched wharf.

Saliel glanced back at him. Athan nodded. *Yes, here.* The spycatcher jerked her forward. "Move."

They walked down the steps. Hands gripped him at the elbow on either side, firm. Athan held the knife lightly. The hilt nestled into his palm. Twelve steps and a landing and then twelve more, with water sluicing down them.

Saliel seemed to stumble as she went down the second flight of steps. She fell to her knees, clutching the spycatcher, dragging him with her.

Athan yanked his right arm free from Hager's grip. He turned and sank his knife into Ottler's throat. The hand that held his elbow spasmed and released. Ottler fell heavily, a look of blank astonishment on his face.

He swung back to Hager. The man pulled a knife from beneath his cloak. His mouth opened in a shout.

It took no longer than a heartbeat—grabbing Hager's wrist and jerking the man toward him, burying his blade high in the man's stomach.

Hager's momentum carried him forward. He fell heavily against Athan, clutching at him.

Athan pulled the knife free. Blood rushed over his hand.

Hager's knees buckled. His head came up. He stared at Athan. A sound came from his mouth, inarticulate. His wrist relaxed in Athan's grip. The knife he held fell to the ground. The rain swallowed the sound it made.

Athan pushed Hager away and spun to face the spycatcher.

The man was halfway down the flight of stairs, struggling to stand. Saliel hung onto his knife arm. The spycatcher's face was a mask of fury. He struck her, sending her sprawling, and pushed to his feet. His lips drew back from his teeth.

Athan kicked him in the chest. The impact was heavy, solid. He felt it in every bone in his body.

The spycatcher fell backward down the steps.

Athan followed, gripping the knife tightly. His boots splashed in red-tinted water.

The spycatcher rolled at the bottom and scrambled to stand, gasping.

"No," Athan said, and punched him in the side of the head. All his weight, all his rage, was in the blow.

The spycatcher's legs buckled, as Hager's had done. He collapsed.

Athan stood looking down at the man, at the reddened water. Then he knelt. He buried his fingers in the spycatcher's hair and pulled his head back.

The man stared up at him, dazed, his pale eyes unfocused.

"You're dead," Athan said, and he cut the spycatcher's throat.

* * *

THERE WAS BLOOD everywhere. He knelt in it. His hands were covered with it.

The sound of rain roared in his ears. No, not rain. The noise was inside him.

Athan dropped the knife. He pushed to his feet, lurching. He was drenched, soaked. In blood. In rain.

He turned slowly to Saliel. She knelt on the steps. Her face was starkly white. "Are you all right?" The words made no sound as they came out of his mouth. He couldn't hear them.

Behind her, on the landing, lay Ottler and Hager.

I just killed three men.

Color leached from his vision. Everything became gray.

"Athan!"

He barely heard his name. It was as faint as the cry of a bird. There was no color except gray. He knew there was blood, knew he stood in it, knew his hands were covered in it—but he saw only gray.

"Athan, are you all right?" She'd been kneeling on the steps, now she stood with her hand on his arm. He hadn't seen her move.

Gray. Rain. Blood.

He turned from her and vomited.

CHAPTER SEVENTY-SEVEN

ATHAN GRIPPED HER hand tightly the whole way—on the wharf, in the carriage. Saliel looked at his face as they reached the Laurentine consulate. The whiteness, the blankness, were gone. His expression was grim, but he was Athan again.

Rain drummed down. The cobblestones ran with water. She glanced at the consulate—a flight of steps, slender columns, white marble—and ducked her head against the downpour.

At the top of the steps, guards barred their path. Their uniforms—blue and gold—made Saliel's throat tighten. *Home.*

"State your business," the most senior of the guards said. He'd seen the blood on their clothes; his hand rested on his saber.

"I must speak with your highest-ranking military officer." There was flat authority in Athan's voice. "Immediately."

The man glanced at the blood again. "And you are?"

"Athan of Seresin."

The guardsman looked at Athan's face more closely. His stance became less challenging. He saluted. "At once, milord."

Three of the guards accompanied them. Saliel's tension eased by slow increments as they walked. The consulate stood on Illymedan soil, but inside this building she was in Laurent.

They crossed echoing vestibules and walked down long corridors. The colors were light, bright. Finally the guardsmen halted before a door. They stood as they had at the top of the steps: to attention, alert-eyed, their hands on their sabers.

Athan's name makes them obey him, but they take no risks.

One of them—a lieutenant—stepped forward and knocked on the wooden panels. Saliel looked down at the floor. The hem of her blue gown was dark with blood. Water dripped from her cloak, pooling on the marble floor. She closed her eyes. Only Athan's hand gripping hers gave her the strength to keep standing.

The door opened. Saliel raised her head.

In the doorway was a General. His face was bullish, with a square jaw and wide nostrils. Medals crowded at his collar and marched across the breast of his tunic, weighing down the fabric.

"General Carel." The lieutenant saluted. "This man claims to be Athan of Seresin. He wishes to speak with you urgently."

The General looked at Athan. His scrutiny was thorough. He bowed. "Milord, you resemble your father."

"So I've been told."

"And your companion?" Iron-gray eyes assessed her, seeing the blood at her throat, the water, the exhaustion. "Are you quite all right, milady?"

"She requires a physician."

"At once, milord." The General snapped his fingers. A guardsman stepped forward. "Escort milady to the physician."

Saliel didn't release her grip on Athan's hand. "But Athan—"

"The physician," he said. "And then you must rest. I'll take care of this."

"Her safety?"

"Is not an issue while you're in this building, milord." General Carel stepped back from the doorway. "Please enter."

The room was square. Shelves of leather-bound books stood on either side of the tall windows. The remaining wall space was hung with maps. He saw the Corhonase Empire, the Illymedes, the nations of the Laurentine Protectorate.

"You have no objection if the lieutenant stays?"

"None."

A large desk dominated the room. Several chairs stood in front of it. The General walked around to stand behind the desk. "You wish to speak with me about a matter of some urgency, milord?"

Athan reached beneath his cloak. "The third Corhonase code book." He laid the package on the desk. Drops of water slid from the oiled cloth that wrapped it. They were faintly pink.

"What?" The General reached for the packet. "Where did you get it?"

"The citadel."

General Carel sliced the stitching open with his dagger.

"There's a Corhonase spycatcher on the wharf," Athan said. "Dead. And two of his men. You may wish to claim the bodies."

The General's head jerked up. He looked at Athan, and then down at the oilskin-wrapped packet and the pink drops of water sliding from it.

"Their vessel will be somewhere. I'm sure you can find it."

"Of course." General Carel laid down the code book. "Where are the bodies?"

"Not far from where the *Morning Star* is moored. A minute's walk. East. And there's a dead woman on the *Morning Star*. The ship's nurse. She's in the suite."

General Carel beckoned the lieutenant forward and gave brisk, concise orders.

"Yes, sir." The lieutenant saluted. He glanced at Athan as he turned away. There was curiosity in his eyes, respect.

Athan sat. He looked down at his hands. Cord still bound his wrists. The gashes he'd made freeing himself bled sluggishly. His clothes were sodden. Water and blood dripped from his cloak. *My blood. Their blood.*

"The citadel."

Athan raised his head.

"I'd heard we had a nobleman somewhere." The General sat down at his desk. He unfolded the oiled cloth and picked up the folded sheets of parchment. "I thought it a rumor."

"There's no one there now. Our guardian was taken."

General Carel glanced up sharply. "What? How long ago?"

"At a guess, some time in the past month."

"Are you certain?"

"Yes."

"This is dreadful news. We must warn—"

"More dreadful than you think," Athan said. "Our guardian revealed everything he knew."

General Carel shook his head. "You can't be certain—"

"The spycatcher had the Eye. He could force the truth to be spoken."

General Carel didn't physically recoil, but Athan saw his shock—the flaring of his pupils, the paling of his face.

"He's dead." Athan gestured at the droplets on the desk. "That's his blood."

The General looked down at the pools of pink-tinted water. He swallowed. "I see." He put the parchment to one side. He leaned forward, his elbows on the desk. His expression was intent, frowning. "Tell me everything."

CHAPTER SEVENTY-EIGHT

DUSK WAS FALLING when Saliel woke. She stared at the unfamiliar ceiling, the window, the door. *Where am I?*

Memory returned: the spycatcher and the wharves, the Laurentine consulate. She pushed aside the bed-clothes and dressed in a gown that wasn't hers—clean, a little too big. The fabric was primrose yellow. She looked in the mirror. *Not a color that suits me.*

The parlor was empty. She walked over to the windows. The panes of glass were flecked with rain. She saw a formal garden: shrubs and paths, a pond with a fountain, slender trees with up-reaching branches.

The consulate flanked the garden on all four sides, pale in the dusk, substantial—offices and reception rooms and living quarters. The solidity of the stone made her feel safe.

Saliel turned away from the windows. The door to the second bed chamber—Athan's—was open. The bed hadn't been slept in.

She lit candles and put fresh logs on the fire. A mirror hung above the mantelpiece. It was carved like the Consort's, with birds and dragonflies and lizards. She reached out to touch the wood. It was smooth beneath her fingers. "Illymedan," she whispered.

The mantelpiece was carved too, with winding tendrils and song birds. Saliel turned her head. Small forest creatures peeped out at her from the arms of the chairs. Lizards climbed the table legs, their tails curving into the grain of the wood; they scurried around the edge of the writing desk. Everywhere she looked she saw mother-of-pearl eyes, bright in the candlelight.

A covered tray lay on the table. She lifted the lid. Cheeses and breads, slices of meat, fresh fruit.

Saliel ate beside the fire. She'd barely finished when the door from the corridor opened. Athan stepped into the parlor. His face was weary. He carried their valises.

She stood. "Athan."

He put down the valises. "Shouldn't you be in bed?"

"I've slept."

"But your throat—"

"Four stitches. That's all. The physician says I'm fine."

Athan wore someone else's cloak. It was wet with rain. He shook water from it and hung it over a chair.

"You've been outside?"

"I went to the *Morning Star*. To see the captain and the surgeon. To explain."

Saliel looked down at her hands. "I shouldn't have opened the door."

"She was already dead, Saliel. She was dead as soon as the spycatcher had hold of her."

"But if I'd—"

"I would have let her in, too. Don't blame yourself." Athan walked across the room to her. His hand touched her hair lightly. "Saliel, you saved us."

She looked up at his face, remembering the blood, the rain. "No, you did."

Athan's mouth twisted. His hand fell from her hair. He turned away.

She watched as he sat. He moved stiffly, as if his muscles ached.

"Have you eaten?"

"Yes." Athan rubbed his face. "While I gave my debrief."

"You've done it already?"

He leaned his head against the back of the chair and closed his eyes. "For both of us. You can sign it tomorrow."

"Athan... how much did you tell them?"

"Everything," he said. "Except your eyes."

Saliel looked down at her gown. She smoothed a crease in the fabric. "Did you tell them I'm from the Ninth Ward?" *How awkward will it be when I step outside that door tomorrow? Will people turn away from me?*

"What? No."

"Thank you."

Athan opened his eyes. "It's none of their business."

Saliel picked up her plate and put it on the tray. "Have you seen your brother?"

"No. No yet."

"Perhaps you can do that this evening."

Athan sighed. "Saliel—"

"I'll go to the shipping office tomorrow morning. I'd like to leave as soon as possible."

Athan looked at her silently, then pulled a folded piece of parchment from his pocket and held it out to her. "The shipping schedule." He pushed up from the armchair. "Would you like some wine?"

She shook her head, clutching the schedule.

Athan poured himself a glass of wine and brought it back to the fireplace. "General Carel has authorized our payment. The money will be available tomorrow."

"Good." Saliel didn't look at him. She opened her hand and unfolded the parchment. She stared at the names of the ships. The destinations. The dates.

The words blurred. She squeezed her eyes shut—*I am not going to cry*—and then opened them again. Athan sat looking at his wine. She saw bandages at his wrists, white.

"You saw the physician?"

"Yes." He raised his head. He didn't stand in the rain with the spycatcher's blood on his hands, but the expression in his eyes was the same—dark and bewildered, as if he'd lost who he was.

Saliel put down the schedule. "Athan, are you all right?"

He swallowed. She saw the muscles move in his throat. "I'm fine."

"Athan, what you did today—"

He put down his wine glass. He looked as if he wanted to vomit again.

Saliel walked over to him. She touched his hair. "Athan?"

He didn't look up at her.

"Athan, you did something no one should ever have to do. That doesn't make you a bad person."

He shook his head.

Saliel sat on the arm of his chair. "Athan," she said quietly. "He was the monster, not you." She pressed her face against his hair. *I love you.* "Thank you for what you did."

For a moment he sat unmoving, tense, then his head lifted slightly and turned toward her. His arms came around her. He held her tightly.

They sat for long minutes, not speaking. He was warm and strong, safe. *I want this to last forever—*

"I must go to bed, Athan."

Saliel stood and looked down at him. The darkness had gone from his eyes. She bent and kissed his cheek. "Find your brother, Athan."

He rubbed a hand across his face. "Saliel—"

"Family is the most precious thing there is. Find yours, Athan. Please."

Athan sighed. "Very well."

CHAPTER SEVENTY-NINE

MUSIC SWIRLED AROUND him. Spring music, light and bell-like. The scent of flowers and perfume filled his nose. On every side was gaiety, laughter, dancing.

Athan strolled, his hands in his pockets. He wore his Marillaqan clothes. They were sober compared to the dancers' clothing, plain and unadorned. He saw ribbons and lace, low-cut bodices, gaudy jewelry—diamonds, rubies and emeralds, sapphires.

The last time he'd seen women in gowns so revealing, they'd been whores.

A stir of conversation marked his path. People turned to look at him—and then glanced at a far corner of the ballroom. Whispers swelled beneath the music.

Athan followed the direction of the glances, strolling, looking around him. The dancers were like exotic birds, with plumages of lace and ribbons and jewels. Beautiful. Ludicrous.

Fashions had changed in the two years he'd been away. Gone were the high head-dresses, the rouge and brilliant eye shadow. The dancers had long ringlets. Their faces were painted white, their lips red.

No one appeared to have any eyebrows.

Athan stifled a snort. *Ridiculous.*

His brother Phelan stood in the far corner of the ballroom, partaking of tiny pastries shaped as butterflies. There was no mistaking him. He wore the Seresin colors—crimson, blue, green—trimmed with gold; a Count's son. A ransom's worth of diamonds sparkled on his fingers, in the lace at his throat and wrists, on the buckles and raised heels of his shoes.

His brother's mouth dropped open. "Athan! Whatever are you doing here?"

He shrugged. "I find myself in the Illymedes."

Phelan put down the pastry he was holding. He held out his hand. The nails were painted crimson.

"You look well," Athan said politely. It was a lie: Phelan's girth had increased since he'd last seen him.

"You don't. You've grown very thin."

Athan shrugged again. "Military life."

"It clearly doesn't suit you." Phelan picked up the pastry again. "How long are you here?"

"I sail the day after tomorrow."

"So soon?" Phelan had no eyebrows to show his surprise. "The revelries have only just begun."

"I'm not here for them."

Phelan glanced at his clothes. "No. That's obvious." He picked up another pastry.

Athan watched him eat. Phelan had their father's face—the bones hidden beneath a layer of fat—and their father's disapproving voice. *In 15 years this will be me. Soft. Arrogant.* His world would narrow, confined by luxury. *Is this who you want me to be, Saliel?*

"I'm getting married," he said.

"Good. It's time you grew up." Phelan picked up another pastry. "Who is she?"

"You may judge for yourself," Athan said. "Tomorrow."

"She's here?"

"Yes." Athan turned and looked at the ballroom. Mouths opened in laughter. Jewels glittered. He saw white faces, red lips, ringlets. He felt the same boredom he had two years ago: the boredom that had made him decide to become a spy. *I don't belong here.*

"How is our uncle?" he asked. "Has he found a wife yet?"

Phelan grunted. "He never looks beyond his wine glass."

Athan stared across the ballroom. He saw the hills behind the Seresin estate. Mist lay in the hollows. The dawn light was pale, flushed with pink.

He blinked and the ballroom came back into focus: gilded woodwork and gold-fringed draperies, a high alabaster-white ceiling painted with roses. Ringlets and lace and red lips.

Our uncle drinks because he chose wrongly.

CHAPTER EIGHTY

SUNLIGHT WAS LEAKING in through the shutters when Athan woke. He shaved the stubble from his face and dressed. The parlor was empty. Saliel had eaten. He saw a plate with crumbs on it, a smeared butter knife, a crumpled napkin.

The door to her bed chamber was ajar. Athan knocked quietly. "Saliel?"

There was no answer, no movement from inside.

Athan pushed the door open. The bedroom was empty.

He swung back to face the parlor. Panic was tight in his chest. *She's gone.*

One of the tall casement windows stood slightly open.

Athan crossed the room. "Saliel!" He pushed the window open and strode out onto a terrace. Birds sang and bells chimed in the breeze. He saw a garden, trees, a fishpond—and Saliel. She stood at the edge of the terrace. She was dressed in her Marillaqan gown. Her hair was as bright as copper in the sunlight. There was sadness in the way she stood, her hands resting on the stone balustrade.

She turned her head and looked at him. "Good morning, Athan."

Athan swallowed. He tried to slow his breathing. "Good morning."

"Is something wrong?"

His heart still beat too fast in his chest. There was sweat on his skin. "I thought you'd gone."

Saliel turned around fully. "I promise I won't leave without saying goodbye. You have my word."

Athan swallowed again. He nodded, and went back inside.

The shipping schedule lay beside Saliel's empty plate. Athan reached for it. He didn't need to search for the ship he wanted; he knew where it was on the list. His eyes found it easily. The *Sea Swallow*. Sailing to Besany tomorrow.

After he'd eaten, Athan took a sheet of parchment from the writing desk. He trimmed a quill and opened the inkpot.

I relinquish all claim to my inheritance, and to everything that my name has entitled me to.

A simple sentence. Black ink on white parchment.

He dipped the quill in ink again and signed his name. *Athan.*

THE TREES HAD slender, gray branches that reached upwards and yellow, wooly blossoms. Pollen drifted down in the breeze. It lay like yellow dust on the surface of the puddles.

Mother-of-pearl bells chimed softly. Everywhere she looked, she saw them—in the shrubs, in the trees, hanging from the roofs, glittering in the sunlight, chiming. She understood the song now: *bells ring to welcome spring.*

Saliel reached up and snapped off a twig. The blossoms were feather-like, downy. Their scent was slightly spicy. It reminded her of the Ladies' Hall, of tiny cakes tasting of ginger and honey.

She heard footsteps above her on the terrace. She turned her head. Athan stood there. "Illymedan eucalypt," he said, looking at the twig in her hand.

"Oh." She let it fall and brushed the pollen from her palm.

Athan smiled. He held out his hand. "Come inside. There's someone I'd like you to meet."

She walked up the steps. "Who?"

Athan took her hand. He drew her indoors.

She halted. A nobleman stood in the centre of the parlor, wearing silk and lace. His clothes were colorful, blue slashed with crimson and gold. Rings glittered on his fingers—ruby and sapphire and diamond. He was as tall as Athan, as black-haired as Athan. She saw Athan in the man's face beneath the white face powder—his nose and jaw, his dark eyes.

She barely heard Athan's words. "I'd like you to meet my brother, Phelan."

I shouldn't be in the same room as him.

"It's a pleasure to meet you." The nobleman bowed.

Saliel swallowed. She removed her hand from Athan's clasp and curtseyed. "The pleasure is mine."

"Have a seat," Athan said. "Saliel. Phelan."

She glanced at him. *I shouldn't.*

Phelan looked at the furniture. She saw it through his eyes: quaint, rustic. He chose an armchair beside the fireplace.

"Have a seat, Saliel," Athan said. His hand was warm in the small of her back. "Please."

She sat, aware of Phelan's gaze. "Athan has told me nothing about you." His voice was polite. "Where are you from? Marillaq?"

"I'm from Laurent."

"Oh?" Phelan's gaze became more intent. "Which House?"

Her chest was tight. It was difficult to inhale, to exhale. *He's going to shun me.*

"No House," Athan said, before she could answer.

Phelan glanced at him. "Is this some jest?"

"No jest."

Phelan's gaze shifted back to her. He wore the clothes of a nobleman, the jewels, but his expression was one she recognized from the slums: suspicion. "What's your birth?" he asked bluntly.

"Phelan, it's none of your—"

"I'm a foundling," Saliel said. "From the Ninth Ward."

Phelan's nostrils flared. She saw revulsion rise in him, anger. He pushed to his feet.

Athan took a step toward his brother. "Don't you dare turn your back on her."

Saliel stood hurriedly. "Athan—"

"She's done more for Laurent than you ever will," Athan said. "A thousand times more."

Saliel laid her hand on his arm. "He has the right to shun me. You know he does."

Phelan ignored her. "Are you insane?" His clothes were bright and frivolous, his face ugly with anger. "She's a foundling from the cesspit! For all you know she's the daughter of a whore."

Athan stared at his brother, then turned to her. "Why don't you go outside," he said. "I won't be long."

She gripped his arm tightly. "Athan, you mustn't fight—"

"I have no intention of fighting with Phelan."

It was the truth. She saw it in his face, heard it in his voice—calmness. She released his arm. "Athan, your House—"

"I know the value of my House. Don't worry."

ATHAN WATCHED SALIEL step out onto the terrace. She was as white-faced as Phelan. He turned back to his brother. "Your manners are execrable."

Color flushed beneath the paint on Phelan's face. "My manners! You let that... that *thing* in the same room as you! As me!"

He had no anger. *I pity you.* He took the folded sheet of parchment from his pocket. "Here."

"What is it?"

"See for yourself."

Phelan hesitated, and then took the parchment. He unfolded it and read the single line of writing. His expression, when he glanced up, was contemptuous. "You truly are a fool."

I used to care what you thought of me, all of you; I no longer do.

"I take it you don't approve?" he said lightly, smiling.

"Approve?" Phelan's mouth twisted as if he wanted to spit. "Of such a monstrosity of a marriage? No one could!" He turned away, stiff with outrage.

"You may tell our uncle he made the wrong decision."

Phelan made no reply. He opened the door with a jerk and stepped into the corridor without a backward glance.

The door swung shut.

Athan stood quietly for a moment, alone. *I am no longer a Seresin.*

There was sadness, but no grief. Instead he was aware of a sense of freedom.

ATHAN STEPPED OUT onto the terrace and walked slowly down the steps into the garden. Saliel sat on a bench carved of white limestone. Her head was bowed.

He walked across to where she sat. "Forgive me. My brother's manners are—"

Saliel's head lifted. "He has every right to shun me. You should shun me too, Athan. It's time."

"No." Athan sat and put his arm around her, pulling her into his body. "Never."

Saliel said nothing. She bowed her head again.

"I wanted you to meet him, Saliel. I wanted you to see what I'll become if I go back to my House."

She stiffened. "If you go back? Athan—"

He pressed his face against her clean, bright hair. "Saliel, please say you'll marry me."

She pulled away from him. "Athan, I've told you—"

"I don't care who your parents were." He reached for her hand. "We make ourselves, Saliel. Don't you see?"

"It's not that, Athan. It's—"

"I'm not afraid of your eyes. Or our children's eyes." He met her gaze squarely. *Listen to me. Believe me.*

She looked away. "I'm like that snake you spoke of. The one that catches its prey—"

"Snake?" Athan shook his head. "No. What you have is a gift, Saliel. Without it we'd both be dead." He tightened his grip on her hand. "Please say you'll—"

"No." She pulled her hand from his clasp and stood. "You've been one of the elite all your life, Athan. You don't know what it's like to live at the bottom."

Athan stood too. "We won't be at the bottom. We'll have a vineyard in the colonies. We'll—"

"No."

He looked at her face, stubborn, pale. "The surgeon said no arguments, Saliel. And I don't want to argue, I don't. But—"

"Then go to your family."

"It's too late. I've left my House."

"What!" He saw her shock, her distress. "Athan, you can't—"

"My House is just a name," he said quietly. "An estate. People I can live without." He reached for her hands again. "We'll make our own family, Saliel."

She pulled her hands free. "You'd regret it! You know you would!" She turned away and began to walk toward the terrace, fast, her head down.

"No. I wouldn't regret it." His certainty was bone-deep. He heard it in his voice, felt it—rooted inside him—as much a part of him as the blood in his veins. *I will not regret it.*

Saliel heard it too. She halted.

"What I would regret is losing you." He walked to where she stood. "There's a place called Besany, Saliel. A month's sailing from here. I think you'd like it." He reached out and touched her face lightly, laying his hand on her cheek. "That's what I want. You. Us. A home in the colonies, where no one cares about the difference between our births." He removed his hand. "Tell me, please... what do you want?"

She lifted her head and looked at him. Misery shone in her eyes.

"The truth," Athan said. "What do you *truly* want?"

He waited, while mother of pearl bells chimed in the breeze and yellow pollen drifted down.

"You," she whispered. "I want you."

Relief swelled in his chest. The future opened out before him: a house built of honey-colored stone. Vines on a hillside. Sea breezes and children's voices. Saliel.

Athan put his arms around her. "You have me."

ABOUT THE AUTHOR

Emily has a Bachelor of Science (Geology) and a Post Graduate Diploma (Rehabilitation). She has lived and studied in Sweden, backpacked in Europe, and travelled overland in the Middle East, China, and North Africa. Her varied career includes stints as a field assistant in Antarctica, a waitress on the Isle of Skye, and a rehabilitation instructor in New Zealand. She currently works in the wine industry in Marlborough, New Zealand. Her first novel, *Thief With No Shadow*, has been shortlisted twice for the Romance Writers of America RITA Awards.

'A finely faceted gem... Bravo!'
– Mindy Klasky

EMILY GEE
THIEF WITH
NO SHADOW

www.solarisbooks.com   ISBN: 978-1-84416-469-1

Aided by the magic which courses through her veins, Melke is able to walk
unseen by mortal eyes. When a necklace she has stolen holds the key to both
saving her brother's life and breaking a terrible curse, she must steal it back
from a den of fire-breathing salamanders. Things are about to get very tough
for Melke, especially when she comes to realise she may have to trust the
very people who were out to kill her.

SOLARIS FANTASY

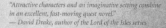

"*Attractive characters and an imaginative setting combine in an excellent, fast-moving quest novel.*"
— David Drake, author of the Lord of the Isles series

GAIL Z. MARTIN
THE SUMMONER

Book One of the
CHRONICLES OF THE NECROMANCER

www.solarisbooks.com ISBN: 978-1-84416-468-4

The world of Prince Martris Drayke is thrown into sudden chaos and disorder when his brother murders their father and seizes the throne. Cast out, Martris and a small band of trusted friends are forced to flee to a neighbouring kingdom to plot their retaliation. But if the living are arrayed against him, Martris must call on a different set of allies: the ranks of the dead...

ⓖ SOLARIS FANTASY

"A rich, evocative story with vivid, believable characters moving through a beautifully realized world with all the quirks, depths and levels of a real place. A terrific read!"
—A.J. Hartley, author, *The Mask of Atreus*

GAIL Z. MARTIN

THE BLOOD KING

Book Two of the
CHRONICLES OF THE NECROMANCER

www.solarisbooks.com IISBN: 978-1-84416-531-5

Having narrowly escaped being murdered by his evil brother, Jared, Prince Martris Drayke must take control of his magical abilities to summon the dead, and gather an army big enough to claim back the throne of his dead father. But it isn't merely Jared that Tris must combat. The dark mage, Foor Arontala, has schemes to cause an inbalance in the currents of magic and raise the Obsidian King...

JAMES MAXEY

BITTERWOOD

"For the sake of humanity, join in Bitterwood's revolt." – Kirkus Reviews

www.solarisbooks.com ISBN: 978-1-84416-487-5

It is a time when powerful dragons reign supreme and humans are forced to work as slaves, to support the tyrannical ruler King Albekizan. However, there is one name whispered amongst the dragons that strikes fear into their very hearts and minds: Bitterwood.

SOLARIS FANTASY